W9-BPG-873

PENDRAGON

JOURNAL OF AN ADVENTURE THROUGH
TIME AND SPACE

Book Three:

The Never War

PENDRAGON

**JOURNAL OF AN ADVENTURE
THROUGH TIME AND SPACE**

PENDRAGON

JOURNAL OF AN ADVENTURE THROUGH TIME AND SPACE

Book Three:

The Never War

D. J. MacHale

Simon & Schuster Books for Young Readers

New York   London   Toronto   Sydney

SIMON & SCHUSTER BOOKS FOR YOUNG READERS
An imprint of Simon & Schuster Children's Publishing Division
1230 Avenue of the Americas, New York, New York 10020

First Simon & Schuster Books for Young Readers edition March 2007

SIMON & SCHUSTER BOOKS FOR YOUNG READERS is a trademark
of Simon & Schuster, Inc.
Book design by Debra Sfetsios
The text of this book was set in Apollo MT.
Manufactured in the United States of America
4 6 8 10 9 7 5
Library of Congress Control Number 2002116463
ISBN-13: 978-1-4169-3627-5
ISBN-10: 1-4169-3627-0

This is for my dad.

ACKNOWLEDGMENTS

Hi to all you readers out there in Halla. Welcome to the next chapter in the continuing saga of Bobby Pendragon and his fellow Travelers. Before you flume off to territories unknown, I'd like to write a few words of thanks to some of the people who help keep Bobby's adventures rolling along.

Writing *The Never War* presented some unique challenges (which I won't tell you about because you haven't read it yet). A very big thank-you must go to Lisa Clancy for providing such wise guidance. Her insight helped me dig deep into Bobby's character and bring out a story that is not only full of adventure, but thought-provoking as well. Thanks, Lisa!

Since *The Never War* takes place in the past of Second Earth, I had to do loads of research to make sure events were historically accurate. I used way too many resources to name here, most of which were on the Internet. So I'm offering a global thank-you to the hundreds of Web sites I accessed for information. (Did you ever hear of someone thanking the Internet for something? I think not!)

A big thank-you goes to the team at Simon & Schuster Children's Publishing for having faith in the series, working hard to make it the best it can be, keeping it on everyone's mind, and always answering my dumb questions.

As always, my business team of Rob Wolken, Michael Prevett, Richard Curtis, Peter Nelson, Corinne Farley, and now Danny Baror have my undying gratitude for being smarter than me.

My wife, Evangeline, continues to be a great critic. Every night she reads the next chapter and every night she yells at me for leaving her with a cliff-hanger. (Unlike you, she can't turn the page to see what happens next, because when she reads, the next chapter hasn't been written yet!)

Finally I'd like to thank all of you who have been reading

the Pendragon books. And a special thanks to those of you who have been writing me through the Web site and telling me how much you enjoy them. I really appreciate it.

Now, enough blah, blah. It's time to open the gate, step into a flume, and head back to the territories.

Hobey-ho,

D. J. MacHale

PENDRAGON

JOURNAL OF AN ADVENTURE THROUGH
TIME AND SPACE

The Never War

FIRST EARTH

That's where I am. First Earth. Veelox was a misdirection. Spader and I flumed to Veelox, but found the action wasn't there. It was here on First Earth.

Where is First Earth? The better question is, *when* is First Earth? I'm in New York City and it's 1937. March of 1937 to be exact. To be *really* exact, it's March 11 of 1937. I'm writing this on my birthday. Here's a weird thought: If I'm in 1937 and it's my birthday, did I still turn fifteen? Kind of freaky, no?

I'll begin this new journal by telling you I stumbled into the most bizarro, confusing, dangerous situation yet. But then again, haven't I said that before? Let me give you a little taste of what happened in only the first few minutes since I got here. . . .

Spader and I were nearly killed. Three times. We were also robbed and witnessed a gruesome murder. Happy birthday to me! The way things are going, I know what I want for my fifteenth birthday . . . the chance to have a sixteenth.

When Spader and I flumed in from Veelox, I had no idea of what "First Earth" meant. Since I'm from Second Earth, I could only guess that First Earth was sometime in the Earth's past. But how far past? For all I knew we were fluming back to a time when quigs were dinosaurs and we'd be on the run from hungry, yellow-eyed raptors.

I was totally relieved to find that when we landed at the gate, it was the exact same rocky room that I had been through many times before. Yes, we had arrived at the gate off the subway tunnel in the Bronx, New York. Phew. At least there were no T-rexes or Neanderthals waiting for us. That was the good news.

Bad news was that we weren't alone. As soon as the flume dropped us off, I saw two guys standing there, facing us. They wore old-fashioned gray suits, like Clark Kent wears in the old *Superman* show on TV Land. Actually, a better analogy is that these guys were dressed like the *bad guys* from that old show, because that's what they were. Bad guys. *Very* bad guys. They wore wide-brimmed hats that were pulled down low and had white handkerchiefs around their noses and mouths like banditos. There's only one word to describe these dudes.

Gangsters.

Their eyes looked wide and scared. No big surprise. They had just seen Spader and me drop out of nowhere in an explosion of light and music. They seemed totally stunned, which was good because there was one other detail I haven't mentioned. . . .

They were both holding machine guns that were aimed at the flume—and at us.

"Down!" I yelled at Spader.

The two of us jumped to opposite sides of the flume just as the gangsters started shooting. I crouched in a ball, totally unprotected as the deadly clatter from their rapid-fire guns echoed off the rocky walls. I thought for sure I'd get hit, but after a few seconds the shooting stopped, and I was still intact. I was afraid to move and even more afraid to look over and see if Spader was okay. The sharp explosions fell off to a distant echo that bounced around the cavelike room. My ears were ringing and the chemical smell of gunpowder burned my nose. I figured this was what it must be like to be in a war.

"Get up!" one of the gangsters ordered. "Hands in the air!"

I cautiously looked over to Spader and saw that he was okay. We stood slowly and raised our hands. The gangsters held their guns on us. I didn't know why. It wasn't like we had weapons of our own. The second gangster kept glancing nervously between the two of us. He looked almost as scared as we were. Almost.

"Th-They from Mars?" he asked his buddy nervously.

Under less terrifying circumstances, I would have laughed. It must have looked like we had just landed from outer space. Not only did we flash in through a storm of light, we were still dressed in our bright blue swimskins from Cloral. For a second I thought about pulling a huge bluff and chanting: "Drop your weapons or we will vaporize you with our mind-heat," or something equally sci-fi, but I didn't get the chance.

"Don't matter," barked the other gangster. He was definitely the one in charge, but I could tell from his voice that he was a little shaky too.

"We done our job," he added.

"S-So what about th-them?" the nervous gangster asked.

The guy in charge looked us over. I could almost hear the wheels turning in his brain. He didn't exactly seem like a rocket scientist, so they must have been very small wheels. I wondered if they hurt when they turned.

"You!" the guy barked at me. "Gimme that ring!"

I couldn't believe it. He wanted my Traveler ring! This was serious. You guys know how badly I need that ring. It shows me where the flumes are, and it's the only way I can get my journals to you. Without this ring, I'm lost.

"It's not worth anything," I said in a feeble attempt to talk him out of it.

"Don't matter," the gangster snapped back at me. "All I want is proof to show you two are real."

"Then take us with you, mates!" said Spader, trying to be friendly. "We're all the proof you need, in the flesh!"

"Those ain't my orders," he snarled.

"Really? What *are* your orders?" I asked.

"Just hand over the ring," the boss commanded. He raised his machine gun to prove he meant business. What could I do? I took off my ring and tossed it to him. He caught it and jammed it into his pocket.

"Let's step outside, nice and easy," the guy said.

This was good. It meant they weren't going to gun us down right that moment. Maybe there was a way out of this after all. The nervous gangster threw the wooden door open, then both stepped aside and motioned with their weapons for us to go through. I looked at Spader. Spader shrugged. We had to play along. With our hands up, we both stepped out of the gate and into the dark subway tunnel.

Everything was familiar, so I made a sharp right, knowing it was the way to the abandoned subway station.

But the gangster had other things in mind. "No, you don't," he ordered. "Keep walking."

We had to walk straight ahead, away from the door. Three steps later we stepped over the rail of the subway track. This was beginning to look bad again.

"Stop! Turn around."

Oh yeah, this was bad. We were both now standing on the train tracks.

"You move, you die," said the first gangster.

Yeah, right. We move, we die. If a train comes along, we *don't* move, we die. Not a lot of wiggle room here.

"Where are we, Pendragon?" whispered Spader.

His answer came in the form of a far off whistle. We both looked to our right and saw the headlight of a subway train rounding the bend, headed our way, on our track.

"What is that thing?" asked Spader nervously. Being from a territory that was covered entirely with water, he had never seen anything like a train before.

"That," I said, trying not to let my voice show the fear that was tearing at my gut, "is a pretty big tum-tigger."

"Hobey," said Spader in awe. "We just got here and we've already lost."

We had been on First Earth for all of two minutes, and we were staring death right in the eye.

Welcome home, Bobby Pendragon.

That's a taste of how our adventure on First Earth began. I don't want to get too far ahead because there was a whole lot that happened between the time I finished my last journal, and when we landed here. But I wanted to explain to you how I lost my ring. This is serious because as I write this journal to you, Mark and Courtney, I'm not really sure if you're ever going to read it. If I don't get that ring back, I'll never be able to send this to you. The only thing I can do is keep writing, hang on to the journals, and hope that I get the ring back soon.

Now, let me rewind to where I finished my last journal and get you guys back up to speed.

I spent my last few days on the territory of Cloral in a haze. We'd defeated Saint Dane, but I didn't feel much like celebrating. That's because Uncle Press was gone, and I kept replaying his last moments over and over in my head. Saint Dane had escaped through a flume and Spader tried to chase him. But a storm of bullets came back at him. Uncle Press realized what was happening, knocked Spader out of the way . . . and took the bullets himself.

He died in my arms. It was the absolute worst moment of my life. The only thing that kept me from totally losing it was that just before he died, he promised me we'd be together again. I know this sounds pretty loopy, but I believe him. If being a Traveler has taught me anything, it's that nothing is impossible. My eyes have been opened to so many new worlds and levels of existence that the idea of hooking up with Uncle Press again doesn't seem all that far-fetched.

Of course, I have no clue how it might happen. That's because I've only scratched the surface of knowing all there is to know about being a Traveler. I wish there were an instruction manual I could buy through Amazon.com that would spell out all the rules and regulations. Unfortunately, it's not that easy. I've got to learn things as I go along. And now I've got to do it without Uncle Press.

Welcome to my life as a Traveler, phase two.

In those last days on Cloral, I knew what my next move had to be, but I was putting it off because, well, I was scared. Things were different now. I was alone. It was a whole new ballgame and I wasn't sure if I was good enough to play in it.

When Saint Dane flumed out of Cloral, he was headed for a territory called Veelox. I knew I had to follow him, but the idea of going after him alone was about as appealing as setting my hair on fire. All things being equal, I think I'd rather have set my hair on fire. So I made a decision that I hope I don't regret.

I asked Vo Spader to go with me.

Don't get me wrong, Spader is a great guy. He's the Traveler from Cloral, after all. He saved my life more than once; he's an incredible athlete; he's about as brave as can be; and most importantly, he's my friend. So why should I be worried about asking him to come with me?

It's because his total, blind hatred of Saint Dane is dangerous. Saint Dane caused the death of his father and for that, Spader wants revenge. Big time. Hey, I don't blame him. But there were a few times on Cloral where Spader got so completely wrapped up in Saint Dane–hating that he nearly got us all killed. Truth be told, Spader's anger toward Saint Dane is one of the reasons Uncle Press is dead.

Since then, Spader promised me he would control himself, and his anger. I can only hope that when we come face-to-face with the demon again, and I guarantee we will, Spader won't do anything stupid. These were some of the conflicted thoughts that were banging around inside my head as I finished my last journal.

"Hobey-ho, Pendragon," Spader said as he strode into my apartment the morning of our departure.

Spader had almond-shaped eyes that looked sort of Asian. They turned up slightly and made him look as if he were always smiling. The truth was, most of the time he *was* smiling . . . when he wasn't obsessing over Saint Dane, that is. His long black hair was still wet, which meant he had been in the water. Spader spent a lot of time in the water, playing traffic cop with the boats and barges that came and went from Grallion. He loved his job, and his life there. At least he loved it before he found out he was a Traveler. Things had changed a little since then.

"It's time," I said.

"For what?" was his quick response.

"Cloral is safe. Uncle Press is gone. And I'm as ready as I'll ever be to go after Saint Dane."

Spader gave me a devilish smile. "Now you're talking, mate! I've been waiting to hear those words for weeks! What if the trail's gone cold?"

"I don't think that's possible," I answered. "Uncle Press always said that time between territories isn't relative."

Spader frowned. "You lost me."

I had to laugh. This didn't make a whole lot of sense to me either, but I had to trust Uncle Press.

"Look at it this way," I explained. "Saint Dane flumed to Veelox a few weeks ago, but since then he may have spent five years there. Or a minute."

"Now I'm totally lost," Spader said in frustration.

"Bottom line is, we're not too late," I said. "It doesn't matter when we go after him, because the flume will put us where we need to be, *when* we need to be there."

"O-kay," said Spader tentatively. "I'll trust you on that."

I'd already said good-bye to our friends on Grallion, and I'd sent my last journal to you. I had explained the importance of journals to Spader and he had already started his own. The person he chose to send them to on Cloral for safekeeping was Wu Yenza. She was the chief aquaneer and Spader's boss. He couldn't have picked a better person.

I took a last look around my apartment. Then we went down to the docks, loaded our air globes and water sleds onto a skimmer boat, and left Grallion for the flume. Spader was the expert, so he drove. As we shot across the water I looked back at the giant, floating farm habitat of Grallion, wondering if I'd ever see it again. I liked Cloral. There were times when I actually had fun on that territory. It gave me hope that being a Traveler didn't mean I always had to live in a state of fear and confusion.

Now the question was, what lay ahead of us? Pretty much a state of fear and confusion. Great. Here we go again.

The trip to the flume was cake. We anchored the skimmer near the reef, popped on the air globes that allowed us to breathe underwater, triggered the water sleds, and quickly sank below the surface. We didn't run into any shark quigs either. I think that once Saint Dane is finished with a territory, the quigs no longer patrol the gates. Still, I wasn't taking any chances. As we sped through the water being pulled by the sleds, I kept glancing back to make sure nothing nasty was sneaking up on us to try and get a nibble.

I didn't relax until we shot under the shelf of rock that led to the gate. Following the glow from my ring, we quickly found the wide circle of light that led up and into the cavern that held the flume. Moments later we were standing together in the cavern, staring up at the dark flume tunnel that was cut into the rock wall high over our heads.

This was it. The last few seconds of calm.

Spader looked at me and smiled. "My heart's thumpin'."

So was mine. We were standing at the starting line and the gun was about to go off. Spader loved adventure. Me? I'd just as soon be home watching toons. Knowing Spader was nervous made me feel like I wasn't such a weenie after all.

He added, "We're in for another natty-do, aren't we, mate?"

"Yeah," I answered. "Pretty much."

"No use in wasting time here then," he said, sounding a lot braver than I felt.

"Yeah," I said. "We're on the wrong territory."

I stood straight, looked up to the dark hole of the flume, and shouted, *"Veelox!"*

The tunnel sprang to life. Shafts of bright light shot from deep inside. The familiar jumble of musical notes could be heard faintly at first, but quickly grew louder. They were coming to get us.

Spader turned to me and smiled. "Hobey-ho, Pendragon."

"Hobey-ho, Spader," I answered. "Let's go get him."

A second later we were swept up by the light and sound and pulled into the flume.

Next stop . . . Veelox.

❂ SECOND EARTH ❂

Mark Dimond and Courtney Chetwynde huddled together in the vault of the National Bank of Stony Brook, reading Bobby's journal from First Earth. It was a journal unlike any of the others Bobby had sent.

First off, the pages weren't loose. They were bound nicely into a book with a deep red cover. And the pages weren't handwritten. They were typed . . . on an old-fashioned typewriter. They knew it was a typewriter because the letters weren't all perfectly lined up and there were a ton of mistakes. Besides, they didn't have computers or printers back in 1937. This new journal was definitely a far cry from the pieces of rolled up parchment paper Bobby had written his first journals on.

The other difference was that Bobby usually sent only one journal at a time. When he finished writing one he'd send it, through his Traveler ring, to Mark's ring. But this time, sitting in front of Mark and Courtney were four journals. After reading what happened with the gangsters on First Earth, Mark and Courtney knew why.

Bobby's ring had been stolen.

The mysterious manner in which the journals arrived was further proof of that. Earlier that day, Mark had gotten a strange phone call from a lady at the National Bank of Stony Brook. She asked for Mark and Courtney to meet her at the bank to discuss something about a Mr. Robert Pendragon. That was all Mark needed to hear. He and Courtney were at that bank in half an hour.

When they arrived, they discovered that Bobby had rented a safe-deposit box at the bank in 1937. Bobby had left explicit instructions that the bank should contact Mark Dimond on this very date—August 21, Mark's fifteenth birthday.

When Mark and Courtney opened up the safe-deposit box, they found the four journals. They had been lying in that box for over sixty years.

This whole episode was another bizarre twist in an already incredible situation. Bobby Pendragon had mysteriously left their hometown of Stony Brook, Connecticut, with his Uncle Press almost nine months before. Since then his family had disappeared, and the journals began showing up. The only people who knew the truth were his best friends, Mark and Courtney. Bobby trusted them to take care of his journals in case he might need them again someday.

But more important, it seemed to both Mark and Courtney that writing these journals helped keep Bobby sane. He was now smack in the middle of an incredible adventure that had nothing less than the future of everything at stake. Writing the journals seemed like a perfect way for Bobby to help keep his head on straight, while everything around him was so twisted. Both knew that one day Bobby's adventure would take him home. But until then, the only thing they could do to help him on his quest was to read his journals, try to understand what he was going through, and keep them safe.

"We're closing," snapped Ms. Jane Jansen, the bank manager, making Mark and Courtney jump.

Ms. Jane Jansen had only just met the two, but she didn't seem to like them. She didn't seem to like much of anything. Her face was in a permanent state of pucker, like she had a lemon in her pocket that she was constantly sucking on.

"Oh, sorry," said Mark, as if he had been caught doing something wrong. "We were reading. Can we come back tomorrow?"

"Tomorrow's Sunday," snapped Ms. Jane Jansen. "And this isn't a library. You children have spent far too much time here already."

Courtney didn't like Ms. Jane Jansen's attitude. And she definitely didn't like being called a child, especially by such a prune.

"So if we can't read here, what are we supposed to do?" asked Courtney politely, trying not to let her distaste for the woman show through.

"The content of that box belongs to you," Ms. Jane Jansen said. "Do whatever you want with it."

"You mean, we can take it all home?" asked Mark.

"I said, whatever you want," said Ms. Jane Jansen impatiently.

"Why didn't you say that in the first place?" asked Courtney. "Or do you always provide such lousy service?"

Mark winced. He hated it when Courtney clicked into wiseass mode.

Ms. Jane Jansen's eyes popped open wide. "Miss Chetwynde, I have been an employee of the National Bank of Stony Brook for over twenty years and I have always provided thorough and professional service."

"I'll be sure to include that in our report to your president," Courtney said. "That's what this is all about, you know. To test how bank employees deal with unusual situations. So far, you haven't exactly rolled with the punches, now have you, Ms. Jane Jansen?"

Ms. Jane Jansen's eyes grew wide. She suddenly turned all friendly and polite. "Well, uh, if you have any complaints I'd be more than happy to personally ensure your complete satisfaction."

"There *is* something," Courtney said. "If you'd be so kind, would you return the empty drawer to our safe-deposit box? We'll be taking the contents with us."

Ms. Jane Jansen clenched her teeth. It wasn't her job to clean up after people. But she sucked it up.

"Of course," she said with a big, phony smile. "I'd be happy to."

Mark quickly scooped up the four journals and stashed them in his backpack. He wanted to get out of there before Courtney got them into trouble.

"Th-Thanks," he said with sincere courtesy. "We'll get out of your hair now." He went for the door, pulling Courtney along with him.

"Thanks for all your help, ma'am," said Courtney sweetly. "You really put the *ass* in *ass*-istance."

Mark yanked Courtney out of the vault, leaving Ms. Jane Jansen with a twisted smile that actually looked painful. A minute later they rushed out of the gray bank building onto Stony Brook Avenue. Courtney was all smiles. Mark was angry.

"Are you crazy?" he yelled. "What if she threw us out of there? We could have lost the journals!"

"No way," assured Courtney. "You heard her. They belong to us. Besides, she deserved it. She treated us like a couple of turds."

"Yeah, well, some things are more important than your bruised ego," Mark muttered.

"You're right, Mark," Courtney said sincerely. "I'm sorry."

Mark nodded, then looked at Courtney and smiled. "She *did* deserve it."

The two burst out laughing. Now that their bank adventure was behind them, their thoughts turned to the important issue. After waiting for months, they had another journal from Bobby! Better, they had *four* journals. In Mark's pack was an entire new adventure. They wouldn't have to wait impatiently for new journals to show up. They had a full story in their hands.

"I don't know about you," said Mark, "but once I start reading again, I'm not going to want to stop."

"Agreed," said Courtney.

"Here's what I'm thinking. It's getting late. How about if we wait till tomorrow?"

"You're kidding!" protested Courtney.

"I'm serious. Tomorrow's Sunday. I'll come over to your house real early, like eight A.M. We'll go down to your father's workshop and won't come out until we're finished."

Courtney gave this some thought. "You promise not to read anything tonight?" she asked.

"Promise," Mark said, crossing his heart.

"Okay, cool," she said. "I'll make some sandwiches. You bring chips. We'll make it a marathon."

"Excellent. I'll bring the Dew, too," Mark said with excitement.

"Whatever." Courtney didn't do the Dew.

"This is gonna be great!" Mark shouted.

The next day at 8 A.M. sharp, Courtney's doorbell rang. Courtney's dad opened the door to see Mark standing there with a loaded grocery bag.

"Morning, Mark," he said through sleepy eyes. "Going on a picnic?"

"Uh . . . no," answered Mark. "Courtney and I are working on a school project in your basement. It's gonna take all day so we need provisions."

"Really?" said Mr. Chetwynde. "It's August."

"Right," said Mark, thinking fast. "Summer school."

"Courtney doesn't go to summer school."

"I know," Mark said, mentally kicking himself for being such a lousy, uncreative liar. "I do."

Mr. Chetwynde looked at Mark. Mark smiled innocently.

Mr. Chetwynde shrugged and yawned. "Whatever, c'mon in." He stepped aside and Mark rushed in.

Mark knew exactly where to go. He and Courtney had used Mr. Chetwynde's basement workshop as a private place to read Bobby's journals many times before. Mr. Chetwynde had set up an entire workshop down there and never used it. He was a lousy do-it-yourself type guy. Mark and Courtney could be there all day, even on a Sunday, and never worry about anybody coming down.

Mark settled into the big, dusty couch as Courtney ran down the stairs. "Sandwiches are in the fridge," she announced. "Ready when we need 'em."

She sat next to Mark on the couch as he pulled the four red-leather journals from his backpack. He put them down reverently on the low table in front of them. The two sat there, staring at the precious stack. Neither made a move to pick one up.

"This is kind of weird," Mark finally said.

"Really," agreed Courtney. "I'm excited and afraid at the same time. I'm dying to know what happened to Bobby, but what if it's bad?"

The two fell silent, staring at the books.

"There's something else," added Mark thoughtfully. "This whole *First* Earth thing makes me nervous."

"Why?" Courtney asked.

"It's like Saint Dane is coming closer. To us."

"You don't know that," Courtney said quickly.

"No, but Second Earth is a territory like all the others. One day Saint Dane is going to come here, too. And when he does, we're going to be doing more than just reading about it."

"Unless Bobby and the Travelers stop him first, right?" Courtney asked hopefully.

Mark didn't answer. He looked at the journals thoughtfully, then reached for the top one. "Let's just read, okay?"

Courtney took a breath to calm down, then said, "Let's try something different this time. We'll read out loud to each other."

Mark was secretly relieved. He was a faster reader than Courtney and always had to wait for her to catch up. This was the perfect solution.

"Yeah, that sounds good," he said, and handed her the journal. "You first."

Courtney took the journal and cracked open the cover. "We left off where Bobby and Spader flumed to Veelox, right?" she asked.

"Right," answered Mark. He sank back into the couch, put a hand behind his head, got comfortable and said, "Go for it."

Courtney turned to the page where they had left off the day before, and began to read out loud.

"A second later we were swept up by the light and sound and pulled into the flume. Next stop . . . Veelox."

FIRST EARTH

Flying through an interstellar tunnel across time and space was never a normal experience, but making the trip with somebody along for the ride kicked it a couple of notches higher on the strange meter.

"I could get used to this!" declared Spader as he did somersaults and flips, looking like an astronaut pulling zero g's.

I had to hand it to the guy—he knew how to have fun. Me? I was more interested in kicking back and looking out at the stars beyond the crystal walls. Whatever. To each his own.

We had only been sailing for a few minutes when the flume dumped us off again. Spader had been flying headfirst and barely had time to spin around and land on his feet. Once the light from the flume was sucked back into the tunnel and the musical notes left us, we found ourselves standing in . . .

Nothing. Seriously. It was pitch-black. I couldn't see an inch in front of my face.

"Whoa, Veelox is dark," Spader declared.

"Yeah, no kidding. Let's wait a second for our eyes to adjust."

They didn't. We stood there for two minutes, but the

place stayed just as inky black as when we landed.

"Get behind me," Spader ordered protectively. "I'll walk with my hand out until I hit—"

"Stop right there!" a voice boomed at us.

Uh-oh. We weren't alone. This had never happened before. Was it Saint Dane? Could the quigs on Veelox talk? Was unseen danger hurtling toward us at this very second?

"Back up," I said softly to Spader.

I took hold of his arm and was about to pull him back into the flume and get the hell out of there, when a light suddenly appeared, hovering in the air over our heads.

"You seeing this, mate?" Spader asked, his voice sounding shaky.

"Yeah," I answered, just as shaky.

The light grew larger. It was all soft and watery at first, but then suddenly snapped into sharp focus to reveal . . .

A girl. Actually, not a full girl. A girl's *head*. No kidding. Just a head. It was big, too. It floated over us like a huge Macy's Thanksgiving Day Parade balloon.

"Who are you?" the head demanded.

Her voice was loud, as though amplified. The girl-head looked normal enough. She had long blond hair tied back in a ponytail. Her eyes were blue, and she wore small, wire-rimmed glasses with yellow-tinted lenses. I'd even say she was cute, for a monster head, that is. She didn't look dangerous, but then again, a giant floating head didn't exactly look normal, either.

"I'm Bobby Pendragon," I said to the head, trying to sound head-friendly.

"And my name's Vo Spader," Spader added. "Who are you?"

"I'll ask the questions!" boomed the head.

I felt like I was standing before the great and powerful

Wizard of Oz. With any luck, there'd be some befuddled old man hiding behind a curtain pulling on levers to control the big thing.

"Where do you come from?" demanded the head.

"I'm from Cloral," answered Spader. "My mate here is from Second Earth. Do you have a body to go with that head?"

The head suddenly dipped down toward us. We both hit the floor. For a second I thought she was going to take a bite.

"I said I'll ask the questions!" she roared.

"Sorry, mate," yelled Spader. "No worries. I'm with you now."

The head floated back higher without taking a chomp. Spader and I exchanged worried looks.

"Why did you come here?" asked the giant blonde girl-head thing.

"Spader and I are Travelers," I said. "We followed someone here. His name is—"

"Saint Dane isn't here now," the head announced.

Whoa. The head was a couple of steps ahead of us . . . no pun intended.

"Uhh, sorry to disagree," Spader said. "But he definitely came here from Cloral."

The big head rolled her eyes like we were annoying her, and said, "I didn't say he was *never* here. I said he's not here *now*. Weren't you listening?"

Spader and I shot each other looks. This was getting even stranger. We were talking to a big, floating, *obnoxious* head.

"Watch," the head said impatiently, as if she were talking to a couple of naughty children. "This happened a few minutes ago."

The head then disappeared. Just like that. It faded out like a movie. I began to wonder if it had really been there or if it were some kind of projection. We were in the dark again, in more ways than one. But not for long.

Another light began to grow. At first I thought the head was coming back, but what appeared right in front of us was another image entirely. It looked like the mouth of the flume! It was like a 3-D movie projected in space. Very cool. That started to explain the giant head. My guess was these guys on Veelox had some hot technology going on.

Spader backed off. "What is this, Pendragon?" he asked nervously.

"It's okay," I assured him. "I think it's like a movie."

"Oh," Spader said. "What's a movie?"

The image of the flume then came to life. Bright light shone from the mouth and the musical notes told us that somebody was about to arrive. And then this strange movie took an interesting turn.

Saint Dane stepped out of the flume.

"Hobey!" shouted Spader in surprise.

"It's okay," I assured him. "It's just pictures."

Saint Dane stood in the mouth of the projected flume. This may have been a hologram movie, but it sure looked real. His long gray hair cascaded over the shoulders of his dark suit, and his piercing blue eyes cut through me as if he were actually standing there. Saint Dane even gave us a wave, as if he knew we were watching him.

Even though I'm still trying to understand where we fit into this whole Traveler picture, there are a few things I know all too well. Mostly they have to do with our mission and with the guy who was standing before us in a hologram—Saint Dane.

Halla is in danger because of him. Halla is everything— every territory, every person, every thing, and every *time* that ever existed. I know, it doesn't make total sense to me, either, but that's what I've been told. Saint Dane is a Traveler who wants to control Halla. In a word, he is evil. But simply calling him evil is like saying Tiger Woods is a good golfer. Saint Dane is the Tiger Woods of bad. He enjoys causing pain and suffering. I've seen what he's capable of. It isn't pretty. If he gets his way and somehow takes control of Halla, well, I don't even want to think about that.

The only thing standing between Saint Dane and his wicked plans are the other Travelers. That's us. Every territory is reaching a critical turning point. Saint Dane is doing his worst to influence these important events so that each territory will fall into chaos. If he succeeds, then all of Halla will fall to him.

We've got to make sure he doesn't succeed.

So far we are 2 and 0. Denduron and Cloral were wins. But it's going to be a long war.

As we stood staring at the hologram of Saint Dane, every fear I had about the guy came screaming back. He was one bad dude. I watched as his recorded image turned back toward the flume.

"*First Earth,*" he commanded.

An instant later the light and music swept him up and carried him into the tunnel. The image then faded out and the flume projection was gone. We were back in the dark.

"Now do you understand?" the girl-head's voice boomed out of the darkness. "He was here. He left. End of story. Now go away."

"Who are you?" I called out to the girl-head. "Why should we believe that?"

Another hologram appeared before us. It was the same view of the flume as before. Again, the tunnel activated with light and music. Who was going to arrive this time? A second later Spader and I watched as . . .

Spader and I stepped out of the flume in the hologram!

"I've gone totally off my nut," Spader said in awe.

"Whoa, Veelox is dark," the projection of Spader declared.

"Yeah, no kidding," the projection of me said. "Let's wait a second for our eyes to adjust."

It was exactly what had happened a minute before.

"My name is Aja Killian," boomed the head voice as our holograms disappeared.

Spader and I spun around to see the big head had returned. It hovered over us like a blond cloud.

"I'm the Traveler from Veelox," she said. "I've got the flume monitored and I record everything that happens. That's why I know Saint Dane isn't here anymore. Any more questions?"

"Yes," I said. "Would you please stop with this giant-head thing and show yourself? If you're a Traveler, then we're all friends here."

I was feeling a little more bold now, and getting tired of staring up at this girl.

"I would," Aja answered. "But I'm nowhere near you."

Spader said, "So you're telling us that Saint Dane flumed in here for a second, then flumed right back out again?"

"I'm not telling you," she said curtly. "I just *showed* you. Don't you believe what you see?"

Spader looked at me and asked softly, "Why did he leave so fast?"

"Because he's wasting his time here," Aja answered quickly. "Veelox is totally under control."

I laughed and said, "Yeah, that's what I thought about Cloral, until people started turning up dead."

"Look," the Aja-head scolded. "Nobody comes or goes through the flume without my knowing. He's not here. So go chase him to First Earth where you can be more useful."

Spader and I shared looks. "I guess she told *you!*" he said with a raised eyebrow.

I looked back up at the Aja-head and said, "If you think he's dumb enough to be controlled by your little home movies, then you're not as smart as you think you are."

That seemed to strike a chord. The big head floated down closer to us and stared me right in the eye. It took all I could do not to back off.

"And what makes *you* the expert on all things Saint Dane?" she asked with disdain.

"I'm not," I answered. "But I've battled him twice and both times been lucky enough to win. How about you?"

Aja-head blinked. I don't think she liked being challenged. She floated back up higher.

"If you take him on alone, you'll lose," added Spader. "He won't get spooked by a big floating head . . . like us."

"I'll try to remember that," she said sarcastically.

Aja Killian was the Traveler from Veelox, and she thought she was smarter than Saint Dane. That was dangerous. I knew we'd be back on Veelox sooner or later. I just hoped that when that time came, we wouldn't have to fight both Saint Dane *and* Aja Killian.

"Go to First Earth," Aja-head scolded. "Have fun, play your little games. Don't worry about Veelox."

With that, the giant head disappeared. Spader and I were once again alone.

"Fun?" Spader said. "I can think of a lot of things to call the tum-tigger we're headed into. Fun isn't one of them."

"Should we believe her?" I asked.

"I'm not sure we have a whole lot of choice," Spader answered. "Looks like Saint Dane came here to throw us off, and the big-head girl caught him."

"Then we're on the wrong territory, again." I said.

"He went to First Earth," Spader said. "That anything like Second Earth?"

"I think we're about to find out."

The two of us then stepped into the mouth of the flume.

First Earth.

Being from Second Earth I couldn't help but think I would be going home. At least that was what I hoped. I didn't know that we were about to flume into the laps of two murderous gangsters who were waiting for us with machine guns.

Yes, the real fun was about to begin.

FIRST EARTH

"You're lucky," Mr. Nasty Gangster chuckled. "It'll be quick. You won't feel a thing."

"How would *you* know?" asked Spader nervously.

The two gangsters held their machine guns on us, keeping us from moving off the subway track. To our right, a subway train was barreling along, headed our way.

This was not a happy homecoming.

"Trust me," the gangster answered. "There won't be enough of you left to feel nothin'."

How's *that* for a grim thought?

"We were just supposed to scare 'em," the nervous gangster said. "Not splatter 'em." The guy looked like he was having second thoughts. I liked this guy. At least I liked him better than the guy who wanted us dead.

"They'll be scared all right," the nasty gangster chuckled. "Just before they catch the train."

Or the train catches us.

"But—" the nervous guy protested.

"Hey, we're on our own now," Nasty shot back. "I'm calling the plays."

The track beneath our feet was now shaking from the imminent arrival of the death train. The headlight was shining on us. The horn shrieked. The trainman must have seen us, but it was too late to stop. The express was coming through whether we were on the track or not.

Believe it or not, in spite of what Mr. Nasty thought, I wasn't scared. That's because I knew how we were going to escape. It was going to be pretty simple. The tricky part would be timing.

"I think we should move, mate," Spader whispered to me. "This could be a messy-do."

"Wait," I said.

"Bye-bye, boys!" shouted the gangster over the screaming horn.

The train was nearly on us.

"Uh, Pendragon?" Spader whined.

"Now!" I shouted.

I grabbed Spader's arm and we both jumped back, off the track. Instantly the train flashed by in front of us. What did those two idiot gangsters think? We were going to stand there and get slammed?

"Run!" I yelled.

The speeding train was now between us and the gangsters. We had a short window of protection. Using the train as a shield, Spader followed me toward the abandoned subway station. With any luck, the train would have enough cars to give us time to get there. It was about forty yards from the gate to the old platform. Not a long run, but it was tricky because we had to do it on another track that ran parallel to the one the train was on. One misstep and we'd go down with twisted ankles.

I shot a quick glance back over my shoulder to see how

long the train was. Luckily there was still a bunch of cars to come. Our luck was holding. I figured we'd hit the station right about the time the train passed us. Then we could jump up on the platform and book out of there. I took another glance back and saw that the last car was almost on us.

"Stay with me!" I shouted back to Spader.

A second later the train whipped by us. I put on the brakes, ready to leap across the track and climb up onto the platform of the abandoned station. But what I saw in the next instant jolted me to a standstill. The two of us stood across from the abandoned station platform to see . . .

It wasn't abandoned anymore!

I couldn't believe it. Everything up until now was exactly as I remembered it: the flume, the gate, the tracks, even the location of the platform. Everything was the same, except for the station. The place was lit up and busy with people. The token booth was open and selling fares to passengers flooding down the stairs; the grimy, broken tiles on the walls looked new and clean; and there was a busy newsstand selling papers to eager customers. How could this be?

"Now's not the time to stop, mate," warned Spader.

He was right. We leaped over the track and hoisted ourselves up onto the platform. People stared at us in shock. I guess they weren't used to seeing people scramble across active tracks, especially not when a train had just blasted through. Spader stood up, winked at an older woman who was watching us, and said with a charming smile, "No worries, mum. Routine inspection. Everything checks out spiff." The woman stared back in total confusion.

An idea hit me and I pushed my way through the passengers toward the newsstand. There was a stack of newspapers right in front. If I was right, the paper would tell me everything I needed to know. I picked it up, stared at the front page, and my whole body went numb.

"What's the trouble?" Spader asked as he came up behind me.

"It's 1937," I said, barely believing my own words. "First Earth is in 1937."

"Right," he said, trying to understand. "What does that mean?"

"It means this is my home territory, but in a time more than half a century before I was born."

The date on the newspaper was March 10, 1937. I couldn't believe what I was seeing, but there it was in good old black and white.

"You gonna buy that paper, mac?" growled the news vendor. "This ain't a lendin' library."

The guy was a pudgy, gruff-looking munchkin who hadn't shaved in a few days. He wore a wool cap with a visor and chewed on a stubby cigar that looked like a rotten stick. It didn't smell much better than it looked. I slowly put the paper down and took a look around the station. Now it made sense. The station was open because it wasn't abandoned *yet*.

I now registered what the people were wearing. It looked like an old-time movie with men wearing suits and hats and women all wearing dresses. I didn't see a pair of jeans or sneakers in the place.

We really were in the past.

"Howdy, Buck Rogers!" came a voice from behind us. "Bring any spare change from outer space?"

We both turned to see a tall, gray-haired African American man in a long, woolen coat walking toward us. Buck Rogers? Oh, right. Spader and I were still wearing the swim clothes from Cloral. We must have stuck out like orange on black.

"Sorry," I answered the man. "I'll catch you next time."

"That's all right," he said with a chuckle. "Give my regards to Ming the Merciless."

Suddenly the sound of machine-gun fire shattered the station.

There were screams of panic as everybody ducked down. I couldn't believe it. Were the gangsters shooting up the place? Spader and I ducked down and looked to the far side of the platform where the shooting came from. Standing there were the two gunmen, still wearing white handkerchiefs over their faces. The nasty guy in charge had fired his machine gun into the ceiling. The weapon was still smoking.

"Everybody freeze!" he shouted. "We're lookin' for a couple of wise guys dressed like spacemen."

That was us. There was no way we could blend into this crowd. I looked around, hoping a cop was on duty. If there was, he was just as scared of these nimrods as everybody else, because he wasn't stepping forward. We were on our own.

The gangsters started walking slowly through the station, scanning the crowd. People were crouched down all around us, afraid to move. I caught the eye of a woman who looked at us with fear. She knew we were the guys they were looking for. But she didn't say anything. Maybe she was afraid of getting caught in the crossfire. Spader and I glanced around, desperate to find an escape route.

"Here! Over here!" somebody yelled. It was the news vendor guy. I looked up and was shocked to see he was leaning out of his newsstand, pointing us out to the gangsters. Nice guy.

Spader and I had no choice but to stand up. Everybody else stayed on the ground. If the gangsters wanted to open fire, they'd have a clear shot at us. I think the term was "sitting ducks." Or maybe it was more like "standing ducks."

The gangsters turned to us and raised their machine guns.

"What is all the ruckus here?"

It was the African American guy who had called me Buck Rogers. He stepped between Spader and me and put his arms around our shoulders. "You think shootin' up these spacemen will get rid of 'em?" he declared. "No sir-ee! I seen this in the movin' pictures! You shoot 'em up and they'll just start duplicatin'! That what you want? Bunch of little blue spacemen running around?"

"Get outta the way, old man," snarled the nasty gangster. "Unless you want to blast off with 'em."

"Now there's an idea!" said the man.

Just then, another subway train entered the station. But rather than speed through, this one slowed down to a stop.

"I always wanted to see what was goin' on up there in outer space!" the old guy cackled. "Maybe now's my big chance!"

The head gangster smiled and brought his machine gun up higher, ready to fire. The second gangster kept glancing nervously between us and his partner. "Suit yourself, old man," said the nasty gangster.

"Oh, I don't think you want to go doin' that," said the old man with such certainty that it actually made the nasty gangster hesitate.

"Look around," he continued. "All these fine people are watching."

The nervous gangster was already looking at all the people whose eyes were fixed on them. Now the nasty gangster took a quick look too. He was having second thoughts.

The subway train came to a stop, the doors opened, and people flooded out onto the platform. A few saw what was going on and quickly jumped out of the way. Others ducked back inside the subway car. The old guy kept his hands on our shoulders and led us over toward the train. As we walked, he kept talking.

"Every one of these good people are witnesses. This isn't some lonely back alley. You can't hide in the shadows. Your dirty work is on display for everybody to see, and remember."

The old guy definitely had the gangsters thinking. Now even the nasty guy looked unsteady. In the meantime, we were moving closer to the open subway door. All I could do was hope it wouldn't close before we got there.

"I believe you two are smart gentlemen," our friend continued. "You understand what I'm telling you."

I didn't think the gangsters understood anything. I thought the old gent was confusing them. But that was okay. If it gave us time to escape, I didn't care what was going through the minds of these bad guys. The old man turned us around so we were still facing the gangsters. Our backs were now to the open subway door. He kept us moving though. He gently pulled us backward and onto the subway train. A few seconds later the three of us stood inside the car. Now I prayed for the doors to shut.

"I am so proud of you gentlemen," said the old man to the gangsters with a smile. "You are two upstanding individuals."

Everyone waited for something to happen. The gangsters stood with their mouths open. Every single person in the station was afraid to move. Spader, the old guy, and I stood just inside the open subway door.

Time stood still.

Then a bell rang on the subway train and the doors started to close. That woke the gangsters up. They both jumped for the train. They were a ways behind us, so they leaped onto the train through the set of doors farther back on our car. At that instant, the old man shoved Spader and me forward. We all jumped off the train and back onto the platform at the exact moment the doors closed behind us . . . with the gangsters trapped on board!

A second later the train began to pull out of the station. The three of us watched as the subway car slid past, along with the two gangsters. The nasty gangster grabbed at the door, angrily trying to pull it open. But it was too late. Next stop for them . . . someplace else. The old guy smiled and gave him a wave as they disappeared into the tunnel ahead. All around us, people started to move again. They all seemed a little shocked, but none more than Spader and I.

"That was incredible!" Spader shouted. "You had them stupefied."

"You saved our lives," I said. "I don't know how to thank you."

The friendly smile dropped off the old man's face. In an instant he went from a warm, charming grandpa to a serious man on a mission.

"Follow me," he said sternly, and walked off.

Spader and I didn't move. "Should we?" Spader asked me.

A second later people started to gather around us. They were moving in like we were two escaped animals from the zoo. We had caused a pretty big disturbance, and they wanted to know why. This was not a good place to be.

"Absolutely," I answered, and ran to follow the old man.

The guy may have been old, but he was quick. He was already halfway up the stairs to the street. Spader and I barreled through the turnstile and ran after him. I was in such a hurry to catch up that I didn't stop to think about what we would see outside. But when we got to the top of the stairs, reality hit me square in the face.

We had arrived in a different time.

This was the same section of the Bronx where Uncle Press first brought me to begin this adventure . . . over sixty years from now. But as much as it was sort of familiar, it was also way different. I recognized many of the buildings. Even in my time there were no modern steel-and-glass structures in this neighborhood, so a lot of these same buildings would be around sixty years from now. The only real difference was that in 1937, they looked clean and new.

The big, obvious difference that jumped out at me was the cars. They were all so old. But they *weren't* old. Here in 1937 they were the latest models. Very strange. Traffic was just as hectic here as in my time, and the street was jammed with ancient vehicles. There was an odd smell, too. It was kind of like chemicals. It took me a while to realize that this was long before people worried about clean air and car emissions and unleaded gasoline and all those things that are supposed to keep pollution down. These cars were all spewing old-fashioned, full-leaded, full-stink emissions. It reeked.

Another thing that caught my eye was the billboards. They were everywhere, advertising things I never heard of. There was one showing a lady with a big smile who brightened her teeth not with toothpaste, but with tooth powder. Another had a guy looking all sorts of happy because he gassed up his car with "Esso" gasoline. Still another showed a group of quintuplets, all girls, who were advertising a soap made with olive oil. Gross. Wasn't that like washing with spaghetti sauce? I knew this was Earth, but it sure felt like a different planet.

Spader stood right by my side, looking dazed. This all must have been strange to him, too. But in a very different way.

"You two going to stand there all day?"

We looked to see the old African American guy standing by a yellow cab, holding the back door open for us.

"Look," I said. "Thanks for bailing us out and all, but we're not gonna get in that cab with—"

"Vincent Van Dyke is my name," he said with a smile. "My friends call me Gunny."

"O-kay, Gunny. Like I was saying, we got things to do so—"

"I know you do," Gunny said. "I know all about it."

"Oh, yeah?" Spader asked. "What do you know?"

Gunny chuckled and said, "I know that if you want to start looking for Saint Dane, you might need my help."

It was like the whole world had stopped again. Did he really say what I thought he said? I turned to Spader. He looked as shocked as I felt.

"Yeah," Spader said. "I heard it too."

The old guy didn't move. He stood with his hand on the open cab door and a smile on his face.

"Who are you?" I asked.

"Like I said, my friends call me Gunny. And I'm pretty sure we're all gonna be good friends, seeing as I'm the Traveler from First Earth."

He held up his hand to show us that he was wearing the familiar silver ring with the dark gray stone in the middle.

Our visit to First Earth was getting more interesting by the second.

FIRST EARTH

"Fifty-ninth and Park, my good man," Gunny said to the cabbie as we got into the car.

It was a big, old-fashioned cab with lots of room in back. I think I have to stop calling things "old-fashioned," though. This was First Earth. This was 1937. This was the past, but it was today. Totally whacked.

The cabbie pulled into traffic and headed toward Manhattan. Along the way I kept looking out the window to see the differences between First and Second Earth. The odd thing was, it really wasn't as different as you might think. I wasn't exactly an expert on history and all things New York, but from the view of a kid from Connecticut who had only been to the city a few times, I was surprised to see how similar things were.

Like I wrote before, the most obvious difference for me was the cars. I'd seen old cars before, but always in some black-and-white movie or picture. When I was a little kid, I thought the whole world was black-and-white in the "olden" days. But I'm here to tell you, things were definitely not black-and-white in 1937. The sky was just as blue, the sun was just as yellow and the grass in the parks was just as green as on Second Earth. But the cars were mostly black. Some were cream colored and a few gray, but black was definitely the most popular color. They rode a little rough, too. The three of us bounced around in the back of that cab every time we hit a pothole. Yeah, they had potholes in 1937 too.

As much as I wanted to check out the wonders of the past, the guy sitting in front of me was more important. He said he was the Traveler from First Earth. I had no reason to doubt him, especially since he wore the ring. But still, he didn't fit the profile of all the other Travelers. First off, he was old. I couldn't tell exactly *how* old, but he had to be up there. Maybe sixty? All the other Travelers were young. Uncle Press was older. So was Osa. But not *this* old. Besides, they were gone. They had passed the torch on to a younger generation of Travelers. Did that mean Gunny's days were numbered too? I decided not to ask him. That wouldn't have been cool.

He seemed like an okay guy. It was incredible the way he had controlled the gangsters and helped us escape. He had a soothing voice that made you feel like everything was all right. As I had learned, Travelers have the ability to be very persuasive. It's like a hypnosis thing. I've tried it myself. It works, sometimes. I'm still not very good at it.

"You two sure do believe in making a dramatic entrance," Gunny said with a chuckle. "My heart's still pounding."

Wow. If he was scared back in that station, he sure didn't show it. Add that to the list. The guy was cool under pressure.

"We didn't expect a welcoming committee," I said. "But we're sure glad you were there."

Gunny nodded thoughtfully. "I'm guessing you're Pendragon," he said, then looked to Spader. "Which one are you?"

"Vo Spader, mate," answered Spader proudly. "Aquaneer supreme from the territory of Cloral."

"I like that!" Gunny laughed. "I have no idea what an aquaneer supreme is, but it sure sounds fine!"

"What's your story?" I asked, still not sure how far we could trust this guy.

"I could bore you for hours with my story."

"Go for it," I said.

"Start by telling us where the name Gunny came from," Spader said.

"The army," Gunny answered. "It's sort of a joke. I signed up back in seventeen to fight in the Great War. Not sure why they called it that, but who am I to say? Trouble was, I couldn't bring myself to fire a gun. I tried, mind you. I really did. But it was the strangest thing. I'd pick up a rifle, point it, but couldn't bring myself to pull the trigger. Didn't matter how much they hollered at me, I couldn't do it. That's when I got the nickname. Spent the rest of the war cooking and cleaning pots."

"Did you know you were a Traveler back then?" asked Spader.

"Nope. Found out two years ago," Gunny said. "I've lived most of a life thinking things were one way. Come to find out it wasn't that way at all. I can't say I'm too happy about it, but I guess I don't have a choice, do I?"

No, he didn't. Neither did we. Welcome to Travelerhood. I glanced quickly up at the cabbie, wondering what he would think of this conversation. My guess was New York cabbies had seen and heard far stranger stories than this.

"How'd you find out?" I asked.

"I work at this hotel," Gunny explained. "Near twenty years now. Started scrubbing pots, now I'm a bell captain. One day this fella showed up. Nice enough gentleman. Soon as I showed him to his room, he started telling me things. Things about me he never could have known."

"Like what?" asked Spader.

"He knew about my family; about where I was raised down in Virginia; about things I said and did forty years before that I near forgot myself. I have to tell you I was a little scared of this fella. But he calmed me down and said everything was going to be fine. He said it was time I knew about my true calling."

"So he laid the whole Traveler gig on you right there?" I asked.

"Not exactly. He asked me to take a trip with him. Uptown. If I had known just how far uptown he meant, I'm not so sure I would have gone with him."

"I guess he took you to the flume," I said.

"That's right. Before I knew it, I was flying through space. I was lucky my poor old heart didn't give out right then and there. We landed at a place called Ta Da or some such thing."

"Zadaa?" I asked.

"That was it. Zadaa. It was this beautiful city in the desert, with a river running under the ground."

Spader and I shared looks. We had been there too. It was Loor's home territory.

Gunny continued, "And he introduced me to the most beautiful lady I had ever seen."

"Osa," I said.

"That was her!" Gunny stopped talking for a second. I could tell his mind was back on Zadaa, with Osa. She was Loor's mother and like Gunny said, an amazingly beautiful woman. Gunny came back to the present and said, "She's the one who told me all about being a Traveler and how it was up to us to stop this Saint Dane fella from causing trouble. I wanted to know why I was chosen, but both of 'em said I'd find out in due time."

"Sounds familiar," I said.

"It was too much for my brain to take in all at once. I'm still not sure I understand it all, even now. The gentleman took me on a few more trips, just to show me more of what was out there. I never thought I'd ever see such wondrous sights. Then he brought me back home. I asked him what I was supposed to do, and he said I didn't have to do anything except wait and keep my eyes open. That was two years ago. After a time I began thinking I dreamed the whole thing. I kept my eyes open, but there was nothing to see. That is, until today."

"The guy who took you to Zadaa," I asked. "What was his name?"

"Went by the name of Tilton. Press Tilton. I suppose you know him."

"He was my uncle," I answered.

"Your uncle!" exclaimed Gunny with a smile. "Now that explains a few things. He told me all about you. Said you'd be showing up someday. He talked about you like you were the upside of buttered bread. Now it makes sense!"

"Upside of buttered bread?" said Spader, giving me a sideways look.

"Hold on," Gunny said. "You said he *was* your uncle?"

"Yeah," I answered quietly. "Uncle Press is dead. I hate to tell you this, but Osa is too."

The smile dropped from Gunny's face. He looked down, letting this information work through his head. "I am truly sorry to hear that," he finally said. "He was a good person. I can say the same for Osa. The world is worse off without them."

"Thanks, but there's more you gotta know," I said.

"I'm not so sure I want to," Gunny shot back. For the first time since we'd met, he looked nervous.

"Those gangsters back at the subway station," I began. "They're the ones who killed Uncle Press."

"No!" exclaimed Gunny. "Press came back?"

"No. We were at a flume in another territory. Saint Dane took off, but before we could chase him, bullets came back at us through the flume."

I could feel Spader grow tense next to me. This was a tough memory for him.

"Uncle Press was killed by those bullets," I continued. "Saint Dane had his hand in it. I'm sure of that. He's the only one who could have activated the flume to send those bullets through."

Gunny looked away. The expression on his face grew dark. He needed to get his mind around this. After several seconds he finally spoke.

"I guess that means it's starting," he said softly.

"What?" asked Spader. "What's starting?"

Gunny was anxious. His mind was racing to places I didn't think he wanted to go. "I hear things, you know?" he said nervously. "Being at the hotel and all, I see and hear it all. Maybe that's why I was chosen for this Traveler business."

"What did you hear?" I asked.

"Those gunmen at the subway station, they are a couple of bad apples. I heard rumors that there was going to be a hit. Somebody was going to get killed, you know? I hear things like that all the time. Usually it's just rumors. But the thing that made me take notice this time was the place it was supposed to happen. It was that subway station. The one with the flume thing. I was hoping it was just a coincidence, but I had to see for myself. That's why I was up there today."

"And then we showed up," I said.

"Yeah," said Gunny. "And a Traveler died. I'm afraid that can only mean one thing."

"Yeah," Spader said to Gunny. "Looks like your days of watching and waiting are over."

"Whatever Saint Dane's plan is for First Earth," I said, "it's on."

The car came to a stop and the cabbie slid the glass partition back that separated the front seat from the back. "Fifty-ninth and Park," he announced.

I wondered how much of our conversation he'd heard. It didn't matter. It wouldn't have made any sense to him.

"Where are we?" asked Spader.

"This is my home," said Gunny. "The Manhattan Tower Hotel. They all come through here sooner or later—movie stars, politicians, captains of industry. And gangsters."

"Gangsters?" I said with surprise.

"Yes," answered Gunny. "After what I've seen and heard today, I've got a feeling they're the reason we've all been gathered together."

"Welcome home," I said to myself and stepped out of the cab.

FIRST EARTH

Gunny paid the cab fare as Spader and I gazed up at the Manhattan Tower Hotel. It was a real swankadelic place. It was thirty stories high and definitely the tallest building in the neighborhood. The front entrance was set back from busy Park Avenue to make room for an elaborate garden in front. There were trees and fountains and everything. It must have been a full-time job for a team to take care of, because even though it was March and kind of chilly, the garden was green and packed with colorful flowers. It was a dense, colorful jungle in the middle of a gray city.

The building itself stood out from the others because of its color. Every other building was some shade of cement. But the Manhattan Tower Hotel had a touch of pink to it. I'm not talking pukey-bright, Pepto-Bismol pink; it was softer than that. It made the place look warm and inviting. I couldn't remember if this hotel was still around on Second Earth. But then again, like I said, I'm not an expert on New York history.

"Let's try something," Gunny said as he joined us on the sidewalk. He took off his long woolen coat to reveal he was wearing his bell captain uniform underneath.

"Hobey!" exclaimed Spader when he got a glimpse. "What a spiffer!"

Gunny had made an amazing transformation. The dark woolen coat he had been wearing made him look like everybody else on the street, but the outfit underneath was spectacular. The jacket was a deep, dark red with shiny brass buttons that went all the way up to the collar. The collar stood straight up and had two lines of golden trim running all the way around his neck. On each cuff of his sleeves were four golden bars. On his left breast was a fancy logo with the letters *MTH* for Manhattan Tower Hotel. On the other breast was a name tag that read "Vincent Van Dyke, Captain." The pants were black, with a gold bar running down the outside of each leg. To finish it off, his shoes were shined to within an inch of their lives. The whole package had a military feel, like he was ready for a parade.

Gunny stood up straight and proud as we admired the uniform. He was a big guy, I'm guessing at least six foot four. But in his uniform, he looked seven feet tall. I think he knew it too. He had a little smile on his face. That was cool.

"Be honest, Gunny," Spader said. "You were kiddin' us before. You're really a royal prince, right?"

Gunny laughed. "Don't I wish," he said. "Come here, Pendragon." Gunny held up his woolen coat for me to put on. "Can't have you guys walking through my hotel looking like Martians," he added.

The coat was about a dozen sizes too big. The sleeves were so long you couldn't see my hands and the bottom dragged on the sidewalk.

"Now I look like a Martian wearing my father's coat," I complained.

Gunny took off the coat and put it on Spader. It looked a

little better on him. At least the bottom only skimmed the ground.

"It'll do," Gunny said. He then turned to me and winked. "We'll take our chances with you looking like a spaceman, shorty."

"Gimme a break, I'm only fourteen!" I said defensively, but I knew he was just giving me a hard time. I was beginning to like Gunny Van Dyke.

Before we could head into the hotel, a big limousine pulled up to the curb near us. I didn't think anything of it, but Gunny got tense.

"Stay right here," he said to us under his breath.

The two front doors to the limousine opened at the same time and four guys in suits jumped out. It all happened so fast it was almost funny. All I could think of were clowns jumping out of a car at the circus. I wondered how many other guys in suits were packed inside. One of the suits hurried to the back door and opened it up. The others stood around, scanning the sidewalk like Secret Service agents. A second later a guy pulled himself out of the back of the limo.

I knew instantly that this was "the man."

He wore a suit like the others, but that's where the similarity ended, because he was big. I'm talking massive. Everything about this dude was huge. His hands, his head, his feet, his body. He wasn't fat. He was just big. His suit was light gray, and I could see he had a big gem stuck in his dark blue tie. I'd bet anything it was a diamond. His hat was the same color as his suit, with a dark blue band around it. A perfectly folded handkerchief that was the same color as his tie poked up from his breast pocket. He had a couple of rings on his fingers that looked pretty expensive too.

This guy seemed like someone who pretty much got whatever he wanted. He stood up, adjusted his suit so everything looked just right, then turned toward the hotel. The other guys gathered around him, forming a protective shield. As they walked, they kept scanning the sidewalk for any threats. No question. They were bodyguards.

"Who is this guy?" I asked. "Some foreign president?"

"I wish," answered Gunny under his breath. "Most foreign presidents aren't killers."

Uh-oh. Not a good answer.

The guy caught sight of Gunny and broke out in a big smile. "Gunny, my friend!" he bellowed. He changed direction and headed right for us. That meant all of his bodyguards had to adjust and follow. It was like a big cargo ship had suddenly changed direction and all the little tugboats around it had to hurry to keep up.

Gunny tried to look casual. Spader and I didn't move.

"You working the street now, Gunny?" the guy asked with a big smile.

"No sir, Mr. Rose," answered Gunny politely. "Just taking a break. Wanted a breath of fresh air."

"Good man," the big guy exclaimed. He reached into his pocket and pressed a dollar bill into Gunny's hand. "Don't work too hard now, understand?" he said, and gave Gunny a friendly cuff on the shoulder.

"Only when I'm working for you, Mr. Rose," Gunny replied.

The guy let out a laugh that was bigger than necessary. But that was okay. If he was a killer, then I wanted him to be in a good mood. It seemed like he thought Gunny was okay. That was good too. But then he looked down at me and stopped laughing.

Uh-oh. Was I in trouble? What should I do? I had this image of King Kong—gazing down on all those poor natives who were running around—getting ready to choose one to pick up and swallow.

"Howdy there, Buck Rogers," he said. "Little late for Halloween."

I wasn't sure of how to react, so I pretended he had made a really funny joke and forced out a laugh. It was the right move because the guy laughed with me. He grabbed my hand and stuck something in it.

"No offense, pardner, just making a joke," he said. "You look real cute." He then walked toward the hotel with his boys scrambling to follow. I looked down at my hand to see he had given me a dollar bill too.

"The spaceman comments are getting old," I said.

"Who was that guy?" Spader asked Gunny.

"Name's Maximilian Rose. He's a businessman who lives in the penthouse here at the Manhattan Tower. He's got more businesses than Heinz got pickles."

"And? . . . " I asked.

Gunny took a quick look around to see if anyone was listening. He continued in a whisper, "And he's about as crooked as a rattlesnake in an accordion factory."

I looked at Spader. Spader shrugged. "Who's Heinz and what's an accordion?"

Gunny continued, "What I'm saying is he didn't make all his money being an honest businessman. He puts up a respectable front, but he is a very bad individual. Trust me on that."

"Those gangsters in the subway," I said. "Do they work for Rose?"

"No, they're from a whole 'nother gang downtown."

"Is there anyone in this town who *isn't* a gangster?" Spader asked.

"I know three for sure," said Gunny. "You, me, and Pendragon."

"Swell," said Spader sarcastically. "It's your basic tum-tigger."

"Tum-what?" asked Gunny.

"Let's just go inside, all right?" I said. Hearing these guys confuse each other was getting almost as old as the spaceman comments.

A few moments later, a doorman wearing a uniform similar to Gunny's held open a heavy, glass door for us and we stepped into the lobby of the Manhattan Tower Hotel. The place was even more spectacular inside than out. It gave me the feeling that I was in some huge, rich-guy mansion. The ceiling of the lobby soared up three stories and was decorated with stained glass scenes of a beautiful green forest. The sun shone down through the glass and sprayed colored specks of light all over the room like a kaleidoscope.

We walked on thick, oriental carpets under giant crystal chandeliers that looked as if they'd come from a European castle. Several sitting areas had red-leather furniture where people sat chatting or reading newspapers. Nobody spoke above a whisper. It was like being in church, or a library. It was pretty obvious that you had to have bucks to stay here. This was no cheaby hotel like the one my parents took me to at Niagara Falls. That place was skuzzy and smelled like b.o. Here you could eat off the floor. Not that you'd want to. Everyone I saw looked as if they had just stepped out of an old-fashioned department-store window. All the men wore suits and hats. The women had on dresses.

There were only two people in the whole room who looked

totally out of place—me and Spader. I was feeling pretty stupid wearing a bright blue suit with shoes to match. Spader didn't look much better in Gunny's big coat.

"We're out of our league here," I whispered to Gunny.

"Nonsense," Gunny replied. "You'll fit right in."

Yeah, right. If we were circus people here to juggle for the good folks.

"Come with me," Gunny said, and walked off.

We followed him, staying close, hoping nobody would notice us. Gunny walked through the lobby like he owned the place. He had a slow, smooth walk that said, "This is my house and I'm proud of it." Several people nodded and smiled at him as they passed. Gunny knew everybody's name and had a little something personal to say to each of them.

"Afternoon, Mr. Galvao, see you again next month. Hello, Mrs. Tavey. I see you've been to our beauty salon. Very lovely. Mr. Prevett, your luggage has all been sent ahead, just as you requested." The guy was good. He knew every guest by name. No wonder he was a captain.

We made it across the lobby and up to a bank of shiny, brass elevators. Gunny hit the button.

"Where are we going?" asked Spader.

Gunny glanced around casually to make sure nobody could hear him. "They're doing a big renovation up on the sixth floor," he said softly. "Nobody will know if we have a couple of spacemen staying there."

That sounded pretty cool to me. We were going to be staying in the swankiest hotel in New York, with a whole floor to ourselves. Not bad. The elevator door slid open and Gunny motioned for us to enter.

There was a guy inside. He was a little dude, about my size, with wire-rimmed glasses, who wore the same uniform as

Gunny. The only difference was he only had two gold stripes on his sleeves and wore a round cap with a flat top.

"Going up!" he announced professionally.

"Sixth floor, please, Dewey," said Gunny.

"Yes sir, Mr. Van Dyke," he said with a squeaky voice. "Sixth floor."

The little guy was the elevator operator. He slid the elevator doors closed, pushed the handle, and the elevator immediately started . . . down. "Oops, sorry," he said. He pushed the handle and the elevator jolted to a stop. He struggled with it and the elevator shook. He finally found the right gear and we started to go up. Phew. The operator gave us a sheepish look of apology. I didn't get his problem. Up, down, start, stop. Not a whole lot of options. I had the strong suspicion that this guy might be a nimrod.

"This is Dewey Todd," said Gunny. "His father built this hotel."

That explained a lot.

Dewey looked up at Gunny with a scowl. "I asked you not to tell people that, Gunny. I don't want people treating me different. I want to make it in the hotel business on my own."

"Well, you've almost got the elevator part, mate," said Spader, trying to hold back a smile. "That's a good start."

Dewey smiled proudly. He didn't get the cut.

"Sixth floor!" he announced, and slid the door open. We all made sure the elevator was safely stopped and everything was cool before stepping out.

"Enjoy the costume party," Dewey said. "Those are great circus outfits!"

"We're spacemen," I corrected.

"Oh, sorry." He closed the elevator doors and we were alone.

"He really is a fine boy," Gunny said, chuckling. "Just a little confused sometimes."

"I know the feeling," I said.

The sixth-floor hallway was definitely being worked on. The walls were bare and there were painting tarps spread out all over the place. As Gunny led us down the corridor he explained, "This was the first floor they finished when the hotel was new, so it's the first they're going to modernize."

Modernize. What a joke. They were trying to make this floor look like 1937. Not exactly "modern" by my standards. We reached the end of the corridor and turned left into another long corridor. Gunny walked up to room 615 and used a key to open it up.

"Welcome home, gentlemen," he said.

The room was huge. Actually, it was a couple of rooms. I think they call this a suite. I could imagine that when the work was finished, this was going to be a pretty fancy place. But right now, while they were doing the renovation, it was being used as a storage area for chairs and sofas.

"You sure this is okay, Gunny?" I asked.

"Absolutely," he answered with confidence. "It breaks about eighteen different hotel rules, but I've been here long enough to pull the right strings. Just don't go ordering room service."

There were a bunch of sofas lined up in a column along one wall. They were up on their arms and reached almost to the ceiling. All we had to do was bring two down and we'd have a comfortable place to sleep. There were big cushy chairs, along with a bunch of stacked tables. There was only one thing missing.

"Where's the TV?" I asked.

Gunny gave me a curious look. "The what?"

Duh. TV wasn't invented yet. "Never mind," I said, feeling like an idiot. "How about a radio?"

"I'm sure there's one around here someplace," answered Gunny. "Are you two hungry?"

"Absolutely," I answered.

"I could go for a kooloo fish and some sniggers," said Spader.

Gunny gave him the same curious look he gave me when I asked about the TV. "I'll see what I can find," he said. "You two make yourselves at home. I'm going to get you some clothes. Is there anything else you might need?"

"Something to write on," I said. "We've got to keep up with our journals."

"Right," answered Gunny. "I'll be back."

Gunny ambled out of the room, leaving Spader and me alone. I walked to the far side of the room, where fancy doors led to a balcony. I opened them and stepped outside. It was close to sunset. From our sixth-floor landing, I got a pretty good view south and west, where the sun was headed down.

"Is this where you grew up?" asked Spader. He was standing right behind me. I hadn't heard him coming.

"No, about thirty miles from here," I answered. "And more than half a century in the future. How weird is that?"

It really was. This was home, but not really. I had an idea that maybe I should try to find my grandparents. They were around in 1937. But then I remembered that my family had disappeared. Did that mean our whole family history disappeared along with them? I had to stop thinking about it. It was making me homesick.

"It's a scary-do," Spader said while gazing out at the city. "I've never seen anything so busy."

"You'll get used to it," I assured him.

"I suppose so," Spader added. "But I'm thinking about Saint Dane. There's a lot of natty-do that monster could get into in a big city like this. How are we going to find him?"

Good question. Saint Dane loose in New York City was a scary thought. "Something tells me he'll find us," I said. "I'm going to take a shower."

The bathroom was almost as big as the living room. This was definitely a suite for hotshot guests. The whole room was covered with white tiles. The bathtub was huge and stood on feet. There was a giant silver showerhead that sprayed enough water to wash a horse. I cranked up the shower, got it good and hot, and stood underneath the spray to let it massage my head.

As I stood there trying to get brain dead, an odd thought hit me: I wasn't going to school anymore.

I know. Weird thing to think about all of a sudden. Maybe it was because I was sort of home. Part of me was psyched. School was important and all, but it wasn't exactly something I looked forward to. On the other hand, school *was* important. It was where you learned stuff. What your parents didn't teach you, school did. As I stood in that shower, I actually started to get nervous. All my friends were going to pass me by. They were learning things that I wasn't.

Then I thought of all the places I'd been that day. Hmmm. Maybe I was getting a pretty intense education after all. I wasn't going to Stony Brook Junior High anymore; I was a full-time student at Traveler U. Maybe that was all the education I was going to need. After batting these ideas back and forth in my head, I came to one solid conclusion:

All this thinking was ruining my shower.

I stood there for another ten minutes, then found a stack of thick white towels, dried off, and left the bathroom to Spader.

A few minutes later I was in the living room, settled into a cushy chair with my feet up while Spader washed away his own thoughts. I was so dog tired, my eyes started to close. It was the first time since we got here that I could let the air out, and it felt great.

Then an urgent knock came at the door.

My eyes shot open instantly. I wasn't asleep anymore. I wasn't even tired. So much for letting the air out.

Spader poked his head out of the bathroom. He shot me a questioning look that said, "What do we do?"

I had no idea. We were busted. It looked like our stay at the hotel was going to be a short one.

FIRST EARTH

This looked bad. How could we ever explain who we were and why we were hanging out on a closed floor of the hotel? In bathrobes. I didn't want to get Gunny in trouble, but I didn't want to get arrested, either.

I snuck quietly over to the door, desperately trying to think up a story that would get us off the hook. None came. I peered through the peephole to get a look at who we would have to deal with and saw . . .

"Room service!" announced Gunny with a big smile.

Phew. Talk about relief. I opened the door and Gunny came in wheeling a big cart that was loaded with those silver domes they put over plates to keep them hot.

"Feeling better?" he asked.

"I am now," I answered. "We gotta get a secret knock or something so we know it's you."

"Secret knock. I like that," Gunny said with a sparkling smile. "Like G-men."

"Like what?" asked Spader as he walked in with a towel around his waist.

"Can we eat now?" I asked.

"All in good time, gentlemen," Gunny said. "We've got business first."

The cart was draped with a white tablecloth that went down to the floor. Gunny reached underneath and pulled out two brown packages. "Try these on for size," he said, and tossed one to each of us. We tore them open to find our First Earth clothes, courtesy of one of the shops here in the hotel. We each had a pair of wool pants with jackets. My pants were light gray with a darker gray jacket. Spader's were a light brown with a matching jacket. We each had plain white shirts.

"What do I do with these?" Spader asked as he held up a pair of long, white boxer shorts.

Gunny laughed. "Don't they wear underwear where you come from?"

"Sure," answered Spader. "But I could make a sail out of these. They'll get all twisted up."

I put mine on and they came down to my knees. But you know what? I didn't care. It felt good to wear regular cotton underwear again, even if I looked like some kind of grandpa. We also had white T-shirts, black socks, and dark leather shoes. The pants had suspenders, too. That was kind of cool. I'd never worn suspenders before. And everything fit perfectly. Gunny was a good judge. After we both got dressed, Gunny looked us over and smiled.

"Now you look like you belong," he said proudly.

"Can we eat now?" I asked.

"Patience, shorty, patience." Gunny reached under the cart and pulled out a stack of white paper and a small typewriter. "You can use this to type your journals," he said. "It's faster than writing."

"What is that thing?" asked Spader.

"I'll teach you," I said. I had only typed on a computer keyboard before, but figured I could learn how to do it the old-fashioned way. "Now can we eat?" I begged. The smell of the food was making me salivate.

"One more thing," said Gunny. "Since you boys are going to be coming and going around here, I figured out a way you can fit right in." He reached back under the cart and pulled out two uniforms like the one Dewey, the elevator guy, wore. "You're going to work here as bellhops."

"What's a bellhop?" asked Spader.

Gunny explained. "You greet guests, help them with their luggage, and run errands around the hotel. It's easy work, and you'll have a terrific boss."

"Who?" Spader asked.

"Me."

"This all sounds good but, can we *please* eat now?" I asked in desperation.

"Have a seat, gentlemen," Gunny said. "It's chow time."

We both sat down while Gunny wheeled the cart in front of us. "I wasn't exactly sure of what to order," he teased. "But after some deep thought, I believe I came up with the perfect menu." With a flourish, Gunny lifted up two of the silver domes.

What I saw made me so happy I wanted to cry.

Since I left home I had eaten some very strange food. It wasn't bad, just different. On Denduron I had lots of vegetables and an occasional rabbit. On Cloral I ate a ton of fish and all sorts of weirdball fruits and vegetables from the underwater farms. On Zadaa, Loor had made us some good crunchy bread along with spicy vegetables. All of the food I had was good, but nothing compared to what was sitting before us right now.

We each had our own big, juicy cheeseburger and pile of golden French fries . . . direct from heaven. Gunny reached under the cart and pulled out a champagne bucket loaded with ice and bottles of Coke.

"What do you think?" he asked.

"I think you're a genius," I said quickly.

Spader wasn't enthused. "What is that stuff?" he asked nervously.

"Cheeseburger, French fries, Coke—food of the gods, my friend," I said. I lifted up my burger, took a delicious whiff, closed my eyes, and wolfed into it. Oh, yeah, I was home.

Spader lifted up a fry, looking at it curiously. "What exactly is a french before it's fried?" he asked.

"White vegetable, cut in strips, fried in grease," I answered. "Stop talking. I'm trying to focus."

We didn't say another word for the rest of the meal. Spader ate reluctantly, but didn't seem to hate it. I put ketchup on our fries and salted them up real good. Man, they were excellent. The whole while Gunny stood over us, smiling. He was like a proud chef who enjoyed the way his food was being appreciated.

Then, for dessert, Gunny lifted two more silver covers to reveal . . . banana splits. Yes! He even had a couple glasses of milk to wash it all down. It was all so incredibly excellent. It had been a very long day, but this dinner made it all worthwhile. I wanted it to last forever, but my stomach was screaming for me to stop. I was totally stuffed and absolutely happy.

"Now don't go expecting this kind of service again," Gunny cautioned. "This is special because you just arrived. After this you eat in the kitchen with the rest of the staff."

"Gunny," I said. "You have no idea how perfect this is."

"Oh, I got a pretty good idea," he said with a smile.

"But it's better than you think," I added. "Tomorrow's my birthday and this is the best present ever."

"Then happy birthday, shorty," Gunny said, beaming. "Many happy returns."

"Happy birthday, mate," said Spader. "Wish I could raise a pint of sniggers."

"Yeah, but this'll do me just fine," I said, holding up a bottle of Coke.

Gunny took the now empty cart and put it by the door. He then came back into the living room and sat down with us. As much as I wanted to kick back, burp, and pretend life was good, that wasn't meant to be. We were here for a reason, and it wasn't to gork out stuffed on burgers.

"This is all new to me," Gunny said. "Chasing Saint Dane, I mean. What do we do?"

It was time to get down to some *real* business. The party was over.

"All the territories are reaching a turning point," I said, holding back a burp. "We've got to figure out what that turning point is here on First Earth, and what Saint Dane is doing to push it the wrong way."

"This should be snappy-do, Pendragon," Spader announced. "You're from this territory. I mean, you're from the *future* of this territory. Think of something big that happened in 1937 that Saint Dane might be messing around with."

The pressure was on. I wasn't very good at history. It all seemed so boring, memorizing dates and places and speeches made by guys I didn't care about. But even though I was historically challenged, it didn't take me very long to come up with an idea. To be honest, it was a no-brainer.

"You've got something, don't you, mate?" Spader asked with a sly smile.

I did, but I wished I didn't. The more I thought about it, the more freaked I got. This was bad. This was *really* bad. My heart started to pump faster and my palms got sweaty.

"What is it?" asked Gunny.

"There *is* something," I began. "I don't remember all the dates. But there is definitely something big about to go down."

"So tell us, mate!" exclaimed Spader.

"The war you were in, Gunny," I said. "The Great War? That became known as World War One."

Gunny's eyes grew very wide. "Are you saying there's going to be a World War Two?" he asked in shock.

I nodded.

Gunny looked down and shook his head sadly. "And they said it was the war to end all wars."

"They were wrong," I said.

"When did it happen?" asked Spader. "Who was fighting?"

I suddenly wished I hadn't slept through Mr. Varady's world history class.

"I don't know all the facts," I said. "There was this Hitler dude from Germany who tried to take over Europe. And Japan tried to take over Asia."

"That's *two* wars," Spader said.

"I think that's why they call it a *world* war," I shot back. "They fought against Russia and the United States and England and China and France and oh, *man*! This is huge! Millions of people died. Millions. It changed the world!"

Spader said, "So maybe we should go over to Germany and talk to this Hitler fella."

I laughed at that. "You don't get it," I said. "We can't just go over to Berlin, knock on Adolf Hitler's door and say, 'Excuse me, Mr. Hitler, you don't know us, but we'd really like you to reconsider this Holocaust thing. Okey dokey?'"

"Why not?" asked Spader innocently.

"Trust me. We're talking about leaders of huge nations ruling millions of people. This is so far out of our league, it's not even funny."

"So when does it all happen?" he asked.

I had to stand up and pace, hoping it would rattle loose some factoids I might have picked up somewhere.

"I don't know the dates. But it wasn't all of a sudden. There was a buildup. The wheels were definitely turning by 1937 but I don't think it got to be a full-blown war until almost 1940. Guys, this sounds *exactly* like something Saint Dane would stick his nose into, and we are *way* over our heads."

Gunny had been listening quietly. It must have been tough for him to hear that the world was about to be turned upside down again. Finally he said, "Don't be so sure about that."

"Are you crazy?" I shouted back at him.

"Think about it," Gunny argued innocently. "We know the war is coming, and we know Saint Dane is here to cause trouble. It all sort of fits. Our job might be to stop this war from happening."

"That's impossible!" I shouted. "There's no way the three of us could stop something so big."

"Maybe," Gunny said thoughtfully. "Or maybe we're thinking about it the wrong way."

"Gunny," I said patiently. "It's a *world war*. Airplanes. Guns. Bombs. Soldiers. Millions of soldiers. We're two kids with big underwear and a tall guy in a fancy suit. I don't mean to sound negative, but I'm thinking Saint Dane may have picked a winner here."

Gunny nodded thoughtfully. "I hear you. There's no way in heaven we could stop something like that once it got going.

But the thing is, what if it's only a little thing that gets it going in the first place?"

"Explain that, please, mate," said Spader.

"I'm saying that you never know what leads to what. There might be a little old something that happens that seems like nothing at first, but it might lead to something else, and that leads to something else, and so on and so on until you find yourself in the middle of a big old war."

"But—"

"Don't 'but' me so quick, shorty," Gunny interrupted. "Think about it first."

"Okay," I said, forcing myself to stop hyperventilating. "You're thinking there might be something small about to happen, that's going to start a chain reaction that will lead to World War Two . . . and we have a shot at stopping it?" I asked.

"Maybe."

"You're dreaming!" I shouted.

"I might be, at that," Gunny said. "But I know we're here for a reason. I also know that Saint Dane is here, somewhere. From what I've heard, he doesn't show up just to sightsee."

"He's right, mate," exclaimed Spader. "What if Saint Dane is here to make sure something happens that leads to the big war? Or what if he's trying to make the war into something bigger than it was going to be already? Hobey, if we find out what it is, we could make sure it doesn't happen."

I wanted to believe it was possible. I really did. But it just seemed too incredible. The idea that we could do something to stop the worst war in history was a total fantasy.

"If you're right," I said, "and I'm not saying you are, then it would have to have something to do with the gangsters Saint Dane sent to the flume to kill Uncle Press."

"Now you're thinking!" Gunny exclaimed. "If we find a

connection between those thugs and what's brewing overseas, I'm guessing it'll lead us straight to Saint Dane."

The three of us looked at each other. Was that it? Was our mission to figure out how Saint Dane was using some gangsters in New York to cause World War II?

"It sounds crazy," I said. "But one thing is for sure: Whatever Saint Dane is doing here, it's definitely got something to do with these mob guys. I don't know if it will have anything to do with the war, but it's where we gotta start."

"Right," Spader said. "With the gangster-wogglies."

Gunny stood up and straightened his suit. "That's where I come in. I've got friends in a lot of places; not all of them are good. I can ask some questions to get us started."

I had no idea where any of this would lead, but I felt confident that we were starting in the right place. Where it would take us was anybody's guess.

"Get some rest," Gunny said. "I'll come get you in the morning when it's time for work. Be ready early."

Gunny took the cart and wheeled it toward the door. "Oh, one more thing. Before work, we'll stop by the barbershop in the lobby. We can't have you two working here looking like ladies."

I hated to admit it, but Gunny was right. My hair was getting long and shaggy. Spader's black hair was almost to his shoulders. These were definitely *not* 1937 cuts.

"What's a barbershop?" Spader asked.

"G'night, gentlemen," Gunny said. "Sleep tight." He opened the door, then turned back to us and said, "How's this?" He rapped twice on the door, then once, then three times.

"The perfect secret knock," I said.

"I always wanted to be a G-man," Gunny said with a smile. He closed the door and we were alone.

"What's a G-man?" Spader asked again.

"It's not important," I answered.

"Then tell me about this World War Two. Is it really the natty-do you're saying?"

"Worse," I answered solemnly. "I don't know the words to describe how bad it was. If there's a chance we could stop it, it would be beyond incredible."

Spader stood up and smiled. "Right then! I have a sudden urge to pee. Not that I'm nervous mind you. I'm just . . . scared to death." He went for the bathroom, leaving me alone with my thoughts.

The ideas we were throwing around were too huge to comprehend. Was it possible that we might find the trigger here in New York that would start a chain reaction to prevent World War Two? A horror like that war was right up Saint Dane's alley. Of course, that meant Saint Dane would be doing his best to make sure we wouldn't find that trigger. That would be the challenge. Same old, same old.

Then three knocks came at the door.

I got up to let Gunny back in, figuring he had forgotten to tell us something. I hoped it was about breakfast. I was stuffed, but the thought of bacon and eggs was a sweet one.

"I can't believe you forgot the secret knock already," I called out as I headed for the door. "You'd make a lousy G-man."

I opened the door and instantly got shoved back into the room. I fell down on my butt, hard. At first I didn't get why Gunny would have done that. When I got my wits back and looked up, I had my answer.

It wasn't Gunny.

Standing over me were the two gangsters from the subway station. The nasty one had a black revolver pointed right at my nose.

"Ain't no G-man around to help you now," he snarled.

FIRST EARTH

I was on my butt, looking up at two guys who only a few hours before had tried to kill me. They didn't even bother covering their faces with handkerchiefs this time. They were a couple of gnarly-looking dudes too. The nasty one was, well, nasty looking. He had a pudgy face and dark, wild eyes. He was one of those guys who had to shave every hour or he'd have a Fred Flintstone thing going on.

The other guy, the tense one, looked a little less tense than before. I'm sure that was because he didn't have an audience now. He had thin features and a sharp, beaklike nose. He still didn't look all too happy about what was going on though. I glanced into his eyes and thought I caught a hint of sympathy. But not enough to call off his bulldog partner. The nasty guy held his pistol on me. It was an old-style revolver with a long barrel. It wasn't high-tech, but I'm sure it could get the job done.

"How did you find us?" I asked while crawling backward.

"We got eyes everywhere," said the nasty one, with a touch of cockiness. "You can run, but you can't hide."

"Why are you after us?" I asked.

"I got nothing against you," Nasty said. "But my associate is another story."

His associate. Who was that? Saint Dane? I wanted to keep these guys talking. Maybe I could use my Traveler hypnosis on him. But that would be tough, seeing as I was too scared to think straight, let alone concentrate enough to use mind powers I wasn't even sure I knew how to use in the first place.

"You have the wrong guy," I said with desperation, though I knew he probably had the exact right guy.

The gangster bent down and stuck the muzzle of the gun in my face. "Winn Farrow don't make mistakes like that."

Winn Farrow. Who was Winn Farrow?

More important, why did he want us killed? It was then that I saw something move out of the corner of my eye. It was Spader. He was behind the gangsters. I tried not to look at him because that would give him away.

"I . . . I don't know any Winn Farrow," I said.

Spader cautiously moved behind one of the sofas that was standing on end.

"I'm not here to argue with you, sonny boy, I'm here to tell you how it's gonna be. Don't go sticking your nose where it don't belong," he said. "If somebody gets in Winn Farrow's way, he won't be there for long, if you catch my drift."

The sofa behind the gangsters started to move. Spader was going to topple it over on them. I had to use every ounce of willpower to keep the gangsters' eyes on me.

"Okay, I hear you. Can I ask you a question though?"

"What?"

"Can I have my ring back?"

The question caught the gangsters off guard. They both looked at me as if I were nuts. Here they were putting on this big strong-arm intimidation show, and all I cared about was my ring. It confused them. Good. It was the perfect time for Spader to make his move. But it didn't exactly work out that way.

Instead, the nasty gangster got this evil gleam in his eye and said, "The hell with orders. I'm gonna end this right here."

Uh-oh. He pulled the hammer back on his revolver. I willed Spader to hurry.

He did.

With a giant shove, the sofa came toppling over. The big couch first nailed the nervous guy, then continued down to take out Mr. Nasty. The gangsters didn't know what hit them. I had barely enough time to roll out of the way before the two thugs hit the floor in a pile of gangster and sofa. I sprang to my feet and dove over the pile toward Spader.

"What took you so long?" I shouted at him.

"It was heavy!"

"C'mon!" I bolted out of the room with Spader right behind me. Those gangsters were going to be back on their feet in seconds, and I didn't want to be anywhere close when that happened. We ran down the hall, turned right, and blasted for the elevators. I hit the button and looked to see that the needle pointed to "1." Bad news. I looked over the second elevator. That needle pointed to "30." Worse news. We were on 6. Not even close.

"C'mon, c'mon!" I coaxed the elevators while furiously hitting the button . . . not that it would do any good.

"Who's Winn Farrow?" Spader asked. "Is it Saint Dane?"

"I don't know. Maybe," I answered breathlessly. "But those guys were only supposed to give us a warning and they decided to kill us."

"You can't trust anybody," said Spader.

"Hey!"

We both looked to our right and saw the gangsters rounding the far corner, headed our way. We had to keep running. Spader and I jammed it down the corridor. Our only hope was to find a stairwell, or at least another corridor. Luckily it was a long hall and we were too far away from the gangsters for them to take a shot at us.

When we got to the end of the corridor, we found a door that probably led to a stairway, but it was blocked by furniture and painting supplies. If we tried to dig through that mess, the gangsters would have us.

"This way," ordered Spader.

We turned right and sprinted down the next corridor. This hallway ran parallel with the corridor where our room was, on the far side of the hotel. It was pretty long too, so we could stay out of bullet range. But we couldn't keep running in circles. We had to find an escape route.

Halfway down the corridor, I saw it. An exit sign. Without stopping to think, I took a right into that door. I was hoping to find a stairway, but no luck. It was a service corridor. We were now running parallel to the hallway with the elevators.

"Maybe we can loop around back to the elevators," I said. "If we're lucky we'll catch one closer this time."

"Hobey-ho," Spader said.

We ran to the far end of the service corridor and stopped. I slowly opened the door to peek out. No bad guys anywhere. So far so good. We quickly ran out, turned right, and sprinted back along the corridor toward our room. We had come full circle.

But this was scary. For all we knew, one of the gangsters could have doubled back and would soon be rounding the corner in front of us. We passed our room and had only a few yards to go before hitting the elevator corridor again, when we heard footsteps coming toward us. Oops. At least one of the gangsters decided to circle back. He would be on us in seconds!

We were done. I froze in panic.

Spader didn't. He grabbed my shirt and pulled me into the last room of the corridor before the turn. There wasn't a second to spare. I caught a glimpse of the gangster coming around the corner.

The two of us dove to the inside of the door. All we could do was hope the gangster wouldn't peek in. A few seconds later we heard footsteps run by. I looked to Spader. He winked at me. We waited a few more seconds, then slowly took a peek outside to see the gangster running full throttle down the corridor, away from us. Excellent.

Now we had to move fast. We booked out of the room and back toward the elevators. We made the right turn again and saw an empty corridor. We also saw one of the elevator doors opening up! We took off on a dead run.

"Going down?" a voice called from inside the elevator.

We were too far away for him to see us. We kept on running, and I saw the elevator door starting to close. At this point it didn't matter if the gangster heard us or not, so I shouted out, "Dewey!"

Too late. The elevator door slid shut. We missed it. A second later the nasty gangster appeared at the far end of the corridor. I guess it *did* matter if he heard us. We were now staring right down the pike at worst case scenario.

That's when the elevator door opened up again! Dewey heard me after all.

"What are you guys doing?" he asked.

We both dove into the open car before the door was all the way open. "Close it! Close the door!" I shouted.

Dewey was totally confused. Both Spader and I started pushing the door closed ourselves. "Hey! That's *my* job!" Dewey whined.

We ignored him and almost had the door shut when the nasty gangster arrived. He got his fingers in the door and tried to pry it open.

"Down, Dewey!" I shouted. "Not that way." I looked up. "*That* way." I looked down.

"But there's another passenger out there!" Dewey complained. That's when the nasty gangster showed his revolver. Dewey got the message. He leaped at the door and helped us close it.

"Get us out of here!" I yelled.

Dewey grabbed the control lever and surprisingly enough, we started down. Dewey was better under pressure than I would have guessed. But he looked wild-eyed and scared.

"Who was that?" he screamed. "He had a pistol!"

"Where's Gunny?" Spader demanded, ignoring Dewey's question.

"I just saw him in the lobby, headed outside. What's going on?"

"Nothing Gunny can't handle," I said. "Forget about what you saw."

"But I gotta tell my father about this," Dewey complained.

"Don't do that!" I shouted. I think I scared the little guy because he backed up against the side of the elevator. I got my head back together and said calmly, "It was just a joke. Like a prank, you know?"

"But, but that guy had a gun," Dewey whimpered.

"Gun?" I faked a laugh. "That wasn't a real gun. That

was . . . that was . . . a costume. For the costume party. You know the clothes we had on before? Those were costumes too. You thought it was a real gun?"

I faked another laugh, looking sideways at Spader. Spader got the idea and he faked a laugh too.

"Yeah," Spader said. "It was a toy."

Dewey wasn't sure we were telling the truth, but I think it was easier for him to accept it than to think there were guys running around his father's hotel flashing guns. That was good. If Dewey called the police, they'd have to question us, and I'm not so sure they'd like the answers we had to give. No, it was better this way. But we had to find Gunny and let him know what was going on. Finally we got to the lobby, and Dewey opened the door.

"Thanks, Dewey. We'll let you know when the next costume party is, okay?" I said.

"Great, thanks!"

Dewey was a simple kind of dude.

We ran from the elevator and went looking for Gunny. We hurried to the front doors of the hotel and booked outside. Night had fallen and the garden was lit up like Christmas, with lights hidden among the greenery.

"There!" shouted Spader, pointing to the sidewalk in front.

Gunny was there talking to a man. We ran down the front stairs of the hotel, through the garden and out onto the street. Gunny saw us. He shook the hand of the man and the guy walked off just as we ran up to him. We were both out of breath and excited.

"What's wrong?" he said, sounding a little angry. "I told you boys to stay put."

"We had visitors," I said.

"The guys from the flume," Spader panted. "They came looking for us."

I didn't like the look on Gunny's face. It was a cross between shock and fear. Bad combination.

"Who is Winn Farrow?" I asked.

For a second I thought Gunny was going to faint. He actually looked unsteady on his feet. Whoever Winn Farrow was, his name made a strong guy like Gunny very scared. This was getting worse by the second.

"I can't believe he sent people here," Gunny said. "That's crossing a very dangerous line."

"Why? Who is he?" I asked.

Gunny looked down at us and was about to answer when we heard a scream.

It was a horrifying, tortured scream that came from far away. Actually, it didn't come from far away, it came from far *up*. The three of us spun quickly to look up at the hotel. What we saw made my knees go weak.

Somebody had jumped out of a window!

The whole building was lit up by floodlights, so the dark figure was easy to see, though I wished I couldn't. The fall took only a few seconds, but those few seconds will stay with me forever. It was horrible. The figure screamed all the way down. Luckily for us, the tall trees in front of the hotel blocked us from seeing the final second. We stood there frozen, then Gunny broke and ran for the building. Spader and I followed right behind him. I didn't want to see what had happened, but I was sure I needed to. Chances were this had something to do with the gangsters and this Winn Farrow dude.

The victim had fallen onto the roof of a car and pretty much caved in the whole thing. There was no way anybody could survive that. I couldn't bring myself to look closer. Neither could Spader. We stood several feet away, while Gunny did the tough thing and walked over to investigate.

While we waited for him, Spader saw something and nudged me. I looked and saw someone standing on the steps of the hotel. It was one of the gangsters. The nervous one. He looked at us like he wanted to say something, but decided not to and ran off. The question was, where was the other guy?

Gunny walked back to us and said softly, "It's him. The ugly one from the subway. He's dead."

That answered my question. Spader and I shared disbelieving looks.

"I guess that means he won't be trying to kill us anymore," Spader said, sounding numb.

This was unbelievable. When I first saw the falling body, I thought somebody had made a suicide jump. Now that I knew it was Mr. Nasty Gangster, nothing made sense anymore. Why would he jump? He had other things on his mind, like hunting for us so he could gun us down.

I stared up at Gunny. He looked sick.

"You gotta tell us what you're thinking, Gunny," I said.

Gunny glanced back at the body. People were starting to gather and stare.

"I'm afraid we're going to have our own war pretty soon," Gunny said. "Right here in our backyard. It may not be as big as the one brewing over in Europe, but it's going to be ugly just the same."

I heard a police siren scream in the distance. It was a far-off, sorrowful wail that was headed our way.

The show was definitely on.

◆　　◆　　◆

I'm going to end this journal here, Mark and Courtney. I wish I had my ring so I could send these pages to you. Hopefully, it'll turn up soon. But until it does, I'll keep these pages safe and keep writing. I'm beginning to get the hang of this typewriter.

I hope this journal finds you well, and that your lives are much simpler than mine.

It's March 11. It's my birthday. Do I still turn fifteen, even though it's 1937?

END OF JOURNAL #9

FIRST EARTH

I'm getting ready to launch to another territory.

It's been nearly two months since I finished my last journal, and I can't tell you how worried I am. I don't want to leave here. At least not now.

But I think we found the turning point.

Gunny was right. I think that if we can change the outcome of this one event, there's a really good chance we can stop World War II. Is that incredible or what? The idea of saving the lives of millions of people is almost too good to be true. Gunny was right. The turning point isn't as big as a war between tribes like on Denduron, or the poisoning of an entire territory, like on Cloral. It's actually one single event. One big, stupid, spectacular event.

But it's going to be hard to stop it from happening. Dangerous, too. Big surprise, right?

Since I wrote you guys last, we have crossed paths with some truly foul characters. It's getting hard to tell the good guys from the bad guys. If we have any hope of stopping this event, we've got to go up against these guys again, and I can't guarantee we'll win.

That's why I'm fluming to another territory. We need some information and there's no way we can get it here. But I'm nervous about leaving because I don't want to miss anything. I'm typing this to you guys on the night of May 5. Tomorrow is the day everything is going to hit the fan. That much we know for sure. We absolutely, positively have to be back in time and leaving now means we'll be cutting it really close. I'm counting on the fact that the flumes always send us Travelers where we need to be, *when* we need to be there. It wouldn't be cool to get back late.

But I think it's a risk worth taking because, like I said before, we need all the help we can get.

The last time I wrote to you it was my birthday, March 11. Spader and I have been here for almost two months. So much has happened since I last wrote that I hope I can remember it all.

When Mr. Nasty Gangster took that header off the Manhattan Tower Hotel, it was truly disturbing. Seeing a man fall to his death is about as horrible and gruesome as it gets. But as bad as that was, it also left us with a mystery. How did he fall? *Why* did he fall? He had been chasing us around on the sixth floor. I couldn't imagine he took a wrong turn and suddenly said, "Oops, this door leads to . . . air! Let's go!" No way.

I also couldn't imagine that he jumped deliberately. Not that I know anything about suicide, but this guy was busy doing other things, like trying to murder Spader and me. Why would he suddenly stop in the middle of the chase and say, "I can't believe I lost those guys. I'm such a lousy gangster, I think I'll just end it all." That didn't make sense either.

The only possible explanation was that he was murdered.

That leads to the bigger question. Who did it? It wasn't his partner, Mr. Nervous Gangster. Spader and I saw him leaving the hotel only a few seconds after Mr. Nasty took the dive. That meant somebody else was guilty. There was somebody else in the hotel who was part of all this, and I could make a pretty good guess as to who it might be.

Yeah, you guessed it too. Saint Dane.

He had to be here somewhere, looking like somebody else. Still, why would Saint Dane murder a guy who was trying to murder us? I guess the bottom line was, we had a ton of questions and not a whole lot of answers. There was only one person who could shed any light on this, and that was Gunny. It was time for him to tell us what he knew about these gangsters.

After Mr. Nasty took the fall, Gunny told Spader and me to go back up to our room. He had to talk to the police and let them know what he saw. Of course he didn't want Spader or me talking to them. They might ask tough questions like: "And where do you live, sonny boy?" or "Give us the name of your parents so we can call them." That would have been tricky. So Spader and I went quietly back up to our room and waited for Gunny.

Once we hit the room though, we weren't quiet anymore. Spader was all worked up.

"He's here. I can smell him," he said while pacing.

"Who?"

"Saint Dane. He's in this building."

"We don't know that."

"C'mon, mate!" Spader exclaimed. "You know he's got to have his slimy hands in this. He sent those gunmen to the flume to kill Press, then he sent 'em after us. How else would those wogglies know we were here?"

"Then how come one of 'em is dead?"

"I'm still working on that; give me some time."

Spader's hatred for Saint Dane was starting to bubble up again. That was bad. We had to keep our eyes on the ball, and that meant not letting our emotions take over.

"Spader," I said cautiously. "You know you've gotta be cool about this, right?"

"Yeah, yeah," he assured me. "Cool as a cooger fish, that's me. Don't worry, Pendragon. I made you a promise. I won't go back on you."

"I believe you," I said. I really, *really* hoped I was right.

That's when the door opened and Gunny walked in. I thought he looked a little older than he had earlier. He was the kind of guy who wanted everything to be just so. Having gangsters plunge to a gruesome death from his hotel wasn't part of his perfect picture.

"I've seen a lot of things happen at this hotel," he said with a shaky voice. "But this beats 'em all."

"Be patient," I cautioned him. "We're just getting started."

Spader said, "What's all this talk about a natty-do around here?"

"A what?" asked Gunny, once again confused by an expression of Spader's.

"You said there was going to be a war here at the hotel," I jumped in. "What's up with that?"

Gunny sat down in one of the easy chairs and let out a tired breath. Spader and I sat across from him on the same couch Spader had toppled over on the gangsters.

"You ever hear of a thing called Prohibition?" he asked.

"Yeah," I said. "Isn't that when the government out-lawed booze?"

"Exactly," said Gunny. "No wine, no beer, no whiskey, no

nothin'. From 1920 until they gave up on it in 1933. It was all against the law, unless you knew where to go. Most people knew where to go."

"Speakeasies, right?" I asked.

"Speak easy?" asked Spader. "I'm losing you two."

"A lot of people got rich during Prohibition," Gunny continued. "Some did it making booze—they called it bootlegging. Others sold it in secret clubs called speakeasies; still others shipped it here, there, and everywhere right under the noses of the police. It was all very illegal. It made a lot of gangsters rich and put a lot of others behind bars. Put a lot of them six feet under dirt, too."

"What's that got to do with us?" I asked.

"There was a gang," Gunny continued. "Operated on the Upper East Side here. They had it all covered—bootlegging, shipping, even ran a couple of speakeasies. Made a lot of money for the two bosses. One of 'em was a gentleman named Maximilian Rose."

"The big guy with the fancy suit we met outside?" I asked.

"One and the same," answered Gunny.

"Who was the other boss?" asked Spader.

"Fellow named Winn Farrow."

Spader and I shot each other a look. "That's who those gangsters were working for!" I shouted. "Farrow and Rose are partners?"

"They *were* partners," Gunny answered. "Long time ago. As I heard it, Rose was the smart one. He knew Prohibition wouldn't last forever, so he started investing his money into other businesses. Some legal, some not. He got his fingers into all kinds of criminal activities like gambling and smuggling and even art theft. When Prohibition ended, he didn't miss a beat. Just kept going on making money."

"What about Farrow?" asked Spader.

"He was just as crooked, but not as smart. He didn't have the same style as Rose. Let's say he was rough around the edges."

"So he was a dumb thug," I said.

"Pretty much," agreed Gunny. "He spent his money fast as he made it. When Prohibition went away, he had nothing to show for it. Rose didn't have any use for him, so they split up. Way I heard it, Farrow didn't like that much. Now the two are what you might call enemies."

"What's Farrow doing now?" I asked.

"He's got his own gang that operates out of an old meat-packing plant downtown. They're a bad bunch. They'll slit your throat just to get your wallet. It's pretty much all they're good at."

"So while Max Rose is hanging out in a fancy penthouse uptown," I said, "his old partner, Winn Farrow, is struggling to get by downtown."

"That about sums it up," Gunny said. "And that's why I'm getting nervous. If Winn Farrow is sending his goons up here to make trouble, and they start falling out of windows, we might find ourselves in the middle of a gang war. People die in gang wars. We may have just seen the first."

"It's worse than that," I added. "Saint Dane has gotta be in this equation somewhere."

"Take it another step, mates," Spader jumped in. "What do these two gangs have to do with setting off this tum-tigger you call World War Two?"

"There's one thing we can say for certain," I added. "Whatever Saint Dane's got in mind for First Earth, I think we're sitting right in the middle of it."

"So what do we do?" asked Spader. "Just sit around waiting for more wogglies to show up with guns, looking for us?"

"I have an idea," said Gunny. "You two have jobs now. Once people get to know you, you can come and go as you please. You might even get closer to Max Rose and his boys. He's got a whole penthouse up there, with people coming and going all the time. There's a lot you can learn just by doing your job in a place like this."

"Sounds like a plan," I said. "Tomorrow we go to work."

And that's how we began our careers as bellhops at the Manhattan Tower Hotel. Our goal was to learn as much about Max Rose and his gangster buddies as we could. We were going undercover. No problem, right?

Yeah, right.

Early the next morning Spader and I put on our spiffy uniforms and reported to Gunny in the lobby of the hotel. Our first duty was to get haircuts. Gunny brought us to the hotel barbershop where Spader and I sat side by side in big, padded leather chairs that spun around. I knew we were in trouble when the barbers didn't start with scissors. They went right for the electric sheers. Gulp. With Gunny behind us smiling, Spader and I got buzzed. We didn't end up with Marine cuts or anything drastic like that, but our hair ended up so short, it wasn't even worth brushing.

The barbers put some kind of goop in our hair that smelled like lemons. It gave us both a slicked-back kind of look that may have been perfect for 1937, but felt greasy and awful. Mental note to self: Wash hair often.

Now that we were all cleaned up and presentable, we went to work. Gunny was right. The job wasn't all that hard. We had to meet guests when they arrived at the hotel and bring their luggage up to their rooms. When they checked out, we'd pick up their luggage and bring it down to the lobby. It was pretty much a no-brainer. The main thing was to be polite and not break anything.

We ate our meals in the big, noisy kitchen with the other bellhops and soon became accepted as regular staff people. That was key because it meant we could pretty much go wherever we wanted in the hotel. Nobody questioned us. The only tricky thing was going back to our room. We didn't want Dewey to start wondering why we always got off on the sixth floor. So at the end of our shift we always climbed the stairs instead of taking the elevator. What a pain.

I could tell you guys more about what it was like to be a bellhop, but that's not the important part of the story. What mattered was figuring out the connection between the gangsters and Saint Dane. That meant we had to watch Maximilian Rose. Easier said than done. He always had these gorilla-look-alike bodyguards surrounding him and we couldn't let them catch us spying on their boss. They might take us out into the alley and rub us out, or whatever it was the old-time gangsters did to people they didn't like. So we had to be careful. Luckily there were three of us, so we could take turns and hopefully not be too obvious.

Rose lived in the penthouse on the thirtieth floor of the hotel. He didn't leave very often. That's because he had a lot of enemies and liked to stay where it was safe. He had tons of visitors though. I guess that's how he did his business. People would come to him. Dewey told me stories about the odd assortment of goons he brought up to the thirtieth floor. What a strange and scary way to live.

Since Rose didn't go out much, we didn't see him much. Mostly all we could do was check out his visitors to try and figure out what he might be up to. But I'm no detective, and it's not like these guys were walking around with big signs saying "Friend of Saint Dane" or anything. They all looked like average guys. Okay, they looked like average *gangster* guys, but you get the idea.

That is, except for one man. His name was Mr. Zell. I knew this because whenever he showed up, he had to pick up the lobby phone and call the penthouse to announce that he was there. Mr. Zell had a style that stood out from Rose's other visitors. His hair was blond and shiny and greased straight back. He always wore these perfect, gray suits that looked real expensive, like they were made for him. His eyes were sharp and always darting around, checking out the room. But he wasn't nervous. Just the opposite. He was real confident. I think he looked around because he always wanted to know exactly what was going on and who was watching him. The word would be "observant." I had to be extra careful not to be observed by Mr. Zell.

But there was one other big thing that made Mr. Zell stand out.

He had an accent. A German accent.

Ordinarily I wouldn't think twice about something like that, but I was in the middle of something that was definitely *not* ordinary. In a few years the United States would be at war with a whole bunch of guys with the same kind of accent. They weren't our enemies yet, but they would be. And since we figured that World War II was probably the turning point for the territory of First Earth, having a German guy hanging out with Mr. Rose definitely caught my attention.

I couldn't help but wonder if hiding beneath that slick, buttoned-up, German-accented appearance . . . was Saint Dane. Of course, I looked at *everyone* as a potential Saint Dane, but this guy jumped to the top of my list. It was making me nuts trying to figure out how to find out what he was doing with Max Rose.

Then one day I got my shot. It was a quiet afternoon and I was hanging in the lobby trying to look busy, when Mr. Zell strode in. I pretended to be polishing a table near the telephone he always used to call the penthouse. I was getting to be a pretty good detective.

Bobby Pendragon, Undercover Traveler.

"Penthouse, please," Zell said into the phone. He listened, then said, "Good morning, this is Ludwig Zell. Yes, I will be staying for lunch today. Thank you." He hung up and walked to the elevators.

Score! He was staying for lunch. That meant they would order room service. One of the other jobs the bellhops had was to deliver room service. This was my chance. I hurried through the lobby, trying not to look like I was hurrying through the lobby, and found Gunny at the bell captain station, reading a newspaper.

"Zell is here," I said quietly. "They're ordering room service."

Without a word, Gunny dropped the paper and headed for the kitchen. He knew what I was thinking. Normally, one of the more experienced bellhops would take the order up to Mr. Rose. It was a sweet gig because the gangster boss always gave good tips. I didn't care about the tip. I wanted to be in the same room with Max Rose and Ludwig Zell. When we got into the kitchen, the head waiter was already on the phone, taking the order. When he hung up, Gunny told him to give the order to me. The head waiter gave me a dirty look that said: "Why should *he* get special treatment?" But he couldn't argue. Gunny was the boss.

I was on.

While we waited for the food to be prepared, Gunny took me aside. "Be careful," he said. "Listen, but don't be obvious about it. If they think you're spying, you'll end up taking a walk off the balcony like that gangster from the subway."

"Don't worry," I answered. I'm not sure why I said that. *I sure as heck was worrying; why shouldn't Gunny?*

"These are bad people, Pendragon," Gunny warned.

"I know. I got it," I assured him. He was making me more nervous than I was already.

Ten minutes later the order was ready. It was spread out on a big cart that was covered with a sharp white tablecloth. There must have been two dozen plates covered with shiny steel lids. I wondered how many people were having lunch because there was enough food here to feed the Pittsburgh Steelers. Gunny gave me a wink of encouragement and I pushed the cart for the elevators.

"Going up!" Dewey announced as he slid open the elevator door.

I pushed the cart in and said: "Thirty, please."

Dewey's eyes grew wide as he closed the door. "You're taking that to Mr. Rose?" he asked with awe. "Whatever you do, don't look anybody in the eye."

"Why not?" I asked.

"I once made the mistake of looking at one of those thugs," Dewey said. "The goon picked me up and shoved me in the laundry chute. Headfirst! It was horrible."

I almost laughed, but that would have been rude. The idea of somebody jamming this geeky little guy into the chute was pretty funny. "How far did you fall?" I asked.

"I didn't," Dewey said. "I stuck my arms and legs out and held on to the sides until he was gone. Then I climbed out. But I could have been killed."

"Thanks for the advice," I said. "I'll be careful." As funny as the image was, Dewey's warning was valid. Max Rose and his pals were not nice guys. If they would jam somebody down a laundry chute for just looking at them, I didn't want to think what they might do if they caught me spying on them. I had to push that thought out of my head or I would have chickened out. Not that I had a choice, because a few seconds later we arrived at the thirtieth floor. The curtain was about to go up.

Dewey pulled the door open and said, "Good luck."

I gave him a weak smile and wheeled the cart outside. I had barely gotten out of the elevator when Dewey slammed the door shut behind me. I guess he didn't want to be sent on another laundry run.

I was met by two thick-looking dudes who stared at me like I was toe jam. One guy made a motion for me to step away from the cart. I took a few steps back, not sure of what was about to happen. As it turned out, this was a security check. While one guy examined the cart, the other guy examined *me*. I guess he was making sure I didn't have a gun or anything. The guy pawed me over pretty good. I felt like a melon being checked for ripeness. But I didn't complain. I didn't want to end up in the laundry chute. After this totally rude once-over, both guys stepped back and motioned for me to pass.

I wanted to complain about the rough treatment, but remembered Dewey's warning and put my head down and shut up. After all, I was on a mission.

Bobby Pendragon, Undercover Traveler.

The door to the penthouse was at the end of the corridor. I wheeled the cart up and was about to knock when I saw that there was a button for a doorbell. Pretty fancy. I pressed it and heard soft chimes ringing inside. A second later the door opened, and I came face-to-face with another tough-looking dude.

"Room service," I announced cheerily. I probably didn't have to say that, since I was wheeling a cart loaded with food, but this guy didn't look like a brain surgeon. I didn't want to take any chances. He motioned for me to come in. I wheeled the cart in and kept my eyes down.

"Wait here," the guy grunted, and walked off. That's when I looked up and got my first glimpse of the penthouse suite. Man, this place was fancy! It looked like I had stepped into some kind of European drawing room. Not that I had ever been in a European drawing room, but I had been in those fancy period rooms in the Metropolitan Museum of Art. I'm not exactly sure why they were called drawing rooms either. It's not like they were doing any drawing.

The furniture was way fancy and kind of fragile looking. On the ceiling was an elaborate painting of some chubby babies with wings, flying around in the clouds, blowing trumpets. Not exactly my taste in art, but I guessed some people thought it was elegant. The room I stood in was a central entrance hall. Corridors spread in three different directions to the rest of the penthouse. As I stood there gazing at the fancy surroundings, one thought came to mind: There must be a lot of money in being a gangster.

Then I heard a gruff voice bellow from somewhere else, "This is what's gonna happen. . . ."

It was Maximilian Rose. He sounded angry. That was bad.

"If he says he needs two weeks, give him one," Rose said angrily. "If he asks for one week, give him three days. If he doesn't like it, I'll have somebody pay him a visit and convince him to like it, understand?" This was followed by the *slam* of a telephone.

A second later a door opened, and Max Rose stepped out. I tried not to look right at the guy, but it was hard not to. He was like a giant storm cloud—big and loud and angry. Though it was afternoon, he was wearing pajamas, a bathrobe, and slippers. It was a fancy robe, all red and shiny, like silk. I caught a quick glimpse into the room behind him. It was an office with a desk loaded with papers. This guy did business in his pajamas. Nice life.

When he stepped through the door, the first thing he saw was me. Before I knew it, we had made eye contact. Gulp. Hello, laundry.

"Hey, Buck Rogers!" he shouted with a smile. He wasn't angry anymore. Phew. "Didn't think I'd remember, did ya?"

I didn't. He had only seen me for a few seconds a couple of weeks ago. Note to self: This guy was observant and had a good memory. Be careful.

"Hello, Mr. Rose," I said politely. "Ready for lunch?"

"I'm starving," he said. "Follow me."

I wheeled the cart across to the far side of the foyer and into a room that was even fancier than the entryway. It was a huge, totally swanky living room. The couches were big and cushy, the tables were intricately carved, and there were tons of giant oil paintings with thick gold frames. But the big deal in this room was the view. One whole wall had nothing but floor-to-ceiling windows that looked out over Manhattan. It was pretty cool.

Again, all I could think was that gangsters sure made a lot of money.

"Set it out there, Buck," he ordered, pointing to a large, dark table.

Buck. Right. That was me. "How many should I set up for, Mr. Rose?"

"How many?" He looked at me like I had just asked him how many arms he had. "There's two of us. How many did you think?"

I then noticed that Ludwig Zell was sitting in an easy chair near the door. The guy looked at me with cold eyes that made me shiver. Was it Saint Dane? If so, he wasn't tipping his hand.

"Yes sir, Mr. Rose," I said. I didn't want to point out that he had more food here than they served to the whole school for lunch at Stony Brook Junior High. Then again, at Stony Brook they didn't serve steaks and lobsters and salads made with vegetables carved into flower shapes. I kept my mouth shut and set the table.

"So, Ludwig," Rose said to the German. "I wanted to make this meal special, like a celebration, you know?"

The German stood up and walked to Rose. "You are too thoughtful, Mr. Rose. This is the beginning of a relationship that will be long and fruitful for both of us. And our people."

This was better than I could have hoped for. I was listening in on these two guys doing business. I didn't want to finish setting out lunch too quickly so I could hear as much as possible, but I didn't want to make it look like I was, well, doing exactly that. This was tricky.

"You know, Ludwig, I've gone out on a limb for you," Rose said. "I've already started to deliver and haven't seen a dime from those people of yours."

"I understand, my friend," answered Zell. "And we appreciate your trust. Now that we have determined the most efficient means of payment, you won't have to work on faith much longer."

"Yeah, but how *much* longer?" asked Rose.

"Your first payment will be arriving May sixth, as promised," answered Zell. "You have my word, and the word of my party."

This was incredible. I was getting all sorts of stuff. Max Rose was doing some kind of work for this Zell guy. But what party was he talking about?

"Hey, spaceman!" barked Rose. "You done or what?"

"Yes sir, Mr. Rose," I said, and stood at attention.

Max Rose walked toward me, digging into the pocket of his bathrobe. Uh-oh. Did I hear too much? Did he have a gun? Was I about to get filled full of lead?

No. He pulled out some dollar bills and jammed them into my hand. It was my tip.

"Now blast off," he said.

"Thank you, sir. Enjoy your lunch," I said, and beat it for the door. I had already gotten more information than I could have hoped for. So while Rose and Zell sat down for their stupid-huge lunch, I closed the door and made a beeline for the front door. I couldn't wait to tell Spader and Gunny what I had learned.

I was halfway to the door when I saw something that made me stop. It was the door to Max Rose's office.

It was open and the office was empty.

I knew instantly that I was faced with a huge opportunity. Sitting on that desk could have been more information about the business that Rose and Zell were in. All I had to do was duck in, take a quick look, and get out. Of course, I could also get caught, and rather than leaving through the front door, I could be exiting the penthouse through a window. Next stop: pavement. I had to make a decision, fast. Every second counted.

I did it. After a quick look around to make sure none of

Rose's goons were close, I shot into the office. It was crazy, but I had to.

As soon as I got inside, I closed the door. If somebody happened to walk by, it would be better if they didn't see a sweaty bellboy flipping through Max Rose's personal papers. That would hurt. Once the door was closed, I turned my attention to the desk. I wanted to be in and out fast, so I moved quickly behind the desk and looked down at the mass of papers.

I had no idea what to look for. It was just a bunch of business papers, contracts, and lists of figures like an accountant would use. My heart sank. Saint Dane's plan on First Earth could have been sitting right in front of me and I wouldn't know it.

I was about to give up and run out when something caught my eye. It couldn't have stood out more from the rest of the pages if it had a flashing red light on it. First off, it looked nothing like any of the other pages. It was a single sheet with a bold logo on top. That alone would have made my eye go to it, but there was one other thing. It was the logo itself. It was something I had seen before, many times. I'd seen it in movies and in books and on TV. But seeing it now, this way, made my stomach do a flip. I knew what this logo represented. And this wasn't a movie.

It was a swastika, the crooked cross that was the symbol of the Nazi party. It was surrounded by a wreath, upon which an angry eagle was perched with its wings spread wide. As I already told you, I'm no expert on World War II history, but I knew for sure that this was a letter from Germany and the Nazi party. The big question was, what was it doing on Max Rose's desk? I did my best to calm down and read the letter. It was short and straight to the point.

April 9, 1937

Dear Mr. Rose:

This letter is to confirm our agreement that the initial payments due to you for services rendered will be arriving in the U.S. via LZ-129 on May 6 of this year and will be available to you immediately. Form and amount of payment is as previously agreed upon. I trust this will be satisfactory and look forward to a long and successful partnership.

Sincerely,

Ludwig Zell

Now I knew what party Ludwig Zell was talking about. The Nazi Party. I couldn't take my eyes off the paper. It was an actual letter from the Nazis to Max Rose, proof they were doing business together. The frustrating thing was that it didn't say what kind of business. All it said was that payment was going to be made on May 6 and it was coming via LZ-129 . . . whatever *that* was.

LZ. Ludwig Zell? Were there 129 Ludwig Zells? Whatever it was, it proved that my suspicions about him were correct. He was not only a German dude, he was working for the big bad guys over in Europe. He was a Nazi.

But the most important thing was that I had found hard evidence of a connection between the Nazis in Germany and these gangsters in New York. Suddenly Gunny's far-fetched theory wasn't looking so far-fetched. Up until then we only suspected that the turning point on First Earth was about World War II. This piece of paper confirmed it. We already knew there was a link between Saint Dane and the gangsters. Now we had a link between the gangsters and the Nazis. Connect the dots. We were getting closer.

There was no way I could take this paper out of here, so I

committed it to memory. No problem. It was short enough that I could remember the most important facts: LZ-129; May 6; payment from the Nazis to Max Rose. Got it.

Now I had to bolt out of there. I snuck back to the door and put my ear to it, listening for sounds of anyone hanging around outside. I didn't hear a thing, so I grabbed the doorknob and gently gave it a turn. What happened next was so impossible, my mind wouldn't accept it at first.

The door was locked. I turned harder, but that didn't make it any less locked. My heart started to race. Maybe it was just stuck. I gave it a jiggle and a twist and a push. But no amount of jiggling or twisting or pushing helped. Nope, the door was locked all right . . . and I was on the wrong side. I looked to see if there was a locking lever that I could flip. There wasn't. There was only an old-fashioned keyhole. But seeing as I didn't have an old-fashioned key, that wasn't any help.

I wanted to scream. How could I have been so dumb as to pull the door closed without checking it first? This was totally my fault. I had snatched defeat from the jaws of victory. It would only be a matter of time before I was discovered, and then any hope of untangling the mystery of May 6 and LZ-129 would die right along with me.

Bobby Pendragon, *Dead* Undercover Traveler.

FIRST EARTH

Things couldn't be worse. I was locked in the private office of a vicious mobster who was going to eat me for dessert. Max Rose had a lot of goons on the payroll. One of them was bound to come by any second. I had to think fast and figure out some other way out of there.

I spun around and scanned the office. Yes! There was another door behind his desk. Why hadn't I seen that before? I ran for it and twisted the knob. It was locked.

Ahhhh! What was it with this guy and locked doors? You'd think he was a crook or something. I had to come up with a Plan B. Fast. Uncle Press always had a Plan B. I really wished he were there to give it to me, because I was coming up empty.

Then I saw the telephone. Of course! Max Rose had slammed down this very phone a few minutes ago. How could I forget? I could call Gunny for help. I wasn't exactly sure of what Gunny could do, but right now, this was my only hope. So I dove for the old (okay, new for 1937) black phone, yanked the receiver off the cradle, and dialed. It was a rotary dial thing, and my hands were shaking as I stuck my finger in the "9" hole. Number 99 was the bell captain's desk. Dialing 9-9 would bring Gunny to me, and hopefully Gunny would bring me to safety. I dialed the first nine and winced as it made a loud, raspy sound like a saw cutting through wood. But I couldn't stop now.

I was just about to dial the second nine when I heard something. It was a quiet sound, but it might just as well have been a nuclear explosion, because I was sure it was going to be just as bad for me.

Someone was opening the door behind the desk.

It was too late to run and there was no place to hide. I was busted. As scared as I was, I made sure *not* to dial the second nine. I didn't want them to know I was calling Gunny. No sense in getting us *all* killed. So I slowly returned the receiver to its cradle and waited for a gun muzzle to be jammed into my back.

"I don't think you're supposed to be in here," came a voice from behind me.

Yeah, right. You think?

But the sound of this voice gave me a flicker of hope. For one, it was the voice of a woman. She didn't sound angry, either. Maybe I could talk my way out of this. After all, I had the Traveler power of persuasion, right? Without turning around I said, "I just brought lunch up to Mr. Rose. The hotel wanted to make it special, but somebody forgot to put champagne on the cart. It was supposed to be a gift, on the house. So I came in here to call down for somebody to bring it up and the door locked behind me."

It was a total bluff, but all I could think of. Would she buy it? Or would she scream for Rose's goons to come in here and toss me out the window? The next few seconds felt like a lifetime.

Finally she said, "Here, take this."

Uh-oh. Was it a bullet?

"Turn around," she said with a laugh. "I won't bite."

I slowly turned around to see who I was dealing with.

Wow. Standing in the doorway was a beautiful woman who looked like some kind of old-time movie star. She was dressed in a long, ivory nightgown that looked as slick as silk. It wasn't embarrassing or anything because she had a silky robe over it. Her hair was dark and done in a perfect do. She wore perfect makeup, too. This wasn't somebody who had just fallen out of bed. She looked ready for a photo shoot. I couldn't tell how old she was, not with all the elegant makeup and all, but I'm guessing she was in her twenties. She had a little smile that told me she knew exactly how scared I was.

Once I got over the shock of seeing her, I saw something else that made my heart leap. She was holding out an old-fashioned brass key on a ring.

"I don't know why he makes all the doors lock that way," she said softly. "Maybe to catch people who go into places they shouldn't." She said this with a smile, like she was needling me. I think she liked to see me squirm. Good for her, because I was definitely squirming. I reached out and took the key.

"Thanks," I said. "It was a big mistake. I never should have come in here."

I went back to the main door and used the key to unlock it. When I opened the door, I was relieved to see that nobody villainous was lurking around in the entryway. I was beginning to think I had a chance of getting out of here alive. Quickly I returned the key to the woman, saying, "I'm very embarrassed."

"Don't worry about it," said the woman. "I'll never tell." She put her finger to her lips to emphasize her promise to "shush." It all seemed kind of flirty. Oh yeah, this was going to work out. I gave her a sincerely grateful smile, then turned for the door and freedom.

"Hey!" she shouted after me. I froze. I was seconds away from a clean escape. What had gone wrong? I turned back to her sheepishly.

"What about the champagne? Aren't you going to make that call?"

Oops. I hadn't followed through with the bluff. I was such a bad liar. Was this going to bite me in the butt? I had to think fast, again. "Uh . . . I really shouldn't be in here," I said. "I'll go downstairs and bring it back up myself."

"Good idea," she said. "You're a smart kid." With that, she left through the door behind the desk..

Ding Dong! The doorbell rang. In a few seconds one of Rose's thugs would appear to answer it, and I was still in the office! I quickly dashed out and across the entryway toward the front door.

"Hey, you still here?" somebody bellowed. It was the guy who first opened the door for me when I arrived.

"Just leaving," I said. The thug pushed past me and opened the door. Standing outside was Gunny, with a bottle of champagne chilling in a bucket of ice.

"For Mr. Rose," he said. "Compliments of the Manhattan Tower Hotel."

I glanced back over my shoulder and saw that the movie-star lady was watching from the corridor. It was perfect. Gunny had cemented my bluff without even knowing it. I was home free.

The thug took the champagne, then pushed me out the door and closed it behind us. Gunny and I made brief eye contact, but didn't say a word. We walked quickly past the two security guards in the corridor, stopped at the elevator, and rang for Dewey. The elevator arrived seconds later and we rode silently down to the lobby. Dewey looked at me the whole way down, dying to know what had happened. But he wasn't going to ask with Gunny there, and I sure as heck wasn't going to tell him anything. When we got to the lobby, Gunny and I stepped out of the elevator and kept walking until Dewey was out of earshot.

Finally Gunny said under his breath, "You were up there too long, shorty. I was getting nervous. I had to make up an excuse to go up."

"It was perfect," I added. "And totally worth it. Wait'll you hear." The two of us parted and went about our business for the rest of the day as if nothing scary had happened.

That night Spader, Gunny, and I met in our room, and I told them everything that had happened in Max Rose's penthouse.

"So these Nazi wogglies," Spader said, "they're pretty nasty characters?"

"Yes," was my simple answer.

"As bad as the gangster boys around here?" he asked.

"Worse," I answered. "These guys aren't just criminals. The Nazis are about taking over the whole territory and murdering millions of people along the way."

"So they're like, Saint Dane–bad," was Spader's conclusion.

"Yeah, they're Saint Dane–bad," I agreed.

"So then, what are they planning together?" Spader asked with frustration.

"That is the big question, isn't it?" Gunny said.

What was Saint Dane trying to do here? Aside from the murderous mission of two gangsters at the flume in the subway, the demon hadn't made his presence known.

"The Nazis are going to pay Max Rose for his services on May sixth," I said while pacing. "I think if we figure out what Max Rose is doing for the Nazis, we'll know what Saint Dane's plan is."

"And what is Ludwig Zell-one-twenty-nine?" asked Spader. "Sounds like some kind of code."

"We don't know if it's Ludwig Zell-one-twenty-nine," I said. "Only L-Z-one-two-nine."

I looked to Gunny, but Gunny only shrugged. LZ-129 might be the key to this whole thing, or mean absolutely nothing.

"I'll keep snooping around," said Gunny.

We ended the meeting by saying we had to keep a closer eye on Max Rose and his band of merry men. We decided to read every newspaper we could get, every day, to see if there was any mention of LZ-129 or Ludwig Zell. You never knew. For the first time since I had gotten to First Earth, I had the feeling that we were on our way to figuring out what Saint Dane had in mind to disrupt this territory.

I was absolutely, totally wrong.

What *really* happened after that meeting was nothing. I'm serious, absolutely nothing. The trail went stone freakin' cold. Max Rose never left the penthouse. Ludwig Zell didn't come by the hotel again. We didn't have any trouble with Winn Farrow and his gang of killers. We read every newspaper from New York, New Jersey, and Connecticut, but didn't find a single reference to Ludwig Zell or LZ-129. Remember, this was long before the Internet. It's not like we could sign on to a search engine, input "Ludwig Zell, evil Nazi mobster plan" and get a complete history of the guy and what he was up to.

This was *way* frustrating.

Gunny even went to some government offices to look for

any documents that showed the kinds of businesses Max Rose was involved in. Good idea, except for one thing. This was 1937. An African American guy walking into government offices looking for information wasn't exactly common. This was long before the civil rights movement. Guys like Jackie Robinson, Martin Luther King Jr., Colin Powell, Clarence Thomas from the Supreme Court, and Nelson Mandela hadn't broken down any barriers yet. They didn't even have very many black movie stars like Will Smith or Eddie Murphy.

So Gunny pretty much walked into a bunch of brick walls.

It would have been a totally depressing situation, if Spader and I hadn't tried to have a little fun along the way. He showed me a good time on his home territory of Cloral, so I wanted to do the same for him on First Earth.

I took him to see a lot of movies. He had never seen anything like a movie before, and it was fun to watch his reaction. He was freaked at first, kind of like when we saw the holograms on Veelox. But after a while he got with the program. The admission price was only twenty-five cents. Can you believe it? I took him to see lots of Marx Brothers movies, my favorite being *A Night at the Opera*. We saw some Westerns with a guy named Tom Mix, and even saw the original *King Kong*. It was fun to see these movies on a big screen instead of television.

We toured all over New York. I took him to the top of the Empire State Building, which was cool because we had just seen King Kong climb the thing. We went to the Statue of Liberty and Grand Central Station and even took a subway out to Coney Island to ride the rides and eat hot dogs.

I think my favorite day was when we went up to the Bronx. No, not to the flume. We went to a Yankees game. I couldn't believe it, but I saw both Lou Gehrig and Joe

DiMaggio play! How cool is *that*? Spader didn't understand the game and it was hard to explain, but it didn't matter. I was in hog heaven.

And speaking of heaven, we also played a lot of basketball.

When it comes to athletic stuff, I have to admit that Spader is better than I am in everything. He's a little older and bigger, which helps. (At least, that's what I tell myself.) But when it comes to basketball, well, that's my game.

At the risk of sounding crude, I kicked his ass. We set up a hoop in an alley behind the hotel and snuck out every chance we got. Gunny found us a crusty old leather ball. The rim was all bent and rusty with no net, but it didn't matter. I recruited some of the other bellhops, and we played two on two. We even got Dewey to play, but he was worse than Spader. Poor guy.

Our games were like minivacations away from Traveler worries. They put my mind back to a time and place when things were a whole lot easier, and the biggest concern I had was whether or not Courtney liked me as much as I liked her. (Yes, Courtney, I used to think about that a lot. I admit it.)

Though our adventures exploring First Earth were excellent, there was always the big old sword of worry hanging over our heads. The longer we went without finding out anything about Max Rose and the Nazis, the more anxious I became. May 6 was drawing closer. It was beginning to look as if nothing would happen until then.

I was wrong. On May 3, things started getting interesting again.

The day started out normally, except that the hotel was expecting a celebrity guest. Her name was Nancy Olsen, but everybody knew her as "Jinx." She was a pilot who flew for the Coast Guard. They didn't have many women pilots back then, and Jinx was a real hotshot. She was touring around the country doing public relations. I guess the idea was to get women interested in signing up for military service. In 1937 women didn't normally do things like fly for the Coast Guard, so Jinx Olsen was unique.

Her tour brought her to New York, where she was going to stay at the hotel for a week while making appearances and giving speeches. There was even a big party planned for her in the ballroom on the twenty-ninth floor of the hotel. It was going to be a big doo-dah with a band and celebrities and politicians and the works. Spader and I had already been asked to be waiters for the party because there were going to be over two hundred guests, and they needed all the help they could get.

When Jinx Olsen arrived at the hotel, I could tell instantly why she was chosen to be the poster girl for the Coast Guard. She was tall and pretty and oozed confidence. Most of the women I had seen on First Earth wore dresses—but not Jinx. She had on khakis and a worn, brown leather jacket. But she didn't look like a guy. No way. She had these dazzling green eyes and a big smile that absolutely lit up the room. When she first strode into the hotel lobby with her duffel bag over her shoulder, the first word that jumped into my head was "adventurer."

The hotel manager, a chubby guy named Mr. Caplesmith, was right there to greet her. "Welcome, Miss Olsen," he said. "We are so honored to have you stay with us."

Jinx stopped short, stared the guy square in the eyes and asked, "Why?"

Mr. Caplesmith got a little flustered and said, "Well, because you're such a famous, uh, pilot person." He had no clue about what made Jinx Olsen tick, and Jinx Olsen knew it.

"Let's be honest," she said. "You're happy to see me because Uncle Sam is paying you to put on a big old party tomorrow night, right?"

Mr. Caplesmith was embarrassed, but he knew better than to lie to her. "Well, you could say that," he said sheepishly.

Jinx smiled and gave him a friendly punch on the arm. "No problem. Just so we all know the score. Where's my room?"

Mr. Caplesmith tried hard not to grab his arm in pain. He looked around and saw me.

"Bell boy!" he ordered.

I ran up and stood at attention. Mr. Caplesmith liked that.

"Please take Miss Olsen up to room fifteen-fifteen." He gave me the room key.

I reached for Jinx's bag, but she didn't give it up. "I can handle it, chief," she said with a smile. "Just show me the way."

"Yes ma'am," I said, and made for the elevator. Jinx followed right after me. I glanced back quickly and saw Mr. Caplesmith massaging his sore arm. It was hard not to laugh. Jinx Olsen was the coolest person I had met since starting work at this hotel, aside from Gunny of course.

"You've got a pretty exciting job," I said. "Making rescues with the Coast Guard and all."

"Yeah, real exciting," she said. It didn't sound like she meant it.

"It's not?" I asked.

"It would be if they actually let me do it once in a while. It's not easy getting the call, being a woman and all." We arrived at the elevator and Dewey started us on our way up. He even got the controls right the first time. He must have been practicing.

"That's not fair," I said to Jinx. "If you've got the chops, you should be flying the missions."

"You know how many times I've told them that?" Jinx said. "But they'd rather trot me out on these public relations tours where I won't get scratched. Heck, I'm a better flier than most of the boys in my squad, but because I'm a woman, well, I don't get the chance."

"Do you know Amelia Earhart?" Dewey asked.

"I've met her," answered Jinx. "Now *that* gal is a flier!"

"Amelia Earhart?" I asked. "Isn't that the woman pilot who disappeared when she was trying to fly around the world?"

Dewey and Jinx looked at me like I was from Pluto.

"You must be mistaken," Jinx said. "She's leaving on her round-the-world trip the end of this month."

Oops. First Earth. I was talking about something that hadn't happened yet. I wasn't wrong though. I remembered seeing a TV show about Amelia Earhart. She never made it. I didn't have the heart to tell them. On the other hand, they never would have believed me because I was talking about the future. Luckily, we had arrived on the fifteenth floor.

"We're here," I announced, and hurried out of the elevator before I had to talk any more about Amelia Earhart. I opened up room 1515 for Jinx and told her that if she needed anything, she should call Gunny, the bell captain, and he'd make sure one of us took care of her. She thanked me and gave me a twenty-five-cent tip. Not exactly a lot of cash, but it would pay for another Marx Brothers movie.

"You know something?" I said. "You may be having a tough time, but someday soon there will be a lot of women fliers. People are going to realize they're just as good as the guys. Things will change. I guarantee it."

This made Jinx smile. She came across as pretty tough, but

I'll bet that was because she had to survive in a macho man's job. But in that brief moment, her guard came down, and I saw beyond the bold front to the real person.

"What's your name, chief?" she asked.

"Bobby Pendragon."

"I'm Jinx, Bobby. Thanks for the kind words. I'll remember them." She winked at me and we shook hands.

I liked Jinx Olsen. Her confidence and cockiness reminded me a lot of Spader. I hoped she was going to get the chance to prove herself someday.

The party in her honor was the following night, and it was a real fancy deal. The ballroom on the twenty-ninth floor was all decked out with red, white, and blue decorations. There must have been a thousand colorful balloons floating up on the ceiling. The men wore tuxedos and the women were in long, formal gowns. I recognized some old-time movie stars, but didn't know their names. There was one guy I definitely recognized though—it was Lou Gehrig. Even out of his Yankees uniform, I knew who he was.

There was a big orchestra playing for people to dance. The musicians all wore white jackets and looked like they had stepped out of an Abbott and Costello movie. I even recognized some of the music they were playing. Like I always said, if you want to learn about classical music, watch old Bugs Bunny cartoons. If you want to learn about old-time swing music, watch Abbott and Costello movies. Who says TV isn't educational?

There was a long table set up on one side of the room for the dignitaries. That's where Jinx sat, right in the middle. She was wearing a dress but looked totally uncomfortable in it. I felt sorry for her. This was the price she had to pay for being allowed to fly. She had to be a goodwill ambassador and put on a happy face for the world. I guarantee she hated it.

The rest of the room was full of tables where people ate and drank. This was where Spader and I did our thing. A whole bunch of other waiters were brought in for the party, and we all wore these short white jackets, black pants, and white gloves. It was pretty cake work. We were each assigned to a table and had to shuttle back and forth to the kitchen, bringing out the food. Basically all I had to do was make sure I didn't spill anything.

The reason I'm telling you guys so much about this party isn't because it was such a gala, fun affair. Bo-ring. It's because of one particular table of guests. Sitting prominently, right near the long head table, was Max Rose and his crew. I couldn't believe it. Here was a swanky party put on by the U.S. government and sitting front and center was a known gangster. My guess was he was there because he was the most important guest of the hotel. I guess when you're the best customer, you get privileges . . . even if you're a mobster.

Gunny made sure that Spader and I were assigned to Max Rose's table. We both hovered around him and his guests, taking care of their every little whim. But what we were really doing was listening to everything being said, hoping to catch some clue as to what LZ-129 was, or what was going to happen on May 6.

"Buck Rogers!" shouted Rose when he saw me. "My favorite spaceman. They got you working as a waiter, too?"

"Yes sir, Mr. Rose," I said. "Nothing but the best for you."

He laughed. I think he liked it when somebody was a little bit cocky. Especially if they complimented him. "Keep the wine coming, Buck," he said. "I'll make it worth your while."

"Yes, sir!" I said. This was good. I planned on being right by his side every chance I got. All the seats were taken by various thugs I had seen coming in and out of the hotel. Unfortunately Ludwig Zell wasn't one of them. But the chair next to Rose was empty. I hoped that it was reserved for our Nazi friend. I had just popped a bottle of champagne and was pouring it for Rose, when the guest who was assigned to the empty chair finally showed up. It wasn't Zell.

"Sorry I'm late, Maxie," came a woman's voice. "It took me forever to find the perfect gown to wear."

I looked up and nearly dropped the champagne bottle. It was the movie star–looking woman who caught me in Max Rose's office.

She looked at me and winked. My heart stopped. I was afraid she'd say something about what had happened in the office. That would be death. My death. She picked up her champagne glass and held it out for me to fill.

"Such a handsome young waiter," she said. "Have we ever met?"

Was she kidding? Did she remember me or was she just pulling my chain?

"I don't think so, ma'am," I lied.

"You must be right," she said. "I'd never forget a handsome young man like you." She gave me a small smile and a wink. She knew *exactly* who I was. She was just messing with me again. I was starting to sweat, so I got away from there fast. This was going to be an interesting night.

Right after dinner there was a bunch of speeches that all sounded alike. A lot of politicians talked about the important role that women were going to play in the military and the Coast Guard and blah, blah, blah. The final speech was given by Jinx herself. I'm sorry to say, her speech wasn't so hot either. She did her best to deliver it like she cared, but I could tell she hated every minute of it.

After the speeches the band kicked in again for people to dance. That's when I got my next surprise. The bandleader stepped up to the microphone and announced in a silky smooth voice, "Ladies and gentlemen, please welcome to the microphone our featured vocalist for this evening, the lovely Esther Amaden."

I looked around to see who the lovely lady was, and who should stand up but Max Rose's girlfriend! Yeow! No wonder she looked so great. She was a professional singer. She was good, too. Not that I'm a big fan of that music, but she had a great voice and looked terrific under the spotlight. She sang a couple of songs that sounded sorta familiar. The people at the party must have known all of them because they each got big applause when she started to sing.

In all, it was a very elegant evening . . . and totally frustrating. After a long night the party was about to wind down, and I hadn't heard a single nugget of useful information from anybody at Rose's table. As far as our mission was concerned, the night was going to be a total bust.

At least, that's what I thought. Truth was, things were about to change dramatically.

There were a lot of waiters working the party. I knew all the bellhops, but didn't know any of the new waiters who'd come on just for the night. There was no reason to. All I was interested in was Max Rose and his table. But as I stood there listening to Esther Amaden sing, I saw something that got me interested in something besides Max Rose real quick.

I was standing near the kitchen door, watching the show. The band was glowing under a warm, blue light. A mirrored ball on the ceiling was spinning and shooting out little white sparkles of light that looked like fireflies. They washed over the band, the dancers, and the tables. Esther looked beautiful in the center of it all in a white spotlight.

I don't know what made me look away when I did, but it was a good thing. What I saw rocked me into Defcon 10. It was one of the new waiters. I think I noticed him because he was walking slowly, with his back to the wall. If there was one thing the waiters weren't doing that night, it was walking slowly. It was way too busy for that. But this guy was just sort of creeping along.

He was holding a big serving tray with a silver dome over it. That wouldn't have been weird . . . two hours before. But now we were done with the food. What was he doing with a serving tray? To make things even more interesting, he was headed toward the table with Max Rose. I took a few steps to get a better look at him, and when I did, my jaw dropped.

I knew this guy! It was Mr. Nervous, the gangster from the subway!

The music was loud. The party was in full swing. People were dancing like crazy.

Nobody saw this guy stalking closer to Max Rose. A moment later he reached under the dome of the serving tray and pulled out a gun. Winn Farrow's men may have been laying low for a long time, but tonight they were back in action. Tonight they were going after Max Rose.

And I was the only one who knew it.

FIRST EARTH

The assassin drew closer to Max Rose.

About a million thoughts clicked through my head rapid fire. Max Rose was a criminal, a killer. A guy in that line of work is bound to have something ugly come down on him sooner or later. That was his business. But Rose and his gang were somehow connected to the Nazis. If he died, our only hope of discovering what they were up to, and what Saint Dane was up to, would die along with him. The future of First Earth depended on what Max Rose knew . . . and that was *my* business.

It took me all of two seconds to realize I had to save Max Rose. But how? If I shouted a warning, the nervous gangster would start shooting and that would be the ballgame. No, I had to act.

Spader walked out of the kitchen at that exact moment. I grabbed him and pointed him toward the stalking gangster. "He's going after Max Rose. We gotta stop him," I said, trying to sound like I was more in control of my emotions than I really was.

Spader didn't question me. He didn't debate or hesitate. As

soon as he saw the situation and knew I wanted it stopped, he clicked into "go" mode.

"I'll take out the wogglie, you go for Rose," he ordered with total authority. A half second later he was pushing through the crowd, headed after the gangster.

The show was on and I had to move. I started running for Max Rose's table. The shortest line was straight through the crowded dance floor. I tried to skirt the swinging dancers, but that was impossible and slowing me down. There was no way I'd make it in time by being polite. I figured everybody's evening was about to be ruined in a few seconds anyway, so why worry? I put my head down and started pumping my legs like a fullback. I blasted through a few unsuspecting bodies, and I'm embarrassed to say that a few of them were ladies. But it didn't matter. I had to make it into the end zone and I would not be denied.

A few seconds later the final dancer between me and Rose's table spun out of the way, and I had a clear shot at my target. Max Rose was sitting on the far side of the big, round table, laughing and puffing on a fat cigar. A quick glance to my left showed me that the gangster with the gun was getting closer. Spader was fighting his way through the crowd to get to the guy, but he was going to be too late. The assassin was only a few steps away from his date with Max.

I looked back to Max Rose and saw there was a whole bunch of table and glassware and even a flowered center-piece between me and him. I had to make a snap decision. My blood was already boiling from my frenzied run across the dance floor, so the choice I made wasn't a tough one. I kicked it into another gear, ran for the table, and launched myself over the top. It all happened so fast that the goons sitting at the table didn't have time to react. I slid across the tabletop, pulling the tablecloth and everything else along with me.

Max Rose saw me coming and his eyes grew wide with surprise. The bodyguard sitting next to Rose went for his gun. But he was too late because just as he pulled the gun from under his jacket, Max Rose got slammed with a wave of tableware, flowers, and Bobby Pendragon, Undercover Traveler.

Rose had begun to stand up and that may have saved his life, because he was a little off balance. The force of me hitting him knocked him straight back. If he had been firmly planted in his chair, I probably would have bounced off him and he would have still been a target. But as it was, we both went over and he landed backward on the floor. He let out a huge grunt as I landed right on top of him. I told you, he was a big guy, and I swear I think I bounced off him like I'd hit a trampoline. The only thing missing was the sound of a timpani drum going *boing!*

It was at that exact instant that I heard a gunshot. I winced, thinking that the bodyguard had shot at me. But it wasn't the guard who fired the shot. As we fell, his gun had clattered down on the floor right next to my head. I must have knocked it away from him in my wild slide across the table. I quickly grabbed it. No way I wanted the bodyguard to pick it up and use it on me.

So where did the shot come from? I looked up to see Mr. Nervous Gangster standing near us, pointing his smoking gun. The look of surprise on his face was almost funny. He must have had Max Rose right in his sights, only to have me come flying through to knock his target away. He fired. He missed. Luckily he didn't hit anybody behind us either.

A second later Spader leaped out of the crowd and knocked the gun out of the assassin's grip. The guy was in shock. He had been a second away from success, only to have his whole plan explode before his eyes.

"Shoot him!" ordered Rose.

It took me a second to realize who he was talking to. It was me! I was sitting on top of him with the bodyguard's gun in my hand. Max Rose wanted me to shoot his would-be assassin. I had never even shot a gun before, let alone one that was aimed at somebody.

"Do it, Buck, shoot him!" shouted Rose.

I was stunned and confused. I turned the gun toward the nervous gangster because that's what I was ordered to do. The guy looked back at me and our eyes locked.

In those eyes I saw something I had never seen before and never wanted to see again. I had his life in my hands. He knew it. It was up to me whether he would live or die. That was a power I didn't want, under any circumstances. It was a frightening moment. This gangster was my enemy. He tried to kill us down in the subway. Worse, he was one of the assassins who killed Uncle Press. Nobody deserved my revenge more than this guy.

But in spite of all that, there was no way I could take his life. That wasn't something I had in me.

So I dropped the gun.

Instantly the gangster ran. You would think with so many people standing around, somebody would have stopped him. But all those fancy folks in tuxedos and gowns were in a state of shock. By the time somebody got their head together enough to shout "Stop him!" the gunman had already ducked out of a service door and was gone.

I looked around and saw nothing but stunned faces. The band had stopped playing and people were now slowly circling us to see what had happened. It was eerie. Nobody said a word; they just stared. I realized I was still sitting on Max Rose's stomach. I looked down to see he was staring up at me with razor-sharp eyes.

"I told you to shoot him," he said flatly.

I was too stunned to say anything.

"Did you hear me, Buck? I told you to shoot him!"

This was a crucial moment. Not only for my own survival, but for the future of our mission on First Earth. I felt like the whole ballgame was right here, right now. I couldn't screw it up.

"Yeah, so what?" I said, trying to sound cocky.

It was a bold move. Max Rose stared right into my brain. I didn't look away. My adrenaline was still spiked way too high to back off now.

"Wasn't it enough that I saved your skin?" I asked. "I'm not hearing any thank-yous."

A moment passed. I felt the hot stares of Rose's bodyguards on me as they waited for Rose to tell them what to do.

After a painfully long few seconds, Max Rose . . . smiled. "Thank you, Buck," he said. "Now would you please get off my stomach?"

Things got pretty hectic after that. People were either scared and jumping over each other to get to the elevator, or pressing in on us to see what had happened. The band started playing again. I guess they were trying to calm everybody down. Isn't that what the band did while the Titanic was sinking? I was getting shoved around by the mass of people. All I wanted to do was get out of there, but it was impossible to move. I thought I was gonna get crushed.

Finally a strong hand grabbed my arm. I looked up to see who it belonged to, and was totally relieved to see Gunny.

"Time to go," he said calmly.

He had my arm in one hand and Spader's in the other. He quickly pushed the two of us through the crowd and back into the kitchen and away from the hubbub. But we didn't stop there. He wanted us out of that place as fast as possible, before anybody could talk to us. Again, once the police showed up there would be a lot of questions asked. The less they knew about us, the better, so it was a good thing we got out of there while it was still a madhouse.

A few minutes later, after a quick ride down on the service elevator, we were safely tucked back into our sixth floor suite, as if nothing had happened.

"Don't come out of here," ordered Gunny. "And don't come to work tomorrow. I want things to calm down first."

"No problem," I said.

"We hear you, mate," added Spader.

Then Gunny smiled nervously. "You were right, Pendragon. We *are* just getting started."

"All in a day's work, Gunny, my friend," said Spader with a touch of his usual cockiness.

Gunny then left and we were alone. My heart slowly stopped sprinting. Spader and I looked at each other. Neither of us knew what to say. Finally we both burst out laughing.

"Hobey, Pendragon!" shouted Spader. "That was amazing!"

"You were great!" I shouted. "You didn't even stop to think before taking off after that guy!"

"Good thing," Spader said. "I probably would have run the other way if I gave it any thought. That was a natty-do, all right!"

"Yeah, yeah, it was," I said.

The two of us fell into chairs, feeling proud of ourselves. We sat there for a while, enjoying the moment, enjoying the victory.

It wouldn't last.

Spader took a final deep breath, blew it out and said, "It's back on, isn't it?"

I knew exactly what he meant. "Yeah," I said. "No more basketball."

As I drifted off to sleep that night, it was with the realization that after weeks of sitting around and spinning our wheels, the curtain was finally about to go up on this show. The scary thing was, we still had no idea what to expect.

I really missed Uncle Press.

The next morning we were woken up by a knock on the door. I figured it was Gunny, but when I looked through the peephole I was surprised to see Dewey.

"I know you're in there, Pendragon," he said. "I know everything that happens in this hotel."

Busted. I had no choice but to open the door. Spader came up from behind me. "What do you want, Dewey?" he asked.

"Did you two really think I didn't know you were living here?" he asked. "How stupid do you think I am?"

Spader and I shared a look. We didn't want to answer that.

"Look at this," he said, and handed us a newspaper. The headline blared: NEAR MISS AT THE TOWER! It was an article about the shooting the previous night. And there was a picture. It was a shot of Max Rose, flat on his back, with me sitting on his stomach. I had no idea somebody had taken that picture. Luckily you couldn't see my face. As far as this big news story went, Spader and I were mysterious waiters who disappeared right after the shooting, along with the would-be assassin.

"Yeah, that was pretty exciting," I said. "I wonder who those two hero waiters were?"

Dewey gave me a sour look. "That answers my question. You must think I'm an idiot."

Suddenly the newspaper was grabbed out of my hand.

"Morning boys," said Jinx Olsen with a smile. "Some party last night!" She then turned to Dewey and touched his cheek. "Thanks, Dewey. You're a peach." Dewey turned all sorts of red. Jinx then pushed past us and into the room.

I wasn't sure of what to do, so I closed the door in Dewey's face.

"Hey!" he protested. Too late.

Jinx strode into the suite, checking out the place. "Nice digs," she said. "Must be tough paying for this on a bell-boy's salary."

Spader said, "Yeah, but there's two of us."

"Ahhh!" said Jinx with a knowing smile. "*Two* bellboy salaries. That must make all the difference." She was being sarcastic.

"What can we do for you, Miss Olsen?" I asked.

"It's Jinx," she said. "Sorry to barge in like this. I just wanted to tell you what a great thing it was you did last night. It was the highlight of my night. No, it was the highlight of my year."

I wasn't sure of what to say. Should we admit it was us? She knew me and obviously saw the whole thing. What was the use of lying?

"We'd just as soon you didn't tell anybody it was us," I said.

"And modest, too," said Jinx with a big smile. "You guys are the perfect heroes. You should be wearing white hats."

"What does that mean?" asked Spader.

"Tell you what," Jinx said. "I want to do something for you boys, seeing as you won't take any credit for being heroes. I want to give you a reward myself."

"You don't have to do that," I said.

"I know," said Jinx as she strode to the door. "But I want to. Get dressed. We're going for a ride. Dress warm." She then blew out of the apartment as quickly as she entered. Spader and I stood there, a little stunned.

"She wants to take us for a ride," Spader finally said.

"But Gunny told us not to leave until things calmed down."

Spader started pulling on his pants. "Pendragon, a beautiful girl just asked us to go on an adventure with her. You can stay here if you'd like, but as for me, I'd like to know what kind of ride she wants to give us."

I'd seen Spader like this before. There was nothing I could say that would talk him out of this. If there was a chance for adventure, then he was going to take it, no matter how irresponsible it might be. I had the choice of staying there by myself, or going along to make sure he didn't get into trouble. To be honest, I liked Jinx and I was kind of interested in what she had in mind too. It took me a solid three seconds to reach for my clothes and start getting dressed myself.

Whatever it was she had planned for us, there was no way I wanted to miss it.

FIRST EARTH

Five minutes later we were downstairs and climbing into a taxicab with the lady flier. I wasn't totally irresponsible though. I told Gunny we were going out with Jinx. He didn't like the fact that we were leaving, but then thought it might be a good idea for us to be away from the hotel for a while. Since the night before, the place was crawling with reporters trying to find the mysterious waiters who saved the life of the notorious Max Rose. Getting away from that circus was probably a smart thing to do.

As we rode in the taxi, Jinx wouldn't tell us where we were headed. She said it was a surprise, but guaranteed we'd like it. To be honest, the thought flashed through my head that she might have been sent by Saint Dane, or even worse, she might actually *be* Saint Dane. But nothing about her set my radar off. I was pretty sure she was exactly who she said she was: Jinx Olsen, an incredible flier for the Coast Guard.

The taxicab took us over to the West Side of Manhattan and the Hudson River. That's when we saw what Jinx had in store for us. When she said she was going to take us for a ride, she really meant it. There, tied up at the end of a pier, bobbing on the water, was Jinx's airplane. Or maybe I should call it a seaplane.

It was a wacky-looking contraption, not at all like the sleek planes of Second Earth. The silver ship floated gently on the swells, looking as if it wanted to be in the air instead of pretending to be a boat. It was a biplane, which meant it had two sets of wings, one on top of the other. Between the two wings was a big, single engine. But rather than the propeller being in front, it faced backward. Weird. There were two cockpits, one behind the other, ahead of the wings. They weren't closed in, either. When you flew in this plane, you were going to feel it in your face, and probably in your stomach, too. Painted on the silver fuselage, just under the front cockpit, was the crossed-anchor emblem of the U.S. Coast Guard.

"That's my baby," she said. "The V-one-fifty-seven Schreck/Viking. She may not look like much, but she's a sweetie in the air."

She jumped aboard and began her preflight check. I was psyched.

Spader pulled me aside so Jinx couldn't hear and said, "Odd looking speeder, that one."

"It's not a speeder," I said. "It's an airplane."

"A what?"

"An airplane. A seaplane, actually. We're going to take off on the water and fly up in the air."

For the first time since I'd known him, Spader looked totally dumbfounded. His mouth actually hung open. No kidding. Wide open. I might as well have said we were going to drink every drop of water in the Hudson. That's how alien a concept flying was to him.

"We're going to fly? Up there? In the air? Like a bird? In that thing?" he asked.

"Yup," I answered.

"That's unnatural!" he exclaimed.

"No more unnatural than putting a clear dome over your head and breathing underwater, but you do that on Cloral every day."

"Yes, but that's simple," he said. "Flying is . . . is . . . impossible."

"Want to bet?" I asked.

Jinx handed us each a brown canvas sack with straps that looked like an old-fashioned backpack. I knew what it was, but I was a little nervous about explaining it to Spader.

"Can't go up without a chute," Jinx said while putting on one of her own. "Just a precaution, like wearing a life vest on a boat." She then demonstrated how to put on the parachute. Uncle Press had taken me skydiving a few times, so I was familiar with the whole deal. Even though this parachute pack was ancient, the principals were the same. I buckled in the way Jinx showed us. Spader did too. He didn't ask what it was for, until we were all buckled up and Jinx did a safety check.

"Looks good," she said.

"What is this for?" Spader finally asked. I looked to Jinx. I didn't want to be the one to break the news.

"It's a parachute, of course," Jinx said as if she couldn't believe he didn't know. "If you fall out, pull on this metal ring. But try not to fall out."

She winked and headed for the plane.

Spader looked at me with a sick expression, "If I fall out, pull this ring?" he repeated. "What happens then? I sprout wings and fly?"

I laughed and said, "Sort of. Don't worry about it. You won't need it."

I pushed him toward the plane, and we boarded. Jinx was at the controls in the forward cockpit. I sat in the back with Spader. It was cramped, especially with the bulky parachute packs, but I didn't care. Jinx gave us each some leather flight caps and floppy goggles to wear. It was a good thing she had warned us to dress warmly. If we were going to be flying around in an open cockpit, it was going to get chilly.

"Buckle in!" Jinx commanded. Spader and I both found some cheesy leather seatbelts and strapped ourselves in. Good idea. Remember, the cockpits were wide open. We didn't want to have to use the parachutes.

"Ready?" she shouted from up front.

"Hobey-ho, let's go!" I shouted.

Spader just grunted. I think he was already nauseous.

Jinx turned over the engine, and with a throaty roar, the giant propeller behind our heads began to turn. Man, it was noisy. I'm not talking about loud. I'm talking about teeth-rattling, bone-jarring, makes-your-stomach-throb-and-your-ears-hurt noisy. At least the leather caps helped to cut some of the noise. I wished I had my CD Walkman.

The whole plane rattled from the force of the engine. I had been in a lot of airplanes—mostly big jetliner-type planes. But Uncle Press had taken me in a few smaller planes. Remember, he was a pilot. So between the flying lessons and the skydiving lessons, I was pretty comfortable in the air. But this plane was rickety. It may have been new in 1937, but by my standards it was only a couple of steps ahead of Wilbur and Orville–time. Still, I trusted Jinx. She was a national poster girl for the Coast Guard, right? She knew what she was doing. At least that's what I told myself.

Spader was another matter. He was scared to death. He had never experienced anything close to this. He sat next to me as stiff as a tree. I could almost feel his heart thumping in his chest. But believe it or not, I knew he wanted to be here. He may have been scared, but he was always up for an adventure.

I had never taken off in a seaplane before. It was a bumpy experience. The water on the Hudson was calm, but even on a calm day there was some chop. So when Jinx turned the plane into the wind and gunned the throttle, we were treated to nearly thirty seconds of bouncing, bumping, and rocking as the plane accelerated over the swells. Then, just when I thought my brain was going to break loose inside my skull, Jinx pulled back on the yoke and we rose into the air. The ride became instantly smooth as we lifted up from the river and headed for the sky.

What followed was an hour that I will remember for the rest of my life.

Jinx treated us to an aerial tour of New York City. We flew up the Hudson and over the newly built George Washington Bridge. We rounded the northernmost tip of Manhattan and got a bird's-eye view of Yankee Stadium. We flew down the East River, watching the barges slowly make their way from the ocean to Long Island Sound. We flew over the Brooklyn Bridge and into New York Harbor, where we were treated to a close-up view of the Statue of Liberty . . . at eye level. Jinx circled the statue four times, then turned back toward Manhattan. We flew north over the island until we got to the Empire State Building, where we did another four turns around.

Somewhere between the Brooklyn Bridge and the Statue of Liberty, Spader began to relax. Up until then he had been clutching the side of the cockpit so hard I thought he'd bend the metal. But gradually he loosened up and enjoyed the tour as much as I did.

"What a great plane!" I shouted to Jinx over the roar of the engine.

"Isn't she?" Jinx shouted back. "We've been all over the country together."

"Isn't it hard to always find water to take off and land?" I asked.

"Don't need it!" she shot back. "She's got wheels for a runway. I can fly this sweetheart wherever the wind takes me. Or the Coast Guard sends me."

The trip ended with a perfect landing on the Hudson, where Jinx guided us expertly back to the pier. She killed the engine and we were treated to something unbelievably fantastic—silence. Once the plane was safely secured, the three of us stood together on the pier.

"Jinx," I said. "I don't know what else to say but 'thank you.'"

"Double for me," added Spader. "I never would have believed it was possible for people to fly."

"You're kidding!" said Jinx with surprise. "Where do you live, under a rock?"

"No," answered Spader. "Under the water most of the time, but I'm not sure what that's got to do with it."

I figured I'd better step in and change the direction of this conversation. "We'll never forget this, Jinx," I said.

Jinx looked at her plane. I thought I sensed a bit of sadness in her. "I love to fly," she said. "Hard to believe it's all going to end."

"What do you mean?" I asked.

"I just got word this morning. After this tour, I'm grounded."

"What? Why?"

"I think the brass is afraid something might happen to me," she said with a hint of anger. "I agreed to do all this public relations stuff so they'd let me fly. Now I've become so famous, they're worried if something happens to me it'll look bad for everybody. Stupid thing is, they're probably right. If I crashed, they wouldn't let another woman in the cockpit for thirty years. Here I thought I was paving the way for women fliers, and all I did was take myself out of the sky."

Neither Spader nor I knew what to say. Jinx then put on her big, trademark smile. "But until they yank me outta the cockpit, I'm going up whenever I get the chance. So thanks, you two, for giving me the excuse to go on this little jaunt."

We all climbed in a cab and headed back to the hotel. Jinx was her old self again, telling us stories about how she learned to fly, and how she once crash-landed in a pasture in Maine and had to dodge a herd of moose. I really liked her and felt bad that soon she would no longer be able to do the thing she enjoyed so much. I really hoped she would find another way to get back into the air.

When we got back to the Manhattan Tower Hotel, Spader and I thanked Jinx again and left her at the front curb. We didn't want to run into any reporters so we ducked into a side entrance. We made it through the kitchen and the dining room and were just about to climb the service stairs to our room, when somebody grabbed both of us by the back of the neck. It was one of Max Rose's bodyguards.

"I've been looking all over for you two," he growled. "Mr. Rose would like a word with you."

Uh-oh. Was this good news or bad news? Was this going to be another chance to learn about Max Rose and his evil plot with the Nazis? Or was he ticked about me not following his order to shoot the gangster and planning to make us both pay the price? The truth was, it didn't matter because we didn't have any choice. We were going to have an audience with Max Rose, whether we liked it or not.

FIRST EARTH

Max Rose's bodyguard kept a firm hold on both of our jackets and marched us to the elevator like two kittens being carried by the neck. I can't speak for Spader, but my feet barely skimmed the ground. Dewey rode us up to the penthouse without a word. He didn't look at any of us. I knew he was thinking about the laundry chute. We hit the thirtieth floor and the bodyguard carried us toward the penthouse. Finally I couldn't take it anymore and pulled away.

"Enough, all right!" I shouted. "We're not going anywhere."

The guy looked at me with fire in his eyes. He didn't like being told what to do, especially by a punk bellhop. For a second I thought he was going to punch my lights out, but he held back. I would have bet anything it was because Max Rose wanted us alive and in one piece. This was good. I started to feel like we weren't being led toward a gangland execution. At least not today, anyway.

We followed the thug into the penthouse and right to the living room where I had set up lunch for Mr. Rose and Ludwig Zell. Max Rose was there waiting for us. He stood behind a bar, dressed in another silky bathrobe, only this one was deep purple. The bodyguard stood at the door with his arms folded. If we had to make a run for it, we'd have to get through him first. That pretty much meant we weren't going to be making a run for it.

"There you are, Buck!" he said with a warm smile. "And we got your sidekick, too. What's your name? Flash Gordon?"

"Vo Spader," answered Spader.

"Vo?" said Max with surprise. "What kind of name is that?"

"What kind of name is Rose?" asked Spader. "Isn't that some kind of flower?"

I winced. I didn't think it was a good idea to match wisecracks with a mobster. Max Rose stared at Spader for a moment, then smiled. "You've got brass, just like your buddy," he said. "I like that, Flash."

Spader gave me a sideways "Who is Flash?" look. But I ignored him.

Rose fixed himself a drink. He poured some amber liquid into a crystal glass, then gave it a squirt of bubbly water that he shot out of a bottle with a trigger. I'd seen those babies before. The Three Stooges used them all the time. I never knew people used them for anything other than water fights though.

The door on the far side of the room opened and in walked Esther Amaden. Actually, "walked" isn't the right word. She slinked in like a cat. She was wearing another long nightgown with a violet-colored shimmery robe over it. Didn't these people ever get dressed?

"You know my associate, Miss Amaden, right?"

"My friends call me Harlow," she said as she draped herself on a couch. "You saved Maxie's life. I think that makes you a friend."

"That's why I wanted to see you boys," said Rose as he lowered his huge frame into an easy chair. "Harlow's right. I think you've got more guts than most of the knuckleheads who work for me." He gestured at the bodyguard by the door. The big goon looked down, embarrassed.

"So I brought you up here to say a proper thank-you," continued Rose. "And to give you a reward." This was looking good. Max Rose felt as if he owed us something. We had to be smart about this.

"We don't want any reward," I said. "We did what we had to do."

"That's a good little spaceman, but I'm telling you, you deserve it."

"Don't disappoint him," Harlow said. "He isn't always so generous."

"You boys name it," Rose said after gulping down some of his drink. "Within reason, of course. What is it you want? Money? You can't be making all that much dough working at this hotel. Or a car? I can get you any ride you want. What is it you little Martians would like?"

This was our chance. It wasn't about money or cars or any kind of reward. This was about Max Rose feeling as if he owed us something. If we were going to find out more about him and about his connection with the Nazis and Saint Dane, this was the time to do it. I had to come up with something fast.

"What do you think, Pendragon?" Spader asked. I could tell by the look on his face that we were thinking the same way. He saw the opportunity here too. The question was, how to handle it?

A thought blasted into my head. It was a dangerous thing to do, but I couldn't think of anything better in a nanosecond. So my mouth started working before my brain could catch up.

"I'll tell you what we want," I said, trying to sound confident. "We want a piece of the action."

Max Rose spit his drink halfway across the room. I swear, he did this huge, wet spit-take. Most of his drink was now on the carpet.

"You want *what*?" he shouted.

"Yeah," said Spader, sounding pretty nervous. "What exactly is it we want?"

I had gotten myself into this. It was time to start making it work or we'd never leave this room. Max Rose stood up and went to the bar to fix himself another drink.

"We hear things, you know," I said, trying to sound cocky but not disrespectful. "Can't help it, working in a place like this."

"Yeah? What is it you hear?" said Rose. He was annoyed. I was going to have to talk our way out of this . . . or into it. Either way, I had to talk fast.

"We hear you're in for a pretty big score, maybe in a couple of days."

Max Rose shot me a look, going from annoyed to angry. I was pushing too hard.

"I'm not saying we want a part of that or anything," I assured him. "We don't deserve nothing like that. I'm just saying we want to be part of your operation. You know, like maybe help you out with whatever it is you got going on."

Max Rose poured his drink and squirted more fizzy water. I could tell he was thinking about what I had said. The question was, *what* was he thinking? The answer would probably mean the difference between life and death for Spader and me.

"What did you hear about this score I got coming up?" he asked.

I shrugged. I had to keep up the tough-guy act or he'd eat

me alive. "Not much," I said. "Just that there's some big pay-off coming in for something you did, and that there might be more where that came from. A lot more."

I didn't want him to know we knew about Ludwig Zell and his connection with the Nazis. That would put us dangerously close to the category of knowing too much. Rose looked at me. I felt like he was deciding whether to keep up the conversation or grab his gun and shoot me. I really hoped he was feeling talkative.

"That's all you know?" he asked.

"That's it," I said. "But you're the smartest, best-connected guy we've ever met. It would be an honor to work for you." I figured throwing in a little butter couldn't hurt.

"So that's it," Max Rose said. "You want a job."

"That's it," I answered confidently.

"Why should I trust you two?" he asked. "You're nothing but snot-nosed kids."

"With respect, mate," said Spader. "We're snot-nosed kids who saved your life."

Max glanced over to Harlow. Harlow raised an eyebrow. "They've got more smarts than any of the clods you got on the payroll now," she said. "Maybe you should give 'em a small job to start. You know, as a test."

Rose looked at Harlow with a mischievous little gleam. "You got something in mind?" he asked her.

Harlow stood up and slinked over to us. She walked around us, sizing us up like a cat plays with a mouse. Of course, right after a cat does that it usually kills and eats the mouse.

"Why don't you send these boys down to see Farrow," she said slyly.

"What for?" Rose asked.

"To give him a message," was the answer. "Have them tell Farrow to lay off. You'll give him a pass for sending his hitman up here, but only if he lays low for a couple of days. Let him know that if he doesn't back off, you'll come down on him, hard. If he listens, you won't have to worry about him until after your score comes in."

"And if he doesn't listen?" Rose asked.

"Then you'll know you've got to take care of business," Harlow answered. "*His* business."

Wow. Harlow may have been beautiful and talented, but she had some cold blood running through her. She liked playing dangerous games. Trouble is, I didn't. There was no way I wanted to go meet this Winn Farrow dude. From what everybody said, he was a psycho and more dangerous than Max Rose.

"I don't get it," I said, trying not to sound chicken. "I thought we proved ourselves last night?"

"Yeah, maybe," answered Rose. "But you turned yellow, Buck. You didn't shoot when I told you to. If somebody's gonna work for me, I gotta know they got the guts to do what I tell 'em, when I tell 'em, no matter how ugly it is."

Harlow walked behind Rose and played with his hair while he spoke.

"I got enemies," he said. "Hard to believe since I'm such a sweet guy, but it's true. That gunman last night, I know him. He works for a competitor of mine."

"We know. Winn Farrow," I said. "Your old partner."

Rose looked up at Harlow. "I told you these boys were smart," she said.

"Yeah, Winn Farrow," said Rose. "I have no beef with the man. He's got his business, I got mine. But lately he's been getting a little, I don't know, jealous. You're right. I got a big score coming in. I don't want Farrow doing anything to mess that up. So here's what I want you to do. Go see my old friend and tell him to back off. That's it. Just tell him to back off. Tell him I'm mad, and by all rights I should hit him back for what he did. Hard. But for old times' sake, I won't. But if he doesn't mind his own business, then I'll come down there and put a hurt on him like he's never seen before."

"That's it?" asked Spader. "All you want us to do is deliver that message?"

"That's it," answered Rose. "Do that for me, and you're in."

"He'll kill us," was all I could say.

Rose laughed. "I figure one of two things will happen. Either you boys make it back in one piece and I'll know I won't have any problems from Farrow, or you'll come back in a bunch of little pieces, and I'll have a war on my hands." He then broke into a grin that can only be described as evil. "So, how bad do you two still want a piece of my action?"

Gulp. I knew the answer to that. We were going to have to accept Rose's offer. But that meant we would have to meet Winn Farrow and his gang of cutthroats. These were the guys who tried to kill Max Rose. These were the guys who tried to kill us. These were the guys who Saint Dane had taken to the flume and used to kill Uncle Press. As suicidal as this mission was, we had to go.

At least we were getting closer to the truth. I had no doubt in my mind that when we met Winn Farrow and his gang, we'd find Saint Dane. I just hoped we'd stay alive long enough to do something about it.

FIRST EARTH

"You're going to what?" shouted Gunny with horror.

"We're going to deliver a message from Max Rose to Winn Farrow," I said.

Spader added, "And that's going to get us in good with Rose so we can find out about the natty-do he's cooking up with the Nazi wogglies. It's perfect."

"It's *not* perfect," Gunny said nervously as he paced the floor of our hotel room. "First off, you're not delivering a message, you're delivering a warning. Winn Farrow doesn't take kindly to warnings."

"But we're just the messengers," I said.

"That's even worse, shorty," Gunny shot back. "He tried to kill Max Rose. Do you think he'd bat an eye over bumping off two messenger kids? No, sir. You boys can't do this."

"I hear what you're saying, Gunny," I said. "But May sixth is tomorrow! We're running out of time."

"This is what we do," Spader added. "It's what being a Traveler is all about."

Gunny stopped pacing and looked at the two of us. Like it or not, what Spader said was true. This was what we were there for. To chicken out and hide wasn't an option. I wished it *were* an option, but it wasn't.

"Then I'm going with you," Gunny announced.

"You can't," I said. "If something happens to us, you're the only one who knows what's going on."

"He's right, mate," Spader said. "You'd have to push on without us."

This was the last thing Gunny wanted to hear.

"That doesn't make me feel any better," Gunny said softly.

It didn't do much for me, either, but it was the truth. "It's not going to come to that," I said with more confidence than I actually felt. "We're going to go down there, give him the message, and get out."

"And what happens if you run into Saint Dane?" Gunny asked.

"I'm counting on it," said Spader with conviction.

I didn't like the way Spader said that. The simple mention of Saint Dane's name always cast a dark shadow over his normally bright personality. Our best hope of pulling this off was to keep our heads on straight and be smart. If Spader lost it and went after Saint Dane, well, then Gunny would probably end up being on his own after all. I couldn't let that happen, mostly because I didn't want to end up on the front page of the newspaper under the headline TWO BELLBOYS RUBBED OUT IN GRISLY MOB SLAYING.

"I'm not going to argue with you anymore," Gunny finally said, sounding tired. "You boys have had more experience with this Traveler business than I have. But I know about Winn Farrow and how he operates. I promise you, the man isn't right."

"We know," I said. "We'll be careful."

I really, really hoped that "careful" was going to cut it.

◆   ◆   ◆

Twenty minutes later we were in a taxicab, headed downtown to meet the infamous Winn Farrow.

I have to admit, I was having second thoughts. What if Winn Farrow was as nutzoid-vicious as everybody said? He might start shooting before we even got in the door. The more I thought about it, the more I worried that we had gotten a little bit too cocky.

Spader must have sensed my tension because he gave me a friendly shove.

"It's gonna be fine, mate," he said, actually sounding oddly cheery. "We're the good guys. We can't lose."

I wished that were true.

"Besides," he added, "nothing's gonna happen to you so long as I'm around."

"How do you figure that?" I asked.

Spader didn't answer right away. I think he was trying to find the right words. When he next spoke, it was with a serious tone I hadn't often heard from him. I'd seen him blind with rage at Saint Dane. I'd also seen him devastated by the death of his father and the disappearance of his mother. But this was different. This was a thoughtful, sincere side of Spader that I hadn't known existed.

"I may not know much about being a Traveler," he said. "But from what I've seen, the key to this whole thing is you, Pendragon."

That took me by surprise. "We're all in this together," I said quickly.

"True, but you're the one keeping us together. I think we're all playing our parts, but I've got no doubt, the most important piece to this natty puzzle is you, mate. If anything happens to you, I'm afraid the show would be over. I won't let that happen."

I didn't know how to react. Though I was slowly starting to accept the fact that I was a Traveler, I wasn't ready to take on the responsibility of being some kind of ringleader. It was tough enough just trying to figure out why I was chosen to be a Traveler in the first place. I didn't want to be in charge, no way. The thought of it actually made me a little nauseous.

"I appreciate it, Spader," I said to him. "And I'll be watching your back too."

"I know that, mate," he said.

I wanted this conversation to end. It was freaking me out more than I was freaked out already. Anyhow, the time for talk was over because the cab had screeched to a stop. I looked out the window and saw we were two blocks away from where we told the cab driver to take us.

"We're not there yet," I said to him. "We need to go another two blocks west."

The cabbie turned around and said, "Maybe *you* gotta go two more blocks, but I sure don't. Ain't safe for cabs to go over there. They see us comin', they think it's Christmas. I been robbed too many times to go in there again. So whether you like it or not, this is as far as I go."

He meant it too. I didn't bother trying to talk him out of it. We got out of the car and paid him. The cabbie then hit the gas and did a quick U-turn with his wheels squealing. He gunned it out of there like he didn't even like being *close* to Winn Farrow territory. We watched him for a second as he made his escape, driving right through a red light.

It didn't help our confidence any.

"Maybe we should rethink this," Spader said.

"I'm tired of thinking," I said. "C'mon."

We started walking west. As I'm sure you've figured out by now, this was a bad section of town. Gunny told us it was the meat-packing district. Historically this was an area of Manhattan where all the slaughterhouses were. It was made up of big, rambling brick buildings where livestock were killed, cleaned, packed, and shipped. A grisly business by anybody's standards. Luckily for us, they didn't do the slaughtering here anymore. The main business was processing and shipping meat. It was a place most people avoided. Can you blame them? It wasn't exactly a fun spot for a Sunday picnic. I guess that's why so many criminals made their homes down here. It was the kind of place that even the cops avoided.

Yet here we were, Spader and I, walking right down the street like we belonged there. Believe me, we didn't. The farther west we walked, the more I felt the hot stares of people's eyes on us. This was the kind of neighborhood where everybody knew everybody else. A stranger stood out like a brilliant light bulb in a dark cave. People watched us from doorways and windows and from passing cars. A few people even whistled. It was their way of taunting us, knowing that we were headed for deep trouble.

"I feel like we just arrived at a party we weren't invited to," Spader said nervously.

"Or like it's feeding time at the zoo . . . and we're a couple of pork chops."

Our destination was an old packing plant that was built onto a pier over the Hudson River. Max Rose told us exactly where it was. It was the place where Winn Farrow and his gang spent most of their time, when they weren't out slitting people's throats, that is.

After walking for a very tense five minutes, we found ourselves in front of a big brick building with the words WILD BOAR MEATS painted in two-foot-high faded white letters over the green, garage-style door.

"This is it," said Spader. "What do we do, knock?"

The answer came quickly. Somebody had walked up behind us. I turned to see that it was more than one somebody. There were five guys, all wearing greasy clothes and worn caps. Their sleeves were rolled up to reveal huge, Johnny Bravo–style arms. I also saw that their hands and arms were stained with dark-brown blotches. I'm guessing these guys worked in the meat-packing plant, which meant those brown stains were actually, gross me out, dried blood.

None of them looked happy to see us. They all had scowls that told me they didn't like strangers and would probably make us pay for invading their turf. Looking at their hands again, I really hoped that those blood stains came from working in the packing plant and not from pummeling bozos like us who wandered into their neighborhood.

"Do you guys work here?" I asked, trying to sound like I wasn't about to pee in my pants.

They didn't answer. Their expressions got darker.

"We're looking for Winn Farrow," Spader said.

Those were the magic words. But it was bad magic, because as soon as they heard the name "Winn Farrow," they circled us, cutting off any hope we had of escape.

"We've got to see Farrow," I said. "We got a message for him."

The thugs started to tighten the circle. Spader and I went back to back. We didn't stand a chance in a fight against these brutes. I could see them clenching their fists, which made the knotty muscles in their forearms flex. Now that they were in close, I could smell them too. Didn't these guys know about deodorant? It was getting real ugly, real fast.

"It's a message from Max Rose," I said in desperation.

The thugs stopped. I actually saw hesitation in their

focused, killers' eyes. We were seconds away from adding to the stains on their hands, but hearing Max Rose's name made them freeze. Better, they looked scared. Up until that moment we had only heard about what a tough guy Max Rose was. Seeing these thugs turn all Jell-O at the sound of his name confirmed it. Max Rose wasn't somebody you messed with.

Suddenly the garage door of the building flew up and four more guys stepped out. These guys were just as vicious looking as the smelly guys surrounding us, except they wore gangster-looking suits. They also had shotguns. I suddenly felt safer with the guys who only worked with their fists. One of the new thugs—I'll call him Shotgun—motioned toward us. Instantly the smelly thugs frisked us up and down, looking for guns. Of course they came up empty.

"We have a message from Max Rose to Winn Farrow," I said. "We don't want any trouble."

Shotgun looked back at the other thugs and laughed. The smelly thugs laughed with him. "You don't want any trouble?" Shotgun laughed. "Well, golly gee-whiz, we wouldn't want you to get into any trouble!"

The thugs laughed even harder. Great. Not only were our lives in danger, we had to be insulted, too.

Shotgun then barked, "Inside!" He motioned toward the garage door with his gun. Spader and I walked inside. The shotgun boys followed close behind us, but the smelly thugs stayed outside. I wasn't going to miss them.

Inside we saw what was once a busy slaughterhouse. Luckily for us, it wasn't in operation anymore. It was a big, open warehouse room that stretched up for three or four stories. There was a track running on either side of the ceiling with ugly metal hooks hanging down. My guess was this was where they strung up the cattle when they did the yucky stuff. There were cement troughs in the floor that I'm sure caught most of the yuk. At the end of the track were long rows of wooden tables where all the slicing and dicing happened. Yuk. It's impossible to overuse the word "yuk" when it comes to this place. I like hamburgers as much as the next guy, but I never wanted to see where they came from.

"What is this place?" asked Spader.

"You don't want to know," I answered.

"Pipe down!" shouted Shotgun. They marched us through this big room to the back of the building, where there was a large, open metal door on the back wall. "In there," ordered Shotgun.

I was starting to get nervous. Okay, I was already plenty nervous, but now I was getting close to that hairy edge of panic. I had a fleeting thought that we were being marched to a quiet back room where these guys would start blasting away.

"Max Rose sent us," I said again. "We want to see Winn Farrow."

I was cut off when Shotgun poked me in the gut with his gun, pushing me into the next room. Spader shot forward and grabbed the gun, but the other thugs jumped him and threw him in the room after me.

The next room was almost as big as the first. There was a big stack of wooden crates full of I don't know what. There were also hundreds of metal hooks that were evenly spaced along the walls and ceiling. A flight of metal stairs led up to a catwalk that ringed the walls over our heads. I'm guessing they stored the sides of beef high and low in here. There were only two doors—the one we came through and another off the catwalk above us. There were no windows.

"Tie their hands," ordered Shotgun. One of the other

thugs pulled out a length of rope and immediately started tying our hands together.

"If Max Rose finds out you wouldn't let us talk to Winn Farrow, there's going to be trouble," I said, trying not to sound too pathetic and desperate.

"Really?" said Shotgun without a trace of concern. "And how's he gonna find out?"

"Oh, he'll find out," was all I could think of saying. Great comeback. I'm not a good bluffer. The thug finished tying our hands so Spader and I were now roped together at the wrists.

"I'm saying this for the last time—" I said.

"You got that right," came a voice from the door we had just come through. "You're doing a lot of things for the last time."

Spader and I shot a look at the door to see a man standing there. I knew instantly that this had to be the one and only Winn Farrow.

It's not that he looked like the tough gangster we were expecting or anything. It was more the way the other guys reacted to him. They all backed off like they were afraid to be in his way.

To be honest, Farrow didn't look all that intimidating. He was a short guy. I'm guessing no more than five feet. No joke. He looked more like a gangster doll, than a gangster. Of course, I wasn't about to tell him that. He had on a suit that was probably nice at one time, but now looked kind of shabby. The material was faded and the elbows were worn through.

That pretty much described all of Winn Farrow's gang. Even though they wore suits, they all looked ragged. Where Max Rose's gang was all spiffed out with expensive, handmade clothes, Farrow's gang looked like they'd been wearing these same outfits for a long time. I guess that's the difference between being a successful uptown gangster and a hungry downtown crook. This was definitely the B team of gangsters.

Farrow entered, followed by two more of his gang. When Farrow walked, he took quick, short strides. He had to. His legs were so short that if he wanted to cover any ground quickly, he had to walk really fast. It was kind of funny looking, like a cartoon. But I wasn't laughing. Oh no. That would have been suicidal.

The men with the shotguns backed off as Farrow moved past them. He stopped in front of us and stood with his legs apart, firmly planted. For a second I thought he was going to put his fists on his hips and shout, "Hi yo, I'm Peter Pan!" Though he may have looked like an elf, his eyes had an insane gleam. I didn't doubt that he was capable of all sorts of mayhem. He was no Peter Pan. After looking us over, he spat on the ground, barely missing my foot.

"So you're the two brats who have been givin' me headaches," he snarled. "I should plug you right here."

"Max Rose wouldn't like that," I said, trying to pull that bluff again.

It was the wrong move. Saying "Max Rose" in front of this guy was like waving a red cape in front of a bull. His eyes lost focus, then rolled back slightly into his head. It was totally creepy. His gang didn't like it any more than I did. They all took a step back, as if expecting him to blow up or something.

A moment later his eyes snapped back into focus. But in my opinion he had just gone another notch higher on the crazy meter.

"You think I care what that rat thinks?" he snarled. "Max Rose is garbage!" He turned to his men. As if on cue, they all chimed in with: "Yeah! Garbage! Rat! Yeah!" Farrow held up his hand and his men instantly shut up. I think they had done this before. It looked rehearsed. Farrow then turned to us and got in close.

"You say he's got a message for me?"

I glanced to Spader, which wasn't hard seeing as we were only about six inches apart. He nodded, giving me encouragement. I had to choose my words carefully. I didn't want to say the wrong thing and set this evil munchkin off. Trouble was, how could I possibly deliver the message I had to deliver without sending him off the deep end?

This plan was now officially stupid. But we were in it now so we had to keep going.

"Yes," I said calmly. "He wants you to know that he's not mad you tried to bump him off. He's willing to forget it ever happened."

"Well," Farrow said with a smile. "Ain't that gentlemanly of him."

So far so good. "But," I added.

"But?" Farrow echoed.

"Yes, there's a but. He'd like you to back off. That's it. He's just asking, very politely, I might add, if you would kindly back off." I hoped I hadn't softened it so much that I sounded like an idiot.

"Oh? Is that all?" asked Farrow. "And what, may I ask, will happen if I *don't* back off?"

We had come to the hard part.

"Well," I went on, clearing my throat. "He said, and I quote, that if you don't mind your own business, he'll come down here and put a hurt on you like you've never seen before."

I winced. That was it. That was the threat. All that was left now was to see how Farrow would react.

At first he didn't. He just kept looking at me like he was

trying to understand what I had said. Then, after a few seconds, Winn Farrow started to laugh. I swear, he burst out laughing. All of his men started to laugh with him, but that didn't mean anything. They only did what Farrow did.

"He's going to come down here and put a hurt on me?" he laughed out. "Who is he kidding? That rat has already hurt me worse than if he put a bullet in my skull." His laughter was slowing down. It was being replaced by anger. "He's the reason I'm in this dump in the first place! We were partners. We ran this town. But he got too full of himself and turned on me. Now he's up there in his castle eating steak and drinking champagne while I'm down here scrambling for crumbs. He's gonna put the hurt on me? He can't hurt me any more if he tried."

He then walked right up to me and stuck his nose in my face. I could smell his sour breath. The guy had been drinking. I guarantee it wasn't expensive whiskey with a shot of Three Stooges fizzy water.

"But I'll let you in on a little secret," he seethed. "I'm gonna get him back where it hurts the most." He turned away from me and made a motion to one of his goons standing at the door.

Spader and I exchanged looks again. What did *that* mean?

The goon walked up to Farrow and handed him something. Farrow then spun back to us with a big smile. He held what looked like a rocket on a stick. No kidding, a rocket. It was red and about a foot long. One end had a pointed nose, the other had fins. Sticking out from between the fins was a wire that had to be a fuse.

Farrow waved the rocket thing under our noses. "I ain't gonna hit him," he said playfully. "I ain't gonna hit any of them saps who work for him neither. You know what I'm going to do? I'm gonna put the mighty Max Rose out of business with this little beauty."

"What is it?" Spader asked.

Farrow pretended to play with the rocket, making it fly up and down like a kid with a toy airplane.

"Oh, just a little toy I got from some friends over in Chinatown. I think this one'll do just fine, but I'm not sure yet. I'd like you boys to help me decide."

"Decide what?" I asked. "What are you gonna do with it?"

"It's very simple," he answered, sounding as if he were talking to a child. "We're going to play a little game. It's called, How many sparklies will it take to light up old Maxie Rose? One? Two? Or maybe even three? That's what we're going to see."

I was beginning to think Winn Farrow was a nutburger.

He turned to his goons and made a motion. Quickly the guy who had tied us up came forward with another length of rope. He tied one end around our wrists and threw the other up and around a meat hook over our heads. This was bad. We were going to be strung up like sides of beef.

"I've got a better idea," I said, trying to think fast. "Why don't we go back to Max and tell him he's the one who's got to back off. Yeah, that's it! I'll tell him you've got a nasty trick up your sleeve and if he doesn't let you back in the gang, you'll use it."

"Yeah," added Spader. "You could be living up in the penthouse yourself!"

Farrow looked at us with dead eyes. All the creepy, happy game stuff was over. "All I want," he seethed, "is to see that scum suffer like I did. I want him to crawl down here and beg me to take *him* in. That's what I want. That's what I'm gonna get."

With a nod, the thug yanked on the rope. First our arms were pulled over our heads, then we were hoisted up into the air with our feet dangling several feet over the floor. Farrow walked over to us and held out the rocket.

"Now, let's see how many of these I'm going to need, okay?" He then turned and hurried out on those short little legs. It wasn't funny anymore.

"What are you going to do?" I yelled with a shaky voice.

"If I told you, it wouldn't be a surprise!" he called back over his shoulder.

Yeah, nutburger. He left through the door, followed by the two guards and the goons with the shotguns. Spader and I were left alone, hanging from the meat hook.

"Now what?" Spader asked.

"We gotta get loose," I said while struggling to get my hands free.

We went to work on the ropes, but it was painful. Our weight made the rough rope dig into our wrists.

Spader glanced toward the door and said, "Hey, what are they doing out there?"

I turned to look and I think my heart stopped. I now understood what kind of game Farrow was planning. The group of gangsters were gathered together about halfway back, in the large slaughterhouse room where we first had entered. The black stick that was attached to Farrow's rocket was now nailed into a wooden crate. The crate was on its side and the rocket was aimed through the door . . .

At us.

"What is that thing?" Spader asked.

I didn't tell him. He was going to find out soon enough.

"Work faster!" I ordered. "We gotta get outta here!" I worked on the ropes, but had to glance back to the other room. Farrow took a cigar from his jacket and plugged it into his mouth. He pulled out a match and struck it against the crate. He then took his sweet time about lighting his cigar.

This was torture. I looked at the ropes to see we were working them loose, but it was going to be too late.

Farrow finished lighting his cigar, then touched the still flaming match to the fuse on the back of the red rocket. Instantly the fuse sparked to life like a Fourth of July sparkler. In seconds the rocket would ignite.

"Pendragon? What is that?" Spader demanded to know. "What's going to happen?" Fear had crept into his voice.

"Keep working on the ropes," I said.

A few seconds later . . .

Ignition.

"Cover your eyes!" I shouted.

Spader turned his head to the wall, but I had to watch. The rocket shot from its makeshift launch pad, flew across the slaughterhouse and sailed right through the center of the open door into the room where we were hanging. Bull's-eye. I turned away at the last instant, ready to get hit.

But the rocket missed us. Instead it blasted into the pile of wooden crates. A few more feet to the right and we would have been torched. We were spared, but not for long. This wasn't your ordinary firework. This was meant to do damage. It must have been loaded with some kind of flammable stuff because it exploded and sent a wave of fire over the crates. In seconds the pile was engulfed with flames.

Spader and I stared at the growing fire with fear and awe. It was growing impossibly fast. I could already feel the heat.

"There's my answer!" shouted Farrow over the roaring flames.

Spader and I turned to see he was standing in the doorway.

"One of those babies is all I'm going to need," he said while puffing on his cigar like a proud papa. "Now, boys," he said, "let's see how fast this dump burns to the ground. Thanks for playing!"

With a laugh, he spun around and strolled out of the room. The door was slammed behind him and I could hear the sound of a heavy lock being thrown. A quick glance at the fire told me that this room would soon be an inferno. All Spader and I could do was dangle there helplessly. Winn Farrow had proven to be as crazy and evil as predicted. Max Rose was going to get his answer. Farrow was not going to back off. The proof would be our deaths.

That's when I heard a voice.

Given that the heat from the fire was already roasting us, I didn't think it was possible, but when I heard that voice, I got a cold chill.

"Hello, Pendragon," the voice said calmly. "Enjoying your visit to First Earth?"

Spader and I both shot a look to where the voice was coming from, to see a man standing on the catwalk over our heads. It was one of the gangsters who had followed Winn Farrow into the room earlier. At least he *looked* like a gangster. His voice told me otherwise. This was a guy from another place and time who finally decided to reveal himself.

"You certainly took your time finding me," he said with a cocky smile. "I was beginning to think you had lost interest."

Saint Dane had dropped by to watch us cook.

FIRST EARTH

The fire spread quickly. It had already engulfed the stack of wooden crates and was creeping across the floor toward us, leaving black, burned wood in its path.

"And hello to you too, Spader," Saint Dane said. "Having second thoughts about teaming up with young Pendragon?"

I looked at Spader and saw the hatred in his eyes. "Forget him," I said softly. "We've got to get loose."

Spader nodded. But while we continued to work on the ropes, Saint Dane worked on us.

"Such a simple territory you come from, Pendragon," he said. "The people are so easy to influence. It's pathetic, really. It's all about money here. Getting it, keeping it, using it for power. Their greed will prove to be their own downfall."

The fire had reached the wall and was starting to climb.

"Winn Farrow and his disgusting little band of ruffians have quite the spectacular plan to bring down Max Rose," Saint Dane said. "Farrow's a feisty little toad, but I admire him. I couldn't have devised a more interesting scenario myself."

I couldn't take it anymore and shouted, "What is it? What are they going to do?"

Saint Dane laughed. "You should have paid more attention in history class, Pendragon. All the clues are there for you. Perhaps you're finding life a bit more difficult without the aid of your dear, departed uncle."

I didn't take the bait. Saint Dane was trying to mess with our minds and I wasn't going to let him. The fire was now climbing the wall near us. I guess I don't have to point this out, but I was scared.

"I'll leave you boys now," Saint Dane said. "I need to help prepare for the big day tomorrow. Too bad you're going to miss it. It's going to be a sizzling-good time."

Saint Dane started for the door, then stopped and looked down to us one last time. "Oh, one more thing," he said. "As I'm sure you guessed, I brought those two gunmen down to the flume and had them fire their crude weapons back to Cloral. I meant it as a warning to you. I had no idea Press would be foolish enough to be standing there. Such a shame. But from the looks of things, you'll be joining him soon. Give him my best, won't you?"

With that, Saint Dane turned and left through the door on the catwalk.

My suspicions had been confirmed. Saint Dane had used those gangsters to kill Uncle Press. It crushed me to think about it. But I had to fight my emotions and stay focused, or we were going to die.

Spader was another matter. I saw a look in his eyes that actually frightened me. Saint Dane's words had touched the dark, raw nerve that he tried so hard to protect. He was ready to explode with anger and hatred.

"Don't go there, Spader," I cautioned. "That's what he wants. Stay focused."

My warning did no good. Spader blew. He frantically

pulled on the rope with a fury like I couldn't believe. He thrashed our hands back and forth so violently I had to lean away or he would have smacked me in the face. When I leaned back, I saw that the fire had crept across the wall over our heads and had reached the rope. The rope was on fire! Spader let out a final ghastly shout of anger and jerked the rope with such ferocity that it broke! The two of us tumbled to the floor and fell together in a heap.

As much as I hated to see Spader lose control, I liked that Saint Dane's needling had backfired. Spader's anger had helped set us free, with a little help from a burning rope. But we weren't safe yet.

"Spader!" I shouted, and yanked his hands to force him to look at me. "You gotta focus or we're gonna die."

"He's a demon, Pendragon. We've got to stop him."

"We will, but first we gotta get outta here." I tried to keep my voice level to calm him down. "Stay with me, all right?"

Slowly, I saw the ferocity leave his eyes. He was back in control. "Yeah, yeah, right," he said, and refocused his attention on saving our skins.

We were off the hook but still tied at the wrists. Spader stretched one way, I pulled the other, and a few seconds later I was able to yank one of my hands free. After that it was easy to untie the rest.

We were loose, but trapped in the middle of an inferno. The flames now covered the walls and licked at the ceiling. If the fire didn't get us, a collapsed ceiling would. I glanced around, desperate to find a way out. It looked hopeless. There was nothing but fire raging all around us.

That's when I saw something strange.

Smoke swirled near the center of the room like a small tornado. The dark funnel moved up toward the ceiling, then shifted direction toward its destination—the door off the catwalk. My eyes followed the smoke and I realized that Saint Dane must not have closed the door all the way, because the twisting cloud of smoke was being sucked outside.

"There!" I shouted. "He left the door open!"

Without waiting for Spader, I ran for the metal stairs that led up to the catwalk. Spader was right after me. The fire had been raging for several minutes now. The heat was unbearable and the metal stairs were burning hot. I felt incredible heat through the soles of my shoes and had to force myself not to use the handrail. That would have fried my hands for sure. Because heat rises, with each step the temperature grew more intense. The smoke was getting bad too. It was tough to breathe. We had to move right through the swirling smoke that was being sucked out the door.

Finally we got up to the catwalk, and I ran for the door. I prayed I was right about it being open and kicked it. The door flew open. Yes! I turned to see Spader was right there with me. We ducked through the door and all I could hope was that it would lead outside.

It didn't. We found ourselves in a long, narrow corridor. Choking smoke filled the narrow, dark space and made it impossible to know which way to go.

"Right or left?" I yelled.

"My eyes are burning, mate. Doesn't matter. Just move!"

I took a chance and turned right and immediately saw good news and bad news. Good news was that in spite of the dark smoke, there was something to guide us forward. The wooden floorboards were so old that there were spaces between them. Through those spaces I could see fire below. It lit up the floor and kept us from running into the walls. But that was bad news too. If there was fire below an old wood floor, it meant the floor was going to burn. All the more reason to get out of there fast. I grabbed Spader's hand and ran. I could only hope that we'd get to the end of the corridor and out before the whole floor caught fire.

We didn't make it. After running about ten steps, I heard a loud *crack!* It was the only warning we had that the floor was collapsing beneath us. A second later we both crashed through in a shower of sparks, smoke, and burning wood. The next few seconds were a blur. I'll try to describe it as best as I can, but it happened so fast, I'm not sure I remember it all.

When we fell through the floor, I lost my grip on Spader's hand. Fire was everywhere. I remember thinking that I was falling into the center of an inferno and that I was gonna roast. But the fire had been burning below for some time and the next floor down was already weak. When I landed, those boards gave way too, and I crashed through again. It was a miracle I didn't break any bones.

The next thing I knew, I was underwater. The slaughterhouse had been built on a pier jutting out over the Hudson River. In a matter of seconds I went from fearing I was going to burn to death, to fearing I was going to drown. Somewhere in my fall I slammed my head pretty hard and couldn't focus. I remember flaming chunks of stuff falling into the water all around me. There was a maze of pilings that must've held up the pier. Every way I turned I seemed to either hit one, or knock into burning debris from the firestorm above. I gulped water. I couldn't breathe. I was exhausted and losing consciousness fast. My head kept going underwater and I was losing the strength to keep pushing myself back up.

Then things got *really* bad. I heard a loud, screeching sound from above. That could only mean one thing. The building was breaking up. The pier was going to collapse on our heads. I had just about given up any hope of getting out of there alive, when I felt a strong grip on my arm.

"Hold your breath!" Spader ordered.

I barely had time to gulp in some air before Spader pulled me under. I totally gave myself over to him and relaxed. While holding on to me with one hand, he swam with a strength that I couldn't believe. No, who am I kidding? Sure I could believe it. Spader was part dolphin. If he wasn't hurt, a swim like this was a piece of cake. I really hoped he wasn't hurt, for both our sakes.

I didn't know how long I could hold my breath, but I knew we were safer under the water than on the surface because I heard the sounds of the building above us collapsing. We had to keep moving and get out from under the structure if we had any hope of surviving. I don't know how long we were below the water. It couldn't have been more than a few seconds because I don't think I could have lasted more than that.

When we finally broke the surface, the first thing I remember seeing was the sun. The next thing I saw was Spader's smiling face as he tread water next to me, looking as relaxed as if he were floating in a kiddie pool.

"Took a little knock there, did you, mate?"

I touched my forehead and felt the lump that was already forming. "I'm a little out of it," I admitted.

"No worries," he said. "On your back, I'll tow you in."

I didn't argue. This was no time to be macho. I gladly let Spader pull me to shore. It only took a minute until we made it to a small, wooden dock. Spader dragged me up onto the platform like a wet doll. We made it. We were alive.

The two of us lay there, trying to get our wind back. After breathing in disgusting smoke for the last ten minutes, the air actually tasted sweet. I closed my eyes and focused on clearing my lungs. I was in pretty rough shape. Besides the slam on the head, I had cuts and burns all over my body. My clothes had protected me some, but they were now less like clothes and more like rags.

Spader spoke first. "It's a horror, mate; it truly is."

I opened my eyes and saw that he was staring at the burning slaughterhouse. The place was nothing more than a giant, twisted, flaming wreck. Black smoke billowed up and drifted out over the Hudson. I wondered why the fire department hadn't shown up yet. My guess was they were afraid to come down to this neck of the woods.

"Farrow said this was a test," Spader said through gasping breaths. "If this was just the test, what are they planning to do for real?"

That was the big question. What was their target? Saint Dane said we had all the clues, but I couldn't put them together.

I saw that Spader was in just as bad shape as I was. His clothes were shredded and burned, and his arms were covered with scratches. "You okay?" I asked.

"I will be just as soon as we finish off Saint Dane," he said angrily.

"You trust me, don't you, Spader?" I asked.

"Of course, mate," he said quickly.

"Then, please, remember that the next time you get all bent out of shape and want to go after Saint Dane," I said. "He's gotta be stopped, but we have to be smart about it."

"Right," Spader said in response. "Smart. Let's be smart now and get out of here."

I felt like he was blowing me off, but now was not the time to argue. We were still stuck in the badlands. As beaten up as we were, we had to move.

The river was about six feet below street level. At the end of the dock was a wooden ladder. I climbed up first and carefully poked my head up and over to see what was going on.

My heart sank.

We were about fifty yards upriver from the wrecked slaughterhouse. Between me and the burning building was nothing but a big empty lot . . . and a group of gangsters. They were all standing there: Winn Farrow, his tattered thugs, the big-armed muscle boys, and of course, Saint Dane. They all stood with their backs to me, no more than thirty yards away, watching their handiwork. If we tried to make a run for it, they'd see us for sure.

But worse than that, parked only a few yards to our right were the gangster's cars. When they went for those cars, they'd find us. We were trapped with no place to hide. In a few seconds we'd be right back where we started.

FIRST EARTH

"What do you see, mate?" Spader asked.

I looked down at him and put my finger to my lips to "shush" him. The last thing we needed was for one of these goons to hear us. If we were going to get out of there, we had to do it before they got tired of watching the burning building. As soon as they went for their cars, they'd see us. The only thing we could do was run. I was pretty sure they'd see us if we ran, but at least we'd have a chance. So I looked around for the best escape route.

Parked about twenty yards from us was a derelict truck with WILD BOAR MEATS painted on its side. It was halfway between us and the street beyond. I thought that if we could run to the truck without being seen, we'd have a shot at making it all the way past the bad guys to the street. From there we could disappear into the city. The crucial move would be from here to the truck. It wasn't going to be easy because we would have to run across the wide open, empty lot. If somebody happened to look back while we were running, well, good night.

I climbed back down and told Spader my plan.

"Right," Spader said. "Me first."

Before I could argue, Spader scrambled up the narrow ladder. He peered over the top, looked back to me, winked, and was gone. I quickly climbed the ladder to watch.

Spader crouched low and ran fast. I held my breath. He was totally exposed. But none of Farrow's goons saw him. He made it to the truck and pumped his hand in the air in victory. Yes! He then peeked over the hood of the truck at the gangsters. They had no idea what was going on behind them. Spader then motioned for me to follow. Gulp. My turn. I bolted over the top and ran.

I wasn't as lucky as Spader. I had only gone a few feet when one of the thugs turned and saw me. It was as simple and stupid as that.

"Hey!" he shouted. Instantly all the gangsters turned and saw me. I made it to the truck and crouched next to Spader. The last thing I saw before ducking down was Winn Farrow angrily grabbing a shotgun from one of his men.

"I guess this was a bad plan," I said.

Bang! Farrow fired the shotgun. The window over our heads shattered, and bits of glass rained down on us. The other gangsters followed his lead. They all started firing at the truck. *Boom! Boom! Boom!* The truck was pounded with rounds of shot. The whole thing rocked each time it was hit. We were protected, but for how long?

"Maybe we should have hid underneath the dock until they left," Spader said.

"*Now* you think of that?" I shouted over the booming shotguns.

"Sorry," he said.

We then heard the sound of a car horn blasting and the

screech of rubber wheels on the road. The gangsters stopped shooting, so Spader and I took the chance to peek out and see what was going on.

I hoped to see a police car screaming to our rescue, but instead saw a black car flying off the street, out of control, headed right for the group of gangsters! The thugs scattered like bowling pins as the car nearly plowed into them. The wild car didn't stop. With its horn blaring, it skidded past the fleeing gangsters and blasted right toward us. The gangsters got themselves back together and now took aim at the careening car. They unleashed their shotguns, this time shattering the car's back window.

But the demon car kept coming.

We had no idea what to do. Was this crazy person going to slam into the truck? We couldn't run or the gangsters would start shooting at us. All we could do was watch and get ready to dive out of the way. The driver accelerated right for our hiding place, then spun the wheel at the last second, barely missing the truck. The car skidded sideways, then the wheels got traction and the vehicle charged forward. A second later it wheeled around to our side of the truck and slowed down. Who was this crazy driver?

"Get in!" shouted Gunny from the driver's seat.

Spader and I didn't hesitate. We both ran for the car and dove into the backseat. Gunny never stopped. He only slowed down long enough for us to get in.

"Go!" I shouted before we got the door closed.

Gunny punched the gas, the wheels spit gravel, and Spader and I were thrown back in the seat. But we weren't safe yet. Two more explosions sounded, and the doors of the car were slammed with shot.

"Stay down!" Gunny commanded. He didn't need to. Spader and I were already down on the floor with all the shattered glass from the rear window. Three more shots were fired, but this time, only one hit the car. We were moving quickly out of range. Gunny bumped over a curb, skidded into a turn, and sped us away from the ugly scene. A few seconds later Spader and I got the guts up to peek out of the back window.

Through the shattered glass we saw the burning slaughterhouse falling away in the distance. We had made it. We were safe, thanks to Gunny.

Spader and I both let out a huge yelp of joy. "Gunny, yeah!" "Hobey-ho!" "You saved us!"

Gunny turned back to us. His eyes were wide with fear. He may have just coolly executed an incredibly daring rescue, but it scared him half to death. "I don't want to do anything like that ever, ever again," he said with a shaky voice. "My heart is trying to bust out of my chest."

"Slow down," I said. "We made it."

Gunny took his foot off the gas and slowed the car to a normal speed. I saw that his hands were shaking at the wheel. "This is gonna cost me my job, you know," he said nervously.

"Why, mate?" asked Spader.

"This car belongs to the hotel manager, Mr. Caplesmith. What's he gonna say when he sees I got it all shot up?"

I'm embarrassed to say that Spader and I both laughed. We didn't mean to, but it was just so . . . funny. What was a shot-up car compared to what we had just been through?

Gunny said, "I don't see anything funny about it at all!"

"I'm sorry, Gunny," I said. "You're right. It's not funny."

Spader added, "Thanks for being there, mate. We owe you."

"You owe me a new car is what you owe me," Gunny said. He then laughed too. He was starting to relax. He looked at us through the rearview mirror and winced. "You two all right? You look like you touched toes with the devil himself."

"That's exactly what happened," Spader said.

"We found Saint Dane," I said. "Or should I say, he found us."

Gunny gripped the wheel tighter. "He have something to do with burning that slaughterhouse?"

"In a way," I answered. "Winn Farrow is the one who lit the match though."

"He burned his own place down?" Gunny asked, confused.

"He's planning something," I said. "They've got these fireworks that explode in a ball of fire, and he's going to use them on Max Rose."

"It's all about revenge," Spader added.

An idea hit me. "The hotel!" I exclaimed. "The Manhattan Tower. If he shot one of those rockets up to the penthouse, it would be all over for Rose."

"That's it!" Spader shot back. "It must be. He's going to torch the hotel. He could do it with one of those fire nasties, easy."

"We should evacuate the building," I said, getting excited. "And tell the police. They can protect the place and—"

"It's not the hotel he's after," Gunny said calmly.

Spader and I both fell silent. "How do you know that?" I asked.

"Because I found out about LZ-one-twenty-nine," Gunny answered with no emotion.

Spader and I were both stunned speechless. Gunny had just casually announced that he had found the critical piece to the puzzle. I had almost forgotten about it. The mysterious LZ-129. We both looked at him. Gunny stared ahead, focused on the road. Finally I couldn't take it anymore.

"So? Are you going to tell us?" I asked.

"What was it that letter said, Pendragon?" Gunny asked me. "You know, the one with the Nazi symbol on it."

I thought back to the letter from Ludwig Zell to Max Rose that I had committed to memory. "It said that payment would be coming to Max Rose on May sixth via LZ-one-twenty-nine," I answered.

Gunny nodded and said, "Whatever Max Rose did for the Nazis, he's going to get his payment tomorrow, and it's coming by LZ-one-twenty-nine. If Winn Farrow really wanted to hurt Max Rose, he could stop him from getting that payment."

"That's what Farrow said," exclaimed Spader. "He was going to hit Rose where it hurts the most."

"So what is LZ-one-twenty-nine?" I asked, getting impatient.

"I saw it in the newspaper today," he answered soberly. "I can't believe I didn't figure it out before. LZ-one-twenty-nine stands for Luft Zeppelin-one-twenty-nine."

"What's a Luft Zeppelin?" Spader asked.

The truth suddenly hit me.

I felt sick. Saint Dane was right. I should have paid better attention in history class. I had the answer staring me in the face all along, but couldn't put it together. It was a famous event in American history. There were movies made about it. There were books written and TV shows made. It was a tragedy as famous as the sinking of the *Titanic* or the destruction of the space shuttle *Challenger*.

"What's he talking about, Pendragon?" asked Spader. "Do you know?"

"Yeah," I answered softly. "I think I do. And it makes a whole bunch of sense."

Gunny reached to the seat next to him where he had a newspaper. "Luft Zeppelin-one-twenty-nine left Germany last week. Tomorrow morning it's going to arrive at the naval air station in Lakehurst, New Jersey."

He threw the paper to us and it landed in my lap. There on the front page was a big picture of Luft Zeppelin-129. It was a giant silver blimp. Only it went by another name that was way better known. That name was written on the silver nose of the air ship.

It was called the *Hindenburg*.

"I'm guessing that Max Rose's payment is aboard that airship, direct from Germany," said Gunny. "I believe that's Winn Farrow's target."

Spader picked up the paper and stared at the picture of the giant airship with the Nazi swastikas painted on its tail.

"This thing flies too?" Spader asked. "It doesn't look like Jinx's airplane."

"It's a big balloon," Gunny answered. "Lighter than air. They've been flying them across the ocean for a few years now. They say it's the wave of the future."

"It's not the wave of the future," I said quietly.

"What do you mean, Pendragon?" Gunny asked. "This is your history. Did you ever hear of the *Hindenburg*?"

I took a breath and swallowed. "Yeah, I heard about it," I answered. "When the *Hindenburg* arrived in New Jersey, it blew up. The balloon burned and the passenger compartment crashed. A lot of people died and the ship was totally destroyed by fire. I don't think they ever figured out how it happened."

The three of us sat in silence for a good long time. Finally Spader said the one thing that was on all our minds.

"Well," he said. "I think we know how the *Hindenburg* is gonna blow up."

"Yeah," I added. "What we don't know is if we can stop it."

FIRST EARTH

$\mathcal{W}$e rode the rest of the way back to the Manhattan Tower Hotel in silence. I think we were all trying to get our minds around the fact that there was going to be a disaster the next day. Winn Farrow was going to light the fuse that would lead to one of the most infamous catastrophes in history. He was going to blow up the airship *Hindenburg*.

There wasn't all that much I knew about the crash. The basic event was one of those things that everybody knew about because it was such a big deal. I'd seen pictures of the *Hindenburg* in flames. I'd seen scratchy news footage of people jumping from the passenger compartment, desperately trying to escape. There was also a famous radio broadcast where some news guy was announcing the arrival of the ship, and then had to keep his head together to describe the horror of the fiery crash.

It was a famous moment in history; it was going to happen the next day. Question was, what were we going to do about it?

When we got back to the hotel, Gunny stayed in the car. "You boys go up to your room," he said. "I've got a friend who can fix this car up like new. No sense in having Caplesmith on my back. We've got bigger fish to fry." He hit the gas and peeled out, leaving us alone on the sidewalk.

"Why are we going to fry big fish?" Spader asked.

"It's just an expression," I said.

"Too bad," he said. "I'm hungry."

We entered the building through the kitchen and grabbed some fruit. Turned out I was pretty hungry too. The next trick was to get back to our room without being seen by any of Max Rose's goon squad. The plan was to dodge them.

We got halfway through the kitchen when we walked straight into the same thug who nailed us the last time. Didn't he ever go home?

"Well, lookee here," he said. "You two boys look like you been through the war. You smell like it too."

"Back off, bozo," I said, trying to act all tough. "We gotta go change and—"

The goon grabbed us by the arms and marched us toward the elevators. I guess I didn't act tough enough. Next thing we knew, we were being shoved into the living room of the penthouse. So much for our plan of dodging Max Rose.

"And don't touch nothing," the goon ordered. "You two are disgusting."

The guy left, giving us a short window to figure out what we would say to Max Rose.

"We gotta tell him," Spader said instantly. "Everything."

"Yeah, right," I shot back. "We'll tell him how I'm from the future and that's how I know the *Hindenburg* is going to explode tomorrow. Perfect."

"Well, you can't say *that*," Spader countered.

"Duh."

"But if we tell him Winn Farrow is going to blow up the

zeppelin, Rose could send his thugs to stop him. They could do the job for us!"

I had to think about that. Spader might be right. If our mission was to stop Farrow and Saint Dane from blowing up the *Hindenburg,* we could use all the help we could get, even if it was from a gang of thugs. This could be a real easy solution. But for some reason, the idea of telling Max Rose what was going to happen made me uneasy.

"You might be right," I finally answered. "But let's not tell him anything yet. Not until we've worked this through."

"We don't have time, Pendragon!" Spader argued. "The sooner we tell him, the better chance he'll have of stopping Saint Dane."

"You mean stopping Farrow," I said.

"Whatever. Hobey, mate, we gotta tell him!"

"No, we don't. Not yet. Don't say anything, all right?"

Before Spader could answer, the door opened on the far side of the room and Max Rose entered with Harlow. Both were dressed in silky pajamas. Big surprise. When he saw us, Max Rose's face lit up with a big smile.

"Buck! Flash! You're not dead!" he bellowed.

Obviously.

Harlow got close to us, took a sniff, and wrinkled her nose. "You boys been playing with fire?"

"No, but Winn Farrow has," Spader said quickly.

I shot Spader a look, willing him to keep quiet.

Rose and Harlow plopped down on the couch, waiting to hear our report. "I'd ask you to sit down, boys, but to be honest, you stink," Rose said.

"No problem," I said. "How 'bout if we get changed and washed up before telling you what happened?"

"Do I look like a patient man?" Rose asked. "Tell me now."

Spader looked at me, expecting me to start talking because that's what I always did. But as I stood there in front of Rose, I didn't know what to say. I was in total brain lock. Nothing was coming.

Rose added, "I guess since you two aren't dead, my old friend Winn is going to respect my request to mind his own business, am I right?"

I needed to come up with a story that would give us time to figure out the best way to handle the news. But I was coming up empty. A second later it didn't matter anymore.

"Winn Farrow is going to blow up the *Hindenburg*," Spader blurted out.

I closed my eyes. There it was. *Bang*. Spader had just set something in motion that was now officially out of our hands.

Max Rose jumped to his feet in surprise. "He's going to . . . ?"

He couldn't finish the sentence. He started to pace nervously. Believe it or not, he not only seemed surprised, he looked scared. That was the last thing I expected. Max Rose was a guy who didn't even blink while staring into an assassin's gun. But now, after hearing that the *Hindenburg* might go down in flames, he was on the hairy edge of cracking. He stormed over to his bar and poured himself a drink. This time he didn't shoot any Three Stooges fizzy water into it either. He wanted it strong.

"How?" he demanded to know.

I didn't answer. This was Spader's show now.

"He's got these rocket nasties," Spader said. "He's going to shoot one at the airship and blow it up."

"You think it'll work?" Rose asked.

"Take a look at us, mate," Spader said. "He shot one of

those bad boys into his slaughterhouse, with us inside. There's nothing left of the place."

Rose gulped down his drink and wiped his mouth with the sleeve of his expensive bathrobe. His hand was shaking. Harlow stood up and slinked over to him.

"Don't worry, Maxie," she said calmly. "Farrow's too dumb to pull off something like that."

Rose was starting to sweat. "Yeah?" he barked at her. "And what if he gets lucky? Do you know how much I got riding on that big balloon?"

I took a chance and asked, "What is it that's coming in?"

I don't think Rose would have answered if he weren't so upset.

"Payment," he shot back at me. "I've done a lot of work for those Germans. I've shipped them equipment and tools and scrap metal and a whole lot of other things. It's cost me millions. I went out on a very long limb for those Nazi creeps. I'm in debt to a lot of people. The kind of people you don't want to be in debt to. If I don't get that payment . . ." He didn't finish the sentence. Whatever it was, it would be ugly. Oh yeah, Max Rose was scared.

"Why don't the Nazis just write you a check or something?" I asked.

"It ain't that easy," Rose answered. "This isn't the kind of transaction you want traced. By anybody. We had to be creative. There's cash on that balloon. Lots of it. They're also sending me bonds and a load of diamonds. Flawless diamonds. I've even got a couple of paintings coming in that were done by some famous dead guys. They're worth millions! That's the way they wanted to pay me and I agreed. They're sending it all in on that blimp so it'll be easier to get through customs. I *knew* it was a rotten idea."

Now I knew what Winn Farrow meant when he said he was going to hit Max Rose where it hurt the most. If Farrow destroyed the *Hindenburg,* it would be the end of Max Rose's business. Worse, going by how scared Rose looked, I'd say it would be the end of Max Rose himself.

"It's okay, Maxie," Harlow said soothingly. "You'll figure something out."

Rose took another drink to calm himself. "You boys did good," he said softly. "I won't forget that. Now get out of here. I need time to think."

Time to think. Yeah, tell me about it. I needed a little of that too. I wished I had more time to think before I let Spader give away the show to Max Rose. Now a chain reaction had started that we had no control over, all because I didn't have enough time to think.

I think I had better start learning how to think faster.

FIRST EARTH

Spader and I backed out of the room and quickly left Max Rose's penthouse. We took the stairs down to the sixth floor to avoid Dewey. We didn't want to explain the way we looked to him or anybody else. As soon as we got inside our room and closed the door, Spader let out a happy shout.

"Hobey, yes!" he yelled. "Rose is going to send his thugs to stop Farrow. We did it. The *Hindenburg* is safe."

I stared at Spader, my anger slowly building. "I asked you not to tell him about Farrow's plan."

"I know, mate, but I had to. That was our chance. You weren't talking so I had to take it."

"And what if it was the wrong move?" I asked, trying not to boil over. "This isn't just about two gangsters who hate each other. We've got a whole territory to worry about."

"C'mon, Pendragon," Spader cajoled. "You know it was the right thing to do. We outsmarted Saint Dane. Again. We won!"

"Man, I hope you're right."

I needed to be alone to think, so I left Spader and headed for the bathroom. I got rid of my burned clothes and stood in the warm shower to clean off the dried blood. The cuts and bruises were nothing that wouldn't heal quickly. We were both very lucky.

As I stood in that shower, I wracked my brain for answers. Not just about the *Hindenburg,* but about Spader. He was driven by his need for revenge. Fine, I wanted to put Saint Dane out of business too. But though Spader and I were on the same side, we had different ideas on how to fight the war. I was afraid this would show up to bite us in the butt someday. Today was that day. Our butts had been bitten.

Still, I didn't want this to be an ego thing. I didn't want to be angry at him just because he didn't listen to me. Who am I? I don't know everything. Maybe he had done the right thing. Maybe the reason we were on First Earth was to do exactly what he had done. By uncovering Farrow's plot to destroy the *Hindenburg* and telling Max Rose about it, we might have saved the airship.

But that led me to the most troubling thought of all. As horrible as the destruction of the *Hindenburg* was going to be, we didn't know what it had to do with Saint Dane's overall plan. Saint Dane's goal was to find the turning point of a territory and push it the wrong way. The question was, what did the *Hindenburg* have to do with the turning point of First Earth? It was a German ship, but did it have anything to do with the coming war? Would saving the *Hindenburg* stop the war from happening?

There were too many unanswered questions for me to think our mission here on First Earth was over.

When I got out of the shower, Gunny was there. Spader had already told him how he felt sure Rose's gang would save the *Hindenburg.* Gunny wanted to be happy, but he had this confused look that told me he wasn't any more convinced than I was. It was time to put everything out there in plain language.

"Here's what we know for sure," I began. "Max Rose has been working for the Nazis. They owe him a bunch of money. He needs the payment, bad, and it's coming in on the *Hindenburg*. Cash, diamonds, bonds, paintings, and who knows what else. It's all flying in over the ocean right now. Winn Farrow, Rose's enemy, knows how important the payment is to Rose, so he's going to blow the *Hindenburg* out of the sky."

"That's an extreme thing to do, just to get revenge," Gunny said.

"Farrow's an extreme guy," Spader shot back. "But now Max Rose knows what he's up to, and he'll stop him from destroying the ship. The *Hindenburg* will be saved! Sniggers for everyone!"

"Maybe," I cautioned.

"He'll do it," Spader said with confidence. "You saw how scared Rose was. He'll do everything he can to stop Farrow."

"But this isn't just about two gangsters who hate each other," I said, trying not to let frustration creep into my voice. "This is about the turning point on First Earth. We haven't figured out why Saint Dane has his hand in any of this."

"Sure we have," Spader said, acting all sorts of cocky. "It's all about the big natty-do war that's coming, right? Isn't that the kind of thing Saint Dane is all about?"

"Yeah, but what's that got to do with the *Hindenburg*?" I asked.

"Maybe everything," Spader shot back. "It's like Gunny said. One little event leads to another and another. I think Saint Dane wants to make sure the war is going to happen, and somehow blowing up that airship will do that. So if we stop them from wrecking that ship, we'll stop the war and Saint Dane loses."

"Maybe Spader's right," Gunny said. "If we can stop the war by saving the *Hindenburg*, it would be like beating Saint Dane."

Spader looked at me with a proud smile.

"Yeah, maybe," I said. "I just wish we could be sure."

"C'mon, Pendragon! How can we lose?" Spader pleaded. "Even if it doesn't stop the war, we'd still be saving the people on the *Hindenburg*. Like you always say, this is a no-brainer."

Spader was making a really strong case, but something was keeping me from buying it a hundred percent. "I just wish we had more to go on," I complained.

We all fell silent for a moment, then Gunny said softly, "I think I know where we can find out more."

"Really? Where?" I asked quickly, grabbing at the lifeline.

"We're Travelers," he said with a matter-of-fact tone. "We can take the flume into the future of this very territory and look back on how things happened."

My heart sank. As much as I loved the idea of going home to Second Earth, I knew it would be a waste.

"It wouldn't help," I said with disappointment. "Sure, we could go to Second Earth and do some research about the *Hindenburg* and World War Two, but that wouldn't tell us anything. We need to figure out what would happen if the *Hindenburg doesn't* blow up."

"Who said anything about going to *Second* Earth?" Gunny said with a mischievous smile.

At first I didn't know what he meant. If we were going to look into the future of Earth, then of course we would go to Second Earth. That is, unless . . .

"Are you saying what I think you're saying?" I asked, barely able to contain my excitement.

"What's he saying?" Spader asked.

Gunny said, "I'm talking about taking a trip to *Third Earth*, of course."

"There's a Third Earth?" I asked, trying not to sound like a giddy geek. "Have you been there? When is it?"

"Yes," he answered with a smile. "I've been there. The year, I believe, is 5010, give or take a year or two."

I had to sit down. The idea of seeing what Earth was like three *thousand* years in the future was making my head swim.

"I am all over this," I said. "But seriously, why would going to Third Earth help us any more than going to Second Earth?"

"I told you, I've been there," he answered. "I went with your uncle Press when he first told me about being a Traveler. It was like something out of a book of fantasies. They have libraries there. But not like the ones we know. There aren't any books or papers or anything you can touch. All this information is kept on little tiny specs of nothing, no bigger than a grain of sand. They had the entire New York City public library on just one of those little things. Imagine that."

Gunny was talking about some kind of computer. At home when you got a computer, it was already outdated. That's how fast advances were being made. I couldn't imagine how far things had gotten in three thousand years.

Gunny continued, "It seemed like they had every little bit of information about everything that ever happened on those little bits of things. I'm guessing if we went there and spoke to Patrick—"

"Patrick?" Spader asked.

"The Traveler from Third Earth. Nice fella. Smart, too. I'm thinking Patrick might be able to tap into all that information and maybe give us a little more idea of what we're dealing with here."

The man was incredible. How many times had Gunny bailed us out already? I'd lost count.

"I think that's a great idea!" I shouted. "Let's go right now."

I couldn't sit still. I had forgotten how bruised and banged up I was and started getting dressed for the trip. But then, in the next second, the air was totally sucked out of my balloon.

"I'm not going," declared Spader.

"What do you mean? We're all going!" I said.

"Not me," Spader said. "There's too much at stake here to go fluming off. We might come back too late."

"It won't be a problem," I said. "Time between the territories isn't the same, remember? We could be gone for a year, but then flume back here an hour from now."

"It's too big a risk, mate," Spader said with conviction. "That airship is due early tomorrow morning. I want to be here when it shows up, just in case Max Rose doesn't take care of Winn Farrow. You're right, mate. We can't rely on Max Rose to do our job. If he fails, it'll be up to us to save the *Hindenburg*." He looked at Gunny and asked, "How far is this Lakehurst place?"

"About eighty miles, give or take," Gunny answered. "It'll take the better part of four hours to drive there. Longer on the bus."

"See?" Spader said. "It's going to take a while to get there. I don't want to risk being late."

"Spader," I said. "I'm telling you, we'll be back in time."

"Sorry, mate," he said stubbornly. "Can't take the chance."

We were slipping into dangerous territory. We were a team. I had to get Spader back with the program.

"Remember what you told me in that cab?" I asked. "You said we were all important, but I was the one who was going to hold us all together. Well, that's what I'm doing now. I'm holding us together. The only chance we've got of beating Saint Dane is if we stay together. You've risked your life to save me, Spader. I need you to be there for me again."

Spader thought about this for a moment. Was I finally getting through to him?

"If you're right," he said, "there won't be a problem. You'll get to Third Earth and back in plenty of time. We'll hook up and take on Saint Dane and his gangster wogglies like you were never gone. But if you don't make it back in time, then somebody's got to be here to make sure they don't blow up that ship. That's why I'm staying."

I didn't know what else to say. He had made up his mind, and to be honest, I wasn't completely sure he was wrong.

Spader then walked up to me and said, "Go to Third Earth. Find out what you can. It might be a big help. But let me stay here and take care of things in case something goes wrong."

I knew Gunny and I would be back in time, but that wasn't the point. What bothered me was that Spader was pulling away from me. He was always a guy who wanted action. Right now he had Saint Dane in his sights and didn't want to let him get away, even if it meant going against what I thought was best.

"Have it your way," I finally said. "We'll meet back here and then we'll all go to Lakehurst. Together."

"Now you're talking!" Spader said, then left us and went into the bathroom to clean himself up.

I didn't want to look at Gunny. I felt as if I had messed up and the team was falling apart.

"When he's got his mind set on something," Gunny said softly, "I don't think it's possible to change it."

"Saint Dane is strong and smart, and he's got way more

power than any one of us," I said. "The only chance we have to beat him is by staying together."

"We'll be back in plenty of time."

"Yeah, probably. But I'm afraid Spader is on his own mission now."

Gunny fell silent. He knew I was right.

I wanted to leave right away, but Gunny said I should get some rest. It had been a busy day and I was beat up pretty badly. Suddenly the idea of a little sleep sounded really good. He left the room, saying he'd be back in a few hours, ready to head uptown.

I lay down on the couch and closed my eyes, ready for sleep. But it didn't come. Even though I was dog tired and needed to recharge my batteries, my mind was working in too many directions to let me nod off. So I got up, hit the typewriter, and finished this journal.

I'm excited and scared at the same time. I can't believe I'm going to see Earth in 5010. How cool is that? I wish this were a trip about fun and discovery, but it isn't. I've got a very bad feeling about the way things are unfolding here on First Earth.

If there's one thing I've learned about dealing with Saint Dane, it's that just when you think you've got things figured out, he changes the rules. He did it on Denduron. He did it on Cloral. Question is, will he do it again here on First Earth?

That's what I hoped to find out on our trip to Third Earth.

I know this is going to sound totally bizarre, but the next time I write to you guys, I will have seen the future. I can only hope that it's a happy one.

END OF JOURNAL #10

THIRD EARTH

This may be the most important journal I've written to you guys.

I'm back on First Earth now. I wrote most of this journal on Third Earth, but I'm adding this little bit to the beginning because I want you to know right away how valuable these pages might end up being. I know, you treat all my journals like they're important, but this one might be the topper. Handle it like gold.

Gunny and I are on a subway train headed back to the Manhattan Tower Hotel. We've returned from Third Earth and we're running out of time. We've got to hook up with Spader and get to New Jersey before the *Hindenburg* arrives. But it's critical that I write down what we discovered on Third Earth because, just as I feared, Saint Dane has changed the rules. No, that's not exactly right. He didn't change the rules. We weren't smart enough to figure out what the rules were. But now we know and I can't begin to tell you how scared I am.

What we found on Third Earth was beyond horrible.

I hope you're reading this, Mark and Courtney. I know I've written that before, but I mean it now more than ever. Because if we fail today, history will be turned upside down, and there's a very good chance you two will never be born. I'm serious. You will not exist. Neither will most anything else as we know it. I don't mean to scare you. In fact, if you're reading this it means we've won. But if you're not reading this, then the journal I'm writing now may be the only record that Mark Dimond and Courtney Chetwynde of Stony Brook, Connecticut, ever existed.

That would be tragic, but only the beginning of the horror to come if we don't stop Saint Dane.

Most of this journal has already been written. I've tried to include every little detail, because in many ways, I'm recording history.

After finishing Journal #10, I put it safely in the desk where I was keeping Journal #9. Gunny planned on taking the journals to have them bound and covered, but not right away.

We first had to take our trip into the future.

Once the pages were put safely away, I closed my eyes and tried to get some sleep. Spader was already conked out. Just as well. I was getting tired of worrying about what he would do next and warning him to be careful. I hoped I could count on him in the future, but right now I didn't want to talk to him.

The plans were set. Gunny and I would flume to Third Earth, and Spader would wait here in case we didn't get back in time. As nervous as I was, I think I caught a few z's. Man, I needed it. But it couldn't have been for long, because before I knew it, Gunny was gently shaking me awake.

"Ready to see the future?" he asked with a smile.

"Absolutely," I answered, wide awake.

The idea of jumping three thousand years into the future had me totally jazzed. Though I wished we were doing it for less intense reasons. Gunny and I took the subway to the

Bronx. We changed trains twice and found ourselves back at the familiar station that I had been through so many times before. It was still kind of strange to see it open for business though. When I thought of this place, my mind always went to the first time I came down here with Uncle Press on Second Earth, when the place was abandoned. Was that a million years ago? It sure felt like it.

With so many people hanging around, it was a tricky thing to sneak down onto the tracks to get to the gate. We didn't want people going all nuts and calling the police because two lunatics had jumped down onto the subway tracks. But Gunny had done this before. We walked to the far end of the platform and waited for the next train to show up. When the train came in, the doors opened, passengers got out, passengers got on, the doors closed, and the train began to roll out of the station. This was the perfect time for us to move because the station was then pretty empty. As soon as the train cleared the platform, we jumped down onto the tracks and ran for the gate.

Nobody saw us. Nobody yelled. Success.

"After you," Gunny said, pointing to the wide mouth of the flume. We had decided to flume separately. Gunny was too big of a guy to flume tandem with and neither of us felt like knocking heads while rocketing across time and space. Besides, I liked fluming solo. It gave me time to think.

"Is there anything I should be ready for?" I asked. "I mean, is there anything on the other end I've got to watch out for?"

"There's plenty to watch out for," Gunny said. "But nothing you have to worry about."

I then stepped up to the mouth of the flume. I have to admit, I had goose bumps. This wasn't an ordinary flume ride—if any flume ride can be described as ordinary, that is.

No, this was more like stepping into a time machine. Next stop: three thousand years from now.

"Third Earth!" I called out.

The flume growled to life. The sparkling light could be seen far in the distance, headed this way. Along with it came the familiar jumble of musical notes that would lift me up and take me into the future of my own territory. I was thrilled, nervous, and terrified all at the same time. Then again, that pretty much defined my life as a Traveler.

"Enjoy the ride!" Gunny shouted.

An instant later I felt the tingling of energy, a slight tug, and I was pulled into the flume.

The ride was uneventful, or at least as uneventful as rocketing through a tunnel headed to a different time and territory can be. It felt good to be alone with my thoughts for a while, and I tried to imagine what Earth might be like in the year 5010. Would it be all Jetson-like and modern? Or did the human race evolve back into monkeys, like in *Planet of the Apes*? I didn't worry too much about the ape thing. Gunny would have filled me in on that little nugget of information.

I don't know how long the trip took. Actually, now that I think of it, it took around three thousand years. Time sure flies when you're having flume. Of course, it only felt like a few minutes. I felt a slight pressure on my chest, then seconds later I found myself standing in a surprising spot.

I was back at the mouth of the same flume, inside the same gate, looking at the same rocky room I had just left.

Huh? Did I make a mistake? Did I say "First Earth" instead of "Third"? Did I somehow make a U-turn somewhere in flumeworld? That's when I heard the musical notes sneaking up behind me. Gunny was incoming. I jumped to the side as he landed in a flash of sparkling light.

"Uhhh, did we make a mistake?" I asked. "We're back on First Earth."

"Nope, everything's fine," Gunny said.

He walked over to the side of the cavern where a pile of clothes lay. I hadn't seen them when I first landed. I was too busy being confused. "Only looks like First Earth," he said as he sorted through the clothes.

Hearing that made me relax a little. We weren't going to step into some bizarro new world. But I have to admit, I was a little disappointed, too. I kind of wanted to step into a bizarro new world.

"I have no idea how these show up," Gunny said as he looked through the clothes.

I joined him and looked through the clothes for myself. "Uncle Press told me it's the acolytes."

"Acolytes?" exclaimed Gunny. "What's an acolyte?"

"I'm not sure. I've never met one. But Uncle Press once told me they're people from the territories who help the Travelers. Beyond that, I haven't got a clue."

I was glad to see the clothes weren't all weird and futuristic. I picked out a pair of normal-looking khaki pants and a navy blue turtleneck. There were even regular old socks and boxers, too! The shoes were the most futuristic thing there. They didn't even look like shoes. They were more like big, white doughnuts. That is, until you slipped them on your feet. As soon as your foot was in, they molded to you and made a perfect fit, kind of like the air globes on Cloral. One size fits all. Cool.

Gunny put on a regular old white shirt with buttons, and a pair of black pants. He chose a black pair of doughnut shoes. White shoes weren't his style. He also put on a black jacket that finished off the look nicely. He then reached into the pocket of his jacket and took out a small, silver square that was about the size of a baseball card.

"What's that?" I asked.

"Some kind of telephone thing," he answered.

"Telephone?"

"Uh-huh. It's how we get in touch with Patrick. Don't ask me how it works—it's all magic to me." He pressed a button on the card and a red light on top blinked twice. It then blinked green and went out. "He knows we're here," Gunny announced. "He'll come get us."

"Cool. Can we, uh, take a look around?"

Gunny smiled. He knew I was dying to see what the future looked like. "That's what we're here for," he said. "C'mon." He led me to the wooden door that was the gate.

Before he opened it, I asked, "Any problems with quigs?"

"Quigs? You mean those yellow-eyed dog things? Nah. If they know you're not scared of them, they don't bother you."

That wasn't what I wanted to hear. I *was* scared of those yellow-eyed dog things. I hoped Gunny gave off enough brave vibes to counter my fear vibes. Gunny then pulled the door open and we stepped out of familiar territory. I expected to see the subway tunnel of First and Second Earth. But that's not what was waiting.

It was a subway tunnel all right, but nothing like the one I was used to. First off, it was bright. White light came from long tubes than ran along the ceiling. The walls were white and shiny and totally clean. This was nothing like the subways I was used to. Along the floor were two silver rails about ten feet apart. I guessed the subway train of the future was a monorail, like at Disney World.

The tunnel stretched far off in each direction. I could see ahead to the lights of the station. It was still there. I wondered if it had reopened since being abandoned in my time of Second Earth.

We then both heard a loud *click* and turned quickly to see the gate had closed behind us. If I hadn't known better, I'd say the door had disappeared, because it was absolutely flush with the wall. You had to look really close to see the outline. Weird. The inside of the gate was the familiar, wooden door. But the outside was shiny white like the rest of the tunnel. There was only one clue that it was even there. Carved into the wall was the familiar star symbol that marked all the gates.

"We best get moving," Gunny said. "Don't want to get caught by a train."

I ran ahead of Gunny because I was so excited. When I got to the platform, I quickly jumped up, then helped Gunny when he caught up with me. I turned around and got my first look at a subway station, Third Earth–style.

What I saw blew me away.

The station was there, all right, and it was definitely open for business. It wasn't very crowded. Only a handful of people wandered about, waiting for their trains. They all looked pretty normal, too. People hadn't changed at all in three thousand years.

But the subway station sure had. I walked a few yards away from the track and was hit with an incredible sight. Standing at a railing, I looked down onto a massive, underground mall. It must have gone down fifty floors below train level! Imagine the biggest mall you've ever seen, then multiply it by like forty times, and you'd have this place. And it was all underground! We were on the very top and could see down to multiple levels that had tons of shops and restaurants, and even a whole section that looked like private entrances. They must have been apartments or something.

People moved around on every level. Some walked, but many rode these odd two-wheel scooters that silently and quickly moved them along. Looking all the way down to the bottom, I saw a humongous pool. It was practically an indoor lake, where people swam and played ball. It was even big enough for people to paddle kayaks around.

This was an enormous, underground city in the Bronx. Or should I say *under* the Bronx.

Gunny had walked up behind me but didn't say anything at first. I think he wanted me to get over the shock.

Finally he asked, "What do you think?"

"Amazing is a good word," I said in awe.

"The way I heard it," Gunny explained, "they were running out of space, so they decided to move into the only unexplored area left on Earth."

"Underground," I said.

"That's right," Gunny said. "From what Patrick tells me, this is nothing. There's whole cities like this all over the world."

I watched as people went about their business, like this was normal or something. I guess to them it *was* normal but . . . wow. I also saw all sorts of people of every race. This wasn't a segregated neighborhood. Maybe people had finally learned how to get along with one another.

"It gets better," Gunny said.

He led me to the escalator that would take us up to the surface. As we walked, I saw a subway train pull into the station. Gone was the clash of wheels on metal and the screech of brakes. The train slid smoothly into the station with a quiet hum. Very cool. Very Disney.

We hopped on the escalator and I had to stop myself from running up faster. I was dying to get my first look at the outside world of Third Earth.

As we rode up Gunny said, "I guess people got smart somewhere along the line. It stopped being about building more and bigger. People began to understand they had to respect what they had or it wouldn't be around for the future."

"So what did they do?" I asked.

"Look," Gunny said.

We had reached the top of the escalator where I was expecting to step out into the middle of the normal, busy Bronx. Well, we were in the Bronx, all right, but it was far from normal.

The first thing I saw was grass. Lots of it. It looked like a park! There was a vast lake where people were fishing under the shade of leafy-green trees. The terrain wasn't flat, either. There were hills and rocky rises and even a foot-bridge over a stream that fed the lake. The sky was clear blue on this amazing, sunny day. I even smelled something familiar. It smelled like—

"Pine trees," Gunny said. "That's what you're smelling."

He had read my mind. The green subway kiosk was built on the edge of a dense grove of pine trees. It was a far different smell from the chemical fume-odor of First Earth.

There were a few odd buildings scattered around that looked like a jumble of boxes stacked on top of one another. They must have been apartment buildings because I saw people out on their balconies, talking and reading and playing and basically hanging out.

There were streets, but rather than the normal grid pattern of a city, these roads gently curved around the natural terrain. There was traffic, but the cars were small, and must have been powered by electricity because the only noise they made was a gentle hum. Many people rode bikes or walked or zipped along on those two-wheel jobs I had seen underground. I also saw a lot of small, dark green shelters scattered around. We had just stepped out from under one of them. My guess was that these shelters marked the entrances to the incredible underground complex below.

"The first time I came here," Gunny said, "I just stood and stared like you're doing right now. Then I got this wonderful, warm feeling."

"Why's that?" I asked.

"Because I realized it may have taken a few thousand years, but we finally got it right."

"It's incredible," I said. "Why didn't you tell us?"

"I figured we had more important things to handle back on First Earth," Gunny answered. "The future would always be here. It's the present we have to worry about."

I then heard a friendly voice call to us. "Looks like we've got a couple of tourists in town!"

A small car slid up behind us that wasn't much bigger than a golf cart. It was much sleeker than a golf cart, though, with a front end that came to a narrow point and had regular-size wheels. It was a silver vehicle, with no top and four seats facing forward.

Behind the wheel was a guy who looked to be in his twenties. He had long brown hair, bright eyes, and a big smile. He was dressed like a normal guy from Second Earth, with jeans and a dark green, short-sleeved shirt.

"Afternoon, Patrick," Gunny said. "Thanks for coming to fetch us so quickly."

Patrick jumped out of the car and gave Gunny a warm hug. "Good to see you, Gunny. Where's the wild man?"

Gunny motioned to me and said, "This is his nephew, Bobby Pendragon."

Patrick shook my hand with a firm grip. "Pendragon! Press

told me you'd be showing up someday. I'm glad to meet you."

"Me too," I said.

"So? Where is he?" Patrick asked.

Gunny gave me a look. The answer had to come from me.

"Press is dead," I said softly. I didn't know how else to say it.

I saw the genuine look of pain on Patrick's face. The three of us stood there silently for a moment, out of respect.

"I'm sorry, Bobby," Patrick finally said. "Your uncle was like a brother to me. I'm going to miss him."

I nodded. Wherever Uncle Press went, no matter how many lives he touched, he always made friends. With everybody but Saint Dane, that is.

"Just before he died," I said, "he told me it was the way it was supposed to be. I have a tough time buying into that."

"I know," Patrick said softly. "But Press believed it. And sure as we're standing here right now, I can't remember a time when he was wrong about anything."

I nodded.

"We need your help, Patrick," Gunny said, getting to business. "I thought you could take us to that library place."

"Absolutely. Hop in."

Since this was my first visit to Third Earth, Gunny got in back and I sat next to Patrick. My new Traveler friend hit the accelerator and we zipped ahead.

"Have you ever been to the New York Public Library in Manhattan?" he asked me.

"I've been by it," I answered. "The place with the big stone lions in front, right? Is it still there?"

"Yes. But, well, things have changed a little."

"Yeah, no kidding," I interrupted.

Patrick laughed. "I've been to First and Second Earth. I hear you," he said. "But there are still many links to the past. There's a strong sentiment that history should be respected and honored. You'll see what I mean."

Saying that things had changed was the understatement of all time. New York City, as I remembered it, was gone.

This was once an area where every square inch was cemented over or built on. It was clogged with traffic and people and noise and air pollution. I'm not saying it was a bad place, but it was definitely a busy place. What New York had become in the year 5010 was very different.

We drove our silent car along a winding road through the country. Trees lined the nearly empty roadway. Off to either side were beautiful, green, rolling hills. Every so often I saw another of those odd, boxy buildings where people lived, but besides that you would think we were driving through Vermont. There were even a few farms with rows of lush fruit trees. When we passed one, I got the definite smell of apples.

"Where is everybody?" I asked.

"I'll give you the short version," Patrick said. "By the mid-twenty-first century, we were running out of natural resources. Pollution was worse than ever and overpopulation was beyond serious. Governments had to start getting smart or it would have been disaster. From then on, Earth functioned as one planet, as opposed to a group of countries with different agendas."

"So they went underground?" I asked.

"That was one solution. It began with manufacturing and energy. There are power plants close to the center of the planet."

"Unbelievable," was all I could say.

"It took more than a thousand years, but by the year 4000, every commercial enterprise was moved underground. From factories to the Gap stores."

"You still have the Gap?" I asked.

"I think that sweater you're wearing came from there."

I took a closer look at the sweater. It didn't look much different than what I could have gotten on Second Earth. Good old Gap. Gotta love 'em.

"The only businesses that stay above ground are farms and some solar power facilities," Patrick explained. "Most of the big power sources are out West in areas that are unpopulated."

"Makes sense," I said.

"Then people began relocating underground as well. There are vast housing complexes just below the surface, all interconnected by a train system."

"Isn't that a little claustrophobic?" I said.

"Not as bad as it was on the surface. We were running out of space. That's what prompted the other move. We not only went down, we went up."

"Up?"

"Space colonies. It started with Space Station Alpha at the turn of the twenty-first century. A few larger orbiting space platforms soon followed. From there we could jump out farther. The next step was the moon. There were colonies of a thousand people each, living on the moon by the year 3000. Mars was next, followed by Venus and two of the moons of Jupiter. By last count there are one hundred and fifty-five million people living off-planet. Combine that with the fact that people finally started getting smart about family planning, and we finally achieved zero population growth."

This was a future that could only be imagined by science fiction writers in my time.

"Are there colonies under the sea as well?" I asked.

"Oh yeah, that too," answered Patrick. "But that's not significant. Maybe only a few million people are in underwater habitats."

"A few million? Not significant? Amazing."

"I'll tell you what was amazing," Patrick said. "Once man began to pull back from the surface, nature began to take charge again. Pollution was reduced. The air and water gradually cleaned up. Forests reemerged, starting with the rain forests in South America. In a lot of ways it was like the world took a giant step backward."

"But what happened to all the stuff? I mean, most of the buildings and roads are gone. Where did everything go?"

"It was all slowly dismantled. It was like a giant recycling project. Much of the material from the surface was retooled and used below to create the underground cities. There were billions of tons of material that couldn't be re-used, like road surfaces. Not to mention all the material that had to be dug out to create the cities below. Most of that was broken down and used to create new terrain. The rolling hills you're looking at were made from the streets and buildings of New York that were demolished. The whole idea was to heal the surface and preserve our resources for the future."

"But some people still live on the surface?" I asked.

"Oh, yeah. There are still cities all over the world. My guess is that it's about half and half, surface dwellers and below grounders. But the below grounders spend a lot of time on the surface, too. People still take vacations to the ocean, or the mountains to ski, and pretty much do most of the things they did on Second Earth. If you want, we can go to a Yankees game."

"There's still a Yankee Stadium?"

"Of course," Patrick answered with a smile. "There are some things that shouldn't be changed."

"It's like . . . perfect," was all I could say.

Patrick laughed. "No, nothing's perfect. But it's better than the direction man was headed."

We rode the rest of the way to the library in silence. Of course I had a million more questions, but I wanted to stop thinking so much and take in the surroundings. Gunny was right. It was a good feeling. It took a while, but it seemed as if mankind had finally figured out the right way to get by.

We sped along the roadway, headed for Manhattan. The closer we got to the island, the more I realized what Patrick meant about preserving the past. Though most of the terrain had been returned to its natural state, there were still a lot of structures on the surface, like the bridges over the rivers that circled Manhattan.

And the Empire State Building was still there. But it now had a shiny, steel surface that made it look like high-tech Empire State. I wasn't sure if it was the exact same building from my time, but it was definitely a huge reminder of the past. Very cool. In general, Manhattan was a little more built up than the Bronx. There were more streets and a lot more of those boxy apartment buildings, and it felt more like a city. Still, it was all very relaxed and civilized.

But something was wrong.

As I saw more of this reborn world, I began to get an uneasy feeling. I couldn't put it into words just then because I wasn't sure what it was, but I was feeling strangely unsettled. I didn't say anything, but a nervous vibe was definitely tickling the back of my brain.

"This is it," Patrick announced as he stopped the vehicle in front of the library.

I was happy to see that the two big stone lions I remembered from Second Earth were still there. The wide cement stairs leading up to the library were the same too. But the building itself was a very different place. I remembered a big, imposing structure, with arches and columns that looked like something you'd see in ancient Rome. But that building was long gone. In its place was a small, modern structure that wasn't much bigger than the library in Stony Brook.

"This is it?" I asked with surprise. "It's kind of . . . small."

Patrick laughed and said, "We haven't used traditional books in about two thousand years. It's amazing how much room they took up. Believe me, you won't be disappointed."

He got out of the car and hurried up the stairs. Gunny leaned over to me and said, "I told you, it's all about those little specks of things. That's where they keep all the information. It's magic."

"Gunny," I said. "I'm kind of nervous."

"About what we're going to find here?"

"Yeah, and about what we've already seen."

We both took a look around at the quiet neighborhood. Some kids were playing kickball on the grass across the street. People rode by the library on their bicycles. A group of musicians played some classical music on the library steps. They all looked relaxed and as happy as could be, not like the frenzied New Yorkers I knew from First and Second Earth.

Gunny took this all in and then said, "This is why I brought you here. You needed to see this. It raises a whole lot of questions, doesn't it?"

"Yeah," I said. "Let's go find some of the answers."

THIRD EARTH

This was like no library I had ever seen because, well, there were no books. Actually, I take that back. There was one book, but it was in the lobby of the building, encased in a heavy glass box like a museum exhibit. I figured this was a book that was here to remind people of the past and the way things used to be. As I walked over to it, I wondered what would be the one book chosen to take this place of honor. Was it a dictionary? A Bible? Maybe the complete works of Shakespeare or some famous poet.

"*Green Eggs and Ham*?" Gunny said with surprise. "What kind of doctor writes about green eggs and ham?"

"Dr. Seuss," I answered with a big smile on my face. "It's my favorite book of all time."

Patrick joined us and said, "We took a vote. It was pretty much *everybody's* favorite. Landslide victory. I'm partial to *Horton Hears a Who,* but this is okay too."

The people of Third Earth still had a sense of humor.

Patrick led us through the large, marble-floored lobby where several people sat in comfortable chairs, reading from flat computer screens. Since space was a problem, this was a good way to go. Still, I loved to read and couldn't imagine not being able to hold a book and turn the pages.

There were several long corridors leading off from the lobby. Patrick led us down one that was lined with doors on either side. Some were open and I could see people inside. I glanced into one room and saw something that made me stop short. Three people were seated around a silver platform that was raised about a foot in the air. Standing in the center of the platform, speaking to them, was Abraham Lincoln! I swear. He was right there. Honest Abe.

" . . . and that government of the people, by the people, for the people, shall not perish from the earth," Abe declared.

"Th-That's Abraham Lincoln!" I said to nobody in particular.

"Yup, Gettysburg Address. Want to listen in?" Patrick asked.

"That's some guy dressed up like Abe, right?"

At that instant Abraham Lincoln disappeared. Zap. Just like that, he faded out and the platform was empty. I shot a quick, questioning look to Patrick. He put an arm around my shoulder and led me farther down the hall.

"Think of how the caveman felt the first time he saw fire," he chuckled. "It probably wasn't much different than you're feeling right now."

"That was no fire, and I'm no caveman," I said in shock. "What *was* that?"

"I'll show you," Patrick said, and led us into one of the rooms off the corridor. This room was pretty much like the one with Abe Lincoln's ghost, but bigger. There were six simple chairs circling a silver platform that was about eight feet across.

"I'm a teacher," Patrick explained. "So I have access to this super deluxe room."

I looked at Gunny. "Have you seen this before?"

"Yeah," Gunny said with a smile. "Like I said, it's magic."

"Take a seat," Patrick said. We did and he closed the door behind us so we had privacy. "The concept is simple. Every bit of information that exists has been stored in the data banks. It's not much different from the computers you have on Second Earth, but about twelve billion times more powerful." He took the center seat, pressed a glowing white button on the armrest, and said in a loud, clear voice: "Computer. New search."

A pleasant woman's voice spoke back to him, saying, "Welcome. How can I help you?"

Whoa. *Star Trek* or what? The lights dimmed automatically, and our attention was shifted to the round stage in front of us.

Patrick touched the button on his armrest and said, "Computer. Lincoln, Abraham. United States president." Instantly the image of Abraham Lincoln appeared on the platform in front of us. But it wasn't just an image, it looked like he was actually standing there in the flesh.

"Oh, man!" I said. "It's a hologram."

"Exactly," said Patrick. He then touched the button again and said, "Gettysburg Address."

Instantly Abe began to speak. "Fourscore and seven years ago our fathers brought forth—"

"Clear," Patrick said, and Abe disappeared.

"How cool is *that*?" I exclaimed. It reminded me of the holograms that Aja Killian showed us on Veelox.

"That was an easy one," Patrick said. "Abraham Lincoln is a common entry."

"Then let's get a little uncommon," Gunny said. "We're here to learn about the *Hindenburg*. Ever hear of it?"

"Are you kidding?" Patrick said, scoffing. "I thought this was going to be tough." He hit the button and said, "*Hindenburg,* zeppelin, early twentieth century."

Before us, floating over the platform, was a familiar sight. The silver airship appeared and hovered in the air, in miniature form, of course.

"Interior views," Patrick commanded.

The full zeppelin disappeared and we were shown a bunch of different views of the passenger cabin of the *Hindenburg.* I can't tell you how cool this was. It was like tearing open a seam in time and peeking back into another era. The *Hindenburg* was a fancy airship. I guess they designed it like an ocean liner. There were staterooms and a dining room, and a long deck where you could stroll around and look down on the world from behind the safety and comfort of glass.

"It was a luxury liner," Patrick said. "Designed to ferry people across Europe and over the ocean in style."

"We're interested in the crash," Gunny said quietly.

"I figured that," Patrick said. He then pressed the white button and said, "Computer. *Hindenburg* disaster."

The full blimp reappeared. Then a second later fire flashed on its right side, near the tail. The fire spread so quickly it was like watching a movie that had been sped up. The tail dipped as flames spread over the silver skin of the balloon. The image was so realistic, I expected to feel the heat. The zeppelin hit the ground, tail first. Then the nose started coming down. I could even see people scrambling out of the gondola underneath and running for safety. It was horrifying, and fascinating.

Finally the entire balloon was engulfed in flames. The skeleton of the structure was revealed as the outer skin burned away. Then, horribly, the frame collapsed into a pile of burning metal. The image stopped moving, like a freeze-frame in a movie.

The computer voice then said, "Zeppelin LZ-one-two-nine. *Hindenburg*. Crashed on first transatlantic flight of 1937. Origin of flight: Frankfurt, Germany. Destination: Lakehurst Naval Air Station, New Jersey, USA. Date of incident: May sixth. Time of incident: 7:25 P.M. Duration of incident: thirty-seven seconds. Passengers and crew aboard: ninety-seven. Dead: thirty-six."

"Thirty-six people died," I said in awe. "And it only took thirty-seven seconds. Unbelievable."

Maybe not so unbelievable. I remembered how quickly the flames spread in that slaughterhouse when Winn Farrow's rocket exploded.

"It landed at 7:25 P.M.?" asked Gunny. "I thought it was supposed to come in the morning?"

Patrick said, "Computer. Reason for delayed arrival."

The computer said, "High winds. Storms. *Hindenburg* delayed until storm subsided."

"Spader will be happy to hear that," Gunny said. "We've got twelve more hours to work with."

Patrick turned to Gunny and asked, "What are you looking for?"

"We want to know what caused the crash," Gunny said. He glanced at me. We thought we knew the answer to that, but it was as good a place to start as any.

Patrick hit the button and said, "Computer. Cause of *Hindenburg* crash."

The pleasant computer voice said, "Several theories. One: Zeppelin filled with flammable hydrogen gas. Possible cause of ignition, residual static electricity from earlier thunderstorm. Two: Shell of balloon covered with volatile aluminum powder.

Potential ignition cause, same static electricity. Three: Lightning strike. Final theory: Sabotage."

"Sabotage?" I asked.

Patrick said, "Computer. More on sabotage."

The computer said, "Potential for explosive device having been placed on board by crew member. Never proven."

"State most likely scenario," Patrick ordered the computer.

The computer answered, "No likely scenario. Cause of disaster unproven."

The still frame of the burned zeppelin then disappeared.

"It's one of the great mysteries of all time," Patrick said. "Why did the *Hindenburg* burn? Even with all our technology, we don't know for sure."

Gunny and I glanced at each other. We knew.

"So this computer has information stored on all people?" I asked. "Not just famous presidents?"

"Every single bit of information that exists is at your disposal."

I thought for a second, an idea slowly forming. "Can I try?" I asked.

Patrick stood up and gave me the chair. "Have fun," he said.

I sat down in the chair, feeling like I had a whole bunch of power at my fingertips. I touched the button and said, "Computer. Rose, Maximilian."

The computer answered, "Over eight hundred thousand entries. More specifics, please."

Patrick chuckled. "The computer cross-references everything in its databases. Give it more to go on."

Okay. I hit the button again and said, "Computer. Rose, Maximilian. United States. 1937. Manhattan Tower Hotel. Criminal."

Bingo. Who should appear on the platform in front of us but Max Rose. He was even wearing one of his familiar silk bathrobes.

"Friend of yours?" Patrick asked.

"Sort of," I answered, then hit the button again. "Computer. Rose, Maximilian. May sixth, 1937."

The computer said, "Maximilian Rose, killed in automobile accident on May sixth, 1937."

Huh? I shot a look to Gunny. Gunny sat up straight. Things were getting interesting. I then said, "Computer. When and where?"

The computer answered, "Six fifty P.M. Intersection of Toms River Road and Route five-twenty-seven, Lakehurst, New Jersey, USA."

"He must have been on his way to meet the *Hindenburg,*" Gunny said.

I hit the button again and said, "New Search." The image of Max Rose disappeared.

"Computer. Farrow, Winn. New York. 1937. Criminal."

Bang. There he was. Winn Farrow, right in front of us. I was beginning to think this computer was as good as Patrick said.

"Computer. Farrow, Winn. May sixth, 1937," I said.

The computer answered, "Received speeding ticket from New Jersey State Police. Four twenty-five P.M."

"That's it for May sixth?" I asked.

The computer answered, "He was driving twelve miles over the speed limit."

"There's gotta be more than that," I said in frustration. "Let me try something." I hit the button again and said, "Computer. Amaden, Esther. New York. 1937."

The image of Winn Farrow disappeared. There was a

second of silence. Nothing appeared on the platform.

The computer said, "No data."

That was weird. I gave it more to go on. "Computer. Add nickname, Harlow. Manhattan Tower Hotel. Singer. Friend of Rose, Maximilian."

A moment, and then, "No data."

"Does this machine ever make mistakes?" asked Gunny.

Patrick answered, "Well, no. Someone named Esther Amaden never existed or the computer would have a record of her."

"What if she changed her name?" Gunny asked.

"The computer would know that. Guaranteed. Who was she?"

Uh-oh. A bad thought hit me and I started getting a sick feeling in the pit of my stomach.

"Computer," I said weakly. "Van Dyke, Vincent. Nickname, Gunny. Manhattan Tower Hotel. New York. 1937."

There was a pause, and then the computer answered, "No data."

Now I started to sweat. Things were happening fast. "Computer. Tilton, Press. Stony Brook, Connecticut. Early twenty-first century. Uncle to Pendragon, Robert. Sister to Pendragon, Kathleen."

A pause, and then, "No data."

Patrick said, "We're Travelers, Pendragon. There wouldn't be any records."

This was getting more horrifying by the second. I was learning something new about being a Traveler. As far as the world was concerned, we didn't exist. That's why my house on Second Earth was gone. That's why my family disappeared.

"Computer! Pendragon, Robert. Nickname, Bobby. Stony Brook, Connecticut."

There was another pause, and then, "No data."

"Don't do this to yourself, Bobby," Gunny said softly.

I was freaking out, but not for the reason Gunny thought. In some ways, I think I knew something like this had to be true. Yeah, it was horrifying to know we had no history. But as frightening as that was, it wasn't what was making my brain explode.

I couldn't sit down anymore. My heart raced. I jumped up, hit the button again and shouted, "Computer! Amaden, Esther. Nickname, Harlow. Girlfriend to Rose, Maximilian. New York. 1937."

The computer paused for several seconds and then said calmly, "No data."

"Uh-oh," Gunny said. He now realized where I was going with this.

"Yeah, uh-oh," I shot back. "Travelers don't have records because Travelers don't have histories. *All* Travelers, not just the good ones."

"Do you think—"

"Yeah, I do. Esther Amaden is Saint Dane. He's been playing the game from both sides from the very beginning."

THIRD EARTH

"He's been playing with us," I said. "He's got Max Rose listening on one side, Winn Farrow listening on the other, and we're the monkeys in the middle."

"You mean to tell me that pretty lady singer is Saint Dane in disguise? That's hard to believe," Gunny said.

"But it's true," I shot back. "He can change himself into anyone. Trust me, I've seen it."

I paced the library room, trying to rethink everything that had happened since I arrived on First Earth. It was a whole different ballgame now that I knew Saint Dane was pulling all the strings. What was he up to?

Patrick said, "Tell me what's going on, maybe I can help."

"We've been thinking the turning point on First Earth is the *Hindenburg*," I explained. "But Saint Dane's plans have to be bigger than the crash of a single ship. World War Two is coming on fast and we thought that if we could prevent the *Hindenburg* from going down, it might somehow stop the war from happening. But we can't know for sure. The tough part is that since Saint Dane is playing both sides of the game, we don't really know what he wants to happen. Does he want the *Hindenburg* to crash or not?"

Gunny added, "We know what happens after the ship goes down. What we don't know is what will happen if that big airship *doesn't* go down."

We all fell silent for a second. That was the problem, exactly. Would saving the *Hindenburg* be a good thing or a bad thing? There was no way to find that answer.

At least, that's what we thought.

"Well, I could help you figure that out," Patrick said casually, like it was no big deal.

"You can? How?" I asked in disbelief.

"I know it's hard for you guys to understand," he began. "But the capacity of our data systems is incredible. What we've been doing here with Abe Lincoln and the *Hindenburg* doesn't even scratch the surface."

"Yeah, it's all pretty cool," I said. "But you can't predict the future."

Patrick smiled and said, "Well, in a way, we can."

Gunny and I looked at each other in surprise. Who was this guy kidding? No computer, I don't care how great it is, can do that.

"Look at it this way," Patrick said. "It's like math. Two plus two equals four. But if you change a two to a three, it doesn't equal four anymore. It equals five."

"And that's how you can predict the future?" I asked. I was losing faith in Patrick, fast.

"Stay with me," he said. "Now imagine a really complex mathematical equation with thousands or even millions of numbers. Same thing. If you change even one number, the whole equation changes, right?"

"Yeah, I guess," I said. "But what's that got to do with predicting the future?"

"Okay," Patrick continued. "Think of all the events that ever happened in the past as numbers in an equation. If you changed even one of those events, it would change all the events that followed. The whole equation would have to be recalculated."

"But numbers are real," I said.

"So is the past," Patrick countered. "As real as any number. I can't predict what will happen tomorrow, but I can definitely predict how changes in the past would play out in the past."

"That's impossible!" I shouted. "That computer would have to know everything about everybody and everything they ever did to make that kind of prediction."

"That's what I've been telling you!" Patrick said with excitement. "That's exactly the kind of data we've got. We can take events from the past and change one of the factors. The computer will cross-reference billions of other factors and calculate the likely new scenario, just like a math equation. It's called variable technology."

He was losing me. And if he was losing me, I knew Gunny was long gone.

"Okay, here's an example of a simple one I did. 1969. Super Bowl Three. The New York Jets beat the Baltimore Colts, sixteen to seven. I brought up all the information I had about that game, the players, the weather conditions, the coaches, everything. I even knew what each of the players had for breakfast. Then I changed one thing. I input that Joe Namath, the Jets' star quarterback, went down with an injury in the first quarter. The final score the computer predicted was very different from sixteen-seven Jets."

"What happened?" I asked. "The Colts kicked butt, right?"

"Well, no," Patrick said. "The Jets actually won the game twenty-four-zip. Weird, no?"

"Predicting a football game is one thing," I said. "Figuring out the course of history is a slightly bigger deal."

"Trust me, Pendragon," Patrick said. "Think of all the things you've seen on Third Earth. If I told you about all this three thousand years ago, would you believe it could happen?"

"Well, yeah, maybe," I said.

"Then believe this too," he said with total confidence. "A big event like the crash of the *Hindenburg* is bound to change things. I can't guarantee that I can predict exactly what will happen if it doesn't crash, but I know I can come up with the big picture."

I looked to Gunny. He was a guy who couldn't even imagine Nintendo, let alone the kinds of things Patrick was talking about. Still, I needed another opinion.

"What do you think?" I asked.

Gunny gave a very wise answer. "As far as I'm concerned, most everything here is impossible. Yet here it is, real as can be. I'm inclined to give Patrick the benefit of the doubt. If he says he can do this, who are we to say he can't?"

That was a pretty good argument. Besides, if Patrick really could do this, we'd have the answers we so desperately needed.

"Okay," I said. "Give it a shot."

Patrick let out a big smile. He was psyched for the challenge. He ran to a cabinet where he pulled out two pads of blue paper and two pens. "I need you two to write down everything you can think of that has to do with the situation. Names, dates, events, locations . . . I mean *everything*. No bit of information is too small."

"I thought the computer does that?" I asked.

"We need to give it as many cross-references as possible," Patrick answered. "The more guidance we give it, the more accurate the result will be."

I looked at the pen he handed me, and chuckled, "You guys still use pens and paper?"

"Not usually," answered Patrick. "But it would take too long to show you how to interface with the computer."

Good point. For the next half hour, we wrote down everything we could think of about the mystery. I made sure to get everything down that I knew about Max Rose and Winn Farrow. They were the key figures here. It was because of their relationship that the *Hindenburg* was in danger. When we finished, we each presented Patrick with many pages of data.

"Now what?" I asked.

"Go outside and relax. It'll take me a while to input all this and start the process. I'll find you as soon as I come up with something."

That was that. Gunny and I left Patrick alone to do his thing. We walked back out to the lobby, where I was hit with the smell of food. I hadn't realized it until that moment, but I was starving. I really hoped there was a cafeteria around and this wasn't some virtual smell coming from somebody using the computer to look up "pizza."

We found a small counter selling simple foods like cookies and drinks. It didn't matter to me. They could have been selling brussel sprouts and I would have bought a bundle. That's how starved I was. Gunny was too. We each picked out a handful of cookies and some juice.

"Uh-oh," Gunny said. "All I've got is First Earth money."

I shrugged and said, "Give it a shot."

Gunny handed the counter guy a First Earth twenty-dollar bill. He looked at it strangely and said, "I'm not really sure what that is, but you don't have to pay for food when you're using the library."

Wow. Free food. That surprised me almost as much as seeing the underground city. Life here on Third Earth was pretty sweet.

Gunny and I took our food outside to the front steps of the library and sat down to eat. We didn't say much at first. We were too busy enjoying the taste of fifty-first century chocolate chip cookies. They tasted the same as the twenty-first century variety. Luckily time hadn't changed everything.

While we ate, I had a chance to think. I wrote before that I had a nervous feeling, but didn't know why. It wasn't until now, as we sat on the steps of the library, that the reason became clear. It had been staring me in the face since we arrived on Third Earth, but I couldn't bring it into focus. Now, as we sat there on that beautiful warm day, I finally got my mind around it. It was totally obvious, too. Maybe that's why I didn't get it at first. It was too simple. But the more I reasoned it through, the more sense it made.

And I didn't like it. My appetite was suddenly gone. I put the last cookie down uneaten.

"What's the trouble, shorty?" Gunny asked.

"It doesn't matter what Patrick comes up with," I said.

"Excuse me?" Gunny replied. "I think it matters a whole lot."

"But it doesn't. I already know what we have to do."

"Really?"

"You know it too, Gunny," I said. "I think we're both hoping that Patrick comes up with something that tells us we're wrong, but he won't."

Gunny stopped eating his cookie and looked out over the scene in front of us. What had once been a busy, congested city was now beautiful countryside. We could see a few modern housing units scattered around, but mostly it was clean, green country full of people enjoying a beautiful, sunny day. In the distance I could see the unpolluted East River. The air smelled fresh. There was no violence. It was perfect. From what Patrick told us, the rest of Third Earth was the same way.

Perfect.

I looked into Gunny's eyes. He was troubled. We were on the same page.

"Doesn't look like a territory that Saint Dane pushed into chaos, does it?" Gunny said.

Exactly. The wreck of the *Hindenburg* was a horrible disaster and classic Saint Dane. We even hoped that by saving it, we might be able to stop World War II. But the truth was, Earth had evolved into a truly wonderful place in spite of the fact that the *Hindenburg* blew up.

"We won't make things better by changing history, will we?" Gunny said.

"No."

Reality was closing in fast. Our mission was about to be turned upside down. If we wanted Earth to evolve into the wonderful territory we were now looking at, we had to make sure history played out the way it was supposed to.

That meant only one thing. Winn Farrow had to succeed. The *Hindenburg* had to go down.

"Saint Dane *wants* us to change history," I said with finality. "That's what this has been about. That's the turning point. If we change history, this is a world that may never be."

Suddenly the whole challenge seemed too huge. I'm embarrassed to say this, but I snapped.

"I hate this!" I screamed, jumping up.

"What's the trouble?" Gunny asked with sympathy.

"The trouble is I don't want to do this anymore. It's not fair. Why are we the ones responsible for saving the territories?"

"Because we're Travelers," Gunny answered.

"Yeah, well, I don't want to be a Traveler. I didn't ask for this. I didn't volunteer. How did I get chosen? How did *you* get chosen? Don't you wonder about that?"

Gunny said softly, "Everyday."

"And it doesn't bother you?"

Gunny took some time to think about this. "To be honest, I think that if I had the choice, I'd still be sitting here with you right now. But it's different for me. I lived a long life before finding out my true calling. I can understand why you're troubled."

"Yeah, you got that right!" I said. "I'm fifteen years old. I had to leave home when I was fourteen. Nobody my age should see the things I've seen. I'm supposed to be playing ball and sweating over tests and zits and hoping girls like me—not making sure thirty-six people die in a horrible accident. I don't want that responsibility!"

The stakes had suddenly gotten very big, very fast, and it scared me to death. I knew I wasn't smart enough, or strong enough to have that kind of responsibility. I wanted somebody else to do the job. I wanted Uncle Press to be there. Or Osa, or even Loor. I didn't want to have to make these kinds of decisions. I wanted to go home. I wanted to see my mom and dad again.

I wanted my old life back.

I was half a second away from going back to the flume and launching myself home to Second Earth for good, when I heard a voice call to us.

"I'm finished."

It was Patrick. He walked down the last few steps to join us. I hope I can do a good job of describing the way he looked. He was shaken. I swear, it was like all the color had left his face. I know this sounds weird, but he looked ten years older than when we last saw him. He didn't even stand up tall, he was kind of hunched over, like there was a tremendous weight on his shoulders.

"Come inside and see what I found," he said softly.

"What is it?" Gunny asked while standing up.

"You're going to have to see for yourself, because you won't believe me otherwise."

"I'm guessing you don't have good news," I said.

Patrick managed a sad smile. "No, no good news, except to say you were right. You found the turning point on First Earth, all right. It's the *Hindenburg*. And you hit the mother lode. It's not just the turning point for First Earth. What happens on May sixth, 1937, is going to affect First, Second, and Third Earth as well."

"Is it as bad as all that?" Gunny asked.

Patrick's only answer was an ironic chuckle. He then turned and walked up the stairs back to the library.

Gunny and I stood there, stunned. I wanted to run home now more than ever. I felt sure that whatever was waiting for us in that library, it would be gruesome. I was truly at a crossroads. I knew how important this was, but I had to convince myself not to run for my life.

"You want to know why we're the ones responsible?" Gunny asked.

I looked up into a pair of wise eyes that had seen far more than mine.

"Because there's nobody else," he said. With that, he slowly walked up the stairs after Patrick.

I stood alone, trying to keep from crying. What Gunny had said was simple, and it was the truth.

I closed my eyes, took a deep breath, and ran up the stairs after them.

THIRD EARTH

"You've got to get back to make sure the *Hindenburg* is destroyed," Patrick said. Though his voice was quivering with fear, he couldn't have been any more clear. "If you don't, everything is going to change."

"I'm guessing it won't be for the better," Gunny said.

"Not even close," Patrick answered.

"Do we want to see this?" I asked.

"No," was Patrick's answer. "But you have to."

We were back in the small library room. Patrick motioned for us to take seats. Gunny sat, but I was too nervous. When I get anxious like that, it's hard for me to sit still.

"Here's the deal," Patrick began. "Remember I talked about mathematical equations and if you changed one number, the whole equation would be altered?"

"Yeah," I answered tentatively.

"Well, it's true, but it also depends on what number you decide to change," Patrick explained. "You might change one number and the overall difference would be small. Or you might change a number that has a much bigger impact."

"What about the *Hindenburg*?" Gunny asked. "How big a change could that make?"

Patrick had to sit down. It was like the weight of what he was about to say was making it hard for him to stay on his feet.

"Saint Dane hit the jackpot," he said. "He found a single event in history that if changed, would turn the future inside out. If he succeeds, he'll push all three territories into chaos."

That was exactly what I didn't want to hear. "How can one change do so much?" I asked.

"That's what I've got to show you," Patrick answered. He hit the white button on his chair and called out, "Computer. *Hindenburg* Variation. Item number one."

Instantly the image of Max Rose appeared before us.

"It's all about this guy Maximilian Rose," Patrick began. "He started doing business with the Nazis in 1935."

"We know that," I said. "He said he was shipping them tools and scrap metal."

"That's not all he was shipping them," Patrick said. "Computer. Item number two."

Appearing before us was a group of men. None of them looked familiar. They were all white guys with short haircuts and wearing suits. They looked like a bunch of dorks.

"Who are they?" Gunny asked.

"Spies," Patrick answered quickly.

"Spies?" I asked. "You mean like James Bond?"

"Industrial spies," said Patrick. "The kind of guys who sell secrets about companies and manufacturing plans and designs. These are all Americans who worked for Max Rose. Some of them did it for the money, others were forced into it by Rose's thugs. Every one of them had valuable secrets the Nazis would have loved to get hold of."

"And Max Rose was selling them these secrets?" Gunny asked.

"Yes. That is, until May sixth, 1937. Computer. Item three."

The gang of spies disappeared and was replaced by an image of a wrecked car. Whatever had happened to this vehicle, it was ugly, because it was a step above scrap metal. I guarantee, nobody could walk away from a wreck like that.

"May sixth, six fifty P.M.," Patrick explained. "Intersection of Toms River Road and Route five-twenty-seven . . . Max Rose is killed in a collision with a state trooper. But that alone wouldn't have stopped his spy business. He had lieutenants who would have picked up right where he left off. Except for one thing. Item four."

The car wreck disappeared and we then saw the familiar image of the *Hindenburg* on fire.

"When the *Hindenburg* went down," Patrick explained, "a huge payment from the Nazis to Max Rose went down with it. Records show there was a shipment on board with four million American dollars, bonds, jewels, and artwork. All gone in thirty-seven seconds."

"Bad for Rose," Gunny said.

"Worse than bad. Losing that money destroyed Rose's organization," Patrick said. "Payments couldn't be made. Ties were severed. Some of the spies sank back into deep cover, never to be heard from again. Others got arrested. Bottom line is the crash of the *Hindenburg* put Rose's spies out of business."

"Okay," I said. "Now we know what happened. What did your computer figure out would happen if the *Hindenburg* didn't crash?"

Patrick hesitated, then stood up and paced.

"I input one single change," he finally said. "I input the variable that the *Hindenburg* arrived safely." Patrick took a deep breath, then continued. "It took the computer twenty minutes to calculate all the changes. Pendragon, that's like saying a computer from Second Earth took a lifetime to calculate pi. That's how extensive the changes were. Every resource, every data bank, every bit of memory was called into play. It knocked everybody else in the library offline. I've never seen anything like it."

"So? Show us," I said.

Patrick sat back down in his chair. He hit the button and said weakly, "Item five."

A man appeared. A lone man with salt-and-pepper-colored hair. He was short, with wire-rimmed glasses and a gray suit. He didn't look familiar at all.

"This is Dani Schmidt," Patrick said nervously, "a physicist working for the Nazis. He never played a big part in history, because he was a failure. The project he devoted the final years of his life to was never finished. He was executed by the Nazis in 1944. His only crime was failure. But that was under the old scenario. If the *Hindenburg* had survived, his life would have taken a different turn. Item six."

The image of Dani Schmidt disappeared, and was replaced by a large, gray piece of equipment that looked like a fat torpedo.

"When the *Hindenburg* arrived safely, the payment was made to keep Max Rose's spy operation in business. More information was stolen from the U.S. and fed to the Nazis. They in turn gave it to Dani Schmidt. It was scientific data they never would have gotten if the *Hindenburg* had crashed."

"So what is that thing?" I asked, pointing to the gray torpedo.

"That was the project Dani Schmidt was working on," Patrick said. "With the scientific information stolen from the

United States, he was able to put the final pieces of his project together." Patrick then took a deep breath. "Item seven."

The image of the torpedo was replaced by an image that looked very familiar. It was a bird's-eye view of Washington, D.C. I could see the Capitol, the Washington Monument, and the Lincoln Memorial.

"May twenty-fourth, 1944," Patrick said with a shaky voice. "The Germans were on the run. The Allies would invade Europe in two weeks. The war would only last another year or so. But on that date, Dani Schmidt's project was brought into play."

We then saw an image that made my knees buckle. There before us, looking as real as if we were watching it from an airplane, we saw Washington, D.C. hit by an atomic bomb. The city was vaporized. The familiar, horrific mushroom cloud rose up over the shattered capital like an evil tombstone.

"That was at ten o'clock in the morning," Patrick said. "There was more to come. Item eight."

The rubble of Washington, D.C. was replaced by a view of Manhattan Island.

Gunny breathed out, "Oh, no."

Boom. New York got slammed too.

"That bomb landed north of Manhattan at ten fifteen. Item nine."

The mushroom cloud over New York was replaced by an aerial view of London. *Boom.* London was history.

"Ten twenty-five. The Nazis sent out long-range bombers with the world's first atomic bombs."

"Shut it off!" I yelled.

"Clear," Patrick said softly, and the destruction of London was gone.

"How can this machine know that?" I demanded. "It's just a guess."

"It's not," Patrick said. "This was always the Nazis' plan. But they never developed a working bomb, so it was never carried out. With the help of the information stolen from the United States by Max Rose's spy network, Dani Schmidt was able to complete his work. There's very little guesswork here. If the *Hindenburg* arrives safely, Germany will be the first to develop an atomic bomb. And they will use it."

"What will happen from there?" Gunny said softly. He looked like he was in shock. "I don't want to see it, just tell me."

"Most of the northeast United States will be devastated by the two blasts. They'll have to deal with radiation for years. Pendragon, your home of Stony Brook, Connecticut, will no longer exist. Earthquakes set off by the blast in New York will see to that."

Now I had to sit down. I wasn't nervous anymore. I was sick.

"Bottom line is, the Germans will win the war," Patrick said. "Adolf Hitler's evil vision will spread throughout the world, just as he planned. As you can imagine, from that point on, the world will take a much different course. Let me show you one last thing. Item fifty-six."

On the platform we saw another overhead view. This was of New York City. The only reason I knew it was New York was because I saw a chunk of building that looked like the Empire State Building. But it wasn't a tall, majestic building anymore. It was only the top few floors. The building must have tumbled when the bomb fell and now only the top few floors were left. We saw several more views of the destroyed city. There were people waiting in line for food. Children slept in the streets, cold and hungry. Tents were set up where the roads had been. Thousands upon thousands of people lived in the rubble like rats.

"Was this right after the bomb fell?" I asked.

Patrick answered. "This is a view of New York City on Third Earth, over three thousand years later. Today."

I then saw something that made me want to cry. Lying on its side, along what was once the busy street of Fifth Avenue, was a green structure that was being used for makeshift housing. It must have covered ten city blocks. Holes were cut in the sides for people to crawl in and out of. The image was stunning, and horrible, because lying there, broken and destroyed among the rubble of once proud buildings, was the Statue of Liberty.

"I'll say it again," Patrick said quietly. "Saint Dane hit the jackpot. He found the perfect moment in time that he could manipulate and send three territories into oblivion. Clear."

The images disappeared. Good thing. I couldn't take it anymore. The three of us sat there in silence. We had just seen doomsday. It's hard to know what to say after that.

"Could there be a mistake?" Gunny asked.

"Specific details may change," Patrick answered. "But the basic situation would be the same. If Max Rose continues to operate his spy network, the Germans will develop the atom bomb first, and they will drop it on England and the United States."

I had heard enough. We already figured that saving the *Hindenburg* would be a mistake. Seeing how great Third Earth was told us that. But now, seeing the horror show Patrick had just presented slammed the point home to me about as hard as possible. Any doubts I had about what I wanted to do were gone.

I stood up and said, "We're on the wrong territory."

Gunny stood up. "Yes, we are," he said with purpose.

"I'm coming," Patrick announced. "I want to help."

Gunny looked at me. I wasn't sure if Patrick coming along was a good idea or not.

"I don't think so, Patrick," Gunny said. "We've got to hit the ground running once we get back. We wouldn't have time to teach you all you'd need to know about First Earth. No offense, but you might end up being more trouble than help."

Gunny was right. Patrick wouldn't know simple things, like how to get across a busy street. We couldn't afford to be slowed down by anything, even a friend.

"I understand," Patrick said, looking disappointed.

"Besides," Gunny said. "You did your part. Now it's our turn." Gunny then turned to me and said, "You ready for this, shorty?"

How could I answer that question? How could anyone be ready for what we had to do? I know why Gunny asked me though. A few minutes before, I was out of control. I wanted my life back. Though I knew stopping Saint Dane from destroying the territories and taking control of Halla was important, it felt like a fantasy. I was tired of living in a fantasy. But after seeing what Saint Dane had in mind for the three Earth territories, the fantasy had suddenly become real. Now he was hitting me where I lived. So how did I answer a huge question like that?

"Absolutely."

Gunny smiled. Next stop, First Earth.

Before hitting the flume, I sat in the library and wrote most of this journal. I didn't want to wait until we got back, because if something happens to me, well, let's just say I wanted to make sure this journal was written. I trusted that the flumes would get us back in time.

Patrick drove us back up to the Bronx and the green shelter that would lead us down to the subway.

"We'll see you again," Gunny said with certainty. "And it will be here on Third Earth. *This* Third Earth."

Patrick nodded. He didn't seem as confident as Gunny. He then turned to me and said, "Pendragon, your uncle told me that if I ever doubted myself, or our mission, that I should put my faith in you. Should I put my faith in you?"

Whoa. Uncle Press said that about me? Patrick was looking for some kind of guarantee that everything was going to be okay. I wished I could give it to him.

"I'm not sure why he'd say that," I answered truthfully. "But I do know one thing. You might as well put your faith in us, because there's nobody else."

On that solemn note, the three of us parted.

A second before we went underground, I took one last look at Third Earth. I really hoped it wouldn't be the last time I saw it like this. Gunny and I then hurried down the escalator, across the platform, down onto the tracks, and back to the gate that led to the flume. There we quickly traded our Third Earth clothes for our First Earth clothes. We didn't even talk. We were both focused on getting back as quickly as possible.

"First Earth!" I shouted at the mouth of the flume. A second later I kissed Third Earth good-bye and shot my way back to 1937.

A few minutes later we found ourselves surrounded by all the familiar sensations of First Earth—the smells, the noise, the people, the energy. It was a rude change from the quiet serenity of Third Earth. But I have to admit, I didn't mind it. It felt like going home.

Once Gunny and I got back to the subway platform, we

waited for the first train downtown and jumped on board. There weren't many subway stops in the Bronx that were underground, so we shortly emerged into rainy daylight. As much as I thought Third Earth was a perfect place, I was glad to see the buildings of old-fashioned New York again. Still Gunny and I didn't speak. We knew what we had to do.

We had returned early in the morning on May 6, 1937. We weren't too late. Our first goal was to get back to the Manhattan Tower Hotel, find Spader, and tell him what we had discovered on Third Earth. From there, we'd decide on a plan to make sure Winn Farrow destroyed the *Hindenburg*. That was a weird feeling. We had to help make sure that a killer succeeded in murdering thirty-six people. But I couldn't think of it like that. It was too horrific. I had to keep telling myself that we were making sure that history played out the way it was supposed to, and that Saint Dane wouldn't change things. That was our mission. That was why we were on First Earth.

As we rode on the subway, I kept my head down finishing this journal. Like I told you up front, this may be the most important journal I've written yet. If we fail, and Saint Dane prevents the *Hindenburg* from burning, the world will change, and this document will be the only proof of the way things were meant to be.

There's one last thing that happened that I should write down. It didn't really affect anything, but it's worth writing about anyway.

The subway car rumbled toward the bridge that would take us across the East River into Manhattan. But I wasn't watching. I was too busy writing. That's when Gunny nudged me. He didn't say a word; all he did was point out the window of the subway car, up toward the skyline of Manhattan. I didn't know what he wanted me to see at first, but a few seconds later I caught sight of it—and it made me catch my breath.

It was just coming into view, high above the tallest buildings. It floated there like a quiet, majestic bird, lazily surveying the ground below. It was Luft Zeppelin-129. The *Hindenburg*. It had arrived in America. I watched the ship in open-mouthed awe. It was way bigger than I had imagined. I also couldn't help but focus on the bold logos on its tail. There were two giant black swastikas on a red and white background, the symbol of the Nazi Party. Seeing them gave me a shiver.

People pressed against the subway windows to get a look at the impressive blimp. They waved, as if expecting the crew and passengers high above to see them. Cars honked their horns, people cheered, other cars pulled over to the side of the street so their passengers could get out and watch. It was like a joyous celebration. People gazed at the airship in awe. To them it was a mighty symbol of the future.

Gunny and I knew differently. The future of the zeppelin was going to be a short one. It had to be.

We're almost at our stop, so I'll end my journal here. It's a horrible feeling. If we fail, this will be the last time I'll be writing to you two, Mark and Courtney. I feel like I want to say good-bye. But I can't think that way. I've got to get it in my head that in a few hours, the majestic zeppelin we just saw floating over Manhattan has to crash to the ground in a flaming ball of fire.

That's our mission. Our future, *your* future depends on it.

END OF JOURNAL #11

FIRST EARTH

As I look back on this last, incredible year, I feel like I've gone through two huge, personal turning points.

The first was the moment I was pulled into a flume for the very first time. That was when I realized the rules of the universe weren't exactly what I thought they were. Ever since then I've had to struggle to keep my head above water in the scary seas of Travelerworld.

The second turning point came in that library on Third Earth. Up until then, the idea of an entire territory falling into chaos didn't really mean anything to me. It was all just theory. But when I saw the images of what Saint Dane had planned for the Earth territories . . . man. It was like everything suddenly came into focus. Saint Dane had to be stopped, now and forever. End of discussion.

Before that moment, I knew it in my brain. Now, I feel it in my heart.

The only people who have a chance of ending his evil campaign are the Travelers. It would be nice if we were a race of invincible superheroes with powers far beyond those of mortal men, but we're not. A stranger group you couldn't find, but only because we're all so normal. It's scary to think that the only force trying to prevent Saint Dane from destroying Halla is a group of regular-old people.

More frightening is knowing I'm one of them.

When I saw those horrifying images of Saint Dane's Earth, something changed in me. It's hard to put this into words, because I'm not sure I understand it myself. Call it anger. Call it outrage. Call it fear. Definitely call it fear. But seeing the evil depths of Saint Dane's vision locked me in. I know I'm in it now, for good. I don't know if my being on this quest is right or wrong or someplace in between. All I know is, I'm here now, and that can't be changed. It's up to me and my fellow Travelers to stop Saint Dane. We're the ones on the spot. I accept that now. I don't like it, but I accept it.

I'm writing all this to you so you'll know where my head is, but also to explain some of the things I did over the past few days. To put it right out there, I messed up. Bad. And the thing is, I'm not so sure that if I had to do it all over again, I wouldn't do the exact same *wrong* thing again. That's what has me so upset right now. Saint Dane must be defeated. Part of that responsibility is mine. But after what happened with the *Hindenburg,* I don't know if I'm up to the job.

The true events that happened on May 6, 1937, will never be reported in any newspaper. They will not be part of recorded history. They will live only in my journals and the journals of my fellow Travelers.

This is what happened.

It was a gray, cold May day. The sky was full of roiling clouds, rain showers, and occasional cracks of thunder and lightning. The *Hindenburg* was supposed to arrive in New Jersey early in the morning, but bad weather forced it to circle the New York area for most of the day. History was playing out the way it was supposed to. So far.

The whole atmosphere had an ominous feel to it. I don't know if that was because of the weather or because I knew what was going to happen. Either way, there was tension in the air.

Gunny and I got back to the Manhattan Tower Hotel as quickly as we could.

But as soon as we got back to our room on the sixth floor, things began to unravel. Spader was gone. He'd left a note for us.

Pendragon and Gunny,

I'm writing this on the morning of May 6. When you two didn't return in time, I thought for sure we had failed. But I heard on the radio-talk-thing that the Hindenburg has been delayed. I'm sorry, mates, I can't wait for you any longer. I'm going to New Jersey on my own. I found out how to take a bus, so that's what I'll do. I promise, I'll do all that I can to save that airship from being destroyed.

Hobey-ho,
Spader

"He's on his way to New Jersey," I shouted to Gunny. "I *knew* we should have stayed together!" I threw the note down in anger.

"It's early," Gunny said reassuringly. "We've got all day to figure something out."

"Yeah, but do you know what this means? Max Rose knows about Winn Farrow's plan. Spader told him, remember? History has already been changed. Strike one. Now Spader's on his own. He's going after Winn Farrow to stop him too. Strike two. Now we've got to stop Max Rose *and* Spader."

"There's a lot that can happen before strike three," Gunny said calmly. "I think the first thing we should do is go see Max Rose."

"Why?" I asked.

"He trusts you. Maybe we can find out how he plans on stopping Winn Farrow."

Okay, that made sense. At least one of us was thinking clearly. It sure wasn't me.

"We'll find out what we can," Gunny continued. "Then we'll take Caplesmith's car and drive down to New Jersey. We might even beat Spader there."

I nodded. This sounded like a plan.

"You all right now?" Gunny asked.

"Yeah, I'm cool," I answered. My heart rate was dropping back down from three hundred beats a minute.

"A wise person once said that the only way we've got a chance here is if we keep our heads screwed on straight and work it through, together."

I looked at Gunny and smiled. "I said that."

"Was that you, shorty?" Gunny asked in fake surprise. "I knew I heard it somewhere."

"Okay, I hear you," I said. "My act is officially back together."

We took the elevator up to the thirtieth floor to see Max Rose. I had no idea what we'd say to him, but it was the obvious place to start. We'd have to wing it once we got there. When we hit the elevator, Dewey looked all sorts of confused.

"What's goin' on?" he asked.

"What do you mean?" Gunny asked him.

"Men have been coming and going from the penthouse all day," Dewey said. "Is Max Rose moving out?"

Gunny and I shared glances. Whatever Max Rose's plan

was to stop Winn Farrow, it was under way. The elevator arrived and Gunny and I jumped out. As usual, Dewey closed the door quickly. It was like he thought the floor was haunted or something.

As soon as we entered the hallway, we knew something was wrong. That's because the two thugs who worked security were gone. There was nobody around to protect Max Rose. Gunny and I ran for the door to the penthouse. We stopped, caught our breath so it wouldn't seem like we were as excited as we were, and rang the doorbell. No answer. We rang again. Nobody came to the door. Gunny then noticed that the door wasn't even closed. He gave it a push with his finger and the door creaked open.

"Hello?" Gunny called. "Bell Captain!"

No response. We took a chance and went inside. Nothing looked out of the ordinary, except that nobody was around.

"Hello?" Gunny called again. Still no answer.

"Do you smell that?" I asked.

Gunny took a whiff. "Smoke," he said.

We both looked around quickly and Gunny spotted it first. Smoke was creeping out from under the door to Max Rose's office. We ran for the door and I threw it open. Instantly billows of smoke blew out. The room was on fire.

"I'll get the hose," Gunny shouted, and ran back into the corridor. A few seconds later he came back into the penthouse pulling a heavy fire hose. "Go turn it on!" he ordered me.

"Don't close that door," I yelled. "It locks automatically."

I ran back to the hallway, following the hose to the source. I quickly cranked the handle and the limp hose jumped to life. I sprinted back into the penthouse in time to see Gunny expertly killing the fire. Billows of smoke and steam blew out from the room as he doused the flames. Seconds later it was over.

"Okay," he announced. "Turn it off."

I ran into the corridor and turned off the water, then returned to the office to check out the damage. What a mess. It looked like the inside of a barbeque grill. It didn't smell so great either. Luckily all the damage was contained in the one room. A few minutes more, though, and it would have spread.

"This was deliberate," Gunny said. He kicked at a few garbage pails that were full of ashes and water. "Burning evidence is my guess."

I saw that the file cabinets were open and empty. The desk drawers were empty too. Max Rose was covering his tracks. Every bit of paper in this room was now a charred memory. There was nothing left that might connect him with his network of spies, or with the Nazis.

"I guess this means everybody's gone," I said.

"Probably," Gunny said. "We should do a quick check though."

We left the wet, smoldering mess and searched the penthouse for signs of life. We checked bedrooms, sitting rooms, the kitchen, and the dining room. Not only were there no people, all the drawers had been emptied too. Max Rose had definitely pulled up stakes and moved out. We knew where he was going, too. He had a date with a zeppelin.

The final stop on our search was the grand living room where I had set out lunch for Rose and the Nazi, Ludwig Zell. Nobody was in there, either.

Gunny said, "We're wasting our time here. I'll get Caplesmith's car so we can get down to—"

We then heard a sound that made the hair go up on the back of my neck. It was the steady sound of somebody clapping.

There was someone in the penthouse after all. Gunny and I looked at each other, then slowly turned toward the door. Standing there looking as beautiful as ever was Esther Amaden. Her friends called her Harlow. Her enemies called her Saint Dane. She was clapping in mock approval.

"Congratulations, boys," the bogus woman purred. "I'm guessing you finally solved the riddle."

"At least have the guts to show yourself," I said defiantly.

The beautiful woman closed the door behind her. Gunny shot me a curious look. It was hard for him to believe that this movie-star-gorgeous woman could be the demon Traveler who was about to turn three territories into rubble. But I knew better. I'd seen it before.

"Whatever you'd like, Pendragon," she said with a smile.

Esther Amaden then went through the transformation that I had seen too many times. Her body became fluid as she left behind the image of the beautiful big-band singer. Her body grew taller until it was near seven feet. Her rosy complexion turned the pasty white color of a corpse. Her short dark hair grew out into a long, gray mane. Her silky bathrobe turned black and changed shape into a black suit that, as I've written before, looked vaguely Asian. The final step was always the toughest to watch. It was the eyes. Harlow's soft, dreamy brown eyes turned razor sharp. They took on the icy blue fire of our nemesis—Saint Dane.

I sensed Gunny's surprise and fear. He took a step back. This was the first time he'd witnessed this transformation. It was also the first time he was seeing Saint Dane in his true form.

"Better?" Saint Dane hissed through a twisted smile. "We really don't spend enough time together, Pendragon, do we?"

It took every bit of willpower I had not to scream.

FIRST EARTH

"I'm disappointed in you, Pendragon," Saint Dane said. "I've left so many clues for you like breadcrumbs in the forest, and it's still taken you all this time to uncover my little plot. Time is growing short. Are you losing interest?"

Saint Dane walked casually around the room with his hands clasped behind his back. Gunny and I kept our distance. It was like being trapped in a room with a wild animal. You never knew what this guy was going to do.

"I suppose the loss of your uncle's sage guidance has made it all the more difficult for you to keep up with me."

Oh, man. This guy loved to hit where it hurt the most.

He then added, "I must admit, you surprised me on both Denduron and Cloral."

"Why's that?" I asked.

"You were a force to be reckoned with. For that, I bow to you. And I must apologize for my own foolishness. It was a mistake to ask you to join me on my quest."

"You got that right," I said quickly. "No way I'll ever join you."

Saint Dane stopped walking and smiled. He was enjoying this.

I wasn't.

"You misunderstand," he said. "My only mistake was asking you too early. It gave you the impression that I was somehow . . . vulnerable." He chuckled. "I assure you, I am not. That's why I chose to play out this latest game on the Earth territories. *Your* home territories. I wanted to demonstrate how easy it is for me to make you dance like a toy puppet. *My* toy puppet. In spite of what you may think due to our past encounters, I am in total control."

"You aren't in control," Gunny said with authority. "Not anymore."

Saint Dane let out a deep, bellowing laugh. I hated that.

"Such an amusing old man," Saint Dane chuckled.

"Old enough to know how to handle the likes of you," Gunny shot back.

"Oooh," Saint Dane bellowed in mock fear. "Forgive me if I don't feel threatened by an old man who doesn't possess the courage to fire a weapon."

"You think you're bothering me," Gunny said without missing a beat. "But you're not."

"Stick around, Gunny," Saint Dane snapped back at him. "By the time we're done, I promise, you will be very, very bothered."

Saint Dane walked to the glass doors that led to the balcony. He threw them open, letting in a chilly wind. He stood with his back to us, looking out over the gray city.

"You see, Pendragon, my victory here on First Earth means much more than the toppling of three territories. What makes this all so wonderfully special is, you're the one who is doing it for me."

That was a strange comment. I didn't like it, one bit.

"We know what's going on, Saint Dane," I said. "We know what will happen if the *Hindenburg* doesn't crash. We went to Third Earth."

Saint Dane spun back to us and exclaimed, "Well, of course you went to Third Earth! I was counting on it. I *wanted* you to know what would happen."

That wasn't the reaction I expected. Gunny and I shot each other a quick look.

Saint Dane chuckled and said, "You still don't understand, do you? I've been leading you and your band of merry men around like trained dogs. Everything that's happened, every turn, every surprise, I've orchestrated. You knew to follow me to First Earth because of the bullets that killed your uncle. But to be sure, I first went to Veelox. That annoying Traveler girl thought she was being so clever by recording my arrival. I couldn't have been any clearer in telegraphing my ultimate destination if I had painted a sign on my back."

I thought back to the hologram that Aja Killian showed us of Saint Dane arriving at the flume on Veelox, then making a show of calling out "First Earth!" before leaving again. Now that I think of it, it *was* pretty obvious.

"Once you were here, my only challenge was to make sure you discovered Winn Farrow's plot to destroy the *Hindenburg*. I knew that once you learned of his plan, you'd do everything possible to prevent that ship from blowing up. The idea of innocent lives being lost is just too horrible a concept for your righteous mind to accept."

As Saint Dane spoke, I thought back to the events that led us to crossing paths with Winn Farrow.

"The gangsters in the subway?" I asked.

"I brought them to the flume to put you on the trail of

Winn Farrow," he answered. "Killing Press was a bonus."

I forced myself not to let that throw me.

"But they tried to kill us. Twice."

"They were supposed to warn you to stay away from Winn Farrow, which I knew would send you running to him like rats to garbage. Killing you was their idea. Idiots. That's why I had to dispose of one of them. Or should I say, Harlow had to."

"The gangster who fell from the hotel was pushed by Harlow? I mean, by you?" Gunny asked in surprise.

Saint Dane answered with a proud bow. Now we knew how Mr. Nasty Gangster died. It was Saint Dane.

"I couldn't let him kill you," he said. "Not before my drama played out. You might say I was your guardian angel, Pendragon."

"In the slaughterhouse," I said, remembering. "You left the door open so we could escape."

"Again, guilty," he said, gloating.

He then took a step back, and transformed. His body grew watery and in a few seconds he became . . . Ludwig Zell.

"You were Zell, too?" I shouted in surprise.

"Not until recently," Zell/Saint Dane said. "Once Max Rose learned of the plot to destroy the *Hindenburg*, I knew he would warn Herr Zell."

Zell/Saint Dane walked over to a closet door.

"I couldn't have our Nazi friend sending the zeppelin back to Germany, so I had to intervene."

Zell/Saint Dane opened the door and a body rolled out. It was Ludwig Zell. The *real* Ludwig Zell. He was pretty dead. No matter how many times I see dead guys, I can't get used to it.

"Poor Ludwig was in the wrong place at the wrong time. Max Rose thought he was giving his Nazi cohort the bad news, but he was actually telling me."

The truth was rushing at me way too fast. I was getting dizzy.

"But why?" I asked. "If Ludwig Zell warned Germany, the *Hindenburg* would be saved. That's what you want, isn't it? What difference would it make *how* it was saved?"

Zell/Saint Dane's attitude grew dark. He took a step toward me, and as he did, he transformed back into his evil-looking self. His horrid eyes locked on mine and he spoke through clenched teeth.

"Because this is about *you*, Pendragon!" he seethed. "I don't care what happens to that airship. I don't care what happens to these pathetic Earth territories. I don't care who wins their silly war or what they do with this useless world afterward."

"You don't?" I said, totally confused.

"In a few short hours the course of your world will be changed forever. The Earth territories will fall into chaos. And who will be to blame? You! If you hadn't come here to stop me, history would have played out the way it was intended. But you couldn't stay away. You put yourself into the equation and because of that, three territories will collapse. Your *home* will collapse."

I stared into Saint Dane's fierce eyes. I'm not sure which I was more afraid of: him or the horror to come. Everything he said was true. If Spader and I hadn't chased him to First Earth, the *Hindenburg* would be destined to crash, the way it was supposed to. But now, because of my meddling, there was a good chance the *Hindenburg* would be saved and the Earth territories doomed. This whole adventure was to prove how easily Saint Dane could manipulate us. Manipulate *me*. The amazing thing was, he was willing to destroy three territories to do it.

Saint Dane then said, "How does it feel, knowing this was all for you?"

The two of us held eye contact. In that one, horrible moment, things became all too clear. I knew where the struggle between Saint Dane and the Travelers was headed. Someday, somehow, somewhere, it was going to come down to Saint Dane . . .

And me. That's why he was doing his best to prove himself to me. What a sickening thought. The only thing that kept me from losing it was knowing that the ultimate day of reckoning wasn't today. No, this was far from over.

"I'll tell you how it makes me feel," I answered with a very small voice. "I feel that as long as you're trying to impress me, I can beat you."

There was a frozen moment.

"You think you understand me?" he said. "You think you have the strength to bring me down? Talk to me again in a few hours, after you've gone to Second Earth to see the scorched world where your friends used to live. Everything you've ever loved will no longer exist, Pendragon. Your home will be turned into a charred pit of death . . . and it will be your fault."

"We still have time," I said. "We can still make sure the *Hindenburg* crashes."

An odd thing happened then. Saint Dane smiled. It wasn't like the sly, knowing smiles he usually threw at me. This was a genuine, wide, Cheshire-cat grin. The guy was actually happy. Being that it was Saint Dane, a sincere smile seemed all the more grotesque. It was totally creepy.

"Yes," he said. "You still have time. Please, make the most of it."

He backed away from me and walked over to the door. He turned the knob and gave a look of mock surprise. "Oh, no, it's locked." he announced. "Max Rose is so paranoid. He's made all of these doors self-locking. But you already knew that, didn't you?"

He then reached into his pocket and pulled out an old-fashioned brass key. He waved it at us, taunting us.

"But no fear," he said. "I've got the key." Saint Dane walked out on the balcony. "Do you think you can stop it, Pendragon?" he asked. "If I let you out of here, do you think you can stop Spader? And Rose? Could you let the *Hindenburg* crash?"

"We can try," I said.

"Of course you can," Saint Dane said as he backed toward the edge of the balcony. "And I want you to. I want you to come close. I want you to feel as if you've beaten me one more time, because that's when victory is the sweetest . . . when your opponent feels as if he actually has a chance to win, just before it all comes crashing down."

He looked out over the city and said, "I think I'll return to Veelox and see what trouble I can stir up. That little girl Traveler is even more sure of herself than you, Pendragon. She's in for a big surprise." He was at the edge of the balcony now.

"Good-bye, my friends. Enjoy your afternoon." Saint Dane gave an exaggerated bow, and in one graceful move, jumped up and off the balcony!

Gunny and I gave each other a quick, unbelieving glance, then ran for the railing. Just as we were about to look over the side, a huge, black raven rose up from below. I swear, it was the biggest crow I had ever seen in my life. It was more like the size of an eagle. The bird rose as if riding on thermals. Then with one quick snap of its wings, it turned and sailed off. But the instant before it left, I saw that it was holding something in its curved beak. It was only a quick flash, but I was certain I had seen it.

It was an old-fashioned brass key.

"You don't think—?" Gunny asked.

"I don't know," I answered. "I don't care. We've got to get outta here."

I ran back into the apartment and over to the door. I tried the knob to make sure it was locked. It was. I took a quick look around and saw another door. I ran to that one. Yeah, it was locked too. Those two doors were the only way out of this room.

"We'll have to break 'em down!" I announced.

I was all set to put my shoulder to the door and start bashing away, when Gunny warned, "Don't!"

"We have to!" I shouted.

"We'll never break those doors down," Gunny said. "Max Rose had them reinforced with steel. This was his fortress. You couldn't knock them down with a battering ram."

I quickly scanned the living room, looking for another way out . . . and saw the telephone. I grabbed it, only to find it was dead.

"He cut the phone lines," I announced. I then looked at my watch. It was almost noon. "Gunny, we're running out of time."

The *Hindenburg* was going to arrive in nine hours.

FIRST EARTH

"This is your hotel!" I shouted. "How do we get out of here? There must be some kind of emergency way to let people know we're in here."

Gunny looked around the fancy living room, then shook his head. "Not if the telephone's out."

This was insane. The world was about to collapse and we were locked in a dumb hotel room.

"I got it!" I shouted. "We can start a fire. It'll set off the smoke detectors."

Gunny gave me a strange look. "What's a smoke detector?"

Oh yeah. 1937. I looked around the room, then ran out on the balcony. Looking over the edge, I hoped to see Saint Dane's smashed body lying on the pavement below. It wasn't. I don't know why, but I wasn't surprised. I thought about that big raven. How weird was that? But I couldn't obsess about it. We had to get out of there.

I looked down to see if there was a ledge we could crawl out on. But the closest foothold was thirty floors down. On the sidewalk. I looked up, thinking we might be able to climb onto the roof. No go. It was out of reach. We really were trapped.

I have to admit, I even stood there for a second and tried to change myself into a raven. What the heck? If Saint Dane was a Traveler and he could do it, maybe I could too.

I couldn't. But just the fact that I tried showed how desperate I was.

I ran back into the room to see that Gunny had come up with a brilliant plan. A dangerous plan, but a brilliant one. He was pulling down the drapes that hung on either side of the balcony doors. With his pocketknife he cut a small tear on one end to get started, then ripped off a long strip of fabric. I knew instantly what he wanted to do. We were going to make a lifeline.

"You keep cutting strips," he ordered. "I'll tie the knots."

I set to work with his knife, tearing off long strips of fabric. Gunny expertly knotted the ends together.

"There's another balcony below us, about thirty feet down," Gunny explained. He then pulled on the fabric, testing its strength. "I'll tie one end onto the railing up here, then lower myself down."

This was a plan. As good as any. But as I cut the pieces of fabric, I knew there was only one thing wrong with it.

"This is gonna work, Gunny," I said. "But you're too heavy. This won't hold you."

"It'll have to," Gunny said quickly. "Because I'm not sending you over the side."

We continued working for a few minutes, until Gunny had fashioned a rope that looked plenty long enough. I tugged on it. It was strong, but still had a little play. Gunny was six foot four and probably weighed 220 pounds. I was five foot five and weighed half that much.

"Gunny, if you go, this'll tear," I said.

Gunny tested the rope himself. I could tell by his

expression he didn't think it would hold his weight either.

"I'm light," I added. "It'll hold me."

I didn't wait for his response. I started tying one end around my chest and under my arms. I had to do it fast, not because I thought Gunny would stop me, but because I was afraid I'd chicken out if I thought too much about it. We were thirty floors up. My mind flashed on the horrible sight of Mr. Nasty Gangster falling through the air.

Note to self: Stop thinking.

"No, Pendragon, I can't let you—"

"We don't have a whole lot of choices," I interrupted. "Either I go, or we hang out here until the housekeeping staff finds us tomorrow morning."

Gunny looked at the floor. If there were any other way around this, he would have taken it. But he knew I was right.

"Let's do it," I said, and carried the makeshift rope out on the balcony.

Gunny tied the loose end securely around the balcony railing. He knew what he was doing. Maybe it was his army training. I trusted that his knots would hold. It was the drape material I wasn't so sure about.

"You're in control," he instructed. "Grab on to the rope near the railing, face the building, keep your feet against the wall and walk backwards. Let the rope move through your hands as you go down. I'll handle the slack."

"I've done this," I said. "It's sort of like rappelling."

Uncle Press had taught me how to rock climb. It seemed like things kept popping up that Uncle Press had prepared me for. I always thought he took me on those great adventures because he was a fun uncle. I had no idea he was training me for life as a Traveler. Because we had gone on a rock-climbing trip when I was twelve, I knew how to rappel down the side of a sheer rock face. The only difference here was, I wasn't secured by a solid climber's rope. I was trusting my life to a raggy piece of drapery. Gulp.

I sat up on the railing and swung my legs over. I made sure not to look down. I didn't need to see how far I would fall if things went south, so to speak. So while pretending I was only a few feet up in the air, I carefully turned around. I stood with my toes on the balcony, holding on to the rail, looking back at Gunny. It all seemed so natural, except that he was standing on the safe side of the railing and my butt was dangling over midtown Manhattan.

"Can of corn," he said reassuringly. But his eyes gave him away. He was scared. Probably not as much as I was, though.

Gunny then threaded the slack rope through the railing and pulled my end tight. As I lowered myself down, he would play out my end of the rope, keeping pressure off the railing knot. It was like being double-secured. At least, that's what I told myself.

I tested the strength of the cloth rope, nodded, and stepped down off the balcony. With my feet firmly planted on the wall, I began to walk down backward.

I flashed on the old *Batman* TV show where those guys used to walk up the sides of buildings with their Bat ropes. That was idiotic. But not as idiotic as what I was doing now. I held the cloth rope tightly, and slowly slid my hands down it as I moved. The only tricky part came when I got to one of Gunny's knots. They were too big to slip through my clenched hands, so I had to let go with one hand at a time and cross over below it. That was scary.

I could hear the cloth rope straining under my weight. Obviously, this material wasn't made to hold so much weight, because I kept hearing tiny little tearing sounds. They were faint, but they might as well have been exploding cherry bombs. If enough of those little tears got together, they'd make one big rip and, well, look out below.

Just to make me even more nervous, I looked up to see that Gunny didn't have enough drape left to hold on to. I wasn't double-secured anymore.

The whole trip only took a couple of minutes, though it felt like I was dangling from that building for a week. Finally I slid my right foot down another few inches and felt air. I had made it to the ceiling of the balcony below! I couldn't see the balcony because it was cut *in* to the building, but I knew it was there. My foot told me so. I was almost home.

That's when the bad news came.

No, the rope didn't break. It wasn't that bad. But it was close. I had another six feet to go before my feet would touch the railing of the balcony below, when I realized the worst: I had run out of rope. We made it too short! I dangled there, twenty-nine stories high over pavement, with the wind blowing and drops of rain beginning to fall . . . with nowhere to go.

"It's too short!" I called up to Gunny. "I can't go any lower."

Gunny winced. "You sure?"

"Uh, yeah." It didn't take a genius to figure this one out.

"You're going to have to climb back up," Gunny called down.

This was a disaster. We blew it. How could we have made such a simple mistake? I had to climb back up and figure out a Plan B. But as soon as I reached my hand farther up the rope, I felt it tear again. It wasn't a little tear either. I must have jolted down an inch. The rope was going to go! If I tried to climb back up, I wouldn't make it very far. I was trapped. There was no place to go but down. Way down.

I then realized that I had one chance. It was horrifying to

think of, but it was the only way. Without stopping to second guess, I grabbed higher up on the rope with one hand and pulled up to take some of my weight off the rope. I then began to untie the knot that secured the rope around my chest.

"Pendragon, what are you doing?" Gunny shouted in horror.

"I need more rope," I called back. "This'll give me another couple of feet."

It was a totally scary maneuver. If I could untie the knot, I could use the extra length of rope that was wrapped around my chest to lower myself down a few more feet. Hopefully that would get me low enough to touch my feet to the railing and swing into the balcony.

Yeah, hopefully. It could also be suicide.

I had to pull myself up with one hand, and untie the knot with the other. To make things worse, if that's possible, the knot was now squeezed into a tiny, tight ball because my whole weight had been pulling on it.

And it started to rain.

The fabric was getting wet and slick. This was insane.

So with one hand I pulled myself up; with the other hand I worked on the knot. It was really hard. After a few minutes my arm started to scream with pain from the stress. I wasn't sure which was going to give out first, my arm or the rope. But I couldn't rest. If I put my weight back on the rope, the knot would pull tight and I'd have to start over.

This was quickly looking like a very bad idea.

After a few agonizing minutes, I managed to loosen up the knot. The next step was the scary one. My right arm was shot. I had to reach up and grab the rope with my left arm to give it a rest. I couldn't let my full weight back on the rope now. The knot was too loose. If I let go, the only thing that would break my fall was the pavement.

With a couple of quick tugs, I pulled the knot entirely free, then grabbed the rope with both hands. I was now hanging by my hands. My really tired hands. I then slipped down a few inches at a time, letting the slick rope slide through my hands. The pain was incredible. I was so tired.

I checked to see how much of the rope was left and saw about a foot until the end. This was going to be close. Then, with only a few inches of rope left, I felt the railing with my toe. I was there!

But I wasn't safe yet. My arms were straight up over my head and I was still staring at building. I was so freakin' close, but still not low enough to swing in. I was going to have to put my full weight on the rail, let go of the rope, and duck under the ceiling. Sounds easy, right? It wasn't. It was totally awkward. Making it worse, the narrow rail was slick with rain.

I eased myself down until my feet were resting on the rail. Man, it felt great to be on something solid again. There wasn't much more than an inch of rope left, but that was okay. For the first time, I thought I was going to make it. I gingerly let go of the rope, putting all my weight on my feet. I then started to crouch down to duck under the ceiling and jump onto the balcony when . . .

My feet slipped.

It all went so fast that I'm not exactly sure what happened. Luckily, when my feet went off the rail, they slipped toward the balcony side, not toward air. That saved my life. But when I fell, I was so close to the rail that my head thumped against the hard, slick metal.

Our escape plan had worked, but we weren't any closer to getting out of there, because that head slam knocked me straight into dreamland.

I found myself lying on a beach. It was the Point in Stony Brook. Best beach in the world. At least it was the best beach in Stony Brook. Mark, how many times did we ride our bikes there to hang out for hours, watching the girls? I can still picture that pink bikini Courtney got last summer. Courtney, hot suit. Yeah, I was lying in the sand at the Point, listening to the waves, kicking back, hanging.

When I opened my eyes I expected to see you, Mark. Or Courtney, or any of the other kids from class, kicking it right along with me. Instead, I saw Dewey.

His eyes were as big as baseballs as he stared down at me.

"Pendragon!" he shouted, all nervous. "Are you alive?"

I wasn't sure. But dead people didn't get headaches, so I figured I was still among the living. I slowly sat up and looked around. All thoughts of the beach at Stony Brook and Courtney's pink bikini were long gone. Oh, well. Dewey's face pretty much ended that. Instead, I saw that I was lying on the floor of the ballroom on the twenty-ninth floor of the hotel. It was the same ballroom where we saved Max Rose's life. It was empty now, except for Dewey and me.

"I was gonna call a doctor, but Gunny told me not to," Dewey whined. "You want me to get one?"

"No," I said quickly. I probably needed one, but now wasn't the time. "I'm fine. Where's Gunny?"

"Downstairs. He told me to wait with you till he got back. Did you really climb down that drapery?"

It all came back to me—Saint Dane, being locked in the penthouse, Ludwig Zell, the trip down the rope, the fall. I really wished I were on that beach in Stony Brook.

"One of the cooks found you lying here," Dewey said. "But you were out cold. He saw the rope hanging down and found Gunny upstairs. Pendragon, there's a dead body up there! Who is that? How did you two get locked in the penthouse?"

"Long story," I said. Then another thought hit me. "What time is it?"

Dewey looked at his watch and said, "Almost three o'clock."

Yeow. If I wasn't awake before, I was now. I had been out for hours! The *Hindenburg* was going to arrive in four hours and we were still in Manhattan!

"I gotta get outta here," I said as I tried to get up. But the pain shot through my head like a bolt of lightning. It pushed me right back down to the floor.

"Don't move," Dewey said. "I'll get you some water." He ran off, leaving me alone.

This was bad. Very bad. Where was Gunny? I forced myself to sit up, then pulled myself into a chair. I had to get my act together and down to New Jersey, or everything would be lost. The *Hindenburg* was going to land at 7:25. Gunny said it was a four-hour drive down to Lakehurst. Even if we left at that very minute, we still wouldn't get down there until almost seven o'clock. That wouldn't leave much time to figure a way to stop Spader and Max Rose.

"We're in trouble," came a voice from behind me. It was Gunny. He jogged across the ballroom toward me.

"I've been out for hours, Gunny! Why didn't you wake me up?"

"Because I was trying to find us a ride down to New Jersey," was his answer.

Good answer.

"I didn't find one," he added.

Ooh, bad answer.

"What do you mean? What about Caplesmith's car?"

"I went to the fella who's been fixing it. It's in pieces all over the garage floor. He said it would take him half a day to put it back together."

"Then we'll take the bus. Gunny, we gotta get down there."

"That's not good," Gunny answered. "The last bus going down that way today left at noon."

"What about a train?" I asked.

"Still no good. Earliest we could get down there would be tomorrow morning."

"This is incredible!" I shouted, jumping up. Bad move. Another bolt of pain shot through my head. It didn't stop my tirade though. "Three territories are going to crumble because we can't get a ride?"

"I'm sorry, Pendragon," Gunny said. "Unless you know some way of flying down there, we're out of luck."

I stopped short. My bruised brain raced. Gunny had said the magic word. Flying.

"C'mon," I said, and ran for the elevator. Gunny was right behind me. We blew right past Dewey, who was headed toward us with a glass of water.

"Where you going?" he asked.

I grabbed him by the arm and pulled him along. After all, he ran the elevator.

Five minutes later we were standing in front of room 1515. I knocked and closed my eyes. I had no idea if she was still staying at the hotel, but this was our last hope. After a few agonizing seconds, the door opened and we stood facing Jinx Olsen.

"Pendragon! Gunny! Here to say good-bye?" she exclaimed. "Come on in." She walked back into her room, where I saw all of her clothes spread out on the bed. She was packing up her duffel bag.

"You're leaving?" I asked.

"Just got the word," she said. "This is it. End of the line. I am officially off active duty." She said this like it was cheery news, but I knew it was eating her up. "I'm headed home to Maine. And you know what? I'm taking the train. Why not? Something different, right?"

Jinx continued to pack. I looked at Gunny. He gave me a nod of encouragement. I wasn't exactly sure what to say, but I had to think of something fast.

"Jinx," I began. "We need a favor."

"Whatever I can do, boys," she answered.

"Can you fly us somewhere?"

Jinx stopped packing. She looked at me, as if it were a strange request, then sat down on the edge of the bed.

"I told you, Pendragon, I'm grounded. No more joy rides."

"This isn't a joy ride," I said. I tried to be as convincing as possible. "We need to get down to Lakehurst, New Jersey."

"Lakehurst?" she said. "That's where the dirigibles come in. The *Hindenburg* is due today."

"Exactly," I said.

"What's so important? You want to be there with all the other lookey-loos to see her float in? To be honest, I think those blimps are a lot of hot air. Get it? Hot air."

I got it. I wasn't laughing.

"That's not it," I said seriously. "I don't really know how to say this. It's a long story and there's no way you'd believe it. But what I'm going to tell you is the absolute truth. If we don't get down there right away, I mean now, something horrible is going to happen that I can't even begin to describe."

"Really?" she said with surprise and a touch of curiosity. "What is it?"

"I can't tell you. I know that sounds stupid, but it's the truth. I'll tell you this much, though, we're asking you to fly the most important mission taken by any pilot, man or woman, ever. I'm not exaggerating."

"He's telling you the truth, ma'am," Gunny added.

It was now up to Jinx. I want to say that it was my brilliant powers of persuasion that convinced her to take us. I want to say that I was smart enough to know she wanted to do something important with her flying and not just be a sideshow. I even want to say I used my Traveler mind powers to convince her. I want to say all those things, but none of them would be true.

"To be honest, Pendragon," she said, "you didn't have to tell me all that other stuff. I was ready to go the second you asked me if I'd fly you somewhere."

I had to smile. Could Jinx be any cooler? "You aren't worried about the Coast Guard?" I asked.

"Nah," she scoffed. "What are they going to do? Ground me? If I've gotta go, I'm goin' out with a bang!"

It was nearly an hour later when we found ourselves strapped into Jinx's V-157 Schreck/Viking, ready for takeoff. I was in the front cockpit next to Jinx because Gunny was a much bigger guy than Spader. He needed the rear cockpit all to himself. The monster engine pounded away as we bounced over the swells of the Hudson River. The weather was still nasty, so the water was pretty choppy. My aching head throbbed each time we hit a swell. I was miserable, but had to gut it out. My bigger worry was that if the weather got any worse than this, I didn't think we'd be able to take off. I looked to the sky and saw that there were still thunderstorms dancing around.

"Can you fly in this weather?" I shouted to Jinx over the roar of the engine.

Jinx gave a quick look around, then said, "What weather?"

That was good enough for me. It was now almost 4:30 P.M. The flight was going to take about an hour and a half, getting us to Lakehurst around 6:00 P.M. The *Hindenburg* was going to land at 7:25 P.M. Not much time to find Spader and Max Rose and figure out a way to stop them. We were cutting it very close.

I looked back at Gunny and shouted, "You ready?"

Gunny was doubled over in the back, puking. He looked up, smiled, and gave me a thumbs up. It was going to be a long flight. Jinx gunned the throttle, the plane bounced over the swells, and after a gut-rumbling thirty seconds, we were airborne.

Just as I feared, the flight was ugly. The little plane was constantly buffeted by gusts of wind and downdrafts. Jinx tried to fly at different altitudes, searching for smooth air, but nothing helped.

Most of the time, we were flying blind. The gray, angry clouds were thick and low. Every time we entered one, I gritted my teeth and held my breath. If there were another plane coming from the other direction, we'd be history. But this was 1937. There wasn't as much air traffic back then, so we were fairly safe. At least that's what I kept telling myself.

A few times I looked back to check on Gunny. The poor guy was having a rough time. His face looked green, but he still gave me a brave thumbs up. At one point I wondered if Gunny thought the thumbs up meant "I'm going to puke again," because that's pretty much all he was doing.

They didn't have radio beacons or radar back in those days. All Jinx had to navigate was a compass, her eyes, and a great sense of direction. As it turned out, she had been down to Lakehurst before, so she knew what landmarks to follow. I think back on that flight and I realize that Jinx's cockiness was deserved. She really was a great pilot. It was too bad nobody recognized her for it.

There was one whopper of a hairy moment that still makes my palms sweaty when I think back on it. We had been flying for almost two hours. That was bad. The flight was taking way longer than Jinx figured. It was because of the weather. We were fighting head winds the whole way. I was getting more anxious by the second.

We then entered a huge cloud bank. This was the darkest, longest one we had been in yet. I kept looking ahead, praying to see light on the far side that would mean we were about to break out. But it wasn't coming. This cloud was huge. No sooner did we enter than we were pelted with more rain. Remember, we were in open cockpits. When it rained, we got wet. We had to keep wiping off our goggles or we would have been totally blinded. I kept reaching forward to wipe off the glass shield in front of Jinx so she could see better. Total waste of time. Visibility was pretty much zero.

I had just finished wiping off the windshield and sat back in my seat, when I saw something that made me stop breathing. There in front of us, only a few yards ahead, was a sight so unbelievable I thought I was imagining it. But I wasn't. It was a giant, floating, black swastika on a white circle, surrounded by a red field.

"Look out!" I shouted.

Jinx banked the plane hard to the right. The engine

groaned, the g force built up so hard that I was crushed back into the seat. I think our wings went vertical. I shut my eyes, ready for the collision, but it never came. Jinx had dodged it. It wasn't until a second later that I realized what we had nearly hit.

It was the tail of the *Hindenburg.*

It had crossed right in front of us. We didn't see it because of the cloud, and we didn't hear it because our own engine drowned out its engines. I swear, we couldn't have missed it by more than a few inches.

Jinx looked at me and smiled. "That was exciting."

Exciting. Okay, that was one word for it. I looked back at Gunny . . . and he wasn't there! My first thought was that he had fallen out. But a second later he sat up and looked at me with watery eyes. He had been doubled over, losing it once again. He couldn't even give me the thumbs up this time. The poor guy wouldn't be the same until his feet were back on solid ground.

"Does that mean we're getting close to the field?" I shouted to Jinx.

"We've still got a few minutes," Jinx shouted back.

That's when we finally blasted out of the cloud bank. I looked down to the ground and saw something that made me sit up straight. It was a long, silver bus moving along the narrow highway. This was a pretty empty section of New Jersey. There wasn't a whole lot of traffic down here. I motioned for Gunny to look down.

"Could that be the bus Spader is on?" I shouted.

Gunny looked, then nodded and gave the thumbs up. Either this was the bus, or he had to puke again. I figured it was the bus. It was a huge stroke of luck. If we could get to Spader, we could stop him from going after Winn Farrow.

Then all we would have to worry about was Max Rose. I quickly turned to Jinx.

"You gotta put us down," I shouted.

"What?" she shouted back. "Why?"

"We've got to get to that bus!" I shouted over the roar of the engine.

Jinx looked down at the ground. She banked the plane right, then left, so she could get a view of the landscape.

"Can't do it, Pendragon," she shouted back. "There's no place to put down."

"Are you sure?" I asked.

"I'm sorry. I would if I could," was her answer. "I won't be able to land until we get to the air station."

That would be too late. I needed to get to Spader now, before he had the chance to mess with Winn Farrow's plans. Stopping him was going to be half the battle. This could very well be the critical moment of the mission. I didn't want to blow it. There had to be a way.

A few seconds later, it came to me. I once again remembered an adventure I had with Uncle Press. Like I wrote before, I now understood that he was preparing me for my life as a Traveler. I learned a lot of skills through him, and I was about to put another one to use. The idea scared me to death, but I knew I could do it. I had to.

"Fly ahead of the bus," I yelled to Jinx.

Jinx didn't question. She gunned the throttle and shot forward. I glanced over at the plane's altimeter to see we were flying at three thousand feet. I then asked her, "Are these parachutes okay?"

She gave me a sideways look and said, "Of course. I packed 'em myself. Don't worry, you won't have to use it."

That's where she was wrong.

"Thanks, Jinx. Make sure Gunny gets to the airfield," I said.

Jinx gave me a strange look. She had no idea what I was talking about. I turned back to Gunny and shouted, "I'll see you at the airfield."

Gunny gave me a strange look. He didn't know what I was talking about either. How could he? There was no way either of them would think in a million years that I was about to do what I was about to do. I glanced at the altimeter and saw we were still at three thousand feet. That was plenty high enough to make a safe jump. At least that's what the book said. Before I had the chance to convince myself I was being an idiot, I clicked out of my seat buckle and turned to Jinx.

"Thanks for the ride, Jinx," I said.

"What are you doing?" she shouted back, stunned.

I showed her. With one quick move I launched myself up and out of the cockpit. A second later I was freefalling through the clouds, really hoping that Jinx was as good at packing parachutes as she was at flying airplanes.

FIRST EARTH

Before today I'd jumped out of a plane exactly three times. Each time I had other, experienced divers with me and always used a static line. That was a line on my ripcord that stayed attached to the plane. After falling for only a few seconds, the static line automatically pulled the ripcord and the parachute came out. I think they do that with new divers to make sure they don't freak and forget to pull the cord. Yeah, right, like there's any chance of *that* happening.

Now, jumping out of Jinx's plane, I was totally on my own. I thought back to all the instruction I'd had. I was taught proper body position and how to sight objects on the ground and all those things that had to do with good form. But as I plummeted away from that plane, all thoughts about good form went right out of my head. All I wanted to do was get down alive.

A second after I left the cockpit, I yanked on that ripcord as if my life depended on it, because, well, it did. I was three thousand feet in the air and dropping fast. This was dangerously low, but if the chute opened the way it was supposed to I'd be fine. I'm happy to report that no sooner did I pull that cord than I felt the familiar tug of the chute and shroud lines being quickly pulled out. Lucky for me, Jinx knew how to pack a parachute. Phew.

Two seconds later I was floating lazily under a beautiful, round white canopy. I looked up to see that the chute was fully open and all the lines were clear. Believe it or not, that's when I got scared. When I decided to jump from the plane, I bolted so fast I didn't give myself time to think about what an idiotic move it was. Now I found myself floating through a thunderstorm. Judging from the bright shots of lightning that were tearing through the sky around me, I'd be lucky to get down to the ground without being flash fried. It wasn't like I could do anything about it though. I had to take deep breaths and force myself to calm down.

I looked up at the chute again and saw Jinx's plane flying on toward the airfield. I also caught another glimpse of the *Hindenburg*. A cloud parted and the giant, silver nose poked its way out. I knew from the history lesson we got on Third Earth that the zeppelin was circling the airfield, waiting for the weather to clear so it could land. Man, that thing was huge! Jinx's plane looked like an ant next to a football. It was awesome. The scary thing was, I was on a mission to make sure it would crash and burn. Worse, if I were successful, thirty-six people would die. This was about as horrible a situation as I could imagine. The only way I could keep going was to bring back the images of the horror that would follow if the *Hindenburg* didn't crash. I had to look away from the zeppelin.

The ground was coming up fast. The key was to straighten up and relax. If all went well, landing was pretty much the same as jumping off a three-foot ladder. If all *didn't* go well, I'd break both my legs and the show would be over. I grabbed the shroud lines, kept my head down, straightened my body perpendicular to the ground, and bent my knees. Soft knees . . . soft knees . . . that was my mantra. Soft knees absorbed the shock. Stiff knees didn't. I hit the ground with both feet and rolled. It wasn't the most graceful landing, but nothing broke. That's a win in my book.

But I wasn't out of danger yet. The parachute then became my enemy. If a gust of wind filled it while I was still attached, it would easily drag me along on an uncontrollable bumpfest. But instinct took over and I quickly released the buckles that held me in the harness. At that exact moment, the wind did kick up. The parachute snapped open as it filled with air and the harness was ripped off my body. If I had waited a second more, I would have been yanked along, out of control. Now the parachute simply flew away from me. I didn't bother chasing after it. I stood and watched it fly away like a giant jellyfish with its tendrils dragging behind. I would owe the U.S. Coast Guard a new parachute.

What a rush! I had leaped out of a plane at three thousand feet and lived to tell the tale. But the truth was, it didn't matter. This wasn't about the jump. This was about getting to Spader. I had to force myself to get my head back together and plan my next move.

I was standing on a lonely road in the middle of nowhere. There was scrubby grass on either side of the road, broken up by a few lonely trees. It was probably farmland for grazing cows. Now what?

I then heard a sound. I didn't know what it was at first, because for the past few hours I had been hearing nothing but the roar of Jinx's engine and the shrill whistle of wind. This new sound was loud, harsh, and getting louder. Whatever it was, it was coming closer. I looked one way up the road and saw nothing. I turned around and saw it.

It was a silver bus, blowing its horn, headed my way. Yes! Jinx had put me exactly where I needed to be. Suddenly my insane jump from the airplane didn't seem so crazy. I had gotten ahead of Spader and we'd soon be back together.

I started waving my arms like crazy. Either this bus was going to stop, or splat me like a bug on a windshield. The sound of gushing air told me that the bus driver was putting on the brakes. I guess he didn't want to scrape me off his windshield. So far so good. The bus rolled to a stop in front of me and I ran to the door as it opened.

"Howdy, Lindbergh," the driver said. "Lose your aeroplane?"

Lindbergh? Aeroplane? Oh, right. I was still wearing the leather flight cap and goggles. What a doofus. I quickly pulled them off and asked, "Okay if I ride to the next stop?"

"Sure enough, Wilbur," he said. "Welcome aboard."

I climbed onto the bus as the driver closed the door behind me. He hit the gas and we were under way. The bus was packed with people. My guess was that they were all coming down to see the *Hindenburg* arrive. There was an excited vibe in the bus, like they were on an adventure. They were ready for the thrill of seeing the big airship.

I walked down the aisle, looking into every seat, expecting to find Spader. But when I reached the back of the bus, I hadn't seen him. I turned back toward the front, double-checking each and every passenger. Could I have missed him? No way. But I got back to the front and still no Spader. It was time to get nervous again.

"Excuse me," I said to the driver. "Did this bus come from New York City?"

"All the way," he said.

"A friend of mine was supposed to be on this bus, but I don't see him."

"Who's your friend?" he laughed. "Orville?"

Orville. Wilbur. Lindbergh. Ha ha, this guy was a real comedian.

"His name is Spader. He's taller than I am and has black hair. His eyes are kind of Asian looking. Did he get on the bus in New York?"

"Look, Ace," the driver said, "I don't remember every Joe who rides my bus. Who do I look like? Sherlock Holmes?"

"No, but, this guy's different looking," I said, pressing the issue. This was 1937. I didn't think there were many Asian-looking people riding New Jersey buses.

"Look," he said impatiently, "if I saw him, I'd tell you. But I didn't, so I can't. All right?"

That was it. Spader wasn't on the bus. But that didn't make sense. If this was the bus from New York, then why wasn't he on it? I fell down into an empty seat, beaten. My death dive from Jinx's airplane was a waste of time and adrenaline. I had no idea what to do next. Worse, I was alone. Gunny was still flying through the storm. All I could do was ride to Lakehurst with the other tourists and figure out something once I got there. I glanced at my watch. It was 6:30. The *Hindenburg* would arrive in less than an hour. Things were looking bleak.

A few minutes later the bus pulled into a gas station. The driver stopped at the pumps, then stood up and spoke to the passengers. "It's another ten minutes to the airfield, folks," he announced. "I need to gas up. It won't take long, so don't go wandering off." The guy then left the bus to fill up.

This was torture. I needed to get to the airfield as soon as possible. Every minute was critical. But I didn't know where I was going or how to get there, so I had to wait it out here with the tourists. I listened in to some of their conversations. They were all talking about the *Hindenburg*. They chatted about how it was such an amazing ship and seeing it was like getting a glimpse into the future. Man, this was freaky. If they had any idea of how horrible that future was going to be, they wouldn't be so happy.

I couldn't stand hearing this anymore, so I tuned out. That's when I glanced out the window and saw something that made me sit bolt upright in surprise.

A black car was on the other side of the pumps from the bus. Sitting in the driver's seat was the goon who worked security for Max Rose! He was the guy who kept grabbing Spader and me in the kitchen of the hotel and bringing us upstairs.

Then, walking out of the gas station, I saw Max Rose himself. I couldn't believe it. These were the guys I was chasing and here they were, right in front of me! I was back in business. I jumped up and ran out of the bus, nearly knocking over the driver who was trying to get back on.

"Mr. Rose!" I shouted. Max looked up, but didn't break out in his usual confident smile. No, he was on his own mission now. He had to stop Winn Farrow from blowing up his criminal empire.

"Buck! I was wondering where you were," he said. "Flash didn't think you'd make it."

Flash? That meant Spader. But when did he talk to Spader?

"Hobey-ho, Pendragon," came a familiar voice.

I spun around to see Spader climbing out of the backseat of the gangster's car! That's why he wasn't on the bus. He had hitched a ride with Max Rose.

A second before, I had thought all was lost. Now I was

standing right in front of the very people I came down here to stop. I still didn't have any idea what to do, but at least I was back in the game.

I ran to Spader, grabbed his arm, and pulled him away from the car. This would be tricky. He was here to help Max Rose and his goons. I had to let him know that things had changed. Drastically.

"Hey, where you going?" Max Rose shouted.

"Be right back!" I shouted. I pulled Spader far enough away so we couldn't be heard.

"What are you doing, mate?" Spader asked. "Don't make him mad. He's on our side, remember?"

"No, he's not," I whispered back. "Don't ask questions; just listen. We've gotta let Winn Farrow blow up the ship."

"What?"

"Max Rose has a spy network that's working with the Nazis. If the ship lands safely, those spies are gonna help Germany build a terrible weapon and win the war. If that happens, three territories are going down."

Spader looked confused. I didn't blame him. It was a lot to swallow.

"I don't understand," he said. "How do you know that?"

"We saw it all on Third Earth. Look, it'll take too long to explain, but believe me, it's true. We have to make sure history plays out the way it's supposed to. Winn Farrow *must* blow up the *Hindenburg*."

"We're leaving!" shouted Max Rose. His car was all gassed up and they were ready to roll. We had to go with them.

"You gotta believe me, Spader," I said.

I then pulled Spader back toward the car. It was strange. I had never seen Spader act like this. Normally he would charge right out front, leading the way into whatever adventure lay ahead. But now, he seemed lost. I guess I couldn't blame him. I had just hit him with some pretty confusing news. Everything he thought to be true had just been turned inside out. Hey, I knew the feeling. I could only hope that he'd get his mind around it fast, so we could come up with a plan.

But all we could do just then was get in the car with Max Rose, stay close to him, and be ready to move when the chance came. *If* the chance came.

Spader and I got in the backseat with Max Rose. Two of Rose's big thugs were in front. It was three on two. I hoped it wouldn't come down to a fight between us, because we'd get pounded. The driver hit the gas and we were on the way to our date with a zeppelin.

"I owe you boys," Max Rose said while wiping nervous sweat from his forehead with an expensive silk handkerchief. "Help me stop that rat Farrow, and I'll take care of you. The deal I've got brewing is bigger than you can imagine."

I could imagine it, all right. The deal he had going was to send the U.S. down the tubes by selling atomic secrets to the Nazis. There was a rat in this equation, but it wasn't Winn Farrow.

"We know how they're getting close to the *Hindenburg*," Rose continued. "They have uniforms and badges like the ground crew wears. Nobody will look twice at 'em."

"How'd you find that out?" I asked.

One of the thugs up front said, "We convinced one of Farrow's boys to come clean." The two laughed, like they were all sorts of proud for having squeezed that information out of him.

My guess was the guy who "came clean" was probably Saint Dane. He wanted Rose to know exactly what Farrow was up to. As always, he was pulling the strings, making us dance.

"I know every one of those boys," Rose continued. "I'll point 'em out, then we take 'em down." He patted the gun that was hidden under his jacket. That was Rose's plan. He was going to find Farrow's men and shoot them. Simple as that. *Bang bang.* Not exactly a complicated Mission Impossible–style caper.

"How are we going to get inside the airfield?" I asked. "We don't have uniforms."

Rose pulled out a wad of cash. "We'll get in," he said. "We're just some innocent tourists who want to see the big ship come in, and we're willing to pay to get a good view. Money talks. Always has, always will."

I stared out the window. Forty minutes to go. As I sat in that car, speeding toward destiny, I had no idea how this would play out.

Then something caught my eye. It was a street sign that showed we were traveling on Toms River Road. We then passed another sign. The intersection for Route 527 was coming up. That was weird. I had never been here before, but it seemed familiar. How could that be?

The car charged forward, headed for the four-way intersection. That's when it hit me. I definitely knew this place. I'd heard about it in the library on Third Earth. History showed that Max Rose died in a car crash, 6:50 P.M. on May 6. Intersection of Toms River Road and Route 527. I glanced at my watch. It was 6:50. Spader and I were in the very same car, charging toward a gruesome date with an innocent motorcycle cop.

We were only a few yards from the intersection now. I quickly glanced to the left and saw it. The motorcycle cop was speeding toward the same intersection. We were seconds away from getting T-boned into oblivion.

There wasn't time to warn the driver. I dove for the front seat and grabbed the wheel.

"Look out!" I yelled and pulled the wheel hard.

We skidded into the intersection, but were moving so fast that the car started to go over. The motorcycle cop hit us, but barely. He only grazed us from behind. If I hadn't pulled the wheel, he'd have slammed us square on, and we'd be dead. The next few seconds were a blur. The car flipped. I don't know how many times. All I could do was cover my head and close my eyes. We were all bounced around like we were in a washing machine. It was a jumble of arms and legs and screams. The sounds were hideous as metal crunched and squealed on the pavement.

Finally the car stopped moving and all was still.

I slowly opened my eyes, not sure if I was dead or alive. Amazingly, the car had ended up back on its wheels and the engine was still running. This was nothing like the wreck the computer had shown me. We had dodged a fat bullet. I was on the floor, wedged between the seat and Spader.

"Spader?" I called out tentatively.

Spader slowly opened his eyes and focused on me. "You all right?" he asked.

"I think so. You?"

Spader squirmed and flexed his arms to see if everything worked. "All in one piece," he answered.

I looked around the car and saw that the driver was now in the passenger seat. He was dazed, but alive. Nobody else was in the car. Max Rose and the other thug must have been thrown out when we flipped.

Spader and I struggled to sit up. He kicked the door open and we had our way out. Carefully we crawled from the battered car. It wasn't until later that I realized how many bruises

I had. At the time I was too shocked to feel them. Besides, my head still hurt from getting conked back at the hotel. That hurt worse than anything else. I was a mess.

We stood up on shaky legs and checked out the accident scene. The motorcycle was on its side behind the car. The cop was next to it. I went to him quickly and saw that he was unconscious, but alive. Phew. The second thug was already on his feet. He staggered around like he was drunk, but it looked like he was going to be okay too. Finally we saw Max Rose on the side of the road. The big guy was struggling to sit up. It was hard to believe, but we all lived through the spectacular wreck.

I was amazed and grateful. But then a thought hit me. Max Rose was supposed to die in this accident. But now, because I had taken the wheel, Max was thrown from the car and he survived. I had changed history. Again. Now Max Rose was still able to stop Winn Farrow. If I hadn't acted, he would probably be dead now and the Earth territories would be safe. By saving Max, I may have sealed Earth's doom.

Did I mention how bad my head hurt?

"Buck!" called Max.

Spader and I went to him. He was alive, but in bad shape. He had a big gash on his forehead and had trouble focusing his eyes. "You gotta stop him, boys," he said. "You gotta stop Farrow. I'm counting on you."

Yeah, right. No chance. That's exactly what we *wouldn't* do. Max then laid back down on the ground. He was out of it. I may have changed history by saving his life, but there was no way he could do anything about saving the *Hindenburg* now. Maybe all wasn't lost after all.

That's when I heard the sound of an engine starting.

Spader and I spun to see that the second thug had gotten his act back together and picked up the cop's motorcycle. He was in the saddle, ready to roll. The sound I heard was him kicking over the bike's engine.

"I got it covered, boss," he shouted to Max. "I'll stop him."

Uh-oh. Rose's gang wasn't out of commission yet. I didn't know what to do. Should I rush the guy and try to tackle him? Should I jump in front of his motorcycle? I had seconds to act, but I didn't. That's when something happened that is going to haunt me for a long time.

Spader ran for the bike.

"I'm coming with you!" he shouted as he jumped on the back.

What was he doing? All I could get out was a confused "Spader?"

"Sorry, mate," Spader said. "We've got to save the people on that ship."

"No!" I shouted. I tried to grab him, but the thug gunned the engine and they lurched forward, just out of my reach.

"I won't let Saint Dane win," Spader shouted as they sped away from me.

There it was. The moment I had feared for months. Spader's hatred for Saint Dane had come roaring back. He was going to avenge the death of his father, no matter what the cost. Spader had promised me he could control his emotions, but he was wrong. Or he lied. It didn't matter which. The fact was, he didn't believe me about what we had found on Third Earth. Maybe I hadn't explained it well enough. Or maybe it was too much for him to understand. Whatever. All he saw was that Saint Dane was about to cause a horrific crash and people would die. He was so blinded by hatred he couldn't believe he was doing exactly what our enemy wanted him to do.

I realized all this as I stood on the road, alone, with no way to follow him or stop him. I glanced at my watch. It was 7:00. In twenty-five minutes the first domino would fall in Saint Dane's plan to destroy Halla.

It would be the end of the Earth territories, now and forever.

FIRST EARTH

There was only one way I could get to the airfield. I had to take the car.

I had driven a grand total of once. I was thirteen years old, my mother was in the passenger seat and we were in an empty parking lot with all sorts of room for error. That experience didn't exactly qualify me for the Indy 500. But hey, I had already jumped out of an airplane in the middle of a thunderstorm, rappelled down the side of a hotel, and lived through a horrendous, flipping wreck. How much worse could driving a car be?

A quick glance around the accident scene told me nobody was going to stop me. Max Rose was lying on the side of the road, unconscious. So was the motorcycle cop. The only guy I had to deal with was the thug who was still in the car, slumped in the passenger seat. Out cold. No way I was taking him along for the ride.

This was the same guy who had grabbed Spader and me and dragged us around the hotel like we were bags of trash. I didn't mind returning the favor, so I grabbed his jacket and pulled. The guy barely moved. He was twice my size and totally limp. It was like trying to maneuver a huge bag of bowling balls.

I guess my adrenaline kicked in because on my second try I was able to drag him out headfirst. His shoulders hit the ground with a dull thud. Sorry, dude. I then dug my legs in and dragged the rest of his bulk out of the seat. I didn't have to feel bad for the guy, he was totally out of it. I made sure to drag his deadweight far enough away from the car so that if something wacky happened with me behind the wheel, I wouldn't run the poor guy over.

I then jumped into the driver's seat and instantly realized I was in trouble.

This was an old-time car. It didn't have an automatic transmission. It had a stick shift on the steering column and a clutch pedal on the floor that I was going to have to learn how to use real fast. My father's car had a stick shift, so at least I knew the basics. I used to sit in his car in the garage with the engine off, pretending to drive. He hated that. He thought I was wearing out the clutch or something. But it was a good thing I had done it because now I knew how to shift. Sort of. The trick was to push the clutch pedal all the way to the floor, put the car in gear, then gently lift the pedal back up while stepping on the gas. If it was done smoothly, the car would move. If it wasn't, the car would stall out. It was a touchy-feely thing. I didn't have the touch or the feel. This was going to be interesting.

The engine was still running, so at least I didn't have to worry about starting it up. I moved the seat as far forward as possible so I could reach the pedals. I put my foot down on the clutch, moved the gear lever up to what I thought was first gear, then gently released the clutch while pressing on the gas.

The car began to roll forward. This was going to work! On the first try, no less. I grabbed the wheel, looked forward, and stepped on the gas.

The car bucked twice and stalled. Man! Not only did I not know how to drive, now I had to figure out how to start the car. I had to force myself not to panic.

There was a key in the dashboard, but when I turned it, nothing happened. For a second I thought the car was officially dead. After all, it had just been through a pretty hairy crash. Still, maybe I was doing something wrong. There weren't a whole lot of control knobs on the dashboard. Remember, this was long before the age of CD players, air-conditioning, and cruise control. I saw one knob that worked the headlights and another that turned on the windshield wipers. That was pretty much it.

Then I spotted a small, silver button below the dashboard. I had never seen a button like this on a car, but then again, I had never been in a car made in 1937 either. What did I have to lose? Unless it operated an ejection seat, it wouldn't hurt to press it. So I did . . . and the engine groaned to life. Yes! I had found the starter button.

The car bucked forward and stalled again. That's because I still had it in gear. What a dope. I jammed my foot down on the clutch pedal to disengage the gears, then hit the silver button again. After a few coughing backfires, the engine rumbled back to life. Excellent. Now I had to move. Four times I tried to get rolling in first gear, four times it stalled out. I was wasting precious time and getting ready to abandon ship and start running.

I decided to give it one more try. This time I gave it lots of gas. When I felt the car start to shake and stall again, I gave it even more gas. I thought the car was going to rattle into pieces, but a second later the ride smoothed out and I was moving. I had done it.

But getting the car to move was only the first step. Now I had to drive. This is where it got scary. I was so focused on getting the car moving, I didn't look at where I was going. As soon as I remembered to look up, I saw Max Rose standing right in front of the car! He had somehow gotten his huge bulk vertical and was now staggering toward me. I yanked the wheel hard and barely missed him. But now I was in the dirt on the side of the road. I didn't dare step on the brakes because I didn't want to stall out and have to go through that whole start-up ordeal again. So I kept my foot down on the gas and desperately cranked on the wheel, trying to get back on the road. After bouncing around and nearly missing a couple of rocks, a tree, and a stop sign, I finally got the tires back on pavement.

I was on my way.

As I pointed the car down the road and focused on keeping it straight, I heard the far-off sound of a siren headed my way. I didn't want to be stopped by a cop. No way. I had to get far away from the accident scene, so I gritted my teeth and put the pedal to the metal.

It was a good thing there wasn't much traffic out there in the boonies because I was all over the road. The steering wheel was huge and turning it was hard. Every little adjustment was an effort. Man, you had to be strong back in those days just to drive! It took me a few minutes, but I kind of got the hang of it. I even changed gears when the engine started to rev really fast. I didn't exactly feel ready to take my driver's license test, but at least I was on my way.

This whole adventure wasted ten minutes. It was 7:10. Fifteen minutes left. But at least I was headed toward the airfield.

Now that I knew I was going to get there, my thoughts turned to what I would do once I arrived. Truth was, I had no idea. Spader and the gangster were going to try to stop Winn Farrow. I had to stop them from stopping him. But how? One step at a time. First I had to get there in one piece. After that, I'd have to wing it.

I pressed the car on even faster. The speed scared me, but I couldn't be late. That point was driven home hard when I rounded a bend in the road, cleared a few trees, and saw a spectacular sight before me. I was driving along a rise that gave me a perfect view of my destination.

It was the airfield. Because I was still a mile or so away, I had a wide-angle view of the scene. The weather had cleared, and though the sun had already slipped below the horizon, the sky was still light enough to give me a pretty good look at the place. It wasn't huge by modern-day standards. It was a lonely airport in the middle of nowhere. There were a few runways that crisscrossed each other, and I saw several planes parked wing to wing. There were a few airplane hangars, but one stood out from the rest. It was giant. I mean *really* enormous. There was only one massive door, which told me this was the hangar where they kept the zeppelins. Aside from that colossal hangar, there was nothing all that unique about this place, except for one other very obvious thing:

The *Hindenburg* had arrived.

I glanced at my watch. It was 7:15. I had ten minutes before Winn Farrow would shoot his rocket to destroy the blimp. But it looked like the *Hindenburg* was already lining itself up for the final approach. There was a big crowd gathered, with floodlights blasting skyward, lighting up the silver-skinned zeppelin as if it were daytime. I'm guessing that the airship was still about a half mile from the landing point.

But with something that big, a half mile wasn't very far at all. It was an awesome and frightening sight.

The ship was traveling from my right to left. It was a scene that looked all too familiar. All the pictures of the burning ship I had ever seen were taken with its nose pointing to the left. The crowd was all gathered to one side—the ship's left side. That's where all the pictures were taken from. Having seen those pictures, I knew exactly where I needed to be. Winn Farrow must be somewhere on the ship's far side. The right side. It was the only place he could be and not be seen by the gathered crowd. The question was, would I get there in time to stop Spader?

As I drove closer to the airfield, I passed the same bus I thought Spader had taken. It was pulled over to the side of the road and all the passengers were out, watching the arrival of the airship. I wasn't sure why they had stopped here, this far away. A few seconds later I had my answer.

As I drove closer to the airfield I saw that a high, chain-link fence surrounded the place. There was a security check set up at the gated entrance, and guys in Navy uniforms were checking people's identification before letting them drive in. That meant they were only letting in authorized personnel.

And I was about as unauthorized as you could get.

There was no way I was going to drive through the front gate and past that security team. I'd probably get arrested for driving without a license, anyway. And arrested for car theft. So before I reached the gate, I turned the wheel and stayed on the road that ran parallel to the fence.

As I cruised past the gate, a few of the Navy guards looked up at me. I sat up extra straight, trying to look like an adult. I'm happy to report that nobody came after me.

But now what? I followed the road that led around the

perimeter of the field, hoping to find another entrance that wasn't being watched as closely. Time was running out. I was beginning to think that I was going to have to go back to the main entrance, gun the car, and blast my way through. What other choice would I have?

Then, halfway around to the far side of the airfield, I found another way in. It was a smaller gate and there were no Navy guys doing security. Yes! I cranked the steering wheel and turned the car into the gate. As I passed through, I saw why this entrance wasn't being guarded.

Two Navy guards were lying in the grass, bound and gagged. Somebody who didn't belong there had jumped them and gotten inside. Was it Winn Farrow and his gang? Or was it Spader and Max Rose's pal? Or both? It didn't matter. I was in the right place. I didn't stop to untie the guards. They were on their own.

It was getting darker. I thought about putting on my head-lights, but I didn't want anybody to see me coming. One glance ahead showed me that the *Hindenburg*'s nose was now pointed to my right. I had made it all the way around to the far side, exactly where I needed to be. Somewhere around here, Winn Farrow was camped out and ready to light the fuse on his deadly rocket. Somewhere around here too, was Spader. I glanced at my watch. It was 7:20. Going by history, only a few minutes were left before all hell would break loose. That meant whatever was going to happen, it was going to happen soon.

That's when I heard a gunshot.

FIR8T EARTH

The shot came from somewhere ahead of me, toward the incoming *Hindenburg*. I stepped on the gas and headed that way. I soon saw a cluster of small wooden huts. They were probably storage sheds. But more than that, they looked like the perfect place where somebody could hide and set up a rocket. I gunned it for those buildings, not really sure what I would find when I got there, or what I would do.

That's when I saw the motorcycle Spader and the gangster had taken off on. They were here, all right. I pulled the car up to the motorcycle and slammed on the brakes. Instantly the car bucked and stalled again. I didn't care. It had gotten me here.

Then I heard another shot. It was coming from around the corner of the small building closest to me. I jumped out of the car and cautiously made my way forward.

The *Hindenburg* was now almost directly overhead. The loud drone of its multiple engines filled the air. Since the floodlights were all on the far side, this side of the ship was thrown into shadow. It felt like a huge, ominous cloud was settling in.

When I rounded the corner of the building, my heart leaped. Right in front of me, crouched down behind some wooden crates for protection, were Spader and the gangster. The two were peering out at another wooden building about twenty yards farther ahead.

I knew Farrow must have been hiding there.

I then heard another shot. A nanosecond later something hit directly over my head, and a splinter of wood was torn away from the wall. I ducked, then took a closer look. The bullet had embedded itself right over my head. Now I knew why Spader and the gangster were hiding. Someone was shooting at them. I crouched down low and ran to join them.

"Spader!" I called out with a loud whisper.

Spader turned toward me quickly. So did the gangster. The thug had a gun and pointed it right at my nose.

"Pendragon!" Spader shouted with surprise. He pushed the barrel of the gun away from me. The gangster saw it was me and quickly turned his attention back to his enemies.

"Farrow's right over there!" Spader said quickly. His eyes were wide with excitement. "There's two of 'em."

"There's only one," the gangster corrected. "I already plugged one. Farrow's alone."

Oh, great. There was already blood spilled.

"It's a tum-tigger, mate," Spader said breathlessly. "He's going to fire the rocket any second."

"Not if I can help it," the gangster declared.

He then did something I couldn't believe. He jumped up from behind his protection and made a kamikaze run toward Farrow. Man, this guy was dedicated. He was making a suicide run to protect Max Rose and his criminal empire. This guy should get the gangster of the month award.

Though he was being very brave, he was also incredibly stupid. There was a twenty-yard stretch of open grass between our hiding place and Winn Farrow. The charging gangster had no protection. He only made it a few steps when three shots were fired. The gangster spun and went down hard.

"No!" Spader shouted, and made a move to jump from behind the crates and do the same thing himself. But I grabbed him.

"You can't!" I shouted.

"He's going to blow up the ship!" he shouted back. "Saint Dane is going to win!"

"No!" I said while holding him back. "This is exactly what Saint Dane wants. He wants us to stop Winn Farrow. Didn't you hear me before?"

"That doesn't make sense!" Spader shot back. "How could you know that?"

I looked Spader right in the eye. There was no way I could quickly explain to him all that we had seen on Third Earth. There was only one way I could convince him. I spoke calmly and directly. I didn't want to let emotions get in the way.

"Do you trust me?" I asked.

"You know I do," Spader answered.

"Then believe me. Our job is to make sure the ship blows up. I know it's horrible, but it's the truth. We've been through a lot together, Spader. You know me; you know what it means to be a Traveler. You've got to put your faith in me."

Spader and I held eye contact. I tried to will him into believing me. I could tell he was wrestling with feelings of trust in me, and what his brain told him was reality.

It kills me to say this, but his brain won. He pushed me away so quickly I didn't have time to brace myself, and I fell back on my butt.

"Sorry, mate," he said. "I can't let this happen."

"Spader, don't!" I shouted.

It was too late. He jumped over the wooden crates, headed for Winn Farrow.

I cringed, ready to hear the gunshots that would hit him like they hit the gangster. But they didn't. I scrambled to my feet, gazed over the crates and saw an incredible sight.

Spader wasn't running. He was standing stock-still in the clearing between the wooden crates and the small hut. He had stopped because Gunny was blocking his way. Gunny had picked up the pistol from the fallen gangster blocking his way and now stood between Spader and Winn Farrow.

Overhead the *Hindenburg* was floating closer to the ground. Guide lines were thrown out from the zeppelin and workers scrambled to grab them and control the huge ship.

"I'm sorry," Gunny said calmly. "I can't let you pass."

I couldn't believe it had come to this. One Traveler was holding a gun on another Traveler.

Spader glanced up at the airship. He knew he didn't have any time left. He looked at Gunny and said, "You won't shoot me, Gunny. You can't."

Gunny flinched. Spader was right. There was no way Gunny would shoot him. It was a bluff. Gunny slowly lowered the pistol.

"The ship has to be destroyed," Gunny said.

Spader wasn't listening. He ran forward, determined to get to Winn Farrow. Gunny bent his knees and tried to grab him, but Spader was too strong. He hit the older man like a fullback and knocked him flat on his back. Now there was nothing to stop him. I expected Farrow to shoot him, but no shots came. He was either out of bullets or focused on his rocket.

I jumped out from behind the crates and sprinted after Spader.

"Spader! Stop!" I shouted. But he couldn't hear me over

the roar of the *Hindenburg's* engines. It wouldn't have mattered anyway. He was on a mission, and no amount of yelling from me would stop him.

When I got to the building, I saw that Spader had nailed Farrow the same way he hit Gunny. He had barreled into Farrow and knocked the crazy little guy to the ground. Now the two of them wrestled in the dirt.

I saw something else. On the ground, a few feet from them, was Farrow's rocket. It was nailed into a board that acted as a makeshift launch pad. Its nose was pointed up at the incoming zeppelin, and the fuse was lit. The deadly rocket was poised and ready to bring the airship down.

The fight between Farrow and Spader was one-sided. Farrow was small, but he was a battler. Spader wasn't. The gangster was too much for him, and the fight only lasted a few seconds. Farrow quickly had Spader pinned to the ground with an arm twisted behind his back. There was no way Spader could get to the rocket now.

My friend arched his neck and saw me standing there. The pained, desperate look on his face made me cringe.

"Pendragon!" he cried. "Don't let those people die!" His voice cracked with emotion. Tears welled in his eyes. In his mind, we were about to let thirty-six people die. He didn't understand the bigger picture.

And at that moment, neither did I.

The reality of what was about to happen hit me like a punch in the gut. What was happening? I suddenly had the lives of thirty-six people in my hands. All I had to do was lean down, move the rocket, and they would be saved. It would be so easy. Farrow wouldn't be able to stop me because he was tangled up with Spader.

"Nothing you can do about it now!" Farrow laughed.

"Max Rose is gonna go down in flames, just like this ship!"

"Please, mate!" Spader begged me, in tears. "They're all going to die!"

I looked up at the ship. The lights were on in the gondola. That's where the people were. The people whose lives would soon be filled with terror. I looked down at the rocket. The fuse was nearly burnt, but I still had time. All I had to do was kick it out of the way. Simple as that. One move from me and the ship would arrive to the cheers of all the spectators. The newspapers would carry a very different, triumphant story and thirty-six people would still be alive.

It was at that moment I realized I couldn't let them die.

The concept of history changing so that the Nazis would develop the atomic bomb and win the war seemed impossible at that moment. But those people up in that airship were very real. They were about to die, and I could save them. So I bent down and reached out to move the rocket.

"Pendragon," came a soft, calm voice.

I turned to see Gunny standing behind me. He was as calm as if standing in the lobby of his beloved hotel greeting guests. He looked at me with his warm, knowing eyes and said the one thing that made sense. It was a phrase I had heard many times before. It was supposed to help explain our lives and the lives of all Travelers. It was supposed to give the feeling that all was well with Halla, and we were on the side of right. It was supposed to explain our sorrow and loss. I heard it when my uncle died, when Osa died, and when my family disappeared. It always seemed to come at the worst possible times.

Gunny said softly, "This is the way it was meant to be."

I held his gaze for a second. He smiled. I looked back at the rocket. A million thoughts flashed through my head. But one thought rose above all the others.

I couldn't let those people die. I didn't have it in me.

"I'm sorry, Gunny," I said. "I can't do it."

I took a step toward the rocket, prepared to kick it away. I'd worry about the consequences later. I was a second away from saving the *Hindenburg* when I felt Gunny's arms wrap around me in a firm bear hug.

"Then let me do it," he said softly.

He was stopping me from kicking the rocket! I struggled to get away. All day I had been desperate to get here to make sure history played out the way it was supposed to. Now I was desperate to save that ship and those people.

"Gunny, let go!" I pleaded. But Gunny held firm.

"No!" screamed Spader in anguish.

An instant later the fuse hit the powder, and the rocket flamed to life. It blasted off its wooden launch pad and streaked into the sky, headed toward a very big target.

FIRST EARTH

How do you describe a nightmare?

A nightmare is an exercise of the mind. It digs up your deepest fears and throws them in your face with only one purpose—to terrify. You can't control a nightmare. The ghastly images come at you like a raging storm. The best you can do is ride it out and hope it will end. And it does end. When you wake up, you know that as real as the frightening experience may have seemed, it existed only in your mind.

The next few minutes could best be described as a nightmare. The only difference being, it wasn't happening in my mind.

We watched as the missile shot toward the dark shadow that was the *Hindenburg*. For the few seconds it took to streak upward, it was like time stood still. I wanted to grab those few seconds and hold on to them, because once they were gone, the horror would begin.

The rocket hit the blimp in front of the tail section. Start the clock. In thirty-seven seconds it would be over.

Gunny said softly, "We should go." His voice cracked. He was shaken as badly as I was.

Winn Farrow had already released Spader. The four of us quickly backed away to get out from under harm's way. We knew what was coming. It was going to be ugly. As we moved back, I kept my eyes on the airship.

The fire spread impossibly fast. First the burning material from the exploded rocket sprayed over a large section of the zeppelin. Then the coating of the balloon caught fire. The flames spread quickly over the skin of the airship, gobbling up the soft, silver covering. In seconds the skeletal frame of the ship was exposed. Then it began to fall, tail first. Once the tail sank, the flames spread up toward the nose, fueled by the burning hydrogen gas that was now being released.

I saw both of the swastikas on the tail crumble into the ground and burst into flames. It was a symbolic moment and the one small victory I took from this calamity.

People scattered, running for their lives. The ground crew dropped their lines and fled in terror. It was all they could do.

Then the passenger gondola under the burning zeppelin hit the ground. Instantly people inside smashed out the windows and jumped to safety. Amazingly, a few people walked down the access stairs and simply stepped off. They were the lucky ones. As soon as their feet hit the ground, they ran for their lives, as bits of burning material fell around them like fiery rain. These people would survive. But there were many people still trapped inside who wouldn't be so lucky.

I had seen all this before, in the computer library on Third Earth. But now I was seeing it for real. Close-up. I felt the heat. I saw the shocked, terrorized faces. I heard the screams. But the most horrible feeling of all was that we could have stopped it from happening . . . and didn't.

I then saw something that was hard to believe. While all the people were fleeing from the disaster, there was one person who actually ran toward it. At first I thought it might be a brave rescue worker who was going to valiantly try to pull people from the dying ship. But as he got closer, I saw who it really was.

It was Max Rose. I had no idea how he got there. Maybe it was the police who picked him up from the scene of the crash, or maybe some of his gang found him on the side of the road. It didn't matter. He was now running crazily toward the doomed gondola. We'll never know what was going through his mind, but I can guess. He was going to try and save his money. As insane as that was, it was the only possible explanation. His mind must have snapped. Or maybe he knew his world was going to crumble anyway, so why not make one last ditch effort to save it?

Nobody tried to stop him. Everything was happening too fast, and there was only one thing on anyone's mind: survival. Max Rose actually made it all the way to the gondola and climbed aboard. It was the last time he was ever seen. In a way, history had returned to normal. Max Rose was destined to die on May 6, 1937. The only difference was that it wouldn't be in a car crash. It was in the burning wreckage of the *Hindenburg*.

A second later the huge, flaming airship collapsed. The framework that was still in the shape of a zeppelin crumpled in on itself. A storm of sparks flew into the air, and the once majestic airship was reduced to nothing more than a giant heap of burning embers.

Thirty-seven seconds.

As I stood there feeling the heat from the massive fire, I saw something that actually gave me a chill. It was a bird. A large, black bird. It soared over the flames like a shadow, made a sharp turn, and shot over our heads. Then with one quick snap of its wings, it flew off into the night. Was it Saint Dane? Had he been there to witness his latest failure?

I didn't think so. I thought he was there to mock me. The Travelers had won, yes. We had insured that history would play out the way it was supposed to. The Earth territories were safe. But did Saint Dane truly care? Or like he said, was this about me?

The truth came clear to me in that one, horrible moment. Everything that had happened, all of Saint Dane's manipulations, were about putting me here, in this exact spot. When the critical moment arrived, I didn't have the strength to stop the rocket. He knew I wouldn't be able to do it. He knew. He wanted to see me fail.

The Travelers may have won the battle here on First Earth, but Saint Dane has won the war. He proved that I was no match for him.

Winn Farrow laughed. He actually laughed. The guy really was a psycho. To cause this kind of disaster just to get revenge on one person is nothing short of lunacy.

"Payback," he said with glee. "Sweet."

"You animal!" Spader shouted, and lunged at the guy. But Gunny caught him and held him back.

"Let it go," Gunny said. "He's none of our concern."

"Yeah," Farrow laughed. "None of your concern." He looked at Gunny and gave him an oily smile. "Thanks, pal," he said. "Couldn't have done it without you."

Gunny winced as though he had been hit. My heart went out to him. He did what he knew was right. He did what I couldn't do. But this poor man who couldn't bring himself to fire a gun had just allowed the destruction of the *Hindenburg*.

No matter how right it was, he was going to have to live with that for the rest of his life.

Farrow then turned and ran into the darkness. I didn't care where.

Spader stepped right up to Gunny and looked him in the eye. His face was twisted with anguish. "You stopped him," he cried. "Pendragon was going to save the ship and you stopped him. Those people are dead because of you! You let Saint Dane win."

Gunny couldn't speak. I thought I saw him shivering.

"He did the right thing," I said.

Spader pulled away from Gunny and shot me an angry look. "Why? Because someone told you it would change history? I don't believe it. How could you know that?"

I didn't answer. Now wasn't the time. Gunny said with a weak voice, "We've got to get out of here."

"I've got a car," I offered.

"No," Gunny said. "Come with me." He hurried off. Spader and I stood there a moment longer, looking at the flaming wreckage.

"Hobey, I hope you're right," he finally said, and followed Gunny.

The airfield was in chaos. Fire trucks raced toward the scene. People were running every which way, trying to help the survivors. Some of the victims were rushed into cars that screamed off, headed for the nearest hospital. Others were loaded into ambulances. There was so much frantic activity that nobody noticed three guys walking calmly away from the action, headed toward the runways.

The flames from the *Hindenburg* lit the airfield up like daytime. I wasn't sure where Gunny was leading us and I didn't care. I didn't want to think anymore. Finally I looked ahead and saw a welcome sight. Sitting on the end of the runway, lit by the flames, was Jinx Olsen's odd little seaplane. After all that happened, I'd forgotten about Jinx.

She came running from the direction of the crash. Her eyes were wild and scared. I'd have been surprised if they weren't.

"Was this it?" she asked with a touch of desperation. "Was this why you had to come here? Were you trying to prevent this?"

We all shared looks. All but Spader. He stared at the ground. I didn't know what to say. Thankfully, Gunny took charge.

"We heard some things," he said. "We thought we could help."

"But we were too late," Jinx said. "It's horrible."

"Yes," Gunny said. "It's horrible." He then walked up to Jinx and looked her right in the eye. He spoke to her in a calm, assured voice. "No one will ever know what happened here. You thought you could help, but there was nothing you could do. There was nothing anyone could do. Remember that."

It was weird. Jinx stared up at Gunny with glassy eyes. All the tension seemed to leave her body. It was like Gunny was hypnotizing her. He was using his Traveler skills to put her mind to rest. I wished he could have done the same for me.

"Right," she said slowly. "There was nothing I could do."

"We should get back," Gunny said to her.

"Yes," Jinx said. "Let's go back."

The four of us got into the plane—Jinx and I in the front cockpit, Spader and Gunny in back. I doubt if anyone took notice of our small plane as we lifted off on the far side of the airfield. Every single person on the ground was focused on the burning zeppelin. As we rose up and away from the destruction, I realized we were leaving behind one of the great mysteries of all time. People would always wonder what really caused the *Hindenburg* to catch fire and crash. Nobody would know of the role two rival gangster mobs from New York had in bringing the massive airship down, or of the part played by Travelers from different territories.

That was the way it was meant to be.

The flight back was uneventful. Thankfully the weather had cleared and it was a smooth trip. Nobody spoke. We were all alone with our thoughts. We landed on the Hudson and got the airplane back to the dock without a problem. The four of us then rode together in a cab back to the Manhattan Tower Hotel. I don't think anyone said more than two words for the whole trip. When we were dropped on the sidewalk in front of the hotel, there was an awkward moment. Spader left us and went inside without saying a word. Gunny and I stood with Jinx. I had no idea how we would leave this with her.

Again, Gunny took charge. "You are a very special person," he said to Jinx. "I'm proud to have known you."

"I hope you get to fly again someday," I added.

"Oh, I will," she said with a wink. "Bet on it."

We all exchanged hugs, then Jinx started inside. But she stopped and turned back to us with a concerned look. "This trip we just took," she said. "Why do I have the feeling there was more to it than there seems?"

"There isn't," Gunny answered. "It was just a trip."

That seemed to satisfy Jinx. She nodded and went inside. In all the accounts of what happened to the *Hindenburg*, there was never any mention of Jinx Olsen having been at the airfield. I can only believe that whatever thoughts Gunny planted in her head, or took away, he made sure that Jinx never said a word to anyone about our flight. It was too bad. All Jinx ever wanted to do was fly and make a difference. She would never know that on that chilly night, she had done exactly that.

Gunny and I stood alone on the sidewalk. Nobody else was around. As I stood there, I really didn't know what to think. Was this an incredible victory over Saint Dane? It sure didn't feel like it. I had to keep reminding myself that if we hadn't been there, things would have been worse. Much worse. But that was something I knew in my head. My heart felt otherwise.

Reality for me was, I had failed. There's no other way of putting it. When it was all on the line, I blew it. If it hadn't been for Gunny, Saint Dane would have won. The Earth territories would have been doomed, and it would have been my fault. And that makes me question my worth as a Traveler. I couldn't help but think of Uncle Press. He had faith in me. He told everyone to trust me. By failing with the *Hindenburg,* I had let him down. What was I supposed to do from here?

"I'm sorry, Gunny," I said softly.

"For what?"

"For putting this on your shoulders."

Gunny looked up at his beloved hotel. The lights reflected in his brown eyes.

"Never in my lifetime did I ever imagine the things we've seen. But now that my eyes are opening up to what life is really about, I have to tell you, I honestly do believe what I said before. This is the way it is supposed to be. Our job is to make sure of it. You didn't put anything on my shoulders, Bobby."

"But I did the wrong thing."

Gunny looked at me. I saw the kindness in his eyes. No, I

felt the kindness. "Maybe. Or maybe today was my day. Maybe the whole reason I'm part of this is to do what I did. You've got a long road ahead, Pendragon. I believe your day is still to come."

We went inside and said good night. I was dog tired and all I wanted to do was fall into bed. When I got to the room, Spader was sitting on the couch, waiting for me. I didn't want to have to deal with him. Not now. But Spader wanted to talk.

"I'm scared, mate," he said. "Everything's been turned inside out. How could Gunny let those people die?"

I didn't say anything at first. I was angry and confused and a little bit scared myself. We had reached a turning point of our own, Spader and me. As great a team as we were, when it came to crunch time, Spader hadn't trusted me. I still needed to convince him that we had done the right thing.

"Tomorrow," I finally said. "Tomorrow I'll show you everything."

That was it. I left him and went to bed. The last thought I had before nodding off was that I hoped I wouldn't have any dreams. Or nightmares.

The next day Spader and I took a trip. We went to the one and only place where he would get the answers he needed. We went to Third Earth.

The trip to the Bronx and the flight through the flume were nothing special to write about. It was amazing to think that something as wild as fluming to a different time and territory didn't seem special anymore. But the truth was, I was getting used to it. We arrived at the gate on Third Earth and changed into the clothes of the territory without saying a word to each other. Hidden in the pile of clothing was the same communicator Gunny had used to contact Patrick, the

Traveler. I hit the button, knowing Patrick would soon be there to pick us up.

I have to admit, I was nervous about what we would find on Third Earth. Had history played out the way it was supposed to? By allowing the *Hindenburg* to be destroyed, had we kept the territories on track? Or did we change something else that might have allowed Max Rose's gang to continue their spy operations?

The moment we stepped out of the gate, I had my answer. The subway was exactly as I remembered it. So was the massive underground mall. When we took the escalator up to the surface I saw the rolling, green hills of the Bronx. What a huge relief.

I'm sure you can imagine the wonder Spader felt as we walked through the territory. He looked every bit as stunned and impressed as I was when Gunny and I first came here. He started to ask me questions, but all I said was, "Ask Patrick." I didn't feel like being a tour guide. Not today.

It didn't take long for Patrick to arrive at the green kiosk that led from the subway. He pulled his small car up to us and gave me an expectant look.

"It's done," I said.

Patrick exhaled with relief.

"Let's celebrate!" he shouted.

Spader and I both got into the car without saying a word. Neither of us were in the mood to celebrate.

"Take us to the library," I said flatly.

Patrick knew something was wrong. He didn't press though. We drove the same route into Manhattan as last time. I asked Patrick to explain to Spader how the Earth territories had come this far. Patrick gave him pretty much the same story he had given me. This was good. I wanted Spader to know just how special a place Third Earth was.

At the library Patrick gave Spader a quick lesson on their computer system and its amazing capacity for information storage. He gave another quick demo, this time bringing up a holographic image of the Beatles singing a song called "She Loves You." Not exactly my kind of music, but it was pretty cool to see four famous guys standing there singing.

As you might imagine, Spader was blown away. It was then time to see what we came for.

I asked Patrick to explain the *Hindenburg* Variation. Patrick first showed Spader history the way it actually happened, with the *Hindenburg* being destroyed. The only thing that had changed from the last time I saw this was that there was no information about Max Rose being killed in a car accident on Toms River Road. This time it showed that Max Rose had mysteriously disappeared on May 6, never to be seen again. Of course, we knew what had really happened. Max Rose died in the wreckage of the *Hindenburg*. History would never know that.

Patrick then took Spader through the alternate scenario, step by step, showing him what would have happened if the *Hindenburg* had arrived safely. He showed Spader Rose's spy network, and the atomic bomb the German scientist Dani Schmidt would create to help the Nazis win the war. He also showed Spader frightening scenes of Third Earth the way it would have existed if the *Hindenburg* had arrived safely.

This is a strange thing to admit, but seeing these horrifying images actually made me feel better, because I knew this was a future that would never be. I would never feel good about the fact that the *Hindenburg* crashed, but any doubts about Gunny having done the right thing were now gone. All we did was keep history on track.

This was the way it was meant to be.

Spader didn't say much during the demonstration. It was a lot to understand. The two of us walked out of the library and sat down on the steps where Gunny and I had sat earlier. It was only yesterday. A lifetime ago.

"I'm sorry, mate," Spader said. "I don't know how else to say it. But look at it through my eyes. I hadn't seen all that stuff back there. I didn't know the same things you did. Hobey, if I had seen what was going to happen if we saved the *Hindenburg,* I never would have done the things I did."

"If we had stayed together," I said. "You *would* have seen all that."

Spader fell silent. I think he was beginning to realize just how badly he had screwed up.

"You're my mate, Pendragon," he answered. "Mates forgive each other."

I didn't say anything at first. In some ways, dealing with Saint Dane was easier than this. With Saint Dane there was good and there was bad. Not a lot of room in between. But this was different. Spader was my mate. He was a Traveler. We were on the same side. That's what made saying what I had to say so tough.

"I want you to go home, Spader," I said.

"What?" he shouted in surprise.

"Go back to Cloral, to Grallion," I continued. "Get back to being an aquaneer."

"But I'm a Traveler now," he protested. "My place is with you."

"Your place is to help the Travelers protect the territories," I corrected. "Until we can trust each other, you can't do that."

"But I *do* trust you, Pendragon," he said sincerely.

I took a breath and said, "But I can't trust *you.*"

Spader looked shocked. No big surprise, these were strong words.

"This isn't about you," I continued. "This isn't about getting revenge on Saint Dane. It's about saving the territories and protecting Halla. I don't think you get that. Until you do, you're better off at home."

There it was. I had laid it flat out. Spader was a good guy. A great guy. But he didn't get it. I didn't pretend to have all the answers, but there were some things I knew for sure. One of them was that the Travelers had to support each other. It was the only chance we had against Saint Dane's evil. Spader had shown that he didn't have that faith. More than once. Together we could stand up to Saint Dane. Scattered, we were lost. Gunny's selfless act at the critical moment was proof of that. I felt so strongly about it that I was willing to turn my back on a guy who had become my best friend. At least my best Traveler friend, anyway.

Spader looked down. I knew he hated hearing this. But I needed him to understand. He was a Traveler. Someday he would play a role again, and when that day came, I wanted him to be ready. His reaction to what I said would be critical to the future of the Travelers, our battle with Saint Dane, and his part in all of it.

"Let's go back to the flume," was all he said. Then he stood up and walked off.

Nothing was resolved.

As Patrick drove us back uptown to the subway in the Bronx, I could only hope that Spader was trying to understand. I didn't push. I didn't want to sound like some kind of parent. Spader had to work this through for himself.

Patrick dropped us off at the green kiosk, and after saying our good-byes, Spader and I made our way back down to the gate and the flume. Still, nothing was said. I worried that Spader would take off on his own without a word. I couldn't let that happen. We had to settle this.

When we got inside the gate, Spader stepped up to the black mouth of the flume. If he had called out a territory, I would have pulled him away.

But he didn't. He turned his back to the flume and faced me. We stood there for a second, then finally he said softly, "I'm with you, mate."

"Are you?" I asked.

"I said it to you before," he continued. "However this natty-do is going to play out, I believe it's you who will bring us through. If you want me to go home, then it's back to Cloral for me."

I was relieved and saddened at the same time. This meant we were officially going our own ways.

"Spader, you're like my brother," I said.

"I feel the same about you, Pendragon," he said with a small smile. "That's why I'm listening to what you say. It's true, I've been wanting to crush Saint Dane since my father died. I've tried to put it out of my head, but it's always there. I've got to find some way to deal with that, and if it means going home and taking time to think things through, that's what I'll do."

Spader then added, "I want you to promise me one thing though."

"What's that?"

"When you find yourself in a tum-tigger, and I know you will, come get me."

That was what I wanted to hear. Spader was the Traveler from Cloral. His spirit and talent had gotten us through in times when I was ready to give up. However this war with

Saint Dane was going to play out, Spader would have to take on a major role.

"Bet on it," I said.

That was what *he* wanted to hear. The two of us hugged. I didn't want to let him go. I didn't want to be on my own again. Especially now, when I was doubting my own worthiness as a Traveler. For a brief second I thought it would be better to deal with Spader's unpredictability than to let him go. But I had to be strong.

He held me at arm's length and said, "I'll be ready."

I nodded. Spader then backed away and glanced into the tunnel.

"Safe trip," I said.

Spader faced the infinite black hole and shouted, "Cloral!"

The craggy tunnel rumbled to life. The far-off light appeared from deep inside, growing closer. The familiar musical notes were on their way. The bright light quickly grew intense. Spader turned to me and smiled.

"Hobey-ho, Pendragon."

"Hobey-ho, Spader."

A second later he was gone.

I don't think I ever felt so lonely. Well, maybe once before. When I stood on the empty lot where my house on Second Earth used to be.

My whole life I was used to having people guide me toward the right answers. First it was my parents. Teachers were there too. So were my friends like you, Mark and Courtney. Of course Uncle Press played a huge part. I didn't always like being told what to do, but it was good to know somebody was always looking out for me.

Now I felt like I was on a highwire without a net. If I was going to get to the other side, the only one who would get me there was me. I had two choices. I could stand here and feel sorry for myself, or move forward.

I turned away from the now quiet flume and changed back into my First Earth clothes. Before doing anything else, I had to get back and let Gunny know what had happened.

"First Earth!" I shouted into the flume.

I then closed my eyes, looking forward to the few minutes of a flume ride when I wouldn't have to worry about anything.

FIRST EARTH

When I walked through the front doors of the Manhattan Tower Hotel, Gunny was the first person I saw. He was at his Bell Captain post, dressed in his spiffy uniform, acting as if nothing had happened. The lobby was buzzing with people, all reading special-edition newspapers that had accounts of the *Hindenburg* disaster. It seemed like everybody had their own theory as to what had caused the explosion and crash.

None of them were right, of course.

Gunny and I took the elevator up to my room on the sixth floor so we could talk in private.

"Everything's cool," I said to Gunny as we entered the room. "Third Earth is exactly the way we left it."

Gunny let out a relieved breath. "Where's Spader?"

"Back home on Cloral," I said. "He needs some time to get his head around what happened."

"Does he understand?" Gunny asked.

"About the *Hindenburg*, yeah," I answered. "The big question is, can we count on him in the future?"

"And?"

"I don't know," I answered honestly. "I hope so."

I sat down on the couch, sinking into the soft cushions. I was suddenly very tired. I think I could have fallen asleep for a week. The tension was finally gone. We had been in overdrive for a long time, and now that we were done, I was ready to crash. But my mind wouldn't let me.

"Gunny, I'm scared," I said.

"About what? Saint Dane?"

"I'm scared about what we had to do to stop him," I said. I spoke slowly, trying to put my thoughts into words. "Letting the *Hindenburg* blow up was . . ."

I couldn't think of a big enough word to describe how horrible it was.

"I hear you," Gunny said.

"And I'm scared of what might happen the next time Saint Dane tries to test me," I added. "What if I don't have somebody like you around to cover my back? Gunny, he didn't care about what happened to the Earth territories. This was about proving he could control us. Control *me*! You know what that means? It means he won. I was going to kick over that rocket."

"But you didn't."

"Only because you were there. Saint Dane proved his point. Gunny, I can't do this."

Gunny sat back in his chair, nodding slowly. When he finally spoke it was with a calm, sure voice that I wanted so badly to believe in.

"None of us asked for this job," he began. "I'd just as soon live out my days here at the hotel, never knowing anybody named Saint Dane or people called Travelers. But that's not the way things turned out."

"Yeah, tell me about it."

"But there's one thing I think about that gives me a little peace of mind. Maybe it'll help you, too."

"Go for it," I said. "I'll take anything."

"Ever since your uncle told me I was a Traveler, I've been wondering why I'd been chosen. Still do. Why us? We're nothing special, just regular folks. But the more I think about it, the more I've got to believe there's something bigger at play here. I think we've each been chosen for a reason. Like last night. I truly believe I was at the *Hindenburg* to do what I did. This may sound silly, but thinking that way gives me a little hope that maybe we just might be the right ones to be doing this after all."

"So, if we were chosen, who did the choosing?"

"Exactly! That's the big question. Who is it that has the kind of vision it takes to see how things should be, and play chess with a guy like Saint Dane? I haven't got a clue. But whoever it is, he wants Saint Dane to fail. That means he's a good guy. And I like the idea of a powerful good guy being on our side." Gunny smiled and said, "Maybe your back is covered a little bit more than you think."

Could it be? Could there be some grand plan at work? Was there a guy out there who wanted to stop Saint Dane and chose us to be his soldiers? If there was, I'd sure like to know. Maybe I wouldn't feel so alone anymore.

"You're a smart guy, Gunny," I said.

"I'm nothing of the sort," he said back to me. "I've just been around a while. I plan on being around a good while longer, too."

I rolled over, closed my eyes, and went to sleep. Right there on the couch. It was the first good night's rest I'd had in a long time.

The next few days were spent finishing this journal and saying good-bye. I tried to see Jinx, but she had already checked out of the hotel. Maybe it was a good thing. I wasn't sure what I'd say if she started asking about the *Hindenburg*. Wherever she was, whatever the future held for her, I silently wished her luck.

I said good-bye to my friends on the hotel staff. Dewey Todd was all sorts of excited because his father had just built another hotel out in Hollywood, and he was leaving New York to run the place. Can you believe it? Dewey was going to get his own hotel. I hoped he had learned more about running a hotel than he had about running the elevator. He wished me well and said if I was ever out in Hollywood to look him up.

As soon as I finish this last journal from First Earth, I'm going to give it to Gunny to have them bound. I wish I could send them to you through my ring, but I'm afraid it's gone for good. There's no way I'm going looking for it. I've had my fill of gangsters.

Tomorrow I'm going to take the train out to Stony Brook and put the journals in a safe-deposit box at the National Bank. This way, when the calendar comes around, you'll be able to pick them up. After that, I don't know what I'll do with my journals.

The next question is, where do I go from here? The logical answer would be to Veelox. Saint Dane said he was headed there. But was that to lure me into another trap? Even if it were, do I have any choice?

I began this journal by telling you guys I had reached my own turning point. Part of that was because I had seen the kind of destruction Saint Dane was trying to cause on the Earth territories. You don't see something frightening like that and shrug it off. If I didn't fully realize it before, I do now.

But maybe more important was the moment when I watched the fuse burning on the rocket that was about to destroy the *Hindenburg*. In that moment I knew what I was supposed to do, but I didn't do it.

When it comes right down to it, was my mistake any different than what I accused Spader of? I let my emotions control me, just as Spader did. As I'm writing this journal, I'm admitting that I have very real doubts about myself as a Traveler. Saint Dane put me at that rocket to prove a point. He knew I wouldn't be able to let the *Hindenburg* crash, which means he knew how to control me.

I can't let that happen again. The stakes are way too high. I know that, now more than ever. If there's anything good that came from my failure on First Earth, it's that I have now totally given myself over to being a Traveler.

One way or another, I'm in it to the end.

As I've written so many times before, I hope you guys are reading this. I have no idea when I'll be able to write again, or from what territory. All I can say is, check the safe-deposit box at the bank every so often to see if there are any new deliveries. I won't stop writing. I can't. Writing these journals has kept me sane. It makes me feel as if you guys are here with me. So until the next time, have fun, be safe, and think about me every once in a while.

Your friend,
Bobby

END OF JOURNAL #12

◉ SECOND EARTH ◉

. . . Your friend, Bobby.

Courtney lowered the final journal and looked at Mark. They had been taking turns reading aloud to each other for the last five hours in Courtney's father's basement workshop. They ate turkey sandwiches and chips and carrots. Mark drank Dew, Courtney stuck with water. They only took breaks for the bathroom. It had been a marathon, and now it was over.

Courtney slammed the journal down on the table in front of them. "I'm totally freaked out," she announced.

"Yeah, m-me too," Mark said, relieved that Courtney admitted it first. "If Gunny hadn't let the *Hindenburg* blow up—"

"We wouldn't be talking about it," Courtney concluded.

"Exactly," Mark said. "No New York, no Stony Brook, no . . . us."

"I'm afraid to look outside," Courtney said. "What if the world has changed?"

"It hasn't," Mark said with authority. "The Travelers made sure of that."

"This is getting serious, Mark" Courtney said with rising panic. "I mean, this is too close to home."

The two stared at the closed journals, letting the thought hang there. Finally Mark said, "Maybe not."

"What do you mean?" Courtney shot back with surprise. "You're the one who said Saint Dane was going to show up here sooner or later, right?"

"Yeah, I did," Mark answered. "I've been worried the battle was going to land on Second Earth from the very beginning."

"And it almost did!" Courtney exclaimed.

"But you know," Mark continued thoughtfully. "After reading this last journal, I'm thinking there's a chance we might be off the hook."

"Seriously?"

"Think about it. If Saint Dane's plan with the *Hindenburg* would have destroyed all three Earth territories, maybe he won't come here after all. I mean, maybe he already took his shot."

Courtney gave a hopeful look to Mark. "You're thinking there might not be a turning point here on Second Earth?" she asked.

"No," he replied. "I'm thinking the turning point for Second and Third Earth might have been the destruction of the *Hindenburg*. Kind of like three-for-one. There's a chance we may have dodged a pretty huge bullet."

Courtney thought about this for a moment, then said, "That would be incredible! But, how will we know for sure?"

Mark answered, "That's the thing. We won't."

The two let this hang for a moment. Courtney studied Mark for a second and then said, "You seem kind of disappointed."

"Me? No, what are you kidding? I'm totally relieved. I just hope I'm right."

Mark put the journals into his backpack. "I think we should keep all the journals in the safe-deposit box at the bank from now on. It's way safer than the desk in my attic."

"Cool," Courtney said. "I'll come by your house tomorrow morning. Eight o'clock. We'll take all the journals in together."

When he got home Mark went to his bedroom and reread some of Bobby's adventure. He was looking for clues that might prove his theory about Second Earth. The more he read, the more he felt certain that Second Earth was safe.

And it bothered him.

Courtney had read Mark right. He *was* disappointed. It wasn't that he wanted there to be trouble on Second Earth; it was more that he was feeling left out. Bobby had a new life now. It didn't help when Bobby referred to Spader as his best friend. That stung. He and Bobby had been inseparable since they were toddlers. Now they were growing about as far apart as possible.

Though he never admitted it to Courtney, Mark had fantasized about the day when Saint Dane would make his move on Second Earth. It meant Bobby would come home, and they could all work together to outwit the demon. Now it looked like that chance would never come. If Saint Dane didn't target Second Earth, Bobby would have no reason to come home.

Mark went to sleep that night feeling as if his one shot at adventure had passed him by.

First thing the next morning Courtney arrived at Mark's house, and they loaded all twelve of Bobby's journals into his backpack. It made them nervous to move them, but they felt sure it was worth it. The vault at the National Bank of Stony Brook was way safer than the wooden desk in Mark's attic.

As they walked to the bank Mark made a decision. He had to tell Courtney how he felt. The two had made a pact to tell each other everything about anything that had to do with Bobby and the journals. When Mark lied to her about Andy Mitchell discovering them, it had led to a total mess. After that Mark promised that he would share everything.

So on the way to the bank, Mark admitted to Courtney that he hoped Saint Dane would still come to Second Earth, so they could join forces with Bobby and battle the evil demon together.

He knew she'd understand.

"Are you crazy?" she shouted back at him.

She didn't understand. Not even a little bit.

"This isn't a game, Mark. It's easy to read those journals while we're eating carrots all comfy on the couch, but getting involved is a whole 'nother ballgame."

"I know that—" Mark said.

"It's like watching reality shows on TV," Courtney went on. "People do crazy stuff like jumping across buildings or living on an island with no food or eating bugs, and it doesn't seem all that hard. But that's because we can turn off the TV, and go to bed, and know breakfast will be on the table in the morning. If Saint Dane shows up here, we can't turn off the TV and go to bed."

"I understand—"

"Do you?" Courtney was getting worked up. "Really? I'll tell you what I think. I think you sound like Spader."

"How's th-that?" Mark shot back, tweaked by the comment.

"Spader is more worried about Spader than about protecting Halla," Courtney reasoned. "That's why Bobby told him to go home. If you're hoping Saint Dane shows up here so you can have an adventure with Bobby, then you're thinking more about you than you are about Second Earth."

"Jeez, all right," Mark shot back. "I get it. It's not like I can do anything about it, anyway. I'm not gonna call Saint Dane up and invite him over for lunch."

The two looked at each other, and laughed. The image of Mark calling up Saint Dane was pretty ridiculous.

"Sorry, Mark," Courtney said with a smile. "I didn't mean to go up on you like that. I'm just scared, is all."

"I am too," Mark said. "But I wanted to let you know how I felt. We promised to do that, right?"

"Yeah, I'm an idiot. I'm sorry," she said. "I get it. It's tough reading about all this stuff and not being able to do anything about it. It's like being on the bench during a big game."

Mark shrugged. He knew exactly what she meant. He'd never been anyplace *but* the bench during big games. It looked like he was going to have to ride the pines during this one too.

They arrived at the bank just as the doors were being unlocked. Courtney went in first through the revolving door. Just as Mark was about to follow, he stopped. He wasn't exactly sure why, but he had an odd feeling. Was somebody watching them?

He glanced around the Ave to see several stores were opening up for the day. Some shop owners were using squeegees on their windows, others were unfurling the colorful awnings that hung over the entrances. There was a policeman standing in the center of the intersection, directing traffic. Nothing out of the ordinary. Mark had no idea why he had the strange feeling, so with a shrug, he entered the bank.

Mark and Courtney marched right up to the desk of Ms. Jane Jansen. The pinched woman was already hunched over her computer keyboard, looking busy . . .

Playing solitaire.

"Working hard?" Courtney asked.

Ms. Jane Jansen was totally embarrassed and closed out her game. When she saw who it was, her face grew even more pinched. Mark thought if she squeezed her cheeks any tighter, her whole face would get sucked in through her mouth.

"Can I help you, children?" she asked through gritted teeth.

"We'd like to get into our safe-deposit box," Mark said politely.

"But if you're busy," Courtney said sarcastically, "we can wait."

"I don't suppose you remembered to bring your key?" Ms. Jane Jansen asked.

Mark reached to the chain around his neck and pulled it out from under his shirt. There were now two keys on the chain. One was to the desk in his attic, the other to the safe-deposit box.

"Surprise!" Courtney said.

"Follow me," Ms. Jane Jansen said as she pulled away from her desk. She looked totally bothered by the interruption.

Mark and Courtney knew the routine. Ms. Jane Jansen led them through the big, round vault door, into the inner vault, and right up to the wall of doors that protected the safe-deposit boxes.

"Would you like me to open it for you?" she asked with a snippy attitude, as if it were the last thing she wanted to do.

"Nah, we can handle it," Courtney said. "Go back to your game."

Ms. Jane Jansen wanted to say something back, but thought better of it. After all, they were clients. Instead, she scowled at them and left.

"I love her," Courtney laughed.

While Courtney opened the door, Mark unloaded all twelve journals from his backpack and placed them into the big steel box. There was plenty of room left over for any new journals that might show up. He then slid the drawer closed, shut the door, and Courtney locked it. The key then went right back to the chain around Mark's neck. The journals were now as safe as they could possibly be.

On their way out of the bank, they didn't bother stopping to say good-bye to Ms. Jane Jansen. They didn't want to disturb her game again. They left the vault, walked through the lobby, and were almost to the front door when—

"Children! One moment please!" It was Ms. Jane Jansen. She hurried up to them, her heels clicking on the marble floor. Her cheeks were rosy and her eyes flared.

"I want you two to understand something," she said angrily. "You may be clients of this bank, but that does not entitle you to messenger service."

Mark and Courtney looked at each other. They had no idea what she was talking about. "Translation, please," Courtney asked.

Ms. Jane Jansen held up a brown paper bag, about the size of a grocery bag, with wet stain marks on the bottom.

"When you two went inside the vault, someone came in and asked that I give this to you," she explained. "This is not appropriate, this is not a service the bank provides, and whatever is in this bag smells."

Courtney took the bag with curiosity.

"Who was it?" Mark asked.

"I have no idea and I didn't ask," Ms. Jane Jansen replied. "As I said, I am not a messenger."

Courtney cautiously unfolded the top of the brown bag and looked inside. What she saw were three white containers, along with a Dew and two cans of ice teas. She showed the bag to Mark. He looked inside and was just as confused as Courtney. There was also a folded piece of paper inside. Mark pulled it out and read aloud, "Never too early in the morning for Garden Poultry fries. Meet me in the pocket park." Mark looked to Courtney and added, "It's signed 'B.'"

Could it be?

"Do we understand each other?" Ms. Jane Jansen asked.

Courtney reached into the bag, pulled out one box of fries

and handed it to the cranky bank lady.

"Absolutely," Courtney said. "Here, have a party."

Courtney and Mark ran out of the bank, leaving Ms. Jane Jansen holding a greasy box of French fries. She was just about to toss it in the garbage, when the oily-delicious smell finally got through to her. She took a deep whiff, looked around to make sure nobody was watching, then turned back to her desk with the greasy treat.

Mark and Courtney blasted out of the bank and ran down the Ave, headed for the pocket park. The Ave cut straight through the middle of downtown Stony Brook. It was loaded with small shops, restaurants, and bookstores. It was definitely the biggest kid hangout in town, but since it was so early, no kids were awake and around.

The pocket park halfway down the Ave was a familiar meeting place. At one time there had been a building where the park stood. Now it was an empty space between two other buildings that had been landscaped with grass, trees, and benches.

Courtney arrived first and looked into the park.

The place was nearly empty. There was only one person there, and it wasn't the person they wanted to find. Mark finally caught up to Courtney and saw the guy. His shoulders sagged. It wasn't Bobby. This guy was older and taller than Bobby. He had really short, spiky, blond hair and wore thin wraparound sunglasses. He looked like a hip-hop skateboard kid from New York, not Bobby Pendragon from Stony Brook. Courtney and Mark walked cautiously up to him.

"Did you send us this?" Courtney asked while holding up the greasy bag.

The guy was slouched down with both elbows on the back of the bench. When he spoke, he didn't even look at them. He was being very cool.

"I guess that answers my question," he said.

"Wh-What question?" Mark asked.

"The question of whether or not anybody would recognize me around here," he answered.

The guy then pulled down his sunglasses to reveal his eyes. He looked right at Mark and Courtney and broke into a huge grin. "Read any good journals lately?"

Oh yeah, it was Bobby.

❂ SECOND EARTH ❂

Mark and Courtney were totally stunned. Bobby jumped to his feet and the three of them clung to each other in a three-way hug. Nobody said anything. No words could add to the feeling. Finally Bobby pulled back.

"We gotta be cool," he chuckled. "The last thing we want is to have people checking me out."

"I swear I didn't recognize you," Courtney said with excitement. "You're . . . older."

"Yeah, well, you guys are too," Bobby said. He gave Courtney an extra look up and down. "Like, a *lot* older." Courtney wasn't sure if she should slug him in the arm, or blush. She did both.

"Ow!" Bobby shouted. He then smiled and said, "Man, it's been almost a year since I've seen you guys. Happy Birthday, Mark."

"Thanks, man," Mark said. "This is a pretty amazing present."

"What's with the blond hair?" Courtney asked.

"I had 'em do this at the hotel beauty shop before I left First Earth. They thought I was nuts. It's not exactly a 1937 look. But I didn't want anybody recognizing me here."

Mark said, "I've got a million questions."

"Let's go someplace else," Bobby suggested. "This is a little public."

The three of them walked farther down the Ave toward Long Island Sound and a big, woodsy town park. There they could lose themselves in the trees and not be bothered. The three friends found a secluded spot in the shade and sat down to a picnic.

"Man, I miss these," Bobby said as he chomped another mouthful of fries. "Best fries in the world. *Any* world."

Courtney and Mark weren't interested in eating. They had Bobby, right here in front of them. There was too much to say to waste time chewing.

"How did you know we'd be at the bank?" Mark asked.

"I figured if you got my journals on your birthday, last Saturday, then this morning would be the earliest you could get back here to check them into the safe-deposit box."

"Smart," Mark said, impressed.

"Lucky guess," Bobby said modestly.

"Why did you come home?" Courtney asked. "You wrote you were going to Veelox."

Bobby didn't answer right away. It seemed to Mark and Courtney that the answer troubled him.

"That was the plan," Bobby answered thoughtfully. "But at the last minute, I couldn't."

"Did Saint Dane turn up somewhere else?" Courtney asked.

"No," Bobby said. "I just thought that, well, to be honest, I need a break."

"I don't blame you," Courtney said.

Bobby continued, "But it's more than that. I'm afraid the more I learn about being a Traveler, the more I forget about being Bobby Pendragon. I feel like I'm changing. I guess that has to happen, but I can't say I'm happy about it."

The three looked at each other. It was true. Time does that. Bobby's memory of Mark and Courtney was absolutely solid, but the two kids sitting in front of him didn't quite fit that memory.

"I guess I needed a reality check," Bobby said. "I didn't want to forget who I am, or where I come from. I thought maybe I could hang out here for a few days, just to chill. You guys know everything that's been going on with me. I want to know what's been happening with you. Is it okay if we hang out for a while?"

"Okay?" Courtney shouted. "It'll be great!"

"But risky," Mark added. "There's still a big search going on for you and your family."

Bobby laughed. "Yeah, I figured. But if you guys didn't recognize me, I don't think anybody else will."

"Aren't your parents in Florida this week?" Courtney asked Mark.

"Yeah," he answered tentatively.

"They leave you alone?" Bobby asked with a smile.

"Hey, I'm fifteen," Mark answered defensively. "They trust me." Then under his breath he said, "And my aunt lives two blocks away."

"Then it's perfect," Courtney declared. "Bobby can stay with you!"

Bobby looked at Mark. "Is it okay?"

Mark thought for a bit, then broke out in a big smile. "Are you crazy?" he shouted. "I'm psyched!"

For the next week Bobby did his best to put any thoughts about being a Traveler out of his head. For these few special days he was going to pretend that he was simply Bobby Pendragon.

Most of their time was spent at Mark's house. Courtney would come over, and the three would sit for hours talking about everything. They filled Bobby in on what bands were hot and who dropped off the face of the earth. They rented movies, and listened to music, and watched bad TV, and gossiped about who was going out with who at school.

Courtney told Bobby all about the softball championship she had been part of, and Mark gave him a demonstration of the killer battle robot that won him first prize in the state science fair. Mark told Bobby about his dreams to one day go to engineering school and maybe get into the space program.

They even went to the town library to do some research. Bobby wanted to know what had become of Jinx Olsen and Winn Farrow. The Second Earth library had about one zillionth the information that the library had on Third Earth, but it was enough. They discovered that Winn Farrow didn't live long enough to enjoy his victory over Max Rose. He was killed during a bank robbery in June of 1937. The secret of who really brought down the *Hindenburg* died along with him.

The news about Jinx Olsen was much better. Bobby was thrilled to learn that when World War II broke out, Jinx joined the Army Air Corps, pretending to be a man! She flew several bombing missions over Germany and received the Distinguished Flying Cross for heroism in flight. Jinx had lived her dream, and then retired to Maine, where she got married and had three kids.

And they ate. Pizza, spaghetti, Chinese food, ice cream, burgers, burgers, and burgers. At least once a day they got fried chicken and fries from Garden Poultry.

They went swimming at the Point, where Courtney was sure

to wear the pink bikini Bobby mentioned in his journal. Bobby appreciated that. He also noticed that Courtney filled it out a little better than the last time he'd seen her wear it, but didn't say anything. That wouldn't have been cool. They also watched Courtney pitch a two-hitter fast-pitch softball game. She hoped to go to a big college to play softball and soccer. Her true love was soccer though. She had dreams of getting on the national team.

When they traveled around, they took pains to make sure Bobby wouldn't be seen and recognized. There was only one close call. The three of them were riding bikes toward the beach and were stopped at a light when Lieutenant Hirsch, the guy who was handling the Pendragon missing persons investigation, pulled up in a car right next to them.

Mark's heart nearly stopped. Courtney was cool though. She smiled and waved. Bobby didn't know who the guy was, so he didn't know enough to be nervous. When the light changed, Hirsch drove on without a second look. It wouldn't have mattered anyway. Bobby didn't look the same anymore.

The three friends packed a year of fun and friendship into one week. In all, they probably didn't sleep more than three hours a night. There was only one rule: Nobody was allowed to talk about anything to do with being a Traveler. No exceptions. There were a couple times when Mark touched on the subject, and Bobby pretended not to have heard him. Mark got the hint. Nothing more was said. They all pretended like there was nothing more important going on than deciding what DVD they should rent, or if the Yankees would whup up on the Red Sox again. It was exactly what Bobby needed. It re-charged his batteries and made him feel human.

But after several days, Bobby began to grow restless. It's

not that he wasn't having fun—he absolutely was—but he knew it couldn't last forever. The change started when he reached the point where he was totally relaxed. That's when his mind started to turn the other way. As much as he tried to forget about it, he always knew that Saint Dane was out there somewhere, plotting a world of grief.

Mark began to sense this in Bobby. It took a day or so for Bobby to relax and get back to his old, fun self. But then Mark noticed Bobby wasn't talking as much. It seemed like there were times when his mind was a million miles away. Mark didn't dare to ask him about it. He was afraid Bobby would close up again, or worse, it would somehow break the magic spell that had given them this great week together. Mark didn't want it to end, though he knew it would have to.

Then one night, while the two of them were trying to fall asleep in Mark's bedroom, Mark took the chance and brought up the taboo subject.

"Bobby?" he asked tentatively. "I want to become an acolyte."

This caught Bobby off guard. "Whoa," he said. "Where did *that* come from?"

Bobby didn't cut him off this time. It encouraged Mark to keep going.

"You know, the acolytes," he said. "The people who help the Travelers. They live in the territories and bring the clothes to the flumes and help you get around and—"

"Yeah, I know who they are," Bobby interrupted. "But I don't know anything about them. I never met one."

"But they're out there," Mark insisted.

"Yeah, I guess so," Bobby said with absolutely no enthusiasm. Reality had returned. Bobby knew he couldn't ignore it anymore. Vacation was over. Time to put the game face back on. He took a deep breath, hesitated one last moment, then clicked back into Traveler mode.

"Why, Mark?" he asked. "What makes you want to be an acolyte?"

"A lot of reasons," Mark answered. "I want to help. It's hard sitting around doing nothing when there's some guy out there trying to bring down the universe and hurt your best friend. Reading your journals has changed things."

Bobby nodded. He understood where Mark was coming from. "Funny thing," he said thoughtfully. "In a couple of days you and Courtney are going to start Davis Gregory High, and all I really want is to forget about being a Traveler and go with you."

"But you can't," Mark said.

"No, I can't."

"There's another reason," Mark added. He took a pause before saying this, because he knew it was a tough subject. "I won't let you down. Not the way Spader did."

Bobby winced. "Spader didn't let me down," he said sharply. "He just lost sight of what was important."

Mark realized he had touched a raw nerve. "I know that," he said quickly, doing damage control. "I just want you to know that I'd always be there to cover your back. No matter what."

"How does Courtney feel about it?" Bobby asked.

"We haven't exactly talked about it," Mark answered. "But I guarantee, if we got the chance, she'd jump right in. You know Courtney."

Bobby chuckled. Yeah, he knew Courtney. "Tell you what," Bobby said. "I'll find out what I can. If there's a chance for you guys to do something, I'll let you know."

That was good enough for Mark. He now had hope that he

might join Bobby on his mission after all. He had trouble falling asleep that night because his mind was so alive with the possibilities.

Bobby had trouble getting to sleep too, but for a very different reason. He knew his time here on Second Earth was over. He needed to be somewhere else, doing what he was destined to do. Tomorrow he would say good-bye to his friends one more time and jump back into the game. That's what rolled through his brain while he tried to get to sleep. But it wasn't easy nodding off to dreamland while one thought kept pushing all others away . . .

Where is Saint Dane? What is he up to? And when I find him, will I be strong enough to beat him?

◐ SECOND EARTH ◑

Courtney arrived at Mark's house early the next morning, all set for another day at the beach. She had made a bunch of salami sandwiches and wore the famous pink bikini under her shorts and T-shirt. There were only two days left of summer vacation, two days before they would begin Davis Gregory High. She knew that once they began this new school, life would change again. Not only would they be leaving the familiar comfort of junior high, but Bobby would be gone. There was no way around that one. These last few days felt like the end of an era. She wanted to make the most of them.

But that wasn't meant to be.

She knew it the second she stepped into Mark's house. The atmosphere had changed. Every time she had come over before, the guys would be playing Nintendo, or watching a game on TV, or cranking up music. Today the house was quiet. Bobby and Mark sat in the living room, talking. The air was heavy. It felt to her like a pregame locker room where everyone had the butter-flies.

"You're leaving today, aren't you?" she asked Bobby.

Bobby nodded.

Courtney plopped down on the couch next to him. "That's it then," she said. "The next time we hear from you, it'll be in some journal?"

"Probably," was Bobby's answer.

There was an awkward silence. They knew that as soon as Bobby walked out the door, their lives would all officially change. It had been a great week, but it was over.

That's when the telephone rang.

"Probably my parents," Mark said, and answered the phone. "Hello?"

A deep voice came through from the caller. "Hello. Is this Mark Dimond?"

"Yeah." Mark didn't recognize the voice. "Who's this?"

"You don't know me, Mark," said the voice. "My name is Vincent Van Dyke."

"Gunny?" shouted Mark in surprise.

Bobby jumped to his feet and grabbed the phone away from Mark. "Gunny?"

"Howdy there, shorty. Enjoying your vacation?"

"What's wrong? Where are you? Are you okay?"

"Whoa, whoa, slow down," Gunny said with a laugh. "Everything's fine. I'm here on Second Earth."

"Yeah, I figured. But where? What are you doing here?"

"I need to see you, Bobby, right away," Gunny said. "Is there someplace we can meet? I can come to you, no problem."

Bobby looked at Mark and Courtney and said, "Gunny wants to meet me. Can he come here?"

"No way," Mark said. "My parents are due back soon."

Bobby looked at Courtney, but she shook her head. "Mom's home. I don't think I could explain this to her."

Bobby thought fast, then an idea came to him. "Where are you, Gunny?"

"New York City."

"Then here's an address. It's in my hometown of Stony Brook. It's Two Linden Place."

Mark and Courtney looked at each other. They knew exactly where 2 Linden Place was. They had been avoiding it all week. It was the address where Bobby grew up. Now it was an empty lot. It had been empty ever since everything that had to do with Bobby Pendragon had mysteriously disappeared.

"I'll find it," Gunny said. "Meet me there in an hour."

"You sure everything's okay?" Bobby asked.

"See you there," Gunny said, and hung up.

"You sure that's a good idea?" Courtney asked. "I mean, isn't it gonna be tough for you to go back there?"

Bobby shrugged. "I can't pretend like things haven't happened."

Two Linden Place was only a short walk from Mark's house, so they had some time to kill before meeting Gunny. They didn't want Courtney's salami sandwiches to go to waste, so they sat at Mark's kitchen table and scarfed them down. They did their best to talk about anything other than what was really on their minds. But it was all just blah, blah. Their minds were elsewhere.

Finally Bobby stood up, saying, "Time to go."

Mark and Courtney weren't sure what to do. Was this it? Was it time to say good-bye?

Mark said, "Make sure you tell us what Gunny had to say in your next journal."

"Why?" Bobby asked. "You're coming with me."

Mark's heart swelled.

"You sure?" Courtney asked.

"Absolutely," Bobby answered. "I've got no secrets from you guys."

The three left the house and walked through the quiet suburban neighborhood toward 2 Linden Place. The last time they had done this, Bobby was expecting to be reunited with his family after his adventure on Denduron. It was a gut-wrenching moment when Bobby first realized his house, and his life, were gone. Everyone knew that going back again would be tough.

It only took them five minutes to get there. Nobody said a word as Bobby stood in front of the empty lot. Grass and weeds had taken over since the last time they were there, making the empty space look all the more forlorn. Bobby started to walk onto the lot, but stopped himself and stayed on the sidewalk. Mark and Courtney shared a look. They saw a tear in Bobby's eye.

A car horn sounded a short hello, and the three turned to see a long, black limousine pull up to the curb. The three exchanged curious looks. This was the last thing any of them expected. But when a back door opened, sure enough, out stepped Gunny Van Dyke. He wore a plain, dark suit and tie that could have been in style any time since 1937.

"Morning, folks," Gunny said with a big grin as he strode over to meet them.

Bobby began to introduce his friends, saying, "Gunny, this is—"

"I know who they are," Gunny interrupted with a warm smile. "Courtney Chetwynde and Mark Dimond. It is a pleasure to make your acquaintance."

They all shook hands.

"You're my hero," Courtney said in awe.

"I am?" Gunny asked with surprise.

"Hey, anybody who saves Earth from annihilation is a hero in my book."

Gunny laughed.

"Is it okay that we're here?" Mark asked. "I mean, you guys have business and all."

"No, it's good you're here," Gunny assured them. "This involves you too."

Mark and Courtney exchanged glances. That was weird. What could Gunny have to say that would involve the two of them?

"What's up? You win the lottery?" Bobby asked, pointing at the limo.

"Don't I wish," Gunny chuckled. "Back on First Earth, shortly after you left the hotel, a fella came by looking for you. Said he had something important to tell you and wanted to give you something. I told him you were gone, but that I could get it to you."

"Who was it?" Bobby asked.

"Don't go jumping ahead, shorty," Gunny chastised. "Let me tell the story. Anyhow, he wouldn't give up. Said he wanted to talk to you himself. When he finally told me what it was all about, I understood why he wanted to see you so bad. I told him I wasn't sure if you'd ever be back and promised to give you the package as soon as I saw you."

"So what is it?" Bobby asked.

"Hang on. So I went to the flume to come looking for you. But when I arrived here on Second Earth, I got an idea. I wondered if the guy who wanted to see you so bad back in 1937 was still around. I did a little snooping and sure enough, he was still alive and living in New York."

"You're kidding? How old is he?" Bobby asked.

"Must be in his nineties, near as I can tell," answered Gunny.

"I looked him up and introduced myself."

"Didn't he wonder why you hadn't aged a single day since the last time he saw you?" asked Courtney.

"He thinks it was my granddad who worked at the hotel back then," Gunny answered. "I told him Granddad never again saw the bellhop called Pendragon, but he never forgot. I said how he handed the package down to his son, and then to me, and I finally tracked down the grandson of that bellhop. That would be you, Bobby."

"And he believed you?" Bobby asked.

"Why wouldn't he? It made sense. A lot more sense than the truth," Gunny added with a chuckle.

"So who is the guy?" Bobby asked.

"Ask him yourself," Gunny said, and motioned toward the limo. "That's his car."

"He's here now?" Bobby said in surprise.

"Go on," Gunny directed. "Talk to him. Just remember, you're not you. You're your grandson."

"Uh . . . yeah," Bobby said, and walked tentatively toward the car.

A driver wearing a black suit jumped from the front seat, ran around back, and opened the rear door. He reached inside and helped his passenger get out. Bobby saw that the guy getting out of the back was indeed very old. He looked a hundred if he looked a day. He was wearing a cream-colored suit and a bright yellow tie. Whoever this guy was, between the limo and the nice clothes, he had some bucks. The driver gave him a cane to lean on. But once he was out of the car, he didn't want any more help. This guy may have been old, but he still had some life in him.

Once he was firmly on the sidewalk, he looked over at Bobby. When their eyes met, the old man actually stood up straighter. Bobby could tell this was a proud man who didn't care much for being trapped in an old body. Bobby didn't recognize him, but then again, he didn't expect to. Yet, as they looked into each other's eyes, Bobby felt something strangely familiar.

"What's your name, son?" the old man asked in a raspy, yet strong voice.

Bobby glanced to Gunny, who nodded encouragement. "Bobby Pendragon," he answered.

"Just like your grandfather," the old man said. "My name is Peter Nelson, though I don't suppose that means anything to you."

"You came a long way to see me, Mr. Nelson," Bobby said with respect. "Do you have something to tell me about, uh, my grandfather?"

Nelson looked away for a moment. He was spinning the memory wheels to get back to 1937. "I've been very successful, young Pendragon," he began. "With business, with family, and with life in general. But I didn't start out that way. In my youth I did some things I wasn't proud of. Things I'm too ashamed to speak about even now. But those were different times, and I was able to put it behind me. I have one person to thank for that . . . your grandfather."

Bobby had no idea what this guy was talking about. He tried to remember something he might have done on First Earth to help somebody out, but came up empty.

"You see," the old man continued, "your grandfather saved my life."

Now Bobby was really confused.

"I was headed down a very dark path," the man said. "Your grandfather gave me a second chance."

"Excuse me," Bobby interrupted. "My grandfather told me a lot of stories, but he never told me about saving anybody's life."

"I'm not surprised," the man responded. "I think that's the

kind of person he was. But he saved my life, all right, sure as I'm standing here before you."

"How?" Bobby asked. This was making him crazy.

Mr. Nelson thought for a second, then said, "I don't know how much I should be telling you, but I guess it's all water under the bridge now. Your grandfather saved *two* lives that day. One was mine, the other was a very powerful man named Max Rose. You see, I tried to kill Max Rose, but your grandfather stopped me. Then Max Rose ordered your grandfather to shoot me, but he didn't. He had my life in his hands and gave it right back to me. I ran off and never looked back. Coming that close to dying, well, it changed my life. I have your grandfather to thank."

It all came flooding back to Bobby. He took a closer look at the old man, and now recognized the thin nose and sharp eyes. Could it be? Yes, it was Mr. Nervous Gangster. He was a million years older, but it was definitely him. This was the guy who attacked Spader and him in the subway and tracked them down to the hotel. As Bobby stood there, the memory of looking into this guy's frightened eyes returned as clearly as if it had happened yesterday. He had held a gun on the gangster while Max Rose ordered him to shoot. He remembered the feel of the pistol and knowing he was close to taking a life. But Bobby dropped the gun and the gangster ran.

Now the guy was here, thanking him, sort of. The old man raised his hand to shake Bobby's, saying, "I wanted to thank him personally, but it didn't work out that way. Thanking you is the closest I'm going to get."

Bobby didn't take the guy's hand.

"I remember now," Bobby said to him. "I mean, I remember the story from my grandfather. Can I ask you a question?"

"Of course," the old man said while dropping his hand.

"My grandfather told me about the first time he saw you. It

was in a cave off a subway station in the Bronx."

Nelson dropped his head. "I've tried to forget that," he said.

"Yeah, well, try to remember," Bobby said sharply. "What were you doing there?"

The old guy squinted, trying to bring back the memories. "What I remember doesn't make a whole lot of sense. There were three of us. Me and my partner, Tony, and a third guy. A strange fella. Real persuasive, if I remember. He wasn't part of the gang very long."

Bobby figured this must have been Saint Dane.

"This guy brought us to that cave with the tunnel," Nelson continued. "He walked up to the tunnel and said something. What was it? Oh, right. I think it was Clorox . . . you know, like the bleach."

Bobby knew exactly what was said. It was Saint Dane, all right, and he had said "*Cloral*."

"Then the damnedest thing happened. The tunnel started lighting up like the Fourth of July. The guy told Tony to take his tommygun and shoot into the tunnel. Tony was a wild guy. He didn't have to be convinced to shoot his gun at anything, so he shot right into the lights. A second later, the lights went out. None of it made any sense."

It made sense to Bobby though. Those were the bullets that were fired through the flume and killed Uncle Press.

Nelson continued. "Then the guy took off. He told us to stay there for a while and if anybody came through that tunnel, to scare 'em and tell 'em to stay away from Winn Farrow. Does that answer your question?"

"Almost," Bobby said. "So you're telling me it was your partner who fired the gun into the tunnel? It wasn't you?" Bobby asked.

"Not a chance," he said adamantly. "I remember that very

clear. I didn't see the point. Tony fired the gun."

Bobby took a breath, then held out his hand and said, "Then on behalf of my grandfather, I'll accept your thanks."

The old man shook Bobby's hand. It was a shake that was as strong and sure as if he were twenty years old. Bobby saw the joy in his eyes because in some small way, he was able to thank the man who saved his life. Of course, the guy would never know that he was actually shaking the hand of the real guy, not his grandson.

"Thank you," Nelson said. "Thank you so much."

He let go of Bobby's hand and started back for the car, when he remembered something.

"Oh, one more thing," he said. He reached into his jacket pocket and took out a small package, wrapped in brown paper. "This is something I wanted to give to your grandfather as a small token of my gratitude. I'm sorry I never got it to him, but I hope you will appreciate it."

"Thanks. I'm sure I will," Bobby said graciously.

Nelson handed the package to Bobby, then looked at Gunny. "Mr. Van Dyke," Nelson called. "Do you need a lift back into the city?"

"I do, Mr. Nelson," Gunny answered. "Can I have a few moments?"

"Take all the time you need," answered Nelson, and walked back to his car, where his driver helped him get inside.

Bobby walked back to the others. They'd heard the whole conversation.

"Unbelievable!" Mark said.

"What did he give you?" Courtney asked.

Bobby looked to Gunny. Gunny had a big smile on his face. "Open it," he said.

Bobby shrugged and tore at the brown paper. "It doesn't look very old," he said.

"It isn't," Gunny said. "I only got it yesterday."

Bobby laughed. Of course. Yesterday Gunny was back in 1937. Bobby pulled off all the brown paper to reveal a small, square black box. He looked at Gunny. Gunny winked. Bobby opened it and . . .

"Oh, man!" Mark yelled with surprise.

Courtney laughed.

Gunny said, "Now you know why I came all the way here to get you this."

Bobby couldn't believe his eyes. Sitting in the box was his ring—his Traveler ring.

"He told me he got it back from his partner after the guy took the fall from the tower," Gunny explained. "He figured getting it back to you was the least he could do, seeing as you saved his life and all."

"Excellent," Courtney said. "We're back in business."

Now Bobby could send his journals back to Mark and Courtney the old-fashioned way. Bobby couldn't stop smiling. In some ways, things had come full circle. He took the ring out of the box and slipped it on his finger. As soon as he did, the ring began to twitch. Bobby held his hand out quickly.

"What's the matter?" Mark asked.

"It . . . it's activating," Bobby said.

"Really? You mean there's a gate around here?" Courtney asked.

The answer came quickly. The gray stone in the ring began to glow, then sparkle. A second later a single beam of light shot from the ring, projecting an image in front of them. There, floating in the air before them, was a girl. Actually, it was a girl's head.

She had blond hair pulled back in a ponytail and wore small, yellow-tinted glasses.

"Whoa," said Courtney.

"Yeah, whoa," added Mark.

"Aja Killian," whispered Bobby in shock.

"Who?" Gunny asked.

"The Traveler from Veelox."

"Where have you been?" demanded Aja's image. "I've been trying to contact you for ages!"

"Long story," Bobby answered.

"I don't want to hear it, Pendragon." Aja shot back. "You'd better get back to Veelox."

"Why?" Bobby asked.

"I'm not saying I made a mistake," Aja's head explained. "This may be a total false alarm, but—"

"Just say it!" demanded Bobby.

"All right!" Aja snapped. "Saint Dane may have slipped through my security system. He is here on Veelox."

Bobby smiled and said, "You're telling me your perfect security system isn't all that perfect?"

"Are you coming or not?" Aja snapped angrily.

"On my way," Bobby answered.

"Don't take your time," Aja said snottily. Her image shot back into Bobby's ring and everything went back to normal.

"Well," said Courtney. "That was . . . strange."

"I guess I'm going to Veelox," Bobby said. Then looked to Gunny and asked, "Want to come?"

"Wouldn't miss it," Gunny answered with a smile. "We'll have Mr. Nelson drop us off in the Bronx."

Bobby turned to face Mark and Courtney. "This has been the best week of my life," Bobby said sincerely.

Courtney then walked up to Bobby and before he realized what was happening, she grabbed him and planted a serious kiss on him. Bobby didn't mind. Once the shock was over, he wrapped his arms around Courtney and held her close.

Kissing Courtney was even better than he remembered.

Mark and Gunny turned away, totally embarrassed. "So?" Gunny asked Mark. "How 'bout them Yankees?"

Courtney and Bobby finally unlocked lips. Bobby's eyes were a little watery, but Courtney's gaze was razor sharp.

"Let's not wait another year before the next one, okay?" she said.

"Uh . . . sure. Sounds good," Bobby said, trying to keep his knees from buckling.

Mark and Courtney each gave Gunny a hug, and the two Travelers started for the limo.

"Remember what we talked about, okay?" Mark called to Bobby.

"I will," Bobby said.

As he and Gunny walked toward the car, Gunny asked, "How are you feeling, shorty? I mean . . . where is your head, you know, with things?"

Bobby didn't answer right away. He wanted to make sure he used the right words.

"I feel like Saint Dane got the better of me on First Earth," Bobby said. "And I'm not gonna let it happen again."

Gunny chuckled.

"What's so funny?" Bobby asked.

Gunny broke out in a big smile and said, "Shorty, you're starting to sound just like your uncle."

Bobby smiled too. Then he and Gunny got into the back of the big car. Bobby opened the window so he could get one last look at his friends. As the car pulled away from the curb he put his arm out and waved to them.

Mark and Courtney watched as the black limo picked up speed along the quiet street, with Bobby's arm still out, waving.

"What was it you guys talked about?" Courtney asked.

"All sorts of things," Mark said with a sly smile. "But I'll tell you one thing, I'll bet we're going to see Bobby Pendragon again, a lot sooner than you think."

They looked back up at the departing limousine in time to see Bobby pull his arm back inside. The car turned onto the main road and disappeared.

To Be Continued

ABOUT THE AUTHOR

D. J. MacHale is a writer, director, and producer of several popular television series and movies that include *Flight 29 Down; Are You Afraid of the Dark?*; *Encyclopedia Brown, Boy Detective; Tower of Terror*; and *Ghostwriter*. Pendragon, his first book series, is a *New York Times* bestselling series. He lives in southern California with his wife, Evangeline; his daughter, Keaton; a golden retriever, Maggie; and a kitten, Kaboodle.